Don't Take Any Wooden Nickels

MINDY STARNS CLARK

HARVEST HOUSE PUBLISHERS

EUGENE, OREGON

Cover by Dugan Design Group, Bloomington, Minnesota

Cover illustration © Gregor Buir / Fotolia; Cover photo © iStockphoto / filo

DON'T TAKE ANY WOODEN NICKELS

Published 2011 by Harvest House Publishers
Eugene, Oregon 97402
www.harvesthousepublishers.com

ISBN 978-0-7369-2957-8

The Library of Congress has cataloged the edition as follows:

Clark, Mindy Starns.
Don't take any wooden nickels / Mindy Starns Clark.
p. cm. — (The million dollar mysteries; 2)
ISBN 978-0-7369-0993-8 (pbk.)
1. Chesapeake Bay Region (Md. and Va.)—Fiction. 2. Women philanthropists—Fiction.
I. Title.
PS3603.L366 D66 2003
813'.54—dc21

2002010021

Printed in the United States of America

11 12 13 14 15 16 17 18 / LB-KB / 10 9 8 7 6 5 4 3 2 1

For my daughter Emily…
Thank you for being exactly who you are:
sweet, talented, funny, giving, beautiful,
and filled with a godly spirit that thrills my heart.
I love you!

Acknowledgments

Many, many special thanks:

To my husband, John Clark, J.D., C.P.A., for your invaluable assistance with legal and financial questions, for incredible writing and editing help, and for all of the things you do that free me to close the door to the office and simply write. As always, without you, this book would not exist!

To Kay Justus, for more than twenty years of friendship and encouragement, countless plotting ideas and suggestions, and never-ending enthusiasm.

To my editor, Kim Moore of Harvest House Publishers, for making the entire editing and publishing process such a joy.

To Ken Weber, for designing my website, and to Shari Weber, for your wonderful research assistance.

To my father, Robert M. Starns, M.D., for brilliant medical information.

To readers Jackie Starns, Sheila Davison, Mary Davison, Theresa Verna, and Kim Furando.

To all of those who filled in the gaps of my knowledge: Hitomi Kimura, Ikuko Nagano, David and Jennifer Clark, Ann and Don Blais, David Starns, Lauren Clark, Jonathan King, Sue and Bob Butler, David Granquist, Sgt. Bruce R. Talbot, Public Affairs Officer Niki Edwards, and so many others I could fill this book with your names. Thank you!

To my fellow authors Debra White Smith, Patricia Sprinkle, and Elena Santangelo, for advice and support.

To Jim and June Ann Murphy, for your hospitality and assistance in the crucial eleventh hour.

To my COS Bible Study group, for biblical wisdom, fellowship, and fervent prayers when my deadlines are looming.

God bless you all!

Do not store up for yourselves treasures on earth...But store up for yourselves treasures in heaven, where moth and rust do not destroy, and where thieves do not break in and steal. For where your treasure is, there your heart will be also.

MATTHEW 6:19-21

One

I heard the gunshots from a distance, sharp and loud in the cool November air. A few seconds later there were more gunshots, then more, then all was silent.

Quickening my pace, I rounded the corner and hurried through two large stone arches into the Glenn Oaks Cemetery, a beautiful, shady old graveyard on the outskirts of Nashville, Tennessee. I had timed this just right, since I didn't really want to get there until the funeral was finished. Now that the honor guard had fired three volleys, I knew it was almost over.

I slowed down a little, found the gravesite, and stopped a respectful distance away. The deceased had been a naval chief petty officer in his youth, and his family had wanted him to have a full honor guard at his burial. Now I could see that nearly half of the 20 or so people in attendance were wearing full military dress uniforms.

I watched as two young soldiers carefully folded the flag that had been draped over the coffin, and then they presented it to the widow. As they did so, an older soldier lifted a bugle to his lips and lightly sounded out the notes for "Taps." The simple tune, always so mournful, sounded especially sad in the middle of this Tennessee graveyard.

Ordinarily, I think, the whole scene would've brought me to tears. Even though I didn't personally know the deceased or his family, I had been widowed myself only three years before, and it still didn't take much to open those wounds. Today, however, I was distracted by other matters. I had an exciting event of my own coming up in just a few hours, thoughts of which were keeping my mind from becoming too absorbed with what was unfolding before me.

Once the service ended, I watched as the tiny crowd dispersed. The seven soldiers I was here to see turned and walked in the opposite direction from me, somberly shouldering their rifles as they marched toward a row of cars. I tried to catch up with them, but the earth was muddy, and the heels of my Joan & David pumps sunk into the ground with the first step. Fortunately, storing away the bugle and rifles took a few moments, allowing me time to walk around the perimeter on the sidewalk and reach them just before they drove away. All of the other mourners had already gone by then, leaving only the seven men crowded into an ancient station wagon and me. I waved at the driver, and he rolled down his window and smiled.

"Can I help you, young lady?" he asked, perfect dentured teeth showing in a tan, wrinkled face. He looked to be in his late 70s, weathered but still handsome in a crisp white naval dress uniform. I guess to him I *was* a young lady, though I didn't always feel young.

"I'm looking for Commander Davis," I said.

"That's me," he replied. He opened the door of the car and stepped out, closing it behind him as the other men peered curiously from inside.

"Callie Webber," I said, reaching out to shake his hand. "It's a pleasure to meet you, sir."

"It's my privilege, ma'am," he replied, glancing down at the envelope I was holding. "Thanks aren't necessary. It's part of the Greater Nashville Honor Guard service. No charge, please."

I realized he thought I was connected to the deceased and that I was here to thank him and pay him for the military send-off. I smiled. I *was* here to give him some money, but not for the reason he thought.

"That's a beautiful service you provide," I said. "Very dignified and touching."

"It's our opinion, ma'am, that every veteran deserves full military honors at their funeral."

"Yes, I agree," I said, aware that although the government will provide a burial flag and two military representatives for a veteran's funeral, it's up to volunteer groups like this one to flesh things out by giving a full military send-off, including the firing party and a live rendition of "Taps." I thought their group provided a valuable community service, and I was happy to be the bearer of good news on this sunny autumn morning—despite my distracted mind-set and the grim surroundings of a cemetery.

" 'Course," he said, "our job is a lot easier on a gorgeous morning like this. Two days ago we were out in the pouring rain."

I smiled, agreeing that it was, indeed, a lovely day. Unbeknownst to him, I had watched him and his little group of veterans at that rainy funeral—though at a distance and from the comfort of my rental car. In fact, I had been in town now for three days and had spent the majority of the time discreetly examining his organization. As an investigator for a charitable foundation, it was my job to scrutinize the finances and activities of selected nonprofits and award grants to them if they passed our rigorous screening process. This gentleman's application had struck me as particularly charming, and I was glad that after a little digging around I had been able to determine that his group was a legit bunch doing good work. A grant would be a big help for them. The handing over of the money, like now, was the fun part that always came at the end of a successful investigation.

For me, however, an even more fun event awaited at the conclusion of this particular investigation. After much frustration and anticipation, I was finally going to meet—face-to-face, for the very first time—my enigmatic boss, Tom. We had known each other for two years now, spending countless hours together on the phone and over the Internet. But we had never actually met in person. Today, however, we were finally going to change that with a brief get-together in the airport as our paths crossed. It wasn't much, but it was better than nothing!

For now, I was trying to put my meeting with Tom out of my mind until I was actually on the plane flying home. As long as there were no glitches, I should be able to finish my work here and make it to the airport in plenty of time for my flight. Guiltily, I glanced at my watch, telling myself to focus.

"I would imagine you have a lot of expenses with something like this," I said, looking at Commander Davis.

"Well, the government provides the blanks for the M-1s," he replied. "Other than that, it's just your basic stuff. Transportation to the funerals, maintenance on the rifles, things like that."

I nodded, thinking back over the information he had supplied in his grant request. I especially liked the section he had written under "Additional Needs": *I guess we could use a few bugles and some bugle lessons, 'cause we don't want one of those fake bugles the government keeps trying to give us, the ones that play "Taps" digitally. Those newfangled things might work for the younger soldiers, but when we send off an old-timer, we want the real thing. Unfortunately, right now the only one in our group who knows how to play is Charlie, but he's getting hard of hearing so sometimes his notes are a little off key.*

"I suppose I should tell you," I said, "that I'm from the J.O.S.H.U.A. Foundation."

"The grant people? Yes, ma'am. I sent in an application a while back."

"Well," I replied, "it made its way to me, and I'm happy to say we will be awarding you a small amount of money for your bugles and bugle lessons."

I handed him the envelope, inside of which was a check for $5000 made out to the Greater Nashville Honor Guard Society. I could see a slight disappointment flash across the man's face, sorry that he hadn't received the money for his primary request, which was $11,000 for a used transport vehicle to carry their small group back and forth to all of the funerals they attended in the region.

"Well now, that's good news. That's very good news," he said finally, tucking the check back inside the envelope. "We sure do appreciate that. Old Charlie, especially. Thanks."

Old Charlie waved to me from the backseat, obviously hanging onto every word of our conversation.

"The best way you can say thanks," I replied, repeating the little speech that always accompanied the handing out of a donation, "is to take that money and use it to further your mission as outlined in your grant proposal. The foundation believes strongly in what you're trying to accomplish, and we just wanted to have some small part in furthering your efforts."

"That's real nice," he said, reaching out to shake my hand. Similar sentiments were expressed from inside the car, which I accepted on behalf of my employer. I told them that I understood if they needed to get going, and I waited until Commander Davis got back into the car before I leaned over and spoke again.

"Oh, and on your way," I said, "you might want to stop off at Henderson Motors."

"Henderson Motors?" the commander asked, concern wrinkling his brow. "Do we have a flat tire or something?"

"No, sir," I replied with a wink. "But they'll have your brand-new Transmaster Eclipse 12-passenger van ready for you in about ten minutes."

"What?" he asked, his eyes suddenly wide with excitement.

"It's all yours, gentlemen, compliments of the J.O.S.H.U.A. Foundation."

Two

I just made it. Returning the rental car had taken a little longer than I had anticipated, which then necessitated a bit of a sprint down the hall once I got through security in the airport. But the important thing was that I was here now. I was on the plane.

At last, I was on my way to the big moment!

The rest of my row was empty, so once we were airborne it was easy for me to settle down and get organized. I retrieved a pillow from the overhead compartment and tucked it behind my back, then I took a minute to undo and resecure my hair into a chignon at my neck. Once that was done, I lifted my beautiful ostrich-skin briefcase, a gift from Tom, onto the seat next to me. I dialed the lock's combination and popped it open. Then I took a few minutes to organize the papers, files, and receipts that had accumulated on this trip, tucking them away into their proper places inside the case. Finally, I closed the briefcase, slid it under the seat in front of me, and leaned back in my chair. I took a deep breath, let it out, and closed my eyes.

Finally, I was on my way to see Tom.

I don't know why I was so excited, or what it was about our situation that made my pulse race every time I thought about it. Tom was my boss, a wonderful man I had grown to like and respect more every time we spoke. Though we interacted as professionals, Tom and I had a rapport that had developed over time and now extended far beyond the bounds of mere employer-employee interaction. Still, no matter how often we spoke or how fond we were of each other, it was kind of hard to call it a "relationship" when we'd never met face-to-face!

An enigmatic multimillionaire who kept an incredibly low profile, Tom was a philanthropist who did his donating anonymously through the J.O.S.H.U.A. Foundation. Tom had made it clear from the day he hired me—over the telephone and on the recommendation of a mutual friend—that though it was primarily his money the foundation would be giving away, he wanted to remain as far removed from the process as possible. He first screened all of the applications, using some personal criteria to narrow them down, but then he always handed the reins over to me for a final recommendation. As an attorney and licensed private investigator, it was my job to investigate those organizations on behalf of the foundation and present funds if we found them to be deserving.

Our system worked well, and we could've gone on indefinitely the way things were. But somewhere along the line, Tom and I found we shared more than just the common goal of philanthropy. Somehow, we shared a connection at a personal level as well—though we rarely verbalized it. Instead, we spent hours talking and laughing on the phone, writing back and forth online, and basically dancing around the idea of finding a way to meet in person.

Today was that day.

Given that we were going to be in the exact same airport at the exact same time, we had finally committed to specific plans to get together, though only for a short while. Tom had flown to Washington, DC, yesterday on business and had spent last night in the apartment the foundation kept near the Watergate. Today, he was heading to New York City and then on to Singapore for an extended business trip, but his flight didn't leave the airport until an hour after mine arrived.

Therefore, God willing, today at exactly 1:10 P.M. I was going to get off this plane, walk to the Executive Club in the Reagan National Airport, and meet my employer. I would at last be able to put a face with the name, with the voice. Sometimes, and in some ways, I felt closer to Tom than to anyone else on earth. After today, I knew there would be a completeness to our entire situation that had always been lacking before.

For now, I needed to relax. This was a two-and-a-half-hour flight, so I still had some time before we would land. I opened my eyes and leaned toward the window, looking down at the autumn splendor of the Smoky Mountains below.

It was a beautiful sight. Beneath a lacing of white mist, the trees on the mountains glowed with brilliant flashes of red and orange among the brown. I loved this time of year, loved the cool days and the cold nights and the obvious changing of the seasons. To me, God always seemed especially close at hand when the splendor of His creation was so evident. I said a quick prayer of thanks for the gorgeous mountains and for a job that could be such fun on a day like today.

I studied the terrain as we flew, thinking about the veterans in Nashville and their reactions to my announcement that we had purchased them a new van. Their thanks had been heartfelt and exuberant, though with the dignity one would expect from a group of retired military men. They had excitedly offered to take me for a spin in the new vehicle, take me to lunch, take me back to the veterans' center and give me a tour. But I had cited a prior commitment and sent them on their way, grinning as they sped from the cemetery toward the car dealership.

Thanks to the foundation, I often had the opportunity to feel benevolent because we regularly gave out substantial amounts of money to all sorts of different groups. I often thought of my job as a dream come true—difficult and challenging at times, to be sure, but also incredibly rewarding.

"Would you like something to drink?"

Startled, I looked up to see a flight attendant standing in the aisle next to me. She held onto a drink cart and waited expectantly. I ordered a ginger ale and lowered the tray in front of me as she efficiently assembled my drink and then gave it to me along with a napkin and two packs of peanuts. Once she was gone, I checked my watch.

It was time to call Tom. Time to reconfirm our meeting.

I used the phone in the seatback in front of me to dial his cell phone. He was expecting to hear from me, because we always talked at the end of a case. This time, however, the conversation would be brief. This time we would be able to continue it in person.

"Let me guess," he said as he answered. "You're calling from the back half of the plane, aren't you?"

"Come on," I said, smiling. "On this flight first class costs almost fifteen hundred dollars more than coach. That much just for a bigger seat and little more personal attention? I don't think so."

"Oh, Callie," Tom said. "Will we ever get you to appreciate the perks of your position?"

"Yeah, here's a perk," I said. "Now we have fifteen hundred extra dollars to give away to some group that really deserves it."

"Fine," he said, laughing. "Let's move on."

"Okay."

We discussed again the details of our meeting. I double-checked the terminal and gate number, and I told him that so far my flight was right on schedule.

"I'll be heading to the airport myself in about an hour," he said, "so it looks like we'll be together soon."

For some reason, just hearing him say those words gave an odd flip-flop to my heart.

"Anyway," he continued, "you can give me the details when we meet, but just tell me quickly about our boys in Nashville. Were they pleased?"

"Extremely," I replied, and then I went on to briefly describe the presentation of funds. Tom especially liked the personal touch I had added in a burst of inspiration. Prior to meeting the men at the cemetery this morning, I had bought a CD of classic military tunes, which I then delivered to Henderson Motors.

"When the van starts up, they'll hear 'Stars and Stripes Forever,'" I said, grinning. "I think they'll get a kick out of that."

"Perfect!" he cried. "I wish we could be there to see that."

"They seemed like such nice men, Tom. I'm glad you decided to spend the thirty thousand on a new van for them. That used one they wanted looked pretty road-weary to me."

"You did a great job, Callie," he said. "As usual. I just hope it wasn't too hard of an assignment for you, considering the nature of their mission."

Tom was aware that, as a widow, I still didn't handle funerals and funeral-related things very well. I didn't have the nerve to tell him that this assignment had not been difficult for me at all, primarily because thoughts of meeting *him* were foremost in my mind, precluding other negative associations.

"So what's next for me?" I asked.

"Well, that depends," he replied, and I could hear papers rustling in the background. "I'll bring along several choices for you. You can take your pick. There's an inner city elementary school in California that wants to start up art and music programs. Pretty straightforward."

"Sounds good."

"We've also got a group of doctors down in Texas who run mercy missions into Mexico. It looks like they're asking for money for medical supplies and travel expenses."

"Okay."

"Finally, there are some Bible translators based in Boston. They're doing some good work there. I've read about them."

"They all sound very interesting," I said, eager to look at the applications.

"I still have a few things I want to check on first," he said. "But I should be ready to give all the paperwork to you by the time I get there."

I swallowed hard.

"So I guess this is really going to happen, huh?" I asked, trying not to sound too eager. Knowing someone so well—and yet not really knowing him at all—was a very difficult position to be in. "How will I recognize you when I see you? Will you be wearing a red carnation?"

He laughed.

"Good idea!" he said. "No, wait, forget the carnation. I'm going to get a red mum."

"A mum?"

"Yeah! I'll be the one wearing the giant red mum on my lapel."

"You're going to sit in the Executive Club wearing a giant red mum?" I teased. "Yeah, right. I dare you."

"I take that dare," he replied. "You just wait and see."

Three

The Reagan National Airport was busy but not unmanageable, and since I had packed light, I didn't need to visit baggage claim. Instead, I pulled up the handle of my carry-on, secured my briefcase to it with a strap, and rolled off in pursuit of the Executive Club.

I made a detour to the ladies' room first to check my hair and makeup and clothes one more time. I had already brushed my teeth on the airplane, but I wanted to take one last look to make sure everything was just so. Today I had worn my favorite Ellen Tracy suit, an azure wool blend people often said accentuated my blue eyes. Now, as I studied myself in the mirror, I thought that might be true.

With my long brown hair and high cheekbones, I wasn't a raving beauty, but I wasn't exactly unpleasant-looking either. I wore my hair pulled back, and I had added an Hermés scarf at the neckline, which softened the look of the suit and showed off the slight tan I had acquired in the last few weeks while on vacation, prior to my trip to Nashville. All in all, I thought, stepping back from the mirror, I looked okay. Better than okay. I looked ready for an important encounter.

I reached the next terminal and went to the gate area where Tom had said I would find the unassuming door that led to the Executive

Club. Until I went to work for the foundation, I didn't even realize that airports had executive waiting rooms. But once I began traveling extensively on business, I found them to be well worth the annual fee. Placed discreetly near the boarding areas, these rooms offered an alternative to the noisy, uncomfortable seating sections around the gates and provided instead quiet, roomy places to work or relax during layovers and long delays.

I had never been to this particular Executive Club, but they were all pretty much alike: luxurious, comfortable, low key. I took a deep breath and stepped inside.

At the front desk, I handed over my bags and showed my membership card. Then I strolled to the main part of the room.

It resembled a nice, well-lit lounge, with large, plush chairs arranged in groupings around low coffee tables. Off of the main room were several smaller rooms. Some had desks, computers, and phone connections, and one had a conference table. I gave the place a quick scan but didn't see any red mums or carnations—or anyone who looked as though he was waiting for someone. Suddenly, it struck me how odd it was that I had no idea what Tom looked like. I may have spoken to him a thousand times on the phone, but I'd never seen a photo nor even heard a description of him.

According to my watch, I was a few minutes early, so I took the time to get a soda and a bowl of pretzels. Then I chose a chair in a small, empty seating area and sat down to wait.

I had only been there a few minutes when I got a text message. Taking out my phone, I saw that it was from Shayna Greer, a young woman I had been helping through a ministry of my church in my spare time. The message said, simply, *Call me! Its urgent!*

"Not a good time, Shayna," I whispered to myself even as I pressed the button to call her back. Shayna was a sweet girl, but she was in the process of trying to pull her life together after a stint in a drug rehabilitation center, and it seemed everything related to her was one crisis after another.

"Callie?" she said as she answered the phone.

"Yes, it's me. What's up?"

She sobbed loudly into the phone.

"It's Eddie Ray!" she cried, referring to an ex-boyfriend who had only recently reentered her life. "He's missing!"

"Missing?"

"We had a big fight last night. He ran off mad, and he still hasn't come back."

I exhaled loudly and looked at my watch. It was already 1:15; Tom was late, but I knew he would be here any second.

"How can *I* help, Shayna?" I asked, trying not to sound exasperated. "I've told you before, you're supposed to call your sponsor or your social worker when something like this comes up. I'm here to help you with work-related issues *only*."

"I know," she said, crying. "But I didn't want to talk to them. I wanted you."

I looked around the room, wondering why people with such complicated personal lives always seemed to seek me out. Maybe it was from my years as a private investigator. Perhaps I gave off the vibe of someone who was used to handling other people's problems.

"Don't you think he just went somewhere to cool down?" I asked evenly. "Running off mad seems to be his pattern, doesn't it?"

"Yeah, but it's different this time," she said, sniffing now. "Something's wrong."

I pinched the bridge of my nose between my eyes.

"How is it different?"

"Because he never came back this morning. He always comes back. I went looking for him, and it turns out he never showed up at Stinky's last night either."

"You've lost me, Shayna."

"That's where he goes to sleep whenever he's mad at me. Stinky's got an enclosed back porch with a cot in it, and he lets Eddie Ray sleep there whenever he wants."

"Did you talk to this 'Stinky' person this morning and ask him if he saw Eddie Ray last night?"

"Yeah. He said Eddie Ray was in the bar for a while, but he doesn't know where he went after that. I talked to, like, ten different people, and that's what they all said."

I glanced up, watching a group of businessmen enter the club. At first, I was afraid that Tom might be among them, but then I realized that they were all in their 50s. One of the few things I knew about Tom was that he was in his early 30s, like me.

"Isn't it possible," I asked, lowering my voice, "that Eddie Ray left the bar with another woman, and that's why nobody will tell you where he went?"

She was quiet for a moment.

"I guess," she said softly. "But I don't think so. He may not be the best boyfriend in the world, but as far as I know he's never cheated on me."

I had to stifle a groan. It seemed that among the long list of Eddie Ray's sins, infidelity wasn't among them.

"Look," I said, trying to make my voice calm. "This really isn't a good time for me now. You're still going to meet me at Advancing Attire at five o'clock, right? We can talk about it more then."

"I can't wait that long. I'll go crazy!"

I glanced at my watch and calculated. Tom's flight was at 2:15, so that meant he would probably want to go to the gate a little before 2:00. If I got out of here then and drove straight home, I could make it to Advancing Attire by 3:30.

"Let's move it up then," I said. "How's half past three?"

"Okay," she whimpered. "But, Callie, what if something's really wrong?"

"We'll deal with it at that time," I said. "I promise."

I managed to get Shayna off the phone, but I couldn't help being upset by her timing. Then I realized I was allowing her emotional meltdown to radically infringe on my special moment. Wishing I had waited before I called her, I slipped the phone into my jacket pocket, closed my eyes, and forced myself to calm down. Shayna's problems with her boyfriend would still be there later. For now, I had more important things going on.

When I opened my eyes, I saw a beautiful blonde woman walking purposefully toward me. She was dressed impeccably in an elegant, understated suit that looked like Armani. She had long legs, a knockout figure, and a humongous diamond ring on the fourth finger of her left hand.

"Kelly?" she asked. "Kelly Webber?"

"Callie," I corrected, standing up. "I'm Callie Webber."

"You're waiting for Tom?"

"Yes."

She came to a stop in front of me and smiled, flashing perfect white teeth.

"I'm so glad I found you," she drawled in a slightly southern accent. "He said to look for a lady with her hair in a bun, so that's what I did."

I blinked, feeling vaguely insulted, though I wasn't sure why.

"Where's Tom?" I asked, apprehension tingling at the back of my neck.

She gestured toward the chairs, so we sat; then she leaned forward, placing a perfectly manicured finger on my arm.

"He is so, so sorry," she said, "but he suddenly had a huge change of plans. I just put him on a plane to New Orleans."

"New Orleans?" I asked. "I thought he was headed to Singapore. For a couple of *months.*"

"No, he had to postpone that whole trip. Something came up."

"Is everything okay?"

She sat up straight, smoothing her hair absently with one hand.

"Oh, I'm sure," she said. "That's just how it goes with Tom sometimes. All of a sudden, he'll drop everything and spin off in another direction, just like that." She snapped her manicured fingers for emphasis. "It drives me nuts," she added, "but that's my Tom!"

I sat back, my mind reeling. Tom had canceled our meeting, canceled his trip to Singapore, and now he was flying south? Unbelievable!

"I hope there's nothing wrong," I said.

"Well, I keep telling him he needs to buy himself a corporate jet. Then he wouldn't have problems like this when he wants to make last minute changes. We had a hard time finding him an available seat. He's flying coach—in a *center* seat, no less!"

I knew there was a stupid look on my face as she continued to babble on. It was taking a moment for everything to compute, for my expectations to align with reality. *My Tom?* Had she really called him "my Tom"? I simply looked at this woman, who was now talking about leg room and bulkheads and exit rows.

"Excuse me," I interrupted finally, "but you are…"

"Oh, I'm sorry," she said. "Janine. Janine McDowell."

Learning her name was fine, but I meant who was she in relation to Tom. His fiancée? His sister? His travel agent?

"How do you know Tom?" I asked.

"Oh, honey, don't get me started," she said, grinning. "We'll be here all night! Suffice it to say, we have an interesting history together."

The way she drew out the word *inter-es-ting* left an odd, empty feeling in the pit of my stomach.

"Anyway," she said, "he asked me to apologize for him and to tell you that he'll try to call you at home tonight."

I looked at my watch, thinking about the rest of my day. I had the appointment with Shayna at 3:30, and then I would be home after that.

"Okay," I said softly.

We stood, and I thanked her before walking away. In a sort of daze, I collected my bags from the front desk and walked toward the door. As an afterthought, I turned back to the woman, who was now in the telephone area, dialing a number.

"Excuse me," I said, going back toward her. She disconnected the call before she had finished dialing it.

"Yes?"

"Did Tom leave some paperwork for me, by any chance? There would've been a couple of files, or maybe some manila envelopes?"

"No," she said. "Nothing like that."

I started to turn away.

"Oh, hang on," she said. "There was one thing."

I turned back and waited expectantly as she opened her purse. From it she pulled a giant silk flower, a mum, resplendent in a vivid red. I took it from her, smiling in spite of myself when I saw a big safety pin clipped to the back.

"He said to give you this," she reported, a puzzled look on her face. "And to tell you that, next time, he dares *you* to wear it."

Four

As soon as I reached my car in the parking lot, I slipped my bag into the back, pulled out my cell phone, and called my friend and coworker Harriet.

She worked in the foundation's main office in Washington, DC, in a small but pleasant-looking building tucked in the heart of the embassy district. I tried to get in there as often as I could, but since I lived almost two hours away, on Maryland's Eastern Shore, I actually spent most of my time working from home or out on assignment.

"Hey, Harriet," I said as soon as she came on the line. "It's Callie."

"Callie?" she twanged in her Texas accent. "You poor thing! I heard what happened at the airport."

"Yeah, so much for finally meeting face-to-face."

"If it helps, hon, Tom felt just awful about it."

"What's going on?" I asked. "Do you know?"

"Not really," she said. "He just called me on his way to the airport to tell me he had a change of plans. He said for me to make sure you knew how sorry he was for standing you up."

I pressed a button on my keychain to disarm the alarm and unlock the doors of my car, a sturdy new SUV. Unfortunately, I had totaled my previous car during a recent investigation, when I was run off the road by a man hired to intimidate me. I never wanted to feel that vulnerable again, so this time I went with the safest, strongest vehicle I could afford.

"He's been planning this trip to Singapore for weeks," I said, swinging the door open and placing my briefcase on the passenger seat. "What could possibly have come up to change his plans?"

"I have a feeling it was some kind of family matter. He said he would fill me in later."

I closed the door, walked to the driver's side, and got in.

"Why didn't he call me himself?"

"You were still on the plane, hon. He tried, but your cell phone was off, and we couldn't figure out any other way to reach you."

"Oh, he reached me all right," I said. "He has some blonde babe meet me at the airport. Who is she?"

"A blonde babe?"

I explained my encounter in the Executive Club.

"You got me," Harriet said when I was done. "You know him better than I do, Callie. I may manage the foundation, but you're the one who spends hours on the phone with him every night."

"It's not hours, and it's not every night."

"You know what I mean. He's never mentioned a fiancée, has he?"

"No, but that doesn't mean anything. He's never mentioned a lot of things about himself."

To say that Tom was a private person was an understatement. I had learned a long time ago not to pry for details, but this whole thing had really thrown me for a loop.

"Did he at least leave any files for me? On the phone he mentioned a couple of different assignments."

"No. He said he didn't have time to finish things up. I'm afraid you'll have to wait till he gets back to you. I have the feeling you might be cooling your heels for a few days."

"You've got to be kidding."

I began weaving my car through the labyrinth of parked vehicles to the exit, thinking this whole fiasco was becoming more frustrating by the minute. On the one hand, I always enjoyed getting a little time off to spend around my home. On the other hand, prior to the trip to Tennessee, I had just spent a wonderful two weeks doing nothing more strenuous than walking my dog and paddling my canoe. Now it was to be more of the same? A little freedom was a good thing, but too much just might make me stir-crazy.

Harriet and I concluded our call with the promise we would let each other know if Tom made any contact. As I put away the phone and pulled into the traffic heading over the Potomac, I felt a heavy weight settle against my heart. Would I ever meet Tom in person? Did he really care if he ever met me?

I drove on toward the Eastern Shore, trying not to think about it, blinking away the tears that had suddenly, inexplicably filled my eyes.

Five

Traffic was moving, but it was fairly dense for early afternoon on a Monday. I usually preferred flying into Baltimore, since the drive to my house from there was much simpler than from downtown Washington. Still, I eventually managed to make my way onto Route 50 toward Annapolis and the bridge that would carry me over the Chesapeake Bay. After a while the traffic thinned out, and once I reached the bridge it was a brief but breathtaking hop to the Eastern Shore.

I began to wind my way south from there to the rural area I called home, feeling myself relax more with every mile. There was something about going from the busyness of the mainland to the country quiet of this area that always soothed my heart and made me feel at peace. That was one reason I had moved here after my husband Bryan died—that and the fact that this had been our favorite getaway spot when we were married, the place where we went when we just wanted to be alone with nature and with each other.

My house was located on a 20-mile-long peninsula—a flat, rambling expanse of land that stretched into the Chesapeake Bay and was flanked by two rivers. At the head of the peninsula was the waterfront borough of Osprey Cove, a quaint little town filled with upscale shops, a few tiny museums, and a number of expensive little bed-and-breakfasts. I usually took the bypass that let me circumnavigate the main drag, which was often clogged with tourists. Today, however, I drove straight into the heart of things, slowing for the traffic that filled the narrow streets.

Except for the congestion problems, Osprey Cove was a charming place—so charming, in fact, that it almost felt fake, like a Disney version of small-town America. There were tiny Cape Code houses and cobblestone streets and lots of window boxes overflowing with the colorful blossoms of spring and summer. In the fall they had crab, oyster, and waterfowl festivals in the large open-air park beside the public docks, and in the winter the streets of the village were graced with white twinkle lights and roving carolers.

The people who lived there were a friendly sort, though I kept my dealings with them to a minimum. I preferred the solitude of my home farther out on the peninsula, and I usually came to Osprey Cove only for groceries or other supplies, as well as the occasional visit to my favorite charity, the place where I helped mentor local young women like Shayna Greer.

The place was called Advancing Attire, and though my church was one of its sponsors, it was basically an independent nonprofit organization. My initial involvement had been simply as a donor, but I was eventually persuaded by the director to put in some volunteer time there as well. Of course, as someone who made a living investigating nonprofits, I did my homework first, evaluating it with the same list of criteria I used with my job. In the end, I had found the organization to be caring and compassionate, with a terrific mission and an efficient, cost-effective operation.

Advancing Attire was located in downtown Osprey Cove, and from the outside it looked like a regular ladies' clothing store. But our "customers" weren't off-the-street shoppers at all—they were indigent women sent to us by the county, and they came by appointment only. Mostly, these were women who possessed the training and intelligence to get better jobs than they'd previously held but lacked the proper "look" to get them through the door. Our mission was to collect used, professional-type clothing from the working women in our area and give that clothing to our clients, who then sought out better job opportunities.

Beyond that, some of us also took it upon ourselves to follow up with the young women we had helped to outfit by guiding them through the job-seeking process and giving them tips for the workplace. Apparently, Shayna thought my help also extended to helping find lost boyfriends, a notion I would need to dispel fairly quickly. From what I had gathered through recent conversations, this fellow she was involved with was a real piece of work. I had no desire to serve as the local missing persons bureau.

I made it to the main strip and found a parking space about a block away. Glancing at my watch as I climbed out of the car, I was pleased to see that I had arrived with a good 20 minutes to spare. I walked up the street to the side door of the building and let myself in with my key.

"Well, if it isn't Callie Webber!"

The program's director, Verlene Linford, came out from behind her desk and headed toward me across the cluttered room, weaving her way around massive piles of clothing. Verlene was one of those perpetually cheerful people, always smiling, always able to make you feel as if, for the moment at least, you were the most important person in the world. That's why she was such a perfect choice to head up Advancing Attire. Her job was to make our impoverished clients, no matter what their circumstances, feel as though they were worthy of a little loving care and attention. Right now, she had her kind brown eyes trained firmly on me.

"We missed you in church on Sunday," she scolded gently, reaching out to stop a mountain of blazers from toppling over next to her. Though she never complained about the cramped space—and she seemed organized enough to be able to lay her hand on any specific item at any given time—I still thought how much easier her work would be if she had a little more room to spread out.

"I was in Tennessee," I replied. "For work."

"What about the Ladies Circle dinner at church? Will you be coming to that?"

"I-I'm not sure."

"Well, I put your name down for a reservation, just in case. It's coming up soon, you know, and I didn't want you to miss out. It's filling up fast!"

Trying not to roll my eyes, I told Verlene that I'd have to see, that it depended on my work schedule, knowing I had no intention of joining the Ladies Circle or any other group.

For some reason, Verlene saw it as her personal duty to keep tabs on me where church was concerned. She hated that I limited my attendance to the Sunday morning worship service—and even then, only when I was in town. As far as she was concerned, I should be on committees and in Bible studies and in the women's group. Despite my protestations, she nagged at me almost every time I saw her. If she weren't so good-hearted, I might be tempted to tell her to mind her own business and leave me alone.

It wasn't that I thought church was unimportant; I knew that the Bible repeatedly stresses the need for "gathering together" with other believers. When Bryan and I lived in Virginia, we were both very active in our church. But here, it was different. Here, I just didn't have the time or energy to invest in the peripheral goings-on of the church community. I was spiritually fed from the Sunday morning service just fine. Everything else—Bible study and outreach projects—I did on my own, and that's the way I liked it.

"Ah well, you lead such a glamorous life," Verlene said, "always jetting off to here and there. When did you get back?"

"Just a while ago," I said. "I have an appointment with Shayna Greer."

"Oh, that's right. I heard she got a job as a medical billing clerk. Good for her!"

We talked about some of the new clothes that had come in since I was here last and what might work for Shayna. At our first appointment, arranged by her social worker, Shayna had been quiet and kind of shy, though very sweet, and we had been able to put together a nice outfit for her to wear to job interviews. Now that she had landed a good job, it was my assignment to provide her with a week's worth of professional-looking clothes, a haircut, and some makeup—

just as we did for all of our clients. Once she started her new job, she and I would probably touch base a few more times; then the case would be closed out and, hopefully, she would be well on her way to a new and better future.

Though I enjoyed the mentoring side of my responsibilities, my favorite task at Advancing Attire was definitely picking out the clothes. Maybe it wasn't much in the grand scheme of things, but I always thought that the self-esteem these women got from their makeovers was priceless. My hope for today was that I would be able to get Shayna's mind off of the missing boyfriend and onto the task at hand.

Verlene and I went into the front room, which was also small but much less crowded and designed to look like an upscale women's boutique. We had slacks, tops, suits, skirts, dresses, accessories, shoes, and even high-quality undergarments organized onto racks and shelves by size and style. Two dressing rooms were in the rear of the store, with a huge three-sided mirror and viewing area between them. Because we didn't charge our clients for the clothes, the only thing missing from our little boutique was a cash register.

"We got a new batch of shoes from Mrs. Reddingham," Verlene said, rolling her eyes and pointing toward the racks. By our previous calculations, Mrs. Reddingham had to have bought an average of one pair of shoes per day for the last ten years to equal the quantity she sent our way. "Oh, and Grace Collins passed away. Did you know her? Of Collins Electronics. Her family has been sending us some of her things for a while, but after the funeral the son brought us a *ton* of stuff. All beautiful, very pricey. She was quite ill for the last several years, so most of it was hardly worn. I think we've gotten it all out on the racks by now."

"Okay, thanks."

"Like Shayna, Grace was very petite. You might find some nice stuff there."

We walked around looking at the different items, and then I sent Verlene back to her work while I made coffee and waited for Shayna to arrive. Once the pot was brewing, I wet some paper towels and tried to repair the damage done to my nice pumps by the mud in the cemetery earlier this morning.

There was a knock on the door just as I was slipping the shoes back onto my feet, and I headed through the boutique to see Shayna standing on the other side of the glass. Her eyes were rimmed in red and filled with tears. I braced myself, unlocked the latch, and opened the door.

Six

"Come on in," I said, holding the door wide. "How's it going?"

Shayna dutifully trooped inside. She wore a denim jacket over a faded T-shirt and carried the outfit we had previously given her draped over her arm. She was pale and thin, with about five inches of dark roots at the top of long hair that had once been bleached a harsh blonde.

"I'm okay," she said softly.

"By the look on your face, I gather your boyfriend hasn't turned up yet?"

"I'm so worried," she answered. "Nobody's seen Eddie Ray anywhere."

I took a deep breath and guided her through the store to the seating area near the dressing rooms. Reluctantly, I sat her down, gave her some coffee, and let her pour the whole story out to me. Apparently, she and Eddie Ray had had a huge, screaming fight the night before, and he had stormed off to the local bar. As she had already explained over the phone, that wasn't unusual. What was unusual was that he had not come back this morning, and no one knew where he had gone after he left the bar last night.

"I even called the police," Shayna said mournfully, "but they told me there was nothing they could do yet. He hasn't been missing long enough."

"He is a grown man, Shayna, free to go if he chooses."

"He wouldn't leave me, Callie. Not again."

"Again?" I asked, alarm bells going off in my head. History seemed to be repeating itself.

"He ran off one other time, a while back," she admitted sheepishly. "He was gone for months, actually. But then he showed up a few weeks ago. He told me he had changed."

I stood and crossed to the counter, retrieving a box of tissues and wondering how to counsel this young woman, who seemed to keep making all the wrong choices.

"Does he take drugs, Shayna?" I asked. "You told me you were in a twelve-step program. If you're in recovery, you shouldn't be around him anyway."

I knew it wasn't really my place to say—as I told her before, I wasn't her sponsor or her social worker, just a volunteer helping her out—but it was hard to hold my tongue.

"No, no," she replied, "he does pot sometimes, I think, but never around me. The problem is that he...he's..." Her voice faded. "Eddie Ray's a big dreamer, I guess you could say. Always got some great thing coming, right around the next corner. He was cooking up something really big this time. He was so excited. That's another reason I know he didn't leave on purpose. He had too much at stake."

"But you said yourself that he's left before."

"I thought it would be different this time."

I pulled out a tissue and handed it to her. She took it gratefully, wiped at her eyes, and then blew her nose.

"Are you in love with him?" I asked gently, taking a different approach.

"I used to be," she whispered. "I'm not sure I am anymore."

"Then don't let him mess this up for you," I said earnestly. "You got a good job—the job you trained for, that you worked hard for. When we finish here today, you'll also have some nice new clothes and a big opportunity. You don't need some guy coming in and messing up your life this way. It's time to focus on *yourself*, Shayna. A nice job can be more rewarding than you'd ever imagine."

My words hung in the air between us, and I could see the doubt on her face. I wished I could make her understand what having a career really felt like—the incredible sense of accomplishment that came with doing a job well, the paychecks that reflected all the training and preparation, the feeling that there was a reason to get up in the morning outside of yourself and your own needs. Still, she was young. Try as I might to share with her the secrets of the workplace, until she lived it for herself, she wouldn't really understand.

"Eddie Ray says my new job is dumb."

"What?"

"He says the life of a nine-to-fiver is boring and stupid. He said that as soon as this thing he's gotten involved in pans out, we'll have enough money so that neither one of us will ever have to work again."

"Ignoring for a moment the fact that Eddie Ray is probably in another state by now," I said, trying to keep the frustration out of my voice, "I thought you *wanted* to work. I thought you *liked* medical billing."

"It's okay."

"Just okay? When I talked to you the other day, you were bursting with enthusiasm. You said you got a great job with good pay in a really nice office. What happened to all of that excitement?"

She looked down at the floor and shrugged.

"Shayna," I said, sitting in the chair in front of her, forcing her to look at me, "just when things are starting to go right for you, why are you letting yourself get dragged back down by a man?"

"I don't know," she whispered, tears spilling down her cheeks.

I felt a surge of sympathy for her. One thing I had observed since I started volunteering with Advancing Attire was that many of these indigent women simply took what life offered—the good and the bad—without it ever dawning on them that they had choices, that sometimes they could take control themselves.

"Shayna," I said, meeting her eyes, "life has thrown a lot of bad things your way. But there are some things you can choose to throw back, you know. You don't always have to take everything as it comes."

She attempted to smile in spite of herself.

"Look," I continued, "you have a real chance here to be a success completely from your own efforts. If Eddie Ray is still around—and if he truly cares for you—he'll have to respect that."

"I...I guess so," she whispered.

"And if he really has skipped town, at least you'll know not to fall for his lines the next time he shows up."

Shayna looked off in the distance, her eyes filled with pain.

"You're right," she said.

"Good," I replied. "I know you told me you've been trying to grow in your faith. Why don't we say a quick prayer and turn this matter over to God? He knows what's best for you. Believing that is about the only thing that will get us through the tough times."

Seven

Shayna seemed better after we shared a short prayer. As a relatively new Christian, she often seemed to have trouble remembering to surrender everything to the Lord. Now that she had, she seemed much more calm. I, too, needed to gain a little perspective for her situation. *It's not my place to mother her,* I reminded myself. *I'm only here to give her the tools she needs for this new start.*

"Now, let's get down to work and find you some new clothes," I said, and she quickly agreed.

As always, I started by laying out on the counter the clothing we had already given her; then I asked her to describe her new workplace and the types of clothing she had observed while there for her interview. It sounded as though the office was what I'd call "dress casual," a look that would be easy to assemble from the clothing we had on hand. Using what we had given her already, we would now attempt to build a mix-and-match wardrobe that would carry her to her first paycheck and beyond.

The next hour passed in a blur as I pulled things from the racks, she tried them on, and we talked about what worked and what didn't. She certainly wasn't very picky—in fact, she seemed thrilled with everything I suggested. Once we had made our final choices, I loaded the list of her new clothes into the computer. When I was finished, I ran a printout and handed it to her.

"Is there any way you could mark what goes with what on this list?" she asked, studying it. "I'm afraid I'm going to get it wrong."

I glanced at the pile of mostly navy, black, and tan items. Thanks to some new things that had come in, we had been able to put together seven separates—plus shoes and accessories—that she could mix and match into about twenty different combinations. Remembering what we had done, I wrote it all down, putting little asterisks next to my favorite combinations.

"Now that we've got you set here," I said finally, sliding the neatly folded items into several bags, "we'll run up the street to get your hair done. Your appointment is in just a few minutes."

"Oh, that's so great," she said excitedly. "I *hate* my hair."

"They'll give you some makeup tips, too, if you like," I said and was pleased to see a genuine grin on her face. I realized she might be very pretty with a more appropriate hairstyle and some artfully applied makeup.

I peeked into the office and told Verlene we were leaving. Then I locked the front door and Shayna and I headed out, her arms weighted down with the heavy bags of clothes and things she insisted on carrying herself. Though I was still upset from the earlier disappointment of not connecting with Tom at the airport, at least I had a bit of a distraction to get me through the afternoon.

"So are you nervous about starting the job?" I asked as we walked.

The air was crisp but not unbearably cold. We were a good two blocks from the bay, but I could still smell the sweet-salty scent of the water.

"Kind of," she admitted. "The people seem real nice, though."

"When do you start?"

"Two weeks from today."

We chatted as we walked the three blocks to the hairdresser's. As we went I noticed that most of the shopwindows were decorated for Thanksgiving, with pumpkins, cornucopias, and lots of fake autumn leaves.

Once we reached the salon, I took Shayna's bags from her and watched as she was immediately led away to get started. I sat on a chic black couch that was attractive but not very comfortable, flipping through a hairstyle magazine from the coffee table in front of me. As I waited, women came and went in a steady pace. Shayna's appointment was with Denise Hightower, the salon's owner. I felt sure Shayna would come out looking great—or at least much better than she had looked going in.

Denise was my regular stylist, though I came in only every few months to have my ends cut blunt. I always wore my dark brown hair pulled back into a tight chignon at my neck, a look that my hairdresser frequently criticized but couldn't talk me out of. I maintained that my style was quick, easy, and professional. That it probably wasn't all that flattering was of no consequence to me.

Despite our disagreements about my hairstyle, I really liked Denise. She had a huge extended family living all over the Eastern Shore. When I first decided to relocate here permanently, Denise's whole family had been very kind and helpful—from Denise's brother, the real estate agent who found me my house, to her cousin, the travel agent who quietly handled all of my traveling needs, going above and beyond the call of duty on numerous occasions. I would've thought them financially opportunistic—going after fresh meat, so to speak—if not for other simultaneous gestures of goodwill that brought them no profit, such as casseroles proffered at my door, invitations to barbecues and parties, and offers of rides to church. Not being a very social person, I rebuffed them so many times that they had finally stopped asking, but I was still grateful for their efforts, and I liked Denise particularly. When I ended up joining their church on my own, the whole family seemed thrilled.

"They didn't tell me you were bringing me a beauty," Denise called out to me now from her station across the room. The place had about ten stations, but usually only two or three women were working at a time. Denise had the best spot, back in the corner, and Shayna was sitting in her chair, a black cape draped around her shoulders, her face radiant in professional-looking makeup, her hair still long, two-toned, and damp. "We decided to do the makeup first," Denise said.

"Now she likes it so much, she's giving me carte blanche with the hairstyle."

"Go for it, Denise," I replied, smiling. "Make her look like someone out of *Vogue*."

Tossing the magazine onto the table, I stood and crossed to Denise's area and sat in the chair in the empty station next to hers. I didn't really need to hang around, and it would've been nice to go on home now and maybe take my canoe out on the river before the sun set. But after being off on my own for three days with the honor guard assignment—not to mention my seclusion during two weeks of vacation before that—something in me didn't really want to be alone right then. Especially after the Tom fiasco.

The three of us chatted as Denise worked on Shayna's hair. She was going short enough so that all of the bleached-blonde part was getting cut off. Soon there were foot-long tresses all over the floor, and I was glad to see that Shayna looked happy with the results. She really did have nice bone structure, and it seemed there might even be some body to her hair now that it wasn't so weighted down by length. Perhaps once she walked into the work force with this new image, she might finally find a little of the self-esteem Eddie Ray was trying to drain away.

By the time Denise was finished, Shayna truly looked like a different person. It wasn't just the outside that had changed; there was something going on inside as well. As Shayna beamed at herself in the mirror, Denise winked at me. We both knew this moment was why we got involved. This moment was what it was all about.

Shayna and I walked back up the street toward her car, and she was nearly bouncing from excitement, a far cry from the miserable girl who had first shown up at the store a few hours before.

"I think when I get home I'll try on all the outfits again, just to see how they look with my new hair."

"That'll be fun."

"I swear, this makeover is just as good as the ones they do in the fashion magazines. You know, in the 'before' picture they're looking all ugly and dumpy, and then in the 'after' picture they're all fixed up and beautiful? Oh, I hope Eddie Ray's back so he can see!"

She prattled on all the way up the street. I let her chatter, wondering what Eddie Ray would do if he were there and she showed up looking so different. Would he pop this bubble as soon as he saw her, or would he like the change and even endorse it?

We were halfway back to Advancing Attire when I looked up to see Verlene striding toward us down the street. She smiled and waved, and as we drew closer she began exclaiming about Shayna's new look. Shayna beamed from ear to ear, obviously proud of how it had turned out.

"I do believe this is one of the best makeovers I've ever seen!" Verlene cried, though I knew for a fact she said that to most of the women who came through Advancing Attire. It wasn't that Verlene was insincere; it's just that she was so genuinely excited about each and every transformation.

"Thank you," Shayna replied earnestly.

"Can I help you with those bags of clothes?" Verlene offered, but Shayna shook her head.

"I'm fine."

Verlene walked with us back toward Advancing Attire.

"I was hoping to catch you before you left, Callie," Verlene said. "I wanted to get your advice in a...in a financial matter. Shayna, I trust you'll keep this information to yourself."

"Yes, ma'am," Shayna replied, looking as if she couldn't care less. Her mind seemed to be on something else entirely.

"The pharmacy is going out of business," Verlene said softly, referring to the store located next to Advancing Attire. "Their lease is up, and the owner wants to retire."

"Are you thinking of taking over their space?" I asked. "That's wonderful! Now you can finally enlarge the place."

Verlene pressed her hands together and brought them to her mouth, bouncing the tips of her index fingers against her lips.

"Yes," she replied finally. "Goodness knows we need the space. But it would...complicate things somewhat. Financially, it may involve bringing in a third party."

"A third party? What do you mean?"

"There's a national group that's interested in signing up with Advancing Attire. I can show you the stuff they faxed me back at the shop. It's all very interesting."

"Signing up? What do you mean?"

"They provide services for nonprofits, like doing payroll and taxes. They also do fund-raising, which is where we come in. They have an anonymous local donor who's willing to sponsor Advancing Attire, including giving us enough money to rent the bigger space."

"Sounds wonderful, Verlene. But if the donor's local, why do you need to involve this other company at all?"

Verlene shook her head, as if she was as confused about that as I was.

"It kind of comes together," she said. "We get the donation only if we sign up with the company."

"That's a little odd," I said, "but I suppose it's worth looking into."

We approached Shayna's car, an aging, beat-up Chevrolet that looked as though it would fall apart at the next stop sign. Even from ten feet away, it stank of rust from the holes along the side, and spots all over the front hood were buffed down to the chrome, like body work that never been finished.

"Here, give me your keys," Verlene said, interrupting our conversation as she held a hand out toward Shayna. "Your arms are full."

Taking the keys from Shayna, Verlene walked straight to the trunk. She unlocked the lid, which popped right open.

Then she screamed.

Shayna and I ran forward to look inside. Immediately, Shayna dropped her bags on the pavement and began gasping for air. I stepped closer, peering at the gruesome scene in front of us.

There was a body in the trunk—from what I could tell, a dead body. It was a man, late 20s, with dark hair, a skimpy mustache, and a deep, fatal head wound. There was also a lot of blood, and it was soaked into the clothing and pooled in dark brown puddles all around the inside of the trunk. I swallowed hard, realizing that what I had smelled wasn't rust from the car, but this man's blood.

Shayna began moaning, a low guttural sound that gave me goose bumps. I turned away from the trunk and pushed her back, waving at the people gathering on the sidewalk so they would give us some room.

"Do you know who that is?" I asked Shayna, my heart pounding. As a private investigator, I had seen my share of dead bodies, but unexpectedly finding one in the trunk of someone's car was still a bit unnerving. Shayna was shivering, and it took a moment to get her to look me in the eye, to get her to speak. When she finally did, it was with a hoarse, tormented whisper.

"That's my missing boyfriend," she rasped. "That's Eddie Ray."

Eight

I don't know what I expected exactly, but I have to say I was impressed by the police conduct in the matter of the murder of Eddie Ray Higgins. Because we were in such a sparsely populated area, I think I had anticipated some two-bit sheriff and his sidekick to "keystone cop" their way through the whole thing. What I found, instead, were careful, astute professionals who seemed to know exactly what they were doing from the moment the first officer arrived.

Within an hour of our discovery of the body, the area had been cordoned off and photographed, the coroner was on the scene, and Shayna, Verlene, and I had been thoroughly questioned by two homicide detectives. Though no charges had been made and Shayna hadn't been read her rights, I could tell she was their number one suspect right off the bat. And, really, why shouldn't she be? The body was found in her car, after all, apparently killed by a whack to the head with something hard and solid.

Still, I knew Shayna hadn't done this. She was meek and timid and shy; this was the work of someone hard and aggressive and angry. Besides, I had seen earlier this afternoon the way she'd agonized over Eddie Ray's disappearance—and I had also seen the shock on her face when his body turned up in the trunk of her car. If she had been faking all of that, then she was one good actress indeed.

It was just starting to get dark when the mood among the police suddenly seemed to change. I realized something was up when a female officer approached Shayna with a pair of handcuffs and asked that she please hold out her hands. Shayna was under arrest, the cop said, for possession of an illegal substance and drug paraphernalia. Shayna paled as the cuffs were locked around her.

"That's a lie!" she cried. "I've been clean and sober for almost a year!"

"Officer?" I asked.

The woman glanced at me, and I thought she looked familiar. I wondered if I had met her somewhere before.

"We found a roach clip hidden under the front seat," she said softly to me, "along with a nice little bag of pot."

She frisked Shayna and then led her toward a waiting police car while reciting her her rights. I stood in place, figuring that Shayna was telling the truth, and that the stash probably belonged to Eddie Ray. The important thing here, I knew, wasn't that Shayna had possessed drugs. It was that the cops wanted to bring her in for murder but, lacking enough evidence, had found a way to take her in for drugs instead. Down at the station they could interrogate her extensively, keep her locked up safely, and generally sequester her until they could prove she'd whacked the man in the trunk. No slouches, these cops.

"Officer, you've got to believe me!" Shayna cried as the policewoman put her hand on Shayna's head and pressed her down into the backseat of the patrol car. For what it was worth, *I* believed her. Drug use was a part of her past, but I doubted very much she was involved in it any longer, and she certainly hadn't seemed under the influence when I had dealt with her in the last few weeks. She just seemed like a normal young woman who had made some bad decisions but had been working to turn her life around.

Now her life was taking a turn, all right, but definitely not in the direction she'd intended. Verlene and I silently watched as the police confiscated the bags of Shayna's new clothes and then drove off, lights flashing but with no siren. I watched the back of her head through the window as they slowly drove away, feeling a surge in the pit of my stomach, anxious for this poor kid and what might happen to her next.

Verlene was shaken and exhausted, and our earlier conversation about rental space and third parties was forgotten in the trauma of the afternoon. Eventually, her daughter showed up to drive her home, and I was relieved to see the girl put one arm firmly around her mother's shoulders and lead her carefully to the waiting car.

Once they were gone, I hung around the scene a bit longer, eavesdropping out of curiosity more than anything else. I tried to figure out who was who among the different people milling around the scene. I had already identified the lieutenant, the coroner, and the detectives, and I figured out which man was the patrol supervisor by the way he spoke to the other uniformed cops and kept a wary eye on the borders of the crime scene.

That left a man in a coat and tie who seemed to hover among the activity without becoming directly involved. He had a thin face with a pointed chin and a hook nose, and I had heard someone refer to him as "Litman." I probably wouldn't have thought much of him at all, except that the lieutenant seemed almost to defer to him, which was odd.

I finally decided Mr. Litman must be with the district attorney's office. In an area like this, they probably didn't get many murders—which meant that when they did, everyone who could possibly get involved came crawling out of the woodwork. The number of police cars, fire trucks, and ambulances that had first responded to the scene was a testament to that.

I wondered who Shayna's public defender would be and if he or she would be any good. Shayna had no way of knowing I was an attorney, and I was glad. As a corporate lawyer, I had never practiced criminal law and wasn't qualified to start now.

But I had also been a private investigator for quite a few years, and that part of me wondered if perhaps I could help now in some way. The poor kid didn't have any money or contacts. Though I hadn't been willing to sign on for her "missing persons" problem earlier today, murder was a different matter. I decided to visit Shayna at the jail the next day to see if we could figure this out. For now, it was time to go home. The sun had set quickly, and the darker it got the colder it became.

I approached the female cop who had arrested Shayna to ask if I was free to leave the scene. She was talking to another officer, so I waited at her elbow, watching as several men extricated the stiff, dead body from the trunk. First, they unzipped a body bag and spread it out on the ground, and then they carefully lifted the body and set it down on the open bag.

As they zipped the bag shut, I noted that the dead man was wearing cheap shoes, polyester pants, and an ill-fitting navy sweater dotted across the back with some kind of seed burrs. Nearly all of his clothing was darkly stained with blood.

The tire iron was carefully removed next, a dark metal rod with one curved end, the diameter of which seemed to match the size and shape of Eddie Ray's head wound. My guess was that they had found their murder weapon. The policeman slid the rod into an extra-long evidence bag and carried it away. I felt sure the police would impound the car.

At last the female cop finished her conversation and turned her attention toward me.

"Hey, Callie," she said. "I'd bet you're about ready to get out of here."

Again, I had that feeling that we knew each other. I didn't want to embarrass myself, but I also didn't want to go any further without making the connection.

"I'm sorry, but how do I know you?" I asked bluntly. "I can't quite put my finger on it."

She looked bemused, and then she took off her hat and grinned.

"I'm Barbara Hightower," she said, smoothing down short, dark bangs. "Denise's sister?"

I smiled, recognizing her now from the beauty salon. She had stopped in once while I was there, and I remembered remarking there was probably a Hightower in every line of work in the county.

"Of course," I said. "I'm sorry. You look just like her. I should've remembered."

"No offense taken," she replied, putting her hat back on. "There are so many of us, even we get confused sometimes."

I told her that my father and brother were cops and that I had been impressed with the police work I'd seen there this evening. I asked if the public defender's office was equally as proficient.

"It's really the luck of the draw over there," she replied under her breath. "Depends on who she gets. You know how it is."

I nodded, saying that I hoped someone competent would be assigned to Shayna's case.

"Excuse me," a man said, interrupting, "but what exactly is your involvement here?"

We turned to see the fellow in the suit, the one I assumed was from the DA's office.

"Mr. Litman, this is Callie Webber," Barbara said, stiffening. "She was with Shayna Greer when the body was discovered."

"Has she been questioned by the detectives?"

"Yes, sir. We're just wrapping things up."

"Very well," the man said, turning away as if he had already dismissed us. "When you're finished, Officer Hightower, please escort Ms. Webber to the perimeter of the police line."

He strutted off and Barbara rolled her eyes.

"Who is that?" I whispered.

"Just a bureaucrat."

Together, we walked toward the perimeter.

"So anyway," Barbara said, "you don't think she did it?"

"No, I don't," I replied. "She doesn't have it in her."

"Maybe not."

"Besides," I said, "like I told the detectives already, Shayna spent half the day sobbing because she thought Eddie Ray had gone off and left her. Trust me, when Verlene opened that trunk, Shayna was as shocked to see the guy there as we were."

Another officer began waving Barbara over to the car, so she told me I was free to leave and then shook my hand, thanking me for my cooperation. She gave me a card with her name and numbers on it, in case I thought of anything else I needed to tell the police. I tucked the card into my pocket, my fingers stiff from the cold. I was more than happy to head home to the warmth of my house.

I started the car and pulled into the line of traffic heading out of town, thinking about Shayna and her plight. The poor girl! Not only had she lost Eddie Ray—admittedly, not the most wonderful guy in the world but certainly someone she'd shared a past with and still had some feelings for—but now she was sitting in jail, about to be charged with his murder. All afternoon, when he was merely "missing," I had told myself that she was being an alarmist, that she had no reason to worry about him.

Apparently, I had been dead wrong.

By the time I made it out of Osprey Cove and onto the highway, the air coming through my heater vents was warm. My brain was spinning, and I told myself that it was time to clear my thoughts. Shayna's problems would still be there in the morning, I knew. I would check up on her then. For now, I decided, I would concentrate on picking up my dog and getting home. I said a prayer for Shayna, and then I put her out of my mind and turned my attention toward the tasks at hand.

Nine

After the confusion and trauma of the afternoon, it did feel good to be going home. Located about ten miles beyond Osprey Cove, my house was my retreat: a cozy two-bedroom cottage on three acres of wooded land right on the waterfront. It was an odd area to live in and had taken some getting used to—especially the lack of city conveniences and the irritating rhythms of tourism. But the problems of living there were well worth the trade-off, for I had merely to stroll across my yard and down the dock to be out on my canoe, where I spent nearly all of my free time paddling up and down the hundreds of rivers, inlets, and tributaries of the wildlife-rich Chesapeake Bay area.

You couldn't see the water from the highway—especially not in the dark, like now. The road was lined with tall pines and dense vegetation, broken here and there by long driveways that wound off out of sight into the trees. To the casual visitor, it was all very deceptive, since most of those plain-looking driveways led to shockingly huge and expensive mansions along the waterfront. I saw everything from the river in my canoe, so I knew just what was hidden beyond those pines, and the opulence was sometimes astonishing. My own home was a true find, a former caretaker's cottage that had been parceled off from an estate and sold for a large but not unmanageable sum. Bought with the full amount of Bryan's life insurance settlement, the place gave me privacy and water access without a million-dollar mortgage.

As I neared my turnoff, I called Lindsey, the teenager who always kept my dog when I was traveling. She was surprised to hear from me so soon but said she would have Sal ready to go when I got there.

Lindsey was as good as her word, and after a quick, two-minute stop, I proceeded to my house with Sal on my lap. She was a good dog, very tiny but not nervous the way so many toy breeds tended to be. She loved riding in the car, and right now she was also happy to have me back.

There was one light on in the house when we got home, the lamp in the front room I kept on a timer. Otherwise, the place was quiet and dark. I didn't mind. I found the solitude peaceful and welcoming.

I flipped on lights as we came in, working my way down the hall to my bedroom at the end. I put my pumps away, took off the suit I had worn all day, and slipped into sweatpants and a warm sweatshirt. I felt weary but wired, and I couldn't believe I had started the day in a graveyard in Nashville. What a lot had happened since then!

I went back to the kitchen and heated some canned soup for myself and scooped some dog food on a plate for Sal. My kitchen was wide and functional, with a door to the carport on one side and a sliding glass door that led to the deck on the other. On summer days I could pull a wonderful breeze all the way through. Now that the days were getting colder, however, I wouldn't be doing that for a while.

The rest of the house was simple and cozy, its rooms all in a row from front to back. First there was the wide front room with a fireplace, couches, and chairs; then the kitchen with its access to the big wrap-around deck; then the back bedroom, with a small adjoining bathroom. The second bedroom, which I used as an office, jutted out from the side of the house on the right, and I had a feeling it had been added to the cottage's original structure at a later date.

Outside, I used the "L" shape of the house to form two sides of a play yard for my dog. I had placed a neat little dog house in the corner and then fenced in the other two sides, putting the gate right next to the carport. In comparison with most of my wealthy neighbors, my home was quite small, but I loved it and found it big enough for my simple needs.

In the kitchen was a perfectly good table and chairs, but now I ate my dinner standing at the counter, still feeling edgy. After Sal and I had both finished eating, I let her out and then washed my dishes, flipped through my mail, and checked my phone messages.

There was nothing there from Tom. I walked down the hall to my home office, turned on the computer, and went online to answer my e-mail. There was nothing from Tom there, either.

I tried calling his cell, his office, and his home phone numbers, but there was no answer at any of them. My frustration surged as I hung up the phone. What was going on with him? What was the emergency, and exactly when was he going to be able to get back to me?

For the first time, I felt truly cut off from him. It made me realize that no matter how much I liked Tom, no matter how well we got along over the telephone, in the end I was just another employee. When this emergency arose—whatever the nature of it was—he was simply off and gone. That I could understand, of course, but what hurt my feelings was the lack of personal contact afterward. I had thought we were more to each other than that.

I stood and crossed the hall into the bedroom, intending to change into a nightgown and go to bed. The more I dug through my nightgown drawer, however, the more upset I became. Finally, I slammed the drawer shut, went to the closest, and started digging for some warm clothes, plus gloves, a scarf, a hat, and a big, strong flashlight.

With everything that was on my mind, I was never going to get to sleep tonight. If I was going to feel this way all evening, I decided, I might as well accomplish something useful in the meantime.

Ten

I left Sal in the house, got back in my car, and headed away from Osprey Cove. I drove for 20 minutes, past the long driveways and hidden mansions toward the less affluent section of the peninsula. As the highway continued, the estates eventually came to an end, and then the road became bumpier and more poorly maintained—and the houses smaller and more clustered together. The highway finally petered out in Kawshek, a village of Maryland "watermen," folks who made their living from the bay.

Though we shared the same road, I usually didn't have many dealings with the people of Kawshek. Occasionally I would see some of the watermen out on the river, but we didn't have much more than a "waving" acquaintance. I was always reading about how many of them were falling on hard times because development and pollution were causing the quantities of oysters and blue crabs in Chesapeake Bay to diminish drastically. As a result, we'd had several Kawshek women come through Advancing Attire fresh from job training, desperate to make a living in some other way. I was happy to work with all of the women who came there seeking our help, of course, but I always felt a special bond with the watermen women, for most of them loved the peninsula and the dark, gentle waves of the Chesapeake as much as I did. To button them into a fancy suit and send them out into the business world of the mainland was actually kind of sad; it seemed to signal the end of a way of life that had been part of this area for hundreds of years.

Shayna, however, had been a different case. She wasn't native to this area; she had only moved to Maryland a few years before—from New Mexico, if I recalled correctly. She had told me the first day we met that she didn't really like life in Kawshek and was eager to head off to more metropolitan surroundings. Now with her new job in Annapolis, she was about to get her wish, unless Eddie Ray's murder derailed those plans permanently.

Once I reached Kawshek, it wasn't hard to figure out which house was Shayna's, because there were two police cars parked in front, lights flashing, with yellow tape stretched around the perimeter. I pulled to a stop in a small parking lot about a half block away. I was not especially eager to see the police again. There was nothing wrong with my being here, but at best they would think I was nosy, and at worst they might think my connection with the murder was something more than peripheral.

I sat in the car for a minute looking around, trying to get a feel for the street. It was dark and there weren't many lights, but I could tell it definitely wasn't the high-rent district—not that Kawshek would have such a thing anyway. The houses were small and clumped close together, and many of the yards were littered with toys and tools. The parking lot where I sat bordered a small cluster of dirty buildings that comprised the entire downtown: Next to a marina filled with trawlers and fishing boats was a one-pump gas station, a little grocery/bait and tackle shop, and a bar. Earlier today, when Shayna told me that Eddie Ray usually got mad and stormed off to the local bar, I hadn't realized that bar was a mere half block away!

At the end of the street, the building that had been roped off by the police was an ugly green two-story box, and from the three front doors I guessed it was an older home that had long ago been divided into apartments. No wonder Shayna was eager to leave here; except for the proximity to the water, I couldn't imagine a more depressing place to live.

I quietly got out of the car and walked over to join a cluster of onlookers who had gathered at the edge of the parking lot. A few of them wore pajamas under their coats, and I was reminded that a waterman's day often began well before sunrise. Though it wasn't yet 9:00 P.M., half of these people had probably already been in bed asleep when the police arrived. The rest had probably been in the bar.

"...tol' her to kick him out, but I didn't think she'd kill him."

"I heard 'em fighting 'fore he came over to the bar last night. It was the loudest one yet."

"I heard she went around looking for him this morning, saying he had disappeared."

The people were talking freely about the incident, and I listened carefully to everything that was said.

"Well, I'm not surprised he got hisself killed. That man was no good. He never was any good."

"I still can't believe he's dead, though! We played a game of pool right here, last night. I bought him a beer."

"Thank the Lord Irene's not still around to see this," one woman said, and the others nodded in agreement. "It's enough to break a mother's heart."

"Dangit, Hank," said another. "I tol' you ya shoulda run Eddie Ray outta town the minute he showed up again."

A big man standing next to me held out his hands in a gesture of helplessness.

"Shayna's free to date who she wants," he said. "If she didn't want me anymore, that was her choice."

"You're too soft, Hank," a man said. "I'd a kicked him from here to Baltimore."

I glanced at the man they called Hank and thought he looked anything but soft. He was huge and burly, with ruddy cheeks and a deep scar across his chin.

"Is that the murder scene?" I asked, pointing toward the police activity.

A few of the people glanced at me, suddenly realizing there was a stranger in their midst.

"Might be," one woman said finally. "You a reporter or something?"

"I'm a friend of Shayna's," I replied.

"Ain't never seen you here before."

They all turned then and stared at me accusingly.

"I-I was with her when we found the body," I said. "We'd been picking out some clothes and getting her hair done."

They were all quiet for a moment.

"Callie? Callie Webber? Is that you?"

A short woman stepped through the crowd and looked up at me.

"Wendy Lentil," she said, grinning a toothless grin. She wore a hat pulled down close to her eyes, and a scarf covered her neck and chin all the way to her bottom lip. "You gave my Lisa some clothes for a job over in Easton."

I recognized the woman now. She had come along with her daughter to Advancing Attire about a year before. It had taken several visits to get Lisa all set, and I had come to know mother and daughter fairly well.

Apparently, the fact that Wendy Lentil knew me was good enough for the crowd. They returned to watching the police activity while Mrs. Lentil and I stepped away and talked a bit about Lisa and how her job was going. Soon I was able to steer the discussion back to Shayna and Eddie Ray, and I tried to get as much information from Mrs. Lentil as possible. According to her, everyone liked Shayna, especially since she stopped drinking and taking drugs.

"She ain't been drunk or high in months, far as I know," Mrs. Lentil said. "Came to the Lord in a tent revival. Got herself cleaned up, and some good work training like my Lisa. I heard she was starting a new job real soon."

"Yes, ma'am, she was."

"Can't blame her for doing in ol' Eddie Ray, though. He was a slimy one, that boy."

"Did you know his family?"

"Don't know who his daddy was. His mother was a friend of mine, and let me tell you, she was the only soul out here who couldn't see Eddie Ray for what he was. He freeloaded offa his poor ol' mama while she waited tables till all hours of the night in the bar. She eventually had to stop, of course, 'cause of her high blood pressure. She died a few years ago. That's when Eddie Ray brought Shayna to live here, right in Irene's house without the benefit of marriage or nothing."

"Really."

She lowered her voice and gripped my arm, pulling me closer.

"I don't even think Eddie Ray loved Shayna," she whispered. "He just *used* her."

"Used her?"

"Yeah, to cook and clean for him once his mama was gone."

"That's a shame."

"Then he finally sold his mama's house and took off. That's when Shayna moved in over there."

I nodded, glancing again at the dismal apartment house up the street.

"Did I hear someone say she was dating again?" I asked softly.

"Here and there. 'Til Eddie Ray showed back up, she was mostly going out with Hank," she whispered, gesturing toward the big man with the scar on his chin. "Kinda new here, but he seems like a good fella."

"How did he feel about Eddie Ray moving in with Shayna?"

"You'd have to ask him," she replied. "From what I heard, he backed right off and left 'em alone."

We were interrupted by another police car coming down the street, lights flashing but without the siren. I turned my face away and stepped back over to the crowd, just in case it was Barbara Hightower or one of the other cops I had dealt with earlier.

"I heard his head was nearly chopped clean off," said a woman. "Must've did it with an axe or something."

"I heard there was blood all over the inside of the trunk," Mrs. Lentil said, tugging at my arm. "Is that true?"

"There was a substantial amount of blood," I admitted.

"Must've been quite a bit," an old man said. "There's a big pool of blood on the ground in front of the house. Looks like an oil drip, but it's Eddie Ray's blood from where it was oozing out of the trunk."

That earned some groans from the crowd.

"Drips all the way down here," the man continued, pointing at the road. I looked to where he indicated and could see a black dot in the dirt. I stepped closer to study it, and then I looked forward to see another dot about ten feet away.

"How far does this go?" I asked, looking off toward the dark end of the road, away from the police activity.

"Don't know," the man said. "At least as far as my house at the end of the block there. I noticed it this morning when I was walkin' over here to get a paper. I thought, 'Uh-oh, somebody's got themselves a bad oil leak.' Then from a distance, I could see the puddle under Shayna's car. I didn't realize it was at the back, not the front. Thought it was oil."

"About what time was this?" I asked the old man. He was stooped and weathered but had a thick, snow white head of hair and a twinkle in his eye.

"Oh, 'bout six-thirty this morning. I considered knocking on Shayna's door to tell her about the leak, but I didn't think she'd appreciate being woke up that early. Not everybody keeps waterman hours."

I nodded, thinking. When the detectives had interviewed Shayna earlier, she told them that her car had sat here from about 8:00 last night until she came into Osprey Cove for her appointment with me at 3:30 this afternoon. But if Eddie Ray had been in the bar last night, drinking beer and playing pool, and these drops had been here at 6:30 this morning, then Shayna was wrong. Her car *had* been driven during the night, with Eddie Ray in the trunk, his blood leaving a telltale trail behind.

"Did anybody see anything suspicious here last night?" I asked. "Or hear anything?"

They mumbled "no's" and shook their heads.

"How about the car?" I persisted. "Anybody notice the car coming or going after eight o'clock last night?"

Again, the answer was negative.

I knew that soon the police would come over here and begin asking these very same questions. Suddenly, I realized what I needed to do.

"I've got to run," I told Mrs. Lentil. We said our goodbyes, and then I slipped quietly away and got back in my car. I drove away from the flashing lights, went about two blocks, and then turned and parked on a side street. I got out and went to the rear of the vehicle.

I opened the hatchback softly, using a flashlight to look through my investigating tools for the item I needed now, a small handheld unit about the size of a soda can. It wasn't anything too high tech, but it would serve my purposes. I grabbed it and shut the hatchback with a click, turned off my flashlight, and headed off on foot to the main street. Once there, I turned away from the flashing police lights in the distance and starting walking up the highway.

The night was freezing cold by now, and I felt chilled to the bone despite my gloves and scarf. I walked fast, hoping to warm up as I went. The streetlights ended at the next block, and soon I was enveloped in silent darkness.

I kept walking, my eyes adjusting as I went. Once I was around the bend and completely out of sight of the police, I pulled out the little handheld unit and clicked it on. It was a simple device, a sort of portable black light I had purchased from a hotel supply company. The light was marketed as an inspection device for maintenance supervisors; in a darkened bathroom, for example, with the unit as the only light, one could see if the maids had cleaned adequately, for the black light illuminated substances a careless worker might leave behind, such as urine and bacteria.

The light also, however, illuminated blood, which was why it was an important tool for a private investigator. Though it had been quite a few years since my investigations routinely dealt with things like murder, I still found myself involved in the occasional odd case where things like this came in very handy. In fact, I had solved a murder case for my boss just two months before, up in Philadelphia. This time, though, the murder had happened much closer to home.

I held the unit pointed at the ground and kept walking up the highway away from Shayna's house, hoping that soon it would pick up another drop of Eddie Ray's blood. I didn't have to wait long. After about five steps I spotted a circle in the road—a splatter that glowed white under the light. If my theory was correct, there would be another splatter ahead.

There was.

Fifteen minutes later, I was still walking, still tracking the dots of blood, and beginning to question the wisdom of doing this on foot. He could've bled for miles, I realized as I went. It was too cold and too dark to walk here much longer—not to mention that I was quite worried that any minute now more police cars would come or go along this main road. Again, I wasn't doing anything wrong, but considering that I hadn't been hired to pursue this case, it seemed a bit odd that I would be out here now, tracking the trail of murder.

Still, I persisted a bit longer once I realized the dots were coming closer together. As I walked I thought over what I knew about blood and death. Once a person's dead, of course, the heart stops pumping and the blood flow ceases. Eddie Ray must've survived for a while after his head injury, albeit unconsciously, because he obviously bled enough to drip all the way home, saturate the trunk, and make a puddle under the car. I was musing over this when I realized the drops were coming very close together now, about every two feet.

Finally, my light picked up some larger splatters, and then beyond them, nothing more. I ran ahead just to make sure, but the dots stopped at the larger splatters and didn't seem to pick up again. I ran back to the area with the splatters, aware that I would have to be very careful not to disturb any evidence, because this had to be the point where Eddie Ray was struck.

I stood in the middle of the dark road, held the black light out in front of me, and turned slowly in a full circle. The light picked up something glowing in the bushes along the side of the road, so I stepped over there carefully and studied what I saw without touching anything. Small flecks of tissue here and there were enough to show the trajectory of the impact. The bush appeared to be something seed-producing, and I thought of the burrs on the back of the dead man's sweater. He had been hit here, at the edge of the road. Perhaps he had even slumped against the bushes after impact before he was loaded into the trunk and driven back to Kawshek, where the car was parked in front of Shayna's apartment building.

I stood up straight, walked back to the center of the road, and turned off my light. The darkness was instant and all-enveloping.

Like most of the peninsula this time of night, all was silent and still. I could smell the water. I could hear the rustle of a light wind in the cattails. Because it was November, there were no grasshoppers or crickets to sing in the dark, no nightbirds to peal in the sky. It was just quiet.

Deathly quiet.

A slow shiver made its way up my spine when it struck me that I might not be alone here. Suddenly, despite the silence in the air, I had the feeling that I was being watched. *Stupid, stupid, stupid,* I thought to myself as I gripped the cell phone in my pocket. To come out here in the dark, alone and without protection, was just stupid.

Suddenly, a new smell wafted its way to me, a smell of something familiar but out of place, like something that didn't belong here in the wilderness. I sniffed, my mind racing. Was it Lysol? Windex?

No, I realized. It was *Clorox.* Inhaling, I detected the distinct odor of bleach.

Resisting the urge to run away, I took a few steps back as I pulled from my coat pocket my cell phone and the business card given to me by Barbara Hightower. I dialed as quickly as I could, hit the "send" button, and put the phone to my ear.

Nothing.

I looked at the screen and saw a blinking message: "Out of service area."

With a chill, I started walking back the way I had come, wondering how far I would have to go before I was in range of a cellular tower. That's always how it was out here—spotty service, gaps in usage—but until this moment it hadn't ever really mattered that much.

My senses were heightened, and I looked around wildly as I continued to walk. It still seemed as though someone were watching me, though I couldn't put my finger on what made me feel that way. I turned around and shined my flashlight into the darkness surrounding me, but all I could make out, up high and far in the distance, was a glowing pair of eyes looking back at me. They looked strange, but I knew they probably belonged to an owl.

I heard rustling close by, along the side of the road, and my heart quickened. Was it a person? An animal? I didn't wait to find out. Instead I turned and took off running, heading back toward Kawshek as quickly as I could.

There were no footsteps behind me, no heavy breathing down my neck, so after a few minutes I slowed down and checked my phone again. According to the little green screen, I was back in calling range.

I stopped and dialed Barbara's number with trembling fingers, praying it was a direct line straight to her.

She answered on the third ring.

"Barbara?" I said. "It's Callie Webber. I've got something important to show you. I think you'll want to come see it right now."

"Where are you?" she asked.

I described my location and reiterated that it was important she come immediately.

"I'm on my way," she agreed tiredly.

"Oh, and Barbara?" I said, wrapping my arm around myself and trying not to shiver. "If you don't mind, stay on the line with me until you get here, okay?"

Eleven

By the time I finally arrived home, I was frozen solid and completely exhausted. Though I would've liked to start a fire, I was just too tired. Instead, I went straight to the bedroom, clicked my electric blanket on "high," and then changed into the warmest pajamas and housecoat I owned.

At least I was allowed to leave the scene of the crime, I thought. My probing around in the dark at night, following Eddie Ray's trail of blood with a Personal Inspection Light, had of course looked a bit suspect at first. But then Barbara Hightower had vouched for me, and the fact that I was a licensed PI helped to smooth over any lingering doubts. In the end, and except for the suspicious bureaucrat Mr. Litman, everyone seemed rather grateful that I had saved them some grunt work by locating the actual scene of the crime.

And, apparently, there hadn't been anyone in the area watching me after all—or if there had been, they had certainly managed to get away without being caught or even making any noise. As for the smell of bleach, it had dissipated by the time the police and I got back to the scene of the crime, and no one seemed quite convinced that what I thought I had smelled actually existed.

"The mind plays tricks on you," one of the cops had said to me with a shrug, though at my insistence he did check with headquarters just to see if there had been reports of any chemical spills in the area tonight, perhaps from a truck or a ship or a nearby factory. There hadn't been. Still, I knew what I had smelled. The acrid odor that had hit my nostrils tonight was indeed the smell of bleach.

For now, putting it all out of my mind, I padded to the kitchen in fuzzy slippers to make myself some warm milk, jumping from one foot to the other as it heated in the microwave. While I was waiting, I noticed the red light on my answering machine, so I pressed the button to hear that there was one message, from about an hour ago.

It was Tom.

"Hey, Callie," his voice said into the empty kitchen, "it's me. I'm sure you're wondering what happened. What can I say, except that I'm really, really sorry. You know I wouldn't have missed seeing you like that without a very good reason."

I leaned forward on the counter, listening.

"It's personal. Sort of a family emergency. Anyway, I wanted to talk to you about it. Guess you're not there now."

He sounded a little lost, kind of sad, and I deeply regretted I hadn't been here to take his call. I was still upset, and somewhat confused, though I did have to admit that just hearing him talk made me feel warmer inside. As always, in his voice there seemed to be a strong undercurrent of what wasn't being said that was nearly as important as what was.

"Okay," he continued, "I guess maybe I'll try you again later. I hope you made it home from the airport all right."

I touched the answering machine, wishing it was that easy to reach out and touch him.

"I've got my phone turned off, so you won't be able to get me. I'll have to call you back. Bye, Callie."

That was the end of the message. I listened to the dial tone for a moment and then reset my machine, somehow reassured despite the fact that he had given me no new information. I took my cup from the microwave, clicked off the light, and went back to the bedroom. The bed was toasty warm when I got there, and I climbed under the covers and leaned back against propped-up pillows. Sal jumped up from the floor and settled in her familiar spot against my leg. I sipped my warm milk, reached for the bedroom phone, and dialed Harriet's number.

"Did I wake you?" I asked when she answered.

"Oh, puh-leeze, you know what a night owl I am. What's up?"

"I heard from Tom."

I described his brief message, and then we tried to decipher it. I wondered aloud if maybe someone was ill or had died.

"Then again, maybe it was a good thing," Harriet said. "There can be good family emergencies."

"Like what?"

"Maybe his mother won the lottery. Maybe his sister decided to get married on the spur of the moment."

"His sister's already married, isn't she?"

"I think she's divorced. I'm not sure."

We tossed around more ideas, good and bad, until eventually the conversation drifted to other things. I considered telling Harriet about the events of my afternoon, but I knew she didn't like mystery, intrigue, or murder. The fact that I had been face-to-face with a dead man several hours earlier would be a bit extreme for her, so in the end I kept it to myself.

"Hey, enjoy the time off while it lasts," she said, steering the conversation back to Tom's sudden absence and the fact that he hadn't left any work for me to do while he was gone. "I'd give anything for a little unexpected vacation."

"I suppose," I said, though suddenly the rest of the week felt long and empty before me. The murder investigation of Eddie Ray would surely wrap up in a day or two as soon as the police stopped concentrating on Shayna and found the real killer. After that, I was left with nothing more exciting to do than clean out a few closets.

"Do something fun, for goodness' sake," Harriet said.

"Well, why don't we try to get together this weekend?" I asked. "I could come into the city. We could go out to eat, do some shopping..."

"I'd love to, hon, but I've got that line dancing competition over in Chincoteague. I'll be up to my ears in the Double Split Pony till Monday."

I smiled, picturing Harriet in all her line-dancing glory.

"You could join us," she continued. "There's always room for one more."

"No, thanks," I replied. "I'm sure I'll find something to do around here by myself."

"That's what I'm worried about," she said. "We've just got to get you out and about more."

"I get out! Goodness, I'm gone more days than I'm here."

"I'm not talking about work. I'm talking about your social life."

"My social life is fine, thank you very much."

"Yeah, right," she replied. "When's the last time you did anything social with anyone else but me? And trying to arrange a quick rendezvous in an airport with your boss doesn't count. Neither does that thing you do with your church, helping out those young women."

I thought of Shayna, currently cooling her heels in jail.

"I'm…I've been busy," I hedged.

"How 'bout when you were on your vacation?"

"I spent most of that time in my canoe."

"Oh, Callie," Harriet moaned. "We've just got to find you a man."

"I don't need a man," I said, bristling. "You know very well I'm perfectly happy on my own."

"Well, at the very least, you need some more friends."

"I've got friends!"

"Count 'em, hon. If it takes more than one hand, I'll be flabbergasted."

"Whatever," I said, trying not to sound hurt. Harriet was half teasing, but there was an undercurrent of truth in her voice.

I changed the subject, but I felt a bit edgy for the rest of the conversation. Once we had hung up, I thought long and hard about her comments. So what if I preferred to keep to myself? Was that really so bad? I knew how to be friendly. I just didn't seek people out.

"There's a difference between being lonely and being alone," I said out loud, defensively, to no one but my dog, Sal. She answered by burrowing her head into the side of my leg, placing her chin on my knee, and then giving a little wag to her tail. *If Harriet wants me to count the number of my friends,* I thought, *then good old Sal is at the very top of the list.*

Twelve

I couldn't sleep. An hour later my mind was still spinning, drifting back to Shayna and the conundrum of who killed Eddie Ray.

By the time I had left the scene of the crime, the police were still busy collecting evidence and floating theories. Shayna remained their primary suspect, though as far as I knew, she still hadn't been charged with anything beyond drug possession. I was comforted to know no other drugs or drug paraphernalia had turned up in her apartment; that lent much more credence to her claims that she was clean and sober and that the bag of marijuana found in her car wasn't hers.

Still, her boyfriend's dead body had been found in the trunk. I thought about that, floating some possible theories of my own. I decided it was most logical that Eddie Ray had taken Shayna's car during the night, some time after he stormed over to the bar and spent a while there. Where he was going in the car so late at night was anyone's guess, but he must've been on his way either away from or back to Kawshek when for some reason he pulled over to the side of the darkened road a few miles out of town. Considering that the physical evidence had been found on the right side of the road, I thought it logical that he was heading away from Kawshek when it happened.

But why had he stopped? It wasn't a flat tire—earlier this afternoon, peering over the shoulders of the police, I had gotten a good look at the lug nuts on all four wheels, and none of them had shown any signs of having been recently tampered with. So what was it? Was someone in the car with him who asked him to pull over? Was someone waiting on the road, waving him down?

Regardless of what it was that got him to pull over, apparently Eddie Ray climbed out of the car, was whacked on the head by someone wielding the tire iron from that car, and then he was shoved into the trunk, where he remained unconscious, slowly bleeding to death. But here was the tricky part: At that point, someone had driven the car, with his bleeding body inside the trunk, all the way back to Shayna's apartment and parked it there. No wonder the police thought she had done it.

The very fact that the car was parked at Shayna's precluded any thoughts about a random killer or some sort of homicidal maniac wandering the Chesapeake. Whoever killed Eddie Ray had known who he was and where the car he was driving belonged, because they had gone to the trouble to deliver it right back there. Was it someone who wanted to frame Shayna for murder? If so, then perhaps the marijuana under the seat had been a part of that frame-up as well. I made a mental note to ask her if she had any enemies.

I also wanted to ask her about the car keys. Did Eddie Ray—or anyone else for that matter—have a duplicate set of keys to her car? If not, where had her keys been the next day when she was ready to drive the car? Surely the killer hadn't delivered the car back to its parking spot *and* quietly put the keys back where they belonged in Shayna's apartment. That would be creepy indeed.

Facts swirling in my head, I climbed out from under my nice, warm covers and grabbed my laptop. I got back in bed, opened it up, and propped it on my knees. This wasn't an official investigation by any means, but it would be a shame not to follow my standard procedure of creating an information database about the case so I could keep track of the data I had gleaned.

A half hour later I had created the database and loaded in all of the information and theories I could possibly think of. I decided I would talk to the public defender in the morning just to make sure Shayna was in good hands. Once that was done, I would offer my cooperation, provide any information I had, and then back away and let the police and the attorney do their jobs. I could offer Shayna support but would try and stay out of the investigation.

I shut down the computer, set it on the floor, and then reached over to click off my light. Now, perhaps, I could put the whole thing out of my mind and try and get some rest. I closed my eyes and, even as wired up as I was, at some point I must've drifted off to sleep.

The next thing I knew, I was waking up in the darkness, vaguely aware of Sal making some kind of noise at my feet. Confused, I propped up on one elbow, trying to peer through the darkness at my dog.

I could feel her pressed against me, closer than usual, and in the silence of the night I listened as a low, gutteral growl bubbled out from her throat.

"Sal?"

Usually, she wasn't a very verbal dog, not much of a barker or a growler. The sound she was making now was almost foreign to me, but I could feel her little body trembling against me even as she continued to growl.

Slowly, the hairs on the back of my neck stood up.

Without speaking, I reached down and put a hand on her shoulders, and for a moment, she stopped. Then she barked, a sharp, sudden yap of warning to whoever or whatever it was that had put her on alert.

Heart pounding, I swung my legs over the bed and reached into my bedside drawer for some kind of weapon. The best I could come up with was a metal "Elvis" back scratcher, a souvenir Harriet had brought me from Memphis. I clutched it in front of me with one hand while I reached out with the other toward the phone.

I wasn't an alarmist, that's for sure, and I definitely knew how to defend myself against an intruder. But until I had figured out what had so spooked my dog, I wasn't taking any chances. I had 911 on speed dial, and I was prepared to use it if necessary.

I waited, my pulse pounding in my head. For the moment, Sal had stopped making any noise at all, though now she was standing on the end of the bed, her body facing the half-open bedroom door, as tense as a pointer with a grouse. The house was silent, but something didn't feel right. If I were a dog, I decided, I would be growling as well.

Suddenly, Sal flew into a barking frenzy as she jumped off the bed and dashed out of the room. She barked all the way down the hall, and then it sounded as if she were at the back door, barking still. I looked at the phone then looked at the hallway, and I made my choice. I wasn't going to call the police based solely on the barking of my dog. Until I knew for sure that I had some sort of intruder, I would attempt to handle this by myself.

I thought the police had heard enough from me tonight already.

Silently, I crept to the bedroom door and peeked out into the hall. Aside from the frenzied Sal, nothing seemed amiss. The back door was shut tightly, and there were no looming shadows in the kitchen that I could see.

Clutching the back scratcher, I ventured forward, creeping along the dark hallway until I reached the window that looked out over Sal's play yard.

I used one finger to pull aside the blinds, hoping that I wouldn't come face-to-face with someone outside, trying to look back in at me! The night was dark, but all I saw was the yard, the grass, the trees. Sal was still barking though, so I squinted and stared harder, praying that if indeed someone were out there I would be able to spot them before they could break through into my house.

Nothing seemed wrong. There was no one at the door or lurking in the shadows of the carport. I sucked in a deep breath, trying to remember if anything like this had ever happened with Sal before. Just once, I realized, last year. When there had been a possum in the trash can.

A possum in the trash can! Of course! I stood up straight and relaxed, dropping the blinds as I exhaled loudly. My trusty guardian was letting me know that the nocturnal animals were at the garbage again.

I flipped on the patio light and looked out at the cans, which were half hidden in the shadows of the storage shed. From what I could see, the cans were, indeed, wide open. With one lid askew and a full bag of trash inside, I had practically been begging for an invasion.

"Come on, girl," I said to Sal, unlocking the door and pushing it open so she could run out. If she needed to defend me against the night's creatures, the least I could do was let her at 'em.

I slipped on a pair of sneakers and then followed her outside, surprised at the burst of cold that hit me as I went out. I hadn't looked at the clock, but judging from the night sky, it had to be very late, maybe 4 A.M.? As Sal ran around the yard, sniffing and yapping and growling, I crunched through the leaves toward the shed, calling out a warning to any animals so they could scamper away before I got there. Once I reached the shed, I worked quickly, raising the trash can lid and setting it on straight, then clicking it shut on the side. First one can, and then the other.

As I worked, I thought of Bryan's dog, the sweet black Lab he had gotten the year before we were married. Hubble was a real barker, and if it had been him here now, he would be barking twice as loudly and twice as frantically as Sal. But I had given him to my brother after Bryan died, unable to keep him around because it was too emotionally painful for me. Hubble was a big, lumbering galoot of a dog who continued to wait at the front door for Bryan to come home every night for two months after Bryan was gone. Even when I would go to bed and call for Hubble to come with me, he would whine and remain at the door, as if he believed that if he wanted it badly enough, eventually it was bound to happen. One night I sat on the floor next to him and sobbed into his fur, begging him to stop waiting, screaming at him that Bryan wasn't coming home, that he wasn't ever coming home again. The next day, I gave Hubble to Michael.

I hadn't seen the dog since.

"Sal, settle down!" I commanded now, a surge of emotion filling my throat. I wiped away angry tears, thinking first that I was mad at Sal, and then wondering if my anger was at the memory of Hubble. Finally, as I marched back toward the house, I realized that it was *Bryan* that I was really angry with.

Bryan, who ought to be here in bed with me at 4 A.M. when possoms invade the trash and the dog starts to growl.

Bryan, who ought to be protecting me, keeping me safe.

Never mind that I had always been able to take care of myself, even when Bryan was alive. He still had no business going off and dying on me. No business at all!

I called Sal back inside when I reached the door, and she obeyed, letting out little yips as she came. Once in, I locked the door, turned off the light, and led her back to the bedroom.

It wasn't until I had washed my hands and was back under the covers that I was able to calm down a bit and look objectively at my anger. I was way beyond this stage in my grief; that such a rage had risen up like this in the middle of the night and reared its ugly head scared me. I thought I was doing so well. Now all it took was one creepy experience and I had regressed nearly all the way back to square one. Sometimes, the grieving process just seemed too complicated to comprehend.

I was almost asleep when the truth finally hit me. It wasn't about Bryan or his death, and it wasn't about the dog. It was about the trash cans.

I sat up in the bed, skin tingling.

Replaying my actions in my mind, I saw myself as I had been less than 20 minutes before, flipping on the outside light, striding brazenly toward the shed, fixing the lids to the trash cans.

Closing my eyes, I realized it only now: There had been a smell out there, a smell as strong and as odd as the one I had detected earlier, at the murder scene. A smell that didn't belong.

The smell of bleach.

Thirteen

After several more hours of tossing and turning, I was up by seven the next morning. I threw on some clothes and did some stretches, and then Sal and I went outside. With an uneasy feeling, I looked all around the shed, all around the house, for signs of an intruder, but I couldn't find anything other than one possible half footprint in some mud behind the shed. The smell was gone, and all that was left was a vague memory of a middle-of-the-night disturbance that seemed a lot less scary now that the sun was coming up.

Finally, I gave up and went down the dock to the canoe. I figured if I wasn't going to be able to sleep in, the least I could do was find some pleasure in a little time on the river. As I pushed off, Sal took her position in the bow, eagerly facing forward, two paws up on the deck plate. Her name, Sal, was short for "La Salle," the French explorer who once traveled about 3000 miles by canoe. True to her name, Sal loved canoeing as much as I did.

The air was cold, but I quickly warmed up by paddling hard against the current. It was stronger than usual, and I liked the pull on my arms, the optical illusion of speed as I sailed along against the flow of the waves. As I paddled, I went into a sort of autopilot, the same nowhere-land my brain inhabited whenever I canoed or went jogging or did some other mindless physical task. The rhythm of it was comforting—plant, stroke, lift; plant, stroke, lift—adding a small twist at the end of each J-stroke for correction.

Oblivious to the surrounding landscape, I breathed in cold air and huffed out white vapor and rowed until I pushed past stinging hands and burning muscles to the deep, pleasurable ache of a good workout. Once I reached the giant deserted osprey nest that marked the five-mile point for me, I stopped paddling and let the canoe simply float. Finally, I executed a slow reverse sweep, and then I held the paddle across my lap, caught my breath, and let myself drift back toward the way I had come.

What a glorious morning! Truly, the Lord had blessed me here with the bouquet of autumn leaves that lined the winding river. We were past the peak fall colors, of course, but there were still hints of orange and yellow among the brown. I let my eyes scan the shore, looking for the telltale shells of unio clams. I had spotted a wily old raccoon at dawn here a few weeks before, sitting among scattered shells on the bank, prying one of them open with his tiny black fingers.

I didn't see the raccoon now, but I did notice a pair of loons floating ahead of us, unremarkable in the gray-brown coats they wore for the winter. Sal remained in her perch at the bow, sniffing at them as we floated by.

We passed one of my favorite landmarks on the river, a point that jutted out from the shore where an unusual tree grew. I called it the "lovers' pine." It was actually *two* trees that at some juncture early in their growth had become intertwined—so much so that it looked as if the two trunks had melded into one. At the base it was still two trees, but several feet up the trunk it almost became a single tree, tall and solid and beautiful, towering over the river like a watchman.

"He has made everything beautiful in its time," I said to my dog, quoting from Ecclesiastes. Certainly, my little corner of the world was a very beautiful place.

Canoeing was often my best time for prayer, so as I gently paddled my way back home I talked to God—out loud, but softly—

about the incident last night, about my surge of anger toward my late husband. Long ago, I had reached a point where I had specifically forgiven Bryan for dying.

Now, as I recalled that past moment in my mind, I felt a surge of peace. I continued to paddle, deciding that maybe I hadn't really regressed in the grieving process at all, but rather this had been just a momentary lapse, a repository of all of the turmoil and confusion of the afternoon and evening.

That led me to think of Shayna and her predicament as well as Tom and whatever issues were besetting him and his family. I prayed for them all, putting everything into God's hands, knowing that He could make something good out of every bad situation.

By the time I arrived back to my dock, I was starving. I fed Sal a can of dog food and then tended to my own breakfast of hot tea, poached eggs, and whole wheat toast. Deviating just a bit from my routine, I also sliced up an orange and set it on the corner of my plate. I sat and ate in the peace and quiet of my empty kitchen, flipping through a mail-order catalog that had come in yesterday's mail.

Once I had eaten, I cleaned my dishes and then phoned Barbara Hightower. She answered on the first ring, her voice sounding muffled and tired.

"It's Callie," I told her. "I'm sorry. Sounds like I woke you up."

"I wish," she replied. "I haven't even gone home yet."

"Busy night?"

"You know the drill. Lots of hurry up and do nothing. How can I help you? Did you find another murder scene for me this morning?"

"Just wondering about how things progressed last night. Any big surprises after I left?"

She hesitated.

"Come on, Callie. I'd like to cooperate with you, but you've got to be more specific than that. You know I can't just sit here and tell you everything."

"Okay. Well, let's start with Shayna. Is she still being held on drug charges, or has that changed?"

"Still just the drugs. But the report on the tire iron should be back any minute. If her fingerprints are on it, all bets are off."

"It was her tire iron from her car. Of course her fingerprints are on it."

"It was the murder weapon, Callie. What can I say?"

I toyed with the phone cord, remembering the sight of Eddie Ray's head wound. It hadn't been pretty.

"Has she been assigned a lawyer yet?" I asked.

"Yeah, she got Max Nealson, over in the PD's office. Nice guy but way overloaded right now. If you're really interested in helping Shayna, you might talk with him, see if he'd like you to do some of the footwork. That is, if you have the time. You said you're off this week, right?"

"It looks that way."

"She's being held here at the barracks, not the detention center. They're going at her pretty hard."

I thought about poor Shayna being interrogated by the police, a murder rap hovering just over her head.

"So what's your take on all of this, Barbara? Do you think Shayna killed Eddie Ray?"

Barbara exhaled slowly, and I could picture her rubbing her forehead with her hand, elbows tiredly propped on top of her desk.

"Look, Callie," she said, lowering her voice. "Some of the guys here knew Eddie Ray Higgins in high school. They say he was a slimeball way back then."

"Really."

"I see it this way. If she did kill him, he probably drove her to it. And if she didn't kill him, then I'd hate to see her life ruined because of an overworked public defender and a little circumstantial evidence."

"She's a nice kid," I said. "I don't know her all that well, but I feel certain there's no blood on her hands, so to speak."

"We'll find out, I guess. We're still looking at other possibilities, though I wouldn't count on anything."

Barbara then gave me the phone number for the public defender's office in Barrington. I thanked her for her help and gave that number a try. After working my way through several different people, I was able to get Max Nealson on the line, and he agreed to see me as soon as I could get over to his office.

After a quick shower, I was on my way. I took the Osprey Cove bypass off of the peninsula before heading due east toward Barrington on an uneven road past miles and miles of farm fields, weathered houses, and the occasional country store. I rarely came this way for anything, and I had forgotten how deserted it was. Barrington was the county seat, though, so as I drew closer to town the houses increased in number, if not in size, and they were punctuated with strip malls, discount stores, and big grocery outlets.

Once there, I found my way to the center of town, to the cluster of buildings that comprised the county's legal hub. At some point early on, at least some of the city planners must've had a little vision as to how things should be laid out, because the courthouse and the county clerk's office and the cluster of other county buildings sat on three sides of a square surrounding a picturesque little park. The fourth side of the park fronted the river, which was wide and lovely and fringed with weeping willow trees. A mother and child were standing near the water's edge with a bag of bread, and as I parked my car and got out I could hear a couple of ducks making a ruckus at their feet.

Strolling up the walk, I found the building I needed and went inside, walking my way along the entire length of the first floor before I located the office I wanted. The sign on the frosted glass door said "Public Defender" and I entered, expecting to find a waiting room filled with agitated people and squirming babies. Instead, there was simply a woman at a desk who informed me that, yes, I was in the right place and that the public-access part of the PD's office was in another building across the way.

The woman pointed me toward the cubicle of Max Nealson, who stood when I entered and shook my hand. He had a receding hairline and wire-rimmed glasses and was a bit older than he had sounded on the phone, perhaps in his mid-forties. To my experience, that was pretty old for this type of work. By his age, most lawyers had burned out on defending the downtrodden and switched to a more profitable area of the legal profession.

"Thanks for seeing me on such short notice," I said, settling into the chair opposite his desk. "I know you're very busy, so I won't take up much of your time."

He sat back down and shuffled through a massive mess of papers, finally coming up with a manila file that he opened in front of him.

"No problem, no problem," he said, flipping quickly through the slim file. "Shayna Greer, right? I've got it right here. Just handed to me this morning."

"How's she holding up?" I asked.

He skimmed the few pages in front of him.

"I don't know," he said absently. "We haven't spoken yet."

I nodded, wondering how quickly things worked around here. I was about to ask when he thought he would get a chance to meet with her when he set down the file and peered at me over the rim of his glasses.

"I hear nice things about you from Officer Hightower," he said, offering a half smile. "I understand you're a private investigator? I'm surprised we haven't connected before."

"Oh, I don't work freelance," I said. "My background is PI work and then law. But I'm with a foundation out of DC now. I'm full-time with that."

"I see," he said. "So what's your interest in this case?"

"I know the defendant. Not really well, but I think she could use a friend right now."

"Oh, yeah, couldn't they all?" he said, rolling his eyes. He was just being facetious, but the callous nature of his comment disturbed me. "I expect the prints will come back with her name on them. I figure with a guilty plea to manslaughter one, she'll get fifteen and serve maybe twelve. That's not too bad."

"It is if she isn't guilty."

"Oh, come on," he said. "From her list of priors alone—"

"Any violent crimes on those priors?"

He looked back down at the file and flipped to the last page, producing a computer printout I assumed had come from the police.

"Let's see. Possession, shoplifting, petty theft..." His voice trailed off as he ran his finger down the list, reading to himself. "No, not really."

"So why do you think she's guilty? Do you know all the details of her situation?"

He dropped the paper and gestured toward the mess on his desk.

"Look, Ms. Webber, I was only assigned this case a few hours ago. I'll have a clearer picture once I've had more time to review the file."

"Meanwhile, she sits in jail."

"Oh, no. She's not in jail."

He went to the file again, this time pulling out the top sheet of paper and waving it toward me.

"They've still got her down at the police barracks," he said. "She signed a Waiver of Prompt Presentment last night, before I was even assigned to the case."

"What's that mean?"

"It means she's locked up, but not at the county detention center. By signing the waiver, she gave them the right to keep her at the barracks. So they can keep questioning her, ostensibly until she cracks."

"She hasn't even been to the commissioner's office?"

"Nope. Still down at the station. Once she signed this waiver, they had a lot more freedom to keep her around."

"Shouldn't you be there with her while they question her?"

"That would be nice," he said. "Maybe I can fit it in between my massage and a leisurely lunch."

"Sir?"

"I don't have the time, Ms. Webber! Get a clue! I've got plenty of other people who need my attention, plenty of other people with problems just as pressing as Mrs. Greer's."

"Miss," I said softly.

"Huh?"

"*Miss* Greer."

"Whatever. If I had the luxury of sitting there and handholding every suspect the police decided to question, I'd never get another single thing done. It's all a matter of priorities."

I thought about that, revising my earlier opinion of this man and his relatively advanced age for a public defender. He may not have left this post physically, but for all practical purposes, it seemed to me he was already long gone.

I decided to change gears, asking if he thought they might let me in to see her.

"I can make a call," he told me, glancing at the phone. "I'm sure it won't be a problem. I expect to talk to her myself this afternoon."

"Better late than never."

"Look, Ms. Webber," he said, gesturing in front of him, his arms wide. "You can see the quantity of cases that comes across my desk. If you don't like the way I handle this particular one, you're more than welcome to hire the woman a private attorney."

"Maybe further down the line," I said. "For right now, I'd like to see what I can accomplish as an investigator, if I may."

"Hey, if you think she's innocent, and you wanna run with this, then fine. Go for it."

Our eyes met in challenge. After a beat, he looked away.

"Obviously," he added, his ears tinting a bright red, "she can use all the help she can get."

I took a deep breath and let it out. Maybe I was judging this man a bit harshly. After all, my legal career had been limited to the board room, not the court room. Perhaps if I did what he did for a living, day in and day out, I'd grow to be a bit cynical as well.

"I'm off from work this week," I said more calmly. "So I'll talk to her and do some poking around in my spare time. If I come up with anything, I'll let you know."

"Good."

"Although, if I get called back to work before we've straightened out this mess, I'll have no choice but to drop everything and go."

"Of course. I'll take whatever assistance you can provide."

"Fine, then. I guess we're on the same page."

"I guess so."

I stood, shook his hand, and then waited as he made the phone call that would get me in to see Shayna. As I made my way out of his building and back to my car, I couldn't help wondering what it was about this case that made me care. Shayna was just some kid from the boonies who had made some bad choices and now was paying for them. Even if she hadn't killed Eddie Ray, she had allowed herself to get involved with him again, had allowed him to move back into her home and her life.

I pictured Shayna's face when she first saw the body and then when the police found the drugs under the seat of her car. She had been genuinely shocked in both instances. Something told me the Lord had put me there at those moments so I would see for myself, so I would believe in her innocence, so I would feel the urge to help this girl.

For now, I was eager to get over to the police station and talk to Shayna face-to-face. If I was going to try and help her, I had some questions that definitely needed some answers.

Fourteen

Shayna looked terrible. Of course, I hadn't exactly expected her to be chipper, but truly the kid looked as though she had been raked over the coals. When the policeman let me into the interrogation room, I found Shayna with her head down on the table, softly crying. She looked up when I entered, confusion blurring her features.

"Callie? What are you doing here?"

"Hey, Shayna," I said. "How are you holding up?"

The door was shut and locked behind me with a click.

"Oh my gosh," she said, eyes wide. "Did they arrest you, too?"

I shook my head, allowing myself a small smile.

"No. I'm here to see you."

She sat up, smoothing her new hairdo back from her face. Even with bloodshot eyes and splotchy cheeks, the flattering effect of the hairstyle was remarkable. I could detect a tremble in her fingers, and I asked if she needed water or coffee or anything.

"They've been real nice with all that," she said. "I'm fine."

There was a chair across from her at the table, so I sat, looking around at the small room. It was a standard interrogation room: one table, a couple of chairs, and blank walls except for a large one-way mirrored window. There was a box of Kleenex on the table, and I pushed it toward her. She took one and tended to her face before rolling it into a ball and clutching it nervously in her hand.

"So they've been asking you a lot of questions, huh?" I asked.

She nodded her head vigorously.

"Oh my gosh, Callie, the stupidest stuff. What did I have for breakfast yesterday. What time did I go to the bathroom. Where do I keep my car keys."

"Where *do* you keep your car keys?"

"In the car! I keep telling them, *everybody* in Kawshek does that. We either leave them in the ignition or under the floor mat. It's not like car theft is exactly a problem out there. Especially with a piece of junk like mine. Who'd want it?"

"Did Eddie Ray ever borrow your car?"

"Yeah, sometimes. He didn't have a car of his own."

"Have you had any flat tires lately?"

"A couple of weeks ago. I drove over a piece of wire. It looked like maybe it had broken off from an old crab trap."

"Did you change the tire yourself?"

"Yeah. I was out on the highway. There wasn't anybody else around."

"You used the tire iron?"

"Of course I did. You think I've got Triple A? It was just a flat tire!"

"I see."

"You see what? You sound just like the cops, asking me all these stupid questions. I don't understand what's going on, Callie."

"They're giving you a lot of rope in the hope that eventually you'll hang yourself with it."

"What?"

"They want to catch you in a lie, Shayna."

She shook her head vigorously.

"But I haven't lied, not once. I swear I don't know where the pot came from. You believe me, don't you? I've been clean since last fall!"

I nodded.

"Now I've got this new job starting," she continued, "and I'll just die if I have to postpone that because of some lousy drug charge. It would be so embarrassing!"

I leaned back in my chair and looked at her, thinking that losing a job was the least of her problems right now.

"Shayna, don't you get it?" I said. "They're not interested in the marijuana. They want you for Eddie Ray's murder."

She looked at me for a moment as that sunk in. She seemed to be reviewing things in her mind, and then finally she looked down and blinked out more tears.

"I'm so stupid," she whispered. "I guess I should've figured that out."

"Did you kill him?" I asked.

"No!"

"Do you know who did?"

"No!"

"Then let's work on getting you out of here. I mean, if you want my help, that is."

Shayna looked up, shock written in her wide-open eyes.

"Oh, Callie," she said, those eyes filling with tears. "I think I need your help right now more than I've ever needed anything in my whole life."

Fifteen

For the next 15 minutes, I listened to a detailed history of Shayna's relationship with Eddie Ray Higgins. Some of the facts I already knew, and some were new to me.

They first met in a truck stop in Santa Fe, New Mexico, where she was a waitress, and he was working as a "mule," smuggling heroin across the Mexican border. Shayna was an addict then, and Eddie Ray was a ready source—not to mention a sweet-talking charmer. After a few weeks of on-again, off-again romance, Eddie Ray learned that his mother had died and left him a small sum of money along with a house in Kawshek. He decided to get out of drug-running and move back home to make his fortune legitimately. He brought Shayna with him.

Once they moved here Eddie Ray had tried all manner of ways to make money, but he seemed to fail at everything he did. Shayna described some of his schemes, from starting a fishing lure mail-order business to opening a fancy restaurant in Easton. Eddie always gravitated to "big" plans—things that were destined to fail simply because of his grandiose nature. He went through his inheritance fairly quickly, and then he took out a mortgage on the house and went through that, too. In the end, he had enough left to make a down payment on a deluxe boat for a water-taxi service, but no money to promote the service or even pay for the upkeep of the boat.

"After the water-taxi business failed, he left me for good," Shayna said. "Like I told you, he just up and left. Then two days later, some men from the bank showed up to foreclose on his mother's house."

"Wow."

"I didn't even know they were coming."

"What did you do?"

"What could I do? I left! I walked out of that house, went over to the bar, and got high. I woke up two days later in a ditch out along the highway, and that's when I realized life just couldn't get any worse."

"Doesn't sound like it."

Shayna went on to describe how the first thing she saw as she walked back to town was a big white tent outside of the community church. There was something going on there, but what drew her were the free donuts and coffee set up on a table nearby. She took as many donuts as her hands could hold and then sat in a metal folding chair, intending to eat and be on her way. Instead, she started listening to the words and the music down front, and soon she was swept into the revival. Before the night was over, she had accepted Christ and decided to turn her life around.

"The people in that church could not have helped me more," she said. "They prayed with me and supported me, but they also showed me how I couldn't keep on with the way things were. They talked me into going to drug rehab so I could dry out, and then I was assigned a social worker and got job training. When I finally got out of rehab, the whole church was so proud of me. One of the deacons let me live rent free in that apartment until I could find a job, and the ladies' group gave me an old car so I could get to interviews. They even gave me spending money in exchange for cleaning the sanctuary every Monday morning."

Tears started to roll down Shayna's cheeks as she talked.

"Oh, Callie, they all believed in me so much. Things were going so well. If even one of them thinks I did this—the drugs or the murder—it will just break my heart. I can't face them!"

I sat back, waiting as Shayna pulled out more tissues and blew her nose. I thought about the crowd that had been watching the police activity near her apartment the night before. Indeed, the way they talked, they all seemed to believe she had killed Eddie Ray—but even so, they had sounded sympathetic to *her*, not to him.

"If things were going so well for you," I asked, "why did you let Eddie Ray back into your life?"

She shook her head.

"He took me by surprise, I guess," she replied. "He said he missed me and he loved me—and I was feeling kind of lonely and scared. I hadn't been with anybody in so long. Not that we did anything this time, you know. I let him move in, but I made him sleep on the couch. Part of me wanted him to leave. But part of me just wanted a man around again. Somebody to hold my hand. Somebody to say nice things to me."

I wondered about those nice things he had said to her. Had he really loved her, or was there some other motive? Perhaps he was just in need of a free place to crash. According to Shayna, he had five dollars in his pocket the day he showed up this time. Maybe she was simply his last resort.

"Yesterday," I said, "at Advancing Attire, you were telling me about some new big plan Eddie Ray had. You said he told you that soon he would have enough money so that neither one of you would ever have to work again."

Shayna rolled her eyes.

"I don't even know what this one was about. He got all excited one day about two weeks ago. He said he'd finally hit the jackpot."

"Another water-taxi service?"

"No, this was different. This time he wouldn't tell me what it was exactly. He just said that as soon as he made his first big chunk of change we would get married, and then I would never have to worry about money again."

"Was he involved with someone locally? Like, in a business deal or something?"

"I don't know. He spent a lot of time at the bar with Russell and the other guys, shooting pool, but that was nothing new."

"Russell?"

"Russell Lynch. One of his old friends."

"Did he have many friends in the area?"

"A few. There's not much to do in Kawshek. 'Round five o'clock every afternoon, folks start coming in from the water. Most of them hang out in either the bar or the store. In a way, everybody is friends with everybody else."

"I understand."

Shayna let out a deep breath, pushing her new bangs from her forehead. She looked exhausted.

"What about Hank?" I asked.

"Hank?"

"The guy you had been dating before Eddie Ray came back to town."

"How'd you know about him?"

I shrugged my shoulders.

"Gossip. Weren't you dating him previously?"

"We went out a few times," she said, "but I kind of broke it off."

"Why?"

This time she shrugged.

"Hank's a fisherman. Ready to live his life out in Kawshek in a little one-room apartment. I don't want that life. I want out of here. So I stopped things before they ever really got started."

"Do you think he could've killed Eddie Ray? Out of jealousy?"

Shayna actually laughed out loud.

"Hank Hawkins? He wouldn't kill a fly with a flyswatter. No, there's no way. He may look tough, but he's really very sweet, like a giant teddy bear. We broke up a couple days before Eddie Ray came back. There were no hard feelings."

I nodded, doubt still lingering in my mind. I tried to picture Hank as I had seen him last night, ruddy and huge, with that nasty scar across his chin.

In any event, I knew our time here was just about out, so I approached things from a different tack, concentrating back on Eddie Ray's latest plan for making big bucks.

"Shayna, do you think it's possible Eddie Ray was working as a mule again?"

I thought that if he had been a drug runner before, there was a chance he was involved with something like that again. In an area like the Chesapeake, where hundreds of ships from all over the world passed by on the waterways every day, smuggling had to be rampant. The kind of people involved with drug smuggling probably wouldn't think twice about committing murder—or stuffing a dead body into the nearest trunk.

"I doubt it," she replied. "He hated smuggling before. Besides, he never made much money from it anyway."

I asked her other questions about Eddie Ray's moneymaking plan, insisting he had to have let something about it slip, even if he'd primarily kept her in the dark. She thought for a while before finally looking up at me in surprise, her eyes wide.

"The nickel!" she said. "It all started with the nickel!"

"The nickel?"

She nodded vigorously.

"Callie, there was this thing, this little wooden disk, shaped like a coin. On one side it said 'Don't take any wooden nickels.' I think with a picture of an Indian's head. And on the other side was an advertisement for something. A website, maybe. Something about treasure."

"Treasure?"

"Buried treasure. I thought it was hokey, but Eddie Ray took the nickel, and then pretty soon after that he started acting all secretive and weird."

I sat back, stumped. Buried treasure?

"Where did this wooden nickel come from?" I asked.

"From you!"

I pulled back, surprised.

"Me?"

"Yeah, sort of." Shayna looked down, her face coloring. "In the blazer you gave me, the first time I went to Advancing Attire. There was a little pocket, up here," she said, patting her chest, "on the inside of the jacket, but I never noticed it. Then Eddie Ray was home when I came back from a job interview one day, and I was still wearing the blazer. About two weeks ago. We were just sitting in the kitchen, shooting the breeze, when I realized there was a pocket there and that something little was in it. I pulled out the wooden nickel."

"Go on."

"Like I said, I didn't think it was anything, but Eddie Ray saw the bit about 'buried treasure' printed on it and said he would look into it."

"Where's the nickel now?"

"I don't know. After he took it from me and slipped it into his pocket, I never saw it again. But two days later, Eddie Ray was talking about big money and hitting the jackpot."

"How do you know the jackpot and the wooden nickel were connected?" I asked.

"I wouldn't have thought that at all," she replied, "except for what he said. He told me, 'Just think, baby. They always say "Don't take any wooden nickels," but this one is gonna turn out to be worth millions.' "

Sixteen

I went straight from the police station to Advancing Attire. My mind was racing with all that Shayna had told me, and I felt suddenly hopeful about my pursuit of the case. *Follow the money,* my investigating mentor, Eli Gold, had often said, and that was going to be my approach here. If Eddie Ray had been involved in some big financial scheme, I was going to track it down. The fact that an item of clothing that had come through Advancing Attire might be connected wasn't a very comforting thought, but still it was as good a place as any to start.

Verlene was busy assisting a client when I arrived, so after greeting them I excused myself and headed straight for the computer. I didn't think it would take long to track down the blazer and its source, and from there I might be able to find out what the "buried treasure" on the wooden nickel was all about.

"Oh, darling, you are absolutely *stunning* in violet!" Verlene cried. Stifling a smile, I glanced over at the client, an older black-haired woman Verlene had fitted with a tailored Donna Karan jacket and slacks. The woman beamed, admiring her stylish figure in the mirror.

I seated myself at the desk and quickly pulled up the computer records for Shayna. According to them, she had first come to Advancing Attire at the end of August and had received a navy skirt, navy blazer, white shirt, silk scarf, scarf pin, pumps, and a half slip. The skirt and blazer had both been donated by the same person, a woman named Grace Collins. That name sounded familiar. I closed the file on Shayna and went into Donor Profiles, pulling up Mrs. Collins to get a look at her information.

According to the address in her records, she lived about halfway between Osprey Cove and my house, probably in one of the hidden estates behind the plain-looking driveways. She had a long history of donations, about four times a year for the previous three years. Her last donation had been in October, and it was much more sizeable than usual. In fact, the list of things ran down for several pages. I was skimming the items when I realized why her name had sounded familiar to me. Verlene had mentioned her only the day before, saying that Grace had been petite like Shayna. Now I recalled she had said that Grace Collins had recently died, and her family had subsequently given us much of her remaining clothing.

I scrolled back up to the top of the profile, took out a pen, and jotted down the address and phone number. I was just closing out of the profile area when the black-haired client went into the changing room, and Verlene strode across the room toward the office.

"Callie! Callie! Callie!" she whispered sharply, reaching out to tug at my sleeve. "I've been dying to talk to you all day! What's going on with Shayna? Is she all right?"

I glanced toward the dressing room, hoping the client would soon emerge. I really didn't feel like getting into any of this now. Still, Verlene deserved to know what little I could tell her, so I explained that Shayna hadn't been charged with murder yet, but she was still being held by the police.

"The truth will come out eventually, I'm sure," I added. "You and I know she didn't do it, but we'll have to wait and see what happens."

"What about her new job? Is she going to be fired before she even starts?"

"Again, we'll have to wait and see. She's supposed to start a week from Monday, so there's still time to get her out of custody. Since her job is in Annapolis, they probably won't even have heard about any of this. There's no reason they should know."

Verlene looked toward the dressing room, wringing her hands.

"These girls," she whispered sadly. "Is all our work in vain? Do they ever really make the kind of changes they need to make to turn their lives around?"

I was disturbed by the despair I heard in her voice. Sure, most of the women we helped had a long, tough road ahead of them—and our informal statistics showed that the majority of them ended up right back where they started, once again jobless and involved with things like drugs or unhealthy relationships or unexpected pregnancies. But for every two women who failed, there was still one who succeeded. It was that one out of three who kept me involved, doing what little I could do to give them a chance.

"Verlene," I said, reaching out to take her hand in mine. I wasn't really one for sentimentality, but I sensed she needed to hear some encouraging words right now. She looked at me, and I was surprised to see tears brimming in her eyes. The dear woman really did care. "You know you've made a huge difference in a lot of women's lives—"

"I know, but—"

"But nothing. You give them some wonderful tools and send them on their way. It's up to them how they use those tools. You can't hold yourself responsible for what happens after they walk out of the door."

She blinked back her tears and attempted a smile.

"Come on, Verlene," I said. "If Shayna—or any of these ladies—messes up, that still doesn't change the fact that they are responsible for themselves. You can be comforted in the knowledge that you did everything within your power to help them succeed."

"I suppose so," she sniffed. "It's just all so upsetting."

"Of course it is," I replied, remembering how shaken she had been the day before in the midst of all the trauma. Things I took in stride—murdered corpses, police interrogations, arrests—weren't the norm for most people, and especially not for a sweet, sheltered woman like Verlene Linford. I felt a surge of sympathy for her.

"Maybe you should've stayed home today," I said gently. "I'm sure this place could survive a day without you."

"I had to come in," she replied. "There's this whole lease thing to worry about, plus this other organization is pressuring me to hurry up and make a decision—"

"What organization?"

"I was starting to tell you about it yesterday, when we," she paled and lowered her voice, "when we discovered the, uh, the body."

"What organization?" I repeated, hoping to keep her on track.

"It's one of those big companies—a big nonprofit, to be exact—that handles peripheral operations for small charities. If we sign on with them, they'll take over our accounting, our payroll, our fund-raising, things like that. Then that frees us up to concentrate on serving our clients. Gosh, for the small fees they charge we get a lot in return, including the opportunity to expand. The woman I spoke with on the phone said that they could provide funding for the bigger space right away. But we've got to make a decision."

"Why are they pressuring you?"

"They're not, really. It's just that we need to work fast if we want to be able to move on the building next door when it becomes available."

"When do you think that will be?"

"Soon. The owner gave me a heads up because he's an old friend of mine. But he said I've only got about a week's jump on everyone else, and then he's going to list with his Realtor. You know how store-front property is in this part of town. That place will be snatched up before you know it!"

"What does one thing have to do with the other? Can't you go ahead and lease the extra space and then worry about this national company later?"

"I wish I could. But without their assistance, Advancing Attire can't afford the extra space. It's just not in the budget."

"I see."

"On the one hand," Verlene said, holding out a palm, "it's almost like the Lord provided an opportunity and the means for that opportunity all at once."

I nodded. I had been thinking the same thing.

"On the other hand," she continued, "I certainly don't want to be hasty. Affiliating ourselves with another group, no matter how successful they are, may not be the best move for us. I just don't want to make a poor decision based on our immediate need."

I looked around, thinking it was no wonder Verlene had come looking for me yesterday in search of a little advice. As an investigator of nonprofits of all kinds, this type of thing was right up my alley.

"Have you spoken to your board of directors?" I asked. "What do they say?"

"The board president called a special meeting night before last," Verlene said. "They agree we need more space, but they were a bit split as to whether this was the way to go about it. They've left it to me to gather more information about this company and get back to them by the end of the week."

She looked at me, her eyes wide, and I quickly realized that she was asking me a question.

"Let me guess," I said slowly. "You want me..."

"...to look into the company!" she finished. "To see if this would be a good thing for us. That is what you do for a living, isn't it? Investigate nonprofits?"

I took a deep breath and let it out. Leave it to me to saddle myself with not one but two cases—all during a week that I was supposed to be off from work entirely!

She took my hesitation as an assent and immediately began gathering papers and shoving them into a manila file folder.

"All I ask is that you look this stuff over," she said eagerly. "Just in your spare time. Get back to me in a few days and let me know what you think."

Before I knew it, she had shoved the file into my hands and was stepping back, a look of great relief radiating across her face.

"Thank you!" she exclaimed. "You have no idea what a big help this will be. We're changing lives here, Callie. We always have to keep that foremost in our minds."

As if on cue, the dressing room opened, and the client who had just a few minutes before looked elegant in Donna Karan now came out wearing a pair of hip-hugging faux leopard-skin pants and a short red T-shirt advertising a rock band. A roll of flesh hung out over the pants, and her pierced belly button sported what looked like a pewter skull and crossbones. The contrast between that and the outfit she had just changed out of was startling, to say the least. Verlene shot a pointed look in my direction, as if to say, "You see?" before putting a smile on her face and turning around to help the client.

I grabbed the opportunity to slip away, tucking the file under my arm. As I went out the door, I fingered the paper in my pocket that held the address for the home of Grace Collins.

Okay, Verlene, you got me, I thought. *But first things first.*

Seventeen

The Collins house wasn't hard to find. As I suspected, the address was along the highway, belonging to one of the driveways that curved off out of sight into dense, tall pines. I hadn't called ahead but instead decided simply to show up. It was often easier to get information when the people you were questioning were taken off guard.

I drove up the driveway and rounded a curve that revealed the house. It was a huge, stunning mansion I had viewed often from the river in my canoe, but I hadn't seen it from this side before. Built probably in the '50s but designed to look as if it had been here for generations, it featured massive antebellum columns flanking a gorgeous mahogany double front door. The driveway circled in front of the house, so I pulled to the side and stopped there.

Resisting the urge to clank one of the giant knockers on the door, I instead pressed the doorbell and then listened as it echoed inside. It took a few moments, but eventually the door was swung open by a good-looking man about my age, wearing a navy sweater and dark gray slacks.

"Hi," he said breathlessly. He was handsome in a rich sort of way, with excellent posture and perfect white teeth.

"Hi," I replied. "Is this the Collins residence—"

"Yes, I'm Kirby Collins. Come in, hurry up."

Startled, I stepped inside. He quickly pushed the door shut behind me.

"Follow me!" he said, and then he took off toward the left, disappearing through a doorway.

I paused, looking around at the massive entranceway. A marble staircase ascended in front of me, curving up past two stories of windows that looked out on a lovely courtyard. The place was striking, but my reception had been so odd, I wasn't sure what to do next.

"This way," the man called to me from the other room. "Come on in here."

Feeling rather like Alice in the rabbit hole, I followed the sound of his voice through a living room and into a formal dining room. Both were decorated beautifully—though a bit ornately for my taste—with antique furniture, expensive fabrics, and a dining table that looked as if it seated at least 20. Sitting at one end of the dining table was an older woman, probably in her 80s, dressed in an elegant silk gown. She seemed to be having a tea party—though without the cups or the teapot. Delicately, she pantomimed pouring, adding sugar, and stirring in the thin air in front of her. I tried to catch her eye, but she was somewhere else, busily serving make-believe tea to nonexistent guests.

"We're almost done," Kirby Collins said, and he seemed to be talking both to me and to another gentleman who stood at the far end of the room, spread-eagle against the wall. In the man's hands were two framed paintings, and he was holding a third painting against the wall by pressing against it with his face. Crouching on the floor next to him was a middle-aged woman, thick and sturdy in a nurse's white uniform, sweeping up what looked like broken glass.

"Okay, Bucky, a little to the left," Kirby said, and the older gentleman holding the paintings groaned as he slid all three paintings and his entire body a few inches to the left.

"Can I help?" I asked.

"Sure, if you don't mind."

Stepping gingerly to avoid the glass, I crossed to the wall and took one of the paintings from the man's hand. He used that free hand to grab the painting held in place by his face, exhaling gratefully.

"Super. Now put the middle one up about six inches," Kirby said. "Now the two sides down another three inches. Great. Ma'am, bring yours up just an inch."

We continued to do as he directed until, finally, he told us to freeze. Then he ran forward with a pencil, made some tiny marks on the wall above each of the pictures, and then said we could take them down.

"I think I've gotten all the big pieces," the nurse said, dumping the contents of the dustpan into a wastebasket. "I'll call Maria in to vacuum."

"Fine," said Kirby.

"And again," the nurse said, "I'm so sorry. All I did was go to my room for just a few minutes—"

"It's okay, Carol," said Kirby. "It happens. She didn't get hurt. That's all that matters."

Looking red-faced and exhausted, the nurse walked to the woman at the dining table and put a reassuring hand on her shoulder. The older man straightened his ruffled clothes, smoothed his hair, and then turned to me and nodded formally.

"I apologize for all of this confusion," he said in a dignified voice. "I'm the Collins' butler. May I help you?"

He was so dignified, I felt an urge to laugh. But he seemed sincere, so I only smiled.

"I'm Callie Webber. It's nice to meet you."

I held out a hand and he shook it, introducing himself as Reginald Buchman. Then he introduced the others, explaining that the lady making "tea" was Eleanor Collins, Kirby's grandmother. The nurse was Carol Knight, Eleanor's daytime attendant.

"I'm afraid we had a little incident here," Mr. Buchman said softly. "Mrs. Collins thought it was time to redecorate the dining room, and she broke a picture."

"Hey, it gives me a chance to rearrange things," Kirby said cheerfully. "I never particularly liked the way we had those pictures anyway."

As we talked, Eleanor seemed to shift gears. Suddenly, she stood and started walking out of the room.

"Are you finished with your tea party?" the nurse asked loudly.

"Oh, yes," Eleanor replied as she shuffled away. "The cucumber sandwiches were especially nice."

They left the room, and Mr. Buchman seemed to visibly relax.

"Again, I'm sorry for the confusion," he said. "How can we help you today?"

I took a deep breath, wondering if this was a bad time or if things were always like this around here. I thought about offering to come back when it was a little more convenient, but then I remembered Shayna, cooling her heels with the police, and I decided to blunder on ahead.

"I'm with Advancing Attire, in Osprey Cove," I said. "I needed to speak with someone regarding some clothes that were donated to our organization. I just have a few questions."

"I'm the one you want," Kirby said, slipping a nail through a picture hanger and tapping it into the wall. "Give me one minute."

I waited as he hung the final picture, and I had to admit the arrangement was unusual but very nice. He obviously had a good eye—not to mention a great attitude and a very cooperative butler!

"Okay," Kirby said, handing the hammer to Mr. Buchman and taking my elbow. "Now that that's all done, let's start over. I didn't mean to be rude. I was just afraid Bucky was going to pull a muscle or something."

I smiled. Kirby Collins was charming and cute, with one definite dimple in his right cheek when he smiled.

"Come on into my office," he said, leading me back to the entranceway and then through to the other side.

"Is your grandmother all right?"

"She suffers from dementia," he said, shrugging. "We have these little adventures once in a while."

We went from the stark but grand entrance hall into an equally grand but much more welcoming room. The walls were lined with books, and a grouping of plush chairs and couches was centered on a deep oriental carpet. There was a lovely fireplace along one wall, with a fire roaring inside, crackling and warm.

"You'll have to excuse the mess," Kirby said, pointing to an antique rolltop desk near the window. Papers were spread out across the desktop. "I was just doing some bookkeeping."

"Not one of my favorite tasks," I replied.

"Mine either," he said. "The amount of paperwork that's required simply to run a household always boggles my mind."

"I can imagine," I said, thinking that with a house this large, the bills would be never-ending.

"Excuse me," Mr. Buchman interrupted from the doorway. "Now that I've finished my morning calisthenics, shall I bring some refreshment?"

"I could use a cup of coffee," Kirby said. "How about you, Miss Webber? Coffee? Soda? Something a little stronger?"

"Tea would be nice," I said, smiling. "No sugar. And, please, call me Callie."

"If you call me Kirby," he replied. "One coffee and one tea then, Bucky."

The man gave a slight bow and left the room.

"He likes to gripe," Kirby whispered, "but he knows it's my antics that keep him young."

I just smiled again, thinking the fellow was probably a little too old to be spread-eagle against a wall.

"Hey, you know, you sure look familiar to me," Kirby said. "Have we met before?"

I studied his chiseled jaw, his broad shoulders. He wasn't the type of man who usually caught my eye, but something about him was very engaging. *No,* I thought, *if we'd met, I certainly would've remembered it!*

"I don't think so."

"It's like I've seen you from a distance. That's the image I keep getting anyway."

"I've done some lecturing for Advancing Attire," I said. "Maybe you were out in the audience."

He shook his head.

"Nah, that was my mother's thing, not mine."

"No telling, then," I said. "It could've been almost anywhere. This is such a small area, we've probably crossed paths in one way or another."

"Maybe."

"In any event," I said, "I need to ask about some of the clothing that was donated to our organization by your mother. We—"

"No, wait," he said. "It's been such a crazy morning. I don't want to talk business just yet. Let's have a conversation, something light. We can get down to business when the drinks gets here."

"Okay," I replied warily. I was in no mood for idle chatter, but if it eventually got me the information I needed, I was willing to play along.

"So where do you live?" he asked amiably, settling into the sofa. "You said you're from the area?"

We chatted for a while, and I eventually found myself relaxing a bit. Though small talk wasn't usually my strong suit, I was enjoying my conversation with Kirby Collins. He knew the family that had originally owned my little cottage, and he shared some stories about the former caretaker and his penchant for collecting driftwood that resembled famous people.

"He had one piece," Kirby said, "that I swear looked just like David Letterman. Believe it or not, he even got on Letterman's show. It was great. I was just a kid then, but I thought that was so cool. I spent months trying to start my own collection, but the best I could do was a clam shell that vaguely resembled Angela Lansbury."

I smiled, saying that *Murder, She Wrote* had been one of my favorite TV shows when I was growing up.

"Oh yeah? My mother loved that one, but I didn't buy it. Too many deaths in one small, coastal town if you ask me. I mean, really, who gets murdered in a quiet, peaceful area like this one?"

He held up both hands, palms upward, oblivious to the irony of his words.

"Then again," he continued, "there's more than one kind of killing at the coast. Just last week I murdered a piece of high tech equipment, totally destroyed it." He went on to tell a long, funny story about how he had gone out on a friend's yacht eager to try out the guy's expensive new fish finder. Unfortunately, Kirby said, he had put the wrong end of the device under the water and ended up shorting out its entire electrical system.

When he finished his tale, we shared a smile, our gaze holding just a bit too long.

Mr. Buchman showed up with our refreshments at that moment, and I sat back, wondering at what was going on here. Was Kirby flirting with me? More disturbing than that, was I flirting back? As the butler carefully set down the cups and a tray of small sandwiches, I used the moment to compose myself. This wasn't me, not at all. Maybe I was just so tired from last night's lack of sleep that I was punchy.

"So what kind of boat do you have anyway?" Kirby asked, a twinkle in his eye, as soon as Mr. Buchman had left the room. "I love getting out on the water."

"Oh, just a canoe," I replied, looking away, wondering whether he was being conversational or if this was a genuine hint for an invitation. "But come on, a deal's a deal. Let's get down to business."

Good as his word, Kirby listened attentively as I explained why I was there. His mother had donated a blazer, I said, and in an inner pocket was a small wooden nickel. I described it for him: the Indian head, the slogan, the website about buried treasure. He listened, nodding, but recognition did not seem to cross his features.

"I need to learn more about this nickel," I said. "It's kind of a long story, but it would be very helpful if you could tell me what it is or where it came from."

"I don't understand," he said. "Why don't you show me the nickel, and we can go from there."

"Well, that's the problem. I don't have it."

"You don't have it?"

I exhaled slowly, wishing I could've found a way to avoid this part. Verlene would kill me if she knew I was here, bothering this man with the travails of one of our more indigent clientele.

"It sort of fell into the wrong hands," I said. "Now a young woman is in jail, and I'm afraid it has something to do with this nickel."

"You've lost me," he said. "Did she steal it from you or something?"

"No, but her boyfriend took it and did something with it. Like I said, it's a long story. Do you have any idea what it was, or why it was in your mother's pocket? Did she collect wooden nickels? Did she use the Internet, or maybe have an interest in buried treasure?"

Kirby put down his coffee and then stood, the expression on his face suddenly far away. I remembered his mother had died recently, and I felt guilty for being here now, adding to his grief.

"No, no, and no," he said thoughtfully. "I have a few wooden nickels I collected when I was a boy, but the collection wasn't worth anything. I just thought they were neat."

"Do you still have the collection? Could I see it?"

"Sure," he said. "If I can find it."

He excused himself and left the room. I finished my tea and headed over to the window. Kirby had alluded to doing household paperwork, and indeed the desk there was covered with spread sheets and bills and a large notebook-style checkbook. But also peeking out from under some of the papers was something that looked like a small circuit board and a tiny pair of needlenose pliers.

Not wanting to pry, I turned my gaze out to the expansive lawn, recognizing the familiar fountain that served as its centerpiece. When I canoed past here on the river, as I did frequently, the figurine in the fountain always looked to me like some sort of sea serpent. From here, however, I realized it was a mermaid, her hair thrown back, water flowing from a giant conch shell she cradled in her arms. Though the flamboyant sculpture wasn't unattractive, it didn't exactly fit in with these elegant and moneyed surroundings.

"I see you're looking at Bertha," Kirby said, reentering the room. Carrying a small glass jar, he strode over to join me at the window.

"Bertha?"

"The mermaid. At least that's the name I gave her. My dad's doing."

"She's interesting," I said diplomatically.

"She's ludicrous," he replied. "But she has great sentimental value. That fountain used to be in a waterfront park in Baltimore, the park where my father proposed to my mother. When he heard they were tearing down the park to expand the inner harbor, he bought it and had it installed here."

"What a sweet story," I said, gazing out at the sculpture. "Very romantic."

I could feel Kirby looking at me, and I was suddenly uncomfortable with his proximity—not that it was inappropriate, just that he was close enough for me to smell the vague scent of his cologne. I took a small step away from him, but before I could change the subject and ask about the nickels, he gave a small gasp.

"The canoe!" he said. "I knew I recognized you! From the canoe!"

I looked at him, and he was smiling widely, pointing out the window.

"You go past here all the time," he said. "I watch you while I'm at my desk."

"You said 'from a distance,'" I replied, nodding. "Sorry I didn't make the connection for you. I never thought of that."

He went to the couch and sat, leaning back happily.

"You're the canoe lady," he said, grinning. "I'm so glad I figured that out. It was driving me crazy."

I returned to my chair, also smiling.

"I even had a bet about you with my girlfriend one time," he continued. "She made me watch your rowing technique so that I could see what proper paddling form looks like. She said I could learn to be that good, too. I told her not a chance, that you were probably part Indian, that it was no doubt in your blood."

I sat back, trying not to look befuddled. Here I thought he'd been flirting with me, when all along he had a girlfriend! Boy, was I out of practice for interpreting male-female interplay.

"Sorry, no Indian blood here," I said lamely.

"Are you sure? 'Cause you know, you have great cheekbones. Out there on the river, if you took your hair down, you'd look just like Pocahontas. You seem to be a natural at canoeing."

I shrugged. "My husband made me take a class before our first white-water trip. Since then I guess I've gotten good at it because I do it so much. Canoeing is a very absorbing hobby for me."

He studied me for a moment, an unreadable expression on his face.

"Husband?" he said finally, sounding disappointed. "You're married?"

"Well, late husband," I corrected, confused. Was this man flirting with me or not? It didn't matter one way or the other, but it still felt odd to be so unsure of myself. "Bryan passed away three years ago."

"I'm so sorry," he said. "I had no idea."

"That was before I moved here."

"Was he ill?"

"No," I said. "He died in a boating accident, actually. Killed by a drunk driver in a speedboat."

"Wow," Kirby said slowly. "How horrible for you."

"It's been tough," I said. "But time helps. And prayer."

He ran a hand through his hair.

"You probably know my mother died a couple of months ago," he said. "I mean, I wouldn't compare losing a parent to losing a spouse, but it has been awfully hard."

"You were close?" I asked gently, remembering my own grief that first year and how much I appreciated it whenever anyone gave me a chance to talk about it.

"Oh, yeah," he said. "My mom was a great lady. Just the best. When we found out she had cancer, I took a leave of absence from the company and moved back home to help out. But it was only a matter of time. We all knew she wasn't going to make it."

"I'm sorry," I said. "I know the pain of loss very well."

"I'm sure you do."

He looked at me, and in that instant we seemed to form a sort of connection. He blinked and shook his head.

"But enough of that," he said. Then he attempted a smile and held up the jar. "How 'bout we take a look at these nickels and figure out just what on earth is going on here?"

Eighteen

Kirby opened the jar and dumped it out onto a marble-topped coffee table. The contents formed a small mound of buttons, badges, coins, and wooden nickels.

"I haven't looked at this stuff in years," he said, pulling a small bronze medal from the pile. "I got this for swimming the hundred meter at summer camp."

While he picked through the pile and strolled down memory lane, I pulled out all of the wooden nickels. There were only five, and though they looked old, the writing and images on them were still legible. On the front of each one was either a company logo, a buffalo, or an Indian head, with the words "Wooden Nickel" or the saying "Don't Take Any Wooden Nickels." On the back of each was the name of some company or organization, a phone number, and either a slogan or a cash value. There was one from the "All Weather Wig Company" worth two dollars toward the purchase of a wig. Another advertised the 1980 convention of the Garden State Numismatic Association. I doubted any of them had any inherent value, though I wondered aloud how we could find out if old wooden nickels carried collectors' prices, like coins or stamps.

"I'm sure they do," Kirby said. "But the one you're talking about wouldn't have been old."

"How do you know?"

"You said it had a website printed on it."

"Oh, of course," I replied, feeling stupid. "It would have to be fairly new. I didn't realize they even made wooden nickels any more."

"Yeah, I see them once in a while. Usually for a bar or something. You bring in the wooden nickel, and you get a free drink. Or some club or group, trying to get you to join."

"So where do you think the wooden nickel your mother had could've come from?"

Kirby described the final months of his mother's life, from her initial diagnosis of ovarian cancer last Christmas to her death in August. According to him, she had been too ill to go anywhere but the hospital and back. We thought about that, finally deciding we needed a better idea of the age of the blue blazer. Who knows how long the nickel had been in that pocket? Although Advancing Attire sent all of our finer donations to the dry cleaners, it was possible that the coin had slipped by unnoticed. I sure hadn't felt or seen it when I was helping Shayna pick out her clothes. And even she hadn't noticed it for a while, since it was hidden in the small inner front pocket.

Kirby used the phone on the desk to call the woman who had been his mother's personal assistant for the last five years. After I described the jacket, the woman felt fairly certain that she remembered it, and that it had been purchased about two years ago at a boutique in Baltimore. But she didn't know a thing about a wooden nickel or buried treasure.

Kirby's face was disappointed as he hung up the phone.

"If she didn't know anything about it, I don't know who else would."

"How about your father?"

"My father?" he asked sarcastically. "Once Mom was diagnosed, my father found it suddenly necessary to work fifteen-hour days and travel for weeks at a time. I doubt he saw enough of my mother to know anything other than the fact that she was dying."

Obviously, I realized, there were some unresolved issues here—issues I had no need to become involved in.

"In any event," I said gently, "if you speak with him, could you ask?"

"Sure. No problem."

Kirby began putting the items back into the jar one by one. It seemed like a good time to depart, so I thanked him for his help and gave him my card, jotting my home number on the back.

"The J.O.S.H.U.A. Foundation?" he said, reading the card. "What's that name stand for?"

"I'm not sure," I hedged. "To me, it's just always been the J.O.S.H.U.A. Foundation."

I didn't add that once upon a time I had asked my boss the same question—and had been told that only he was privy to that information.

"Is the clothing place a branch of that?"

"No, Advancing Attire is purely a volunteer effort I do on the side," I said. "Work for the foundation is my regular job, but the card lists my home office phone and fax and e-mail and all of that, so you can reach me if you hear anything more."

He walked me to the door, tucking the card in his front pocket.

"I will figure this out and call you," he said. "No reason you should have to waste your time digging around about some wooden nickel."

"What about *your* time?" I asked. "It looks like you have a lot on your plate already."

"Listen," he said, putting a hand on my elbow, "if we're going to be friends, then the first thing you need to know about me is that I always use any possible excuse I can find to take a break from things around here."

Nineteen

I drove straight home, suddenly famished. I'd had an early breakfast, and now the clock was creeping toward afternoon. Sal was glad to see me, as usual, and after I gave her a treat and let her out, I turned my attention toward making a quick meal. There wasn't a lot of food in the house, mainly because I hadn't expected to be here this week. I found a can of tuna, though, and some limp lettuce, and as I fixed a light lunch I checked my messages.

The first call had come just after noon from Barbara Hightower. She wanted me to know that the tire iron in Shayna's trunk had come back covered with Shayna's fingerprints and no one else's. Shayna had been formally charged with first-degree murder.

I listened to the message again and absorbed the information, heart pounding. The poor kid!

Next, I found that Tom had called twice, the first time leaving just a quick hello, the second time sounding a bit concerned.

"Come on, Callie, answer the phone," he said. "I'm starting to wonder if something's wrong there."

I held the lettuce under the faucet, wishing there was some way for me to reach him.

"Here's what I want you to do," he continued. "Call my voice mail and let me know what would be a good time for me to call you. I don't mean to be so much trouble; it's just that they won't let me keep my cell phone on in intensive care."

Intensive care?

"My mom had a stroke, a really bad one. Right now it's still kind of touch and go. But I want to talk to you. I need to talk to you. Call me."

Then the line went dead.

I turned off the machine and sat on the stool beside the counter. His mom had a stroke! No wonder he had raced off to Louisiana like that. I was deeply ashamed of how self-centered I had been in all of this. Here I had been feeling ignored and rejected and sorry for myself, when all along Tom had been dealing with a family tragedy! I felt very sad.

Immediately, I closed my eyes and prayed for Tom and for his mother. I didn't know much about his family situation—whether he had aunts and uncles to help share the load—or even if his dad was still around. But whatever the circumstances, I asked the Lord to put a loving hand over all of them, to give wisdom to the doctors, to give healing to Tom's mother.

Once my prayer was done, I finished making my lunch and then sat and ate at the table, looking absently out of the window at my beautiful wooded yard. Sal was at the edge of her little fenced-in area, chewing away on her favorite toy. I thought about my own parents over in Virginia, both still in good health, thankfully. Their biggest problem these days seemed to be worrying about me and the isolated life I had created for myself here. But physically, they were both fine. I couldn't imagine either one of them rendered incapacitated by a stroke.

After eating, I reached for the phone and called Tom's voice mail, telling him how sorry I was to hear about his mom. I said that I was heading out in just a while but that I would make a point to return to my house by 8 P.M. I would also leave my cell phone on, in case he wanted to call me on that.

"I'm sorry you were worried about me," I added, wishing we could talk face-to-face. "Everything is fine here. I've just been doing some volunteer work, since I don't have any assignments."

I didn't add that my "volunteer work" had me in hot pursuit of a murderer. Tom obviously had enough on his mind already.

"So call me when you can," I concluded. "I'll be thinking about you."

I hung up the phone and wondered for the thousandth time if he felt as close to me as I did to him. Even though we'd never met in person, even though I knew next to nothing about his private life, sometimes it was as if I could just *feel* him with me. Now was one of those times.

But there was work to do, not just with Shayna's case, but also with Verlene's. I cleaned my dishes and then retrieved the file that Verlene had given me and opened it onto the table. I didn't have much time to spare, but I thought I should at least take a look at things and get myself oriented with this company that had approached Advancing Attire about forming an alliance.

From what I could tell, the introductory letter and company information looked like fairly standard stuff. The group was called Comprehensive Nonprofit Alliance, or CNA for short, and just as Verlene had said, it was a national nonprofit company that handled other nonprofit organizations' peripheral duties, such as accounting and fund-raising, freeing the employees and volunteers of the local organizations to focus on their primary services. According to the letter, there were 42 charities across the country already being served by CNA, and they were actively seeking to expand the operation to eventually cover nonprofit companies in all 50 states.

For a nonprofit, the letter did come across as a bit aggressive, but then again, that wasn't necessarily a strike against them. Verlene herself could be aggressive when she wanted something—as witnessed by the fact that I was sitting here at my kitchen table doing this research, despite never actually agreeing to it! I grinned, thinking of Verlene and indeed all the good charity heads I had had the pleasure to know. If they had one thing in common, it was their ability to pull other people into their own enthusiasm.

My procedure for investigating nonprofit groups was always to follow a list of fairly standard criteria. Over the years, I had developed a roster of "Ten Qualities of a Good Nonprofit" that I used as my guide. This investigation would be no exception, since CNA was essentially a nonprofit that just happened to serve other nonprofits.

The first criteria, that the agency "serves a worthwhile cause," was a matter of opinion. I supposed that organizations like this had their place. According to their literature, they provided a number of services in a variety of categories: accounting, fund-raising, public relations, and even purchasing. Certainly, some of these services could be worthwhile, as I often advised charities to hire out the more tedious tasks, such as payroll. In the end, the extra expense was almost always worth it.

For now, then, I would go ahead and give a yes to the first criteria, albeit a qualified yes. In theory, this place served a worthwhile cause. The bigger question was how that theory translated to reality.

My second criteria, that the agency "adequately fulfills its mission statement, showing fruits for its labors," was going to be a bit harder to discern. Without actually going to all 42 agencies and looking for myself, how could I know whether CNA was doing a good job for them or not? I scanned the list of charities that they served, grabbed the phone, and started calling for references.

By the fourth call, I was able to reach a manager, a man in Dallas, Texas, who apparently ran a cars-for-the-needy-type of group. He was a retired repairman, he explained to me, whose group took donations of old clunkers, fixed them up, and then gave them to ladies at a local battered-women's shelter.

According to him, he had been affiliated with CNA for about a year, and he had mostly positive things to say. CNA had taken over all of the duties the man used to pass off to his wife, like the bookkeeping, freeing her to handle fund-raising and car donations while he was left with doing the actual repairs.

"I thought CNA handled the fund-raising for you," I said.

"No, when you first hook up with them, you can check off the services you want them to perform. We didn't check fund-raising assistance. We just turned over the payroll, bookkeeping, things like that. Oh, and for an extra fee, they do our taxes at the end of the year, too."

"But you secure your own funding?"

"Yes, ma'am," he drawled. "We have a big barbecue dinner the first Saturday of every month. Most of the food is donated by local businesses, so we keep the money we make and that pays for our operations. It works out real well all the way around."

We talked a bit further, and by the time I had hung up the phone I was most impressed with the man and his agency. The dedication and ingenuity of some people never ceased to amaze me. Glancing at the clock, I decided to spend a half hour making similar calls before switching back to my other investigation and continuing the search for Eddie Ray's killer.

The list was easy to follow, and though I left a lot of messages for people to call me back, every second or third call netted me someone of authority who was free to talk and able to give a reference for CNA. Most were positive, though one woman in Los Angeles told me she had a bit of a personality issue with the first rep they were assigned.

"At first, they put us with their Small Agencies Division," the woman told me. "Since, technically, we fell right under the line."

"The line being where?" I asked, wondering how Advancing Attire would stack up.

"If your charity has an annual budget of three hundred thousand or less, they qualify you as a small agency," the woman said. "Once we crossed that, we were switched to a different rep and things seemed to go much more smoothly."

I asked for the name of the person that they didn't like, but the woman became hesitant and said that she'd rather not say. I thanked her for her help, hung up, and made a note to myself to find out more about the Small Agencies Division, since that's the one Verlene would be dealing with.

When my half hour was almost up, I decided to stop making calls and send out a few e-mails instead. Since CNA was based in Cleveland, Ohio, I wrote to a colleague of mine in Akron, a private investigator who owed me a favor, and asked if he could do a quick evaluation of CNA, its facilities, its executives, and its board of directors. Then I wrote a simple e-mail asking for references for CNA and sent it to various contacts I had across the country, people who might have crossed paths with CNA and its service before. In the e-mail, I said that I was assisting a local nonprofit in their decision as to whether to link up with CNA, and I would appreciate any insight and experience they could provide. All conversations would be confidential, of course.

Having done that, I felt like I'd put in enough time on the CNA investigation for now, and I turned off my computer, put away the file, and walked back up the hall to the kitchen. After bringing Sal back into the house, I locked up and went out to the car.

I needed to do a little footwork on Shayna's case, and now that it was nearing three o'clock, that meant a trip back to Kawshek, where I hoped to gather some more information about the late, not-so-great Eddie Ray.

Twenty

People had already put out flowers, I realized as I slowly drove past the scene of the crime. It was just a spot in the highway—the place I had discovered last night by tracking dots of blood to where Eddie Ray had been killed. There was nothing remarkable about it. But now, where a remnant of yellow police tape still hung from a bush, a small collection of flower arrangements had been placed on the ground.

Unpopular fellow that Eddie Ray was, I was surprised to see anything there at all. I pulled over and got out without turning off the car to get a closer look at the flowers. I counted five arrangements, three of which had notes attached.

"See you in heaven," said one card with no signature.

"Farewell," said another.

"Rest in peace," said the third.

I was stepping toward the car when the glint of something shiny in the distance caught my eye. I stood on my tiptoes and peered through the woods, trying to make out what it was: some sort of metal structure, a tin-roofed building that seemed to hang out over the river.

Odd. I hadn't noticed it before, but it had been dark last night. Now, however, I thought it might be significant, considering its proximity to the murder scene. On impulse, I got back into the car, pulled it far to the side of the road, and parked. It was time to do a little exploring.

I tucked my pants into my socks and then stood in the road for a moment, trying to figure the best way to the building through the thick pines and waist-high brush. I walked up and down along the edge of the road until I found what I had been looking for: weeds that had recently been crushed down—by the police, by the murderer, or by both, I wasn't sure. Before I went, I made a quick call to Barbara Hightower, but she wasn't available, and I was passed to one of her colleagues. Fortunately, he and I had met last night, so he already knew who I was and how I was involved with the case.

"I just wanted to double-check something," I told him now. "I was driving past the scene of the murder, and I realized that there's some kind of old building out there. It was so dark last night, I didn't notice it. Did you guys find it after I was gone?"

"You talking about the place with the tin roof, set back from the road a piece?"

"Yes."

"It's an old boat repair shop," he said. "We took a look, but nothing seemed to have been disturbed. One of the guys remembered it from back in the seventies—said that the fellow who owned it had since retired and moved away. Far as we could tell, nobody's bothered it in years, 'cept maybe some birds and a few squirrels."

"Okay," I replied lightly. "I just wanted to make sure you folks knew it was there."

Once I hung up the phone and slid it into my pocket, I took a deep breath and plunged forward through the grass. I really hadn't needed to call, but if this was a significant part of the crime scene, then I knew my presence could compromise it. Unlike the place in the road where Eddie Ray was murdered, I couldn't tiptoe carefully around here and not disturb any evidence. In fact, I had no choice but to crash noisily through the brush, stomping all over anything that might be in my way.

It was slow going. Among the tall grasses were bushes and brambles I kept having to work around. A good machete would've helped, but I didn't think it would be a wise idea to leave such a blatant trail behind—not to mention that I didn't have a machete with me anyway. It became a little easier as I neared the building, mainly because there were shells on the ground, obviously remnants of an old parking lot, which kept more of the undergrowth to a minimum.

Itchy and hot, I finally reached the door, which was old and rusted and half hanging from its hinges. I gingerly pulled it open and stepped through to see that the building was basically just a sheltered dock, with one whole side open to the water. Though it was empty now, the roof was obviously high enough to accommodate yachts and large boats. For smaller boats there was a boom-and-winch system rigged from a metal crossbeam of the ceiling.

I stepped fully into the room and looked around at the refuse of the old repair shop: tools scattered along a table, a few oily rags, a faded calendar tacked to the wall. The cop had been right; this place looked as though it hadn't been touched in 20 years. A thick layer of dust seemed to coat every surface, and there were no bottles of bleach or signs of any bleach use that I could see.

Stepping carefully, I walked from one end of the big structure to the other, looking for what, I wasn't sure. There were some footprints in the dirt on the floor, but since they looked like the tread of standard-issue uniform boots, I felt sure they belonged to the cops who had come in here last night to investigate.

Looking up, I could see evidence of a number of deserted bird nests in the rafters, as well as some wasp nests I could only hope were deserted as well. Strung from the winch system by a combination of chains and canvas straps was a huge, rusted boat motor, and it hung over the workbench like a rat hung by its tail. By the looks of it, it had probably been hanging there for years.

I walked slowly around the perimeter of the room again, studying the scattered debris along the workbenches. The dust really was thick and undisturbed. A spray of graffiti colored one wall, but, again, it looked quite faded and old—evidence of teenage vandals, perhaps, but probably from a few years back. I walked to the door and stood in the doorway looking out at the thick brush, knowing in my gut it wasn't a coincidence that Eddie Ray had been killed near here. I thought back to the moment I had found the murder scene on the road, in the dark, and I remembered feeling as if someone were watching me. I had shined my flashlight in this direction, and two glowing eyes had looked back at me. I had thought they belonged to an owl up in a tree, but now I had to wonder if what I had been looking at were the lenses from a pair of binoculars.

With a shiver I walked around the outside perimeter of the building, somehow not surprised to find a ladder propped against the far side. I tested it with a tentative foot and then stepped up, slowly making my way to the top. It brought me to the flat tin roof of the building, and I stepped out, careful not to disturb the distinct dirt footprints that led from the ladder to the front of the roof. I walked along next to them and peered outward, confirming that this location afforded a perfect view of the road.

I knelt down, examining the prints of what looked like a single pair of shoes, probably sneakers. There was nothing distinctive about the prints, though I was no expert in reading shoeprints. I decided that when I got back to the car I would call Barbara Hightower and let her know about this, so the police could bring in one of their people to collect and interpret this information.

For now I headed back down the ladder and returned to the inside of the building. With one wall simply wide open to the river, anyone could've come here by boat. It would've been easy, I realized, to dock here, make their way through the brush to the road, flag Eddie Ray down, and clobber him there. Then, if the person was working alone, they could've driven Shayna's car to her driveway, left it there, walked the two-and-a-half miles or so back to here, and sailed away in their boat. My theory worked even better if there was more than one person involved; while someone drove the car to Kawshek, the other person could've driven the boat there and picked the killer up at the dock once the car was returned.

Either way, if anyone had come here recently, I decided, chances are they would've tied off onto one of these cleats. There were six cleats along the work area, and I went to them one at a time, knelt, and studied them. The first five were dusty and untouched. The sixth, however, was suspicious enough to make me take a closer look.

It wasn't dusty like the others; that was obvious. More importantly, in the dirt around the base of the cleat I could see splatter marks, like little drips of water that had fallen into the dust and then dried there. That, combined with the footprints on the roof, was proof enough for me: I felt strongly that this building had played a part in the murder of Eddie Ray.

Suddenly, I had that feeling again, as if I were being watched. I stood straight and looked out at the river. It was beautiful as usual, dark and flowing and empty. I could see no one on the far shore, though in places the trees were thick enough so that someone could've been watching me from a hidden vantage point. With a shiver, I brushed off my pants and left the building, heading as quickly as possible through the "jungle" back to the road. The brush was so thick that at one point I found myself immobilized, unable to move forward. Heart pounding, I tried to retrace my steps, stumbling as I worked my way around the brambles and the weeds.

My hands were shaking by the time I reached my car, and I didn't feel safe until I was inside, doors locked, motor running. While I caught my breath, I picked burrs from my clothes and then methodically tended to my hair, taking it down, shaking out bits of grass, and then pinning it back up.

Finally, I put the car in gear and drove on to Kawshek. Whether someone had been watching me or not, I felt certain I had stumbled onto something important in the old boat repair shop. The police had combed through the brush surrounding the murder scene last night looking for clues, but I thought it odd they didn't catch cleat number six inside the old building. It was fairly elementary, as Holmes would say.

Putting it out of my mind for now, I reached Kawshek and easily found the little combination of stores near Shayna's apartment. I pulled to a stop in the parking lot and exhaled slowly, glad to see that my hands were no longer shaking.

Looking around, I decided that the town really was quite dingy. Though the water in the distance was beautiful, as always, there was something dirty and depressing about the buildings and streets. From the crumpled trash that dotted the parking lot to the broken fences and littered yards of the houses nearby, Kawshek seemed to speak loudest of apathy. It looked simply as if no one cared.

I got out of my car and walked nonchalantly to the Kawshek General Store, the place where Shayna had said many of the townspeople frequently gathered. I wasn't even sure why I was there, really, or what I hoped to accomplish. I just wanted to learn more about the town, about the people here, about the folks who knew Eddie Ray. To my mind, usually the smaller the town, the more everyone knows everyone else's business. *Get hold of the right person,* my old mentor Eli Gold always said, *and they'll talk your ear off.*

A bell jingled over the door as I stepped into the store. Two older men looked up from a small round table in the corner where they sat mending a fishing net. One of them had a thick head of white hair, and I recognized him as the fellow who had first seen the dots of blood in the road the night before. The other man looked familiar, though not from last night. With deeply lined ruddy cheeks and a dirty yellow kerchief around his neck, I knew I had seen him in his boat from time to time, out on the water.

Both men nodded at me and went back to their mending. I walked past them toward a refrigerated compartment in the back of the store. I took my time choosing a soda, carefully scanning the small selection and pretending to decide what I wanted.

"Hey, Stinky, you got a customer!" the white-haired man yelled. There seemed to be no one else in the store, but then I heard a grunt from somewhere in the back.

"I'm in no hurry," I added, my heart pounding. According to Shayna, Stinky was the man with the cot Eddie Ray liked to crash on whenever they had an argument. I knew that eventually I would have to talk to this man and find out more about the whole situation. For now, if Stinky was too busy to come to the register right away, more the better. I wanted to be here in the store if any conversations started—or to start a conversation myself. Of course, it would've been easy enough to identify myself as an investigator and start asking questions, but I had a feeling that folks around here would be a lot more tight-lipped if they knew I had come in an official capacity.

I took a soda from the cooler and then walked over to the snack section to spend some time looking at rows of prepackaged crackers with cheese and cookies. I noted that the store was bigger than it looked from the front, with the back jutting out toward the marina. Through a dirty, multipaned window on the back door, I was able to see a single dockside gas pump near a ramshackle bathroom. Boats were lined along the dock, and several men and one woman sat on the tops of dock pilings, hosing out some coolers. As I lingered, the bell on the front door rang three separate times as people came in, spoke to the two fellows there, took a newspaper, and left their change on the counter.

I chose a pack of crackers with peanut butter, went to the cash register, and waited for Stinky. As I stood there, I turned my attention back to the two men who were silently working, a pile of gray cord netting between them on the ground.

"Doing a little mending?" I asked.

"Yup."

"That must get pretty tedious."

"Yup."

Obviously, I wasn't going to draw the two of them into conversation.

I heard the jingle of the bell again and watched as a woman dressed in tight jeans and a navy sweater entered the store. She was pretty, though her teased-up punk-like hairstyle was about 20 years out of date. She came straight to the counter, and I waved her in front of me.

"You go ahead. I'm in no hurry," I said.

"Thanks," she replied, and then she starting banging her car keys on the counter.

"Stinky!" she yelled. "Get out here! I gotta hustle!"

The two men cackled loudly.

"You heard her," the white-haired man yelled toward the back. "Gotta have that nicotine on the double."

"I'm comin', I'm comin'," a man replied. After a moment, he shuffled out from a door behind the counter, wiping his hands on his apron. He looked to be in his early 50s, with tufts of gray hair and about two days' growth of beard on his chin.

"Why don't you buy a whole carton and stop driving me crazy every ten minutes?" he grumbled to the woman in front of me.

"Shut up and give me my smokes," she replied. "I can't afford a whole carton at once."

The two men laughed.

"Can't afford a whole carton but comes in here for a pack every day," the man in the kerchief said. "What's the difference?"

"The difference," said Stinky, choosing a pack of Virginia Slims Menthol Lights and slapping them down onto the counter, "is that she can slip seven bucks out of Russell's wallet without him seeing, but she can't slip out seventy, no way."

"That's about right," the woman said. "Hey, you got any more of that crab soup you had the other day?"

"I was just in the back making some now. Be ready in about fifteen minutes."

"Never mind, then."

She paid for her cigarettes and left as quickly as she had come in. I looked out of the window to see her get into an old, beat-up, black Camaro, which roared with the distinctive sound of a busted muffler as soon as she started it up. She drove away, the sound fading with the distance. Listening to her go, I wondered if the "Russell" the men had spoken of was her husband, and if that was the same Russell who had been friends with Eddie Ray.

"That be all?"

I turned to see Stinky looking at me, one finger poised over the cash register.

"Uh, no," I said. "I'll take a pint of that crab soup she just mentioned."

"Won't be ready for 'bout fifteen minutes," he said again.

"That's okay," I replied. "I'll wait."

He shrugged.

"Suit yourself," he said. Then he turned and shuffled back out of sight back into the rear of the store.

I relaxed against the counter, glad I had found a way to buy 15 more minutes of hanging around.

"So was that Russell's wife?" I asked the two men. The one in the kerchief stopped what he was doing and looked up at me.

"Who're you?"

"I'm a friend of Shayna Greer's," I said, trying to smile warmly. "My name's Callie."

The other man glanced at me, recognition showing on his face.

"Hey, she's the one who followed the drops of blood I saw," he said loudly. "She figured out where ol' Eddie Ray got whacked."

"That so?"

I nodded.

"I've seen you out on the water, too, haven't I?" the man in the kerchief asked.

"Yes, I live just up the road."

That I was a "local" seemed to be enough for these two men. They pointed to a barrel that was lying near the wall and offered me a seat, all smiles now.

"I'm Murdock and this is Dewey," said the man in the kerchief. "You might as well sit a spell while you're waiting for yer soup."

I rolled the barrel over closer to their table and sat, commenting on the activity in front of them. Murdock explained the fine art of net mending, concluding that it was a much more constructive hobby than doing jigsaw puzzles. As he talked, a loud group of teenagers came into the store to buy night crawlers. I half listened to their conversation until they left again, box of bait in hand.

"Looks like this place gets pretty busy this time of day," I said, and both men agreed. We chatted for a few more minutes, and then finally I managed to steer the conversation back to the subject of Eddie Ray.

"He was no good," said Dewey, shaking his head. "Bound to end up that way sooner or later."

"I still can't believe little ol' Shayna Greer did him in, though," added Murdock in a softer tone. "She's a tougher gal than I'd a give her credit for."

His voice sounded almost respectful.

"We're all innocent until proven guilty," I said. "Maybe Shayna didn't do it."

"Aw, she did it," Murdock said. "I heard her and Eddie Ray having a big fight night before last. The night she killed him."

"What was the fight about?"

"'Bout money and getting a job and quit freeloading. Same thing they always fought about."

"I understand Eddie Ray would go sleep at Stinky's house whenever he and Shayna had a fight."

"Nah, not Stinky's house," Murdock said. "Here at Stinky's store. Out back. There's a cot on the porch next to the empty beer kegs."

"I see."

"Yep," said Dewey loudly. "Whenever you heard the two of them yelling, you knew ol' Eddie Ray would end up getting drunk in the bar and then climbing onto the cot out back."

"Alone?" I asked.

Dewey hooted.

"Far as I know!" he said. "Hey, Stinky, get out here."

Griping all the way, Stinky shuffled to the counter.

"What?"

"Eddie Ray ever bring any women with him when he spent the night here?"

"He better not have," Stinky said. "I'd a whopped him upside the head with my chowder pot."

I shifted my position on the barrel, glad to know that perhaps Shayna had been correct when she said Eddie Ray didn't cheat on her.

"The night he died," I asked Stinky, "did he come here at all?"

Stinky glowered at me, but at least he answered my question.

"Like I told Shayna yesterday morning," he said, "I heard the fight, and later I saw Eddie Ray in the bar. But as far as I could tell, he never came and used the bed."

With that, Stinky turned and left the counter area.

"So did they fight often?" I asked the two men in front of me.

"Maybe not all that often, but when they did, it was always loud," Murdock said.

"You could hear it all the way over to my house," Dewey added. "Nothing new there. Eddie Ray was always rilin' somebody up. Had words with Russell Lynch less than a week ago. Had a fistfight in the bar with someone else a few days before that."

"Wasn't Russell his friend?"

"Yeah, they was friends," Murdock answered. "But friends sometimes argue."

"What was the argument about?"

Murdock shrugged his shoulders, measuring out a long length of gray thread.

"Hey, Dewey," he said, "that fight between Eddie Ray and Russell Lynch. What was that about?"

"When?"

"When we heard them yelling out on the water." Murdock glanced at me. "Not that we was trying to listen, of course."

"Of course."

"Something about the boat," Dewey replied. "You owe me this, you owe me that. Money, money. With Eddie Ray, it was always about money."

"Russell's boat?" I asked.

Murdock nodded, carefully snipping the thread with scissors.

"It's not a fishing boat. It's more like a tourist runner. Russell and Eddie Ray bought it together a couple years ago so they could start a water taxi. The whole idea kind of folded, but I think Eddie Ray came snooping around again, looking for some money out of it."

"Where's the boat now?"

"Russell keeps it at his farm," Murdock said. "Uses it for night fishing sometimes, I think."

"Did Eddie Ray still own half?"

"I doubt it. From what I recall, when the water taxi went belly-up as a business, Russell took over the payments. Been paying on it ever since. I think he figures he paid back Eddie Ray's share and then some."

I sat back, wondering if a fishing boat would constitute Eddie Ray's idea of a "fortune."

"What's a boat like that cost?" I asked.

"Depends," said Murdock. "Probably forty or fifty thousand. Not exactly chump change."

"No."

I sat quietly for a moment, thinking, as the men continued mending the huge net. There was something hypnotic about their movements, measured and even with the thick thread. I wondered suddenly if fishermen ever soaked their nets in bleach, perhaps to clean them up.

"That net looks pretty gray," I said, feeling kind of stupid but blundering forward anyway. "You should soak it in some Clorox."

This earned a chuckle from Dewey and no response at all from Murdock.

"I don't think the fish care what color the nets are," Dewey said. "And long as I'm catching fish, I don't much care either."

I nodded, trying again.

"I thought I saw some bleach bottles," I said. "I thought maybe that's what they were for."

"Nah, somebody must be cleaning something," Murdock said, shrugging, as he sewed. "Bleach is used as a disinfectant, right?"

"My mama used to clean our outhouse with it," Dewey replied. "Kills germs real good."

My bleach conversation was going nowhere, so I tried a different tack.

"Tell me about the fight in the bar," I said. "The one that Eddie Ray had."

"Oh boy," Dewey replied, tying a knot with his teeth.

"Over a pool game," Murdock added, lowering his voice. "Eddie Ray picked the wrong man to try to hustle."

I leaned forward and used softer tones myself.

"Who? Russell?"

"No. This was a different argument entirely. This was one a them Tanigawa boys—Kenji or Shin, I don't know which one. They're twins. I can't tell them apart, 'cept that only Shin speaks English."

"Tanigawa?" I asked. "Is that Japanese?"

"Yeah. And they're bad news, both of them. When they come to town, I always steer clear of 'em."

"What happened with Eddie Ray?"

"What happened is Eddie Ray was an idiot," Murdock said softly. "Tried to hustle a pool game. When Tanigawa said he cheated and wouldn't pay up, Eddie Ray punched him in the jaw."

"Yikes! Must've been some fight."

"Not really," Murdock said. "That Japanese fella gets up and whips out a switchblade, one of them martial arts things, yea long, kind of curved-like. He wasn't fooling around. Eddie Ray took one look at that knife, turned around, and ran away!"

Both men laughed loudly. I tried to picture Eddie Ray picking a fight and then discovering he was in way over his head. I wondered how I could find out more about these two Japanese brothers—and if the police had also realized there might be some potential suspects there.

"So where do these guys live?" I asked. "I don't think I've ever met them."

"They're down the bay a bit from here," Dewey said. "They come to Kawshek for gas, groceries, and a drink. Like Murdock said, when we see 'em, we just steer clear."

"Well, I done a little business with them from time to time," Murdock amended. "But mostly I keep my distance. They really are kind of scary, if you want to know the truth."

"Soup's ready."

I looked up, surprised to see Stinky standing at the counter, roughly lowering a pint container into a small paper bag. Once the container was in, he threw in a pack of crackers, a plastic spoon, and a napkin.

"Oh, thanks," I said, wishing I'd had just a few more minutes to talk. Finding Dewey and Murdock had been like striking gold; my conversation with them had given me several new things to consider.

"Them Japanese fellows are good customers here," Stinky said grumpily. "I wouldn't be talking bad about 'em."

"Yeah, yeah, yeah," Murdock said. "In other words, they always got a pocket full of cash, and they don't complain about your high prices."

"You see some other store out here to buy your groceries?" Stinky said defensively. "You're free to leave."

Murdock let out a hoot.

"And miss all the fun in here? I don't think so."

Stinky rang me up on the register and I paid; then I took the chance of buying a few more minutes of conversation by opening the soup right there, sitting back down on the barrel, and taking a bite of the spicy red concoction. It wasn't bad, though I was a bit concerned about the hygiene of the chef. Anyone who looked like that, and whose name was Stinky, probably shouldn't be whipping up a pot of soup for general sale.

"So what about Hank Hawkins?" I said chattily to my two new friends, thinking of the big fellow with the scar on his chin who had recently been dating Shayna. "Do you think he could've killed Eddie Ray? Out of jealousy?"

Surprised, Murdock shook his head.

"Hank wouldn't hurt a fly. Besides, I don't think him and Shayna was all that serious about each other anyway."

"If you're looking for jealousy as a motive," Dewey said, "you'd do better to look in other directions."

Something about the gossipy nature of his tone of voice made me look up.

"Oh?"

"Aw, don't be bringing that up again," Murdock said, shaking his head. "That's old news."

"What is?" I asked, trying not to appear eager.

"Shayna and Russell," Dewey whispered loudly. "They had themselves an affair a while back."

"Speak of the devil!" Murdock whispered sharply just as the back door to the store swung open.

"You see," Dewey continued, unaware of what Murdock had said or that the man who had come in was almost within hearing distance, "Russell and Tia had just moved out to the farm and—ow!"

Dewey was cut short by a sharp kick to his shin from Murdock. Just then the man reached the table and nodded at the three of us.

"Afternoon, Dewey. Murdock. Ma'am."

"Afternoon, Russell." Dewey said, his ears burning red.

I had to assume this was Russell Lynch, the man Dewey had been talking about. He was tall and broad, with a pleasant-looking face under a ragged khaki hat. He wore faded jeans and a flannel shirt, both flecked with splotches of mud, and he smelled strongly of sweat.

"Hey, Stinky," he said, leaning over the counter. "You got any stock wire?"

"What d'you think I am?" Stinky called from the back. "A hardware store?"

"Come on. I just need about ten feet to fix a hole in my fence."

"Try Buster's."

"I did. He only sells it by the roll."

"So buy a roll."

"For a hundred dollars? No way!"

Russell looked at us and winced.

"Hey, fellows, either one of you got any stock wire I could borrow? I'll replace it next week."

Both men shook their heads.

"I might have some," I volunteered, heart pounding at my lie. I didn't even know what stock wire was. "How much do you need?"

"Ten feet or so. Just enough to fix a break in my fence."

I nodded.

"What kind do you want?" I asked.

"Stock wire," he said, blinking. "You know. Wire fencing, like Keystone Red? Little squares down near the bottom, bigger squares up near the top?"

Like the fencing around Sal's play yard.

"I probably have that much. Where do you live? I'll bring it out to you."

"Oh, you don't need to go to all that trouble," he said. "I'll just wait here while you go get it."

My mind reeled, wondering what to do. I figured it might take me 45 minutes to race into Osprey Cove and buy the wire from a hardware store. Then I could come back out here and deliver it personally to his farm and maybe get a better idea of who this man was and how he might fit into the puzzle of Eddie Ray's death.

"Well, I'm not headed straight home," I hedged. "But I could have it out to you in about an hour, hour and a half."

Russell smiled.

"Do you have a boat?" he asked. "If you do, it's no big deal. If not, it's quite a drive."

"Russell don't live right in Kawshek no more," Dewey said, chuckling. "He's a regular farmer now."

"I live across the river and around the bend," Russell continued. "As the crow flies, my farm is just right there. But by land it's a bit of a trip."

"Oh, that's no problem," I said. "I'm going to Osprey Cove first anyway."

He hesitated and then finally spoke.

"If you really don't mind..." he said. "It sure beats me having to buy a whole three-hundred-and-thirty-foot roll."

"Sure. You'll have to tell me how to get to your place, though."

"I'll draw you a map. And we haven't really met, by the way. I'm Russell Lynch."

"Callie Webber," I replied, shaking his hand. "Nice to meet you."

"You, too. I sure do appreciate this."

He seemed glad—but not suspicious—about my offer, and I realized that this was simply how things were done out here. Neighbor helping neighbor.

I packed away my soup as he took a napkin from the counter and began sketching out the series of roads that would take me to his farm. When he was finished, he handed me the napkin, and I studied the crude map. His farm was far. Apparently, I would have to drive all the way east to Osprey Cove, then north on the main highway, then back west to the end of the next big peninsula.

It would be past sunset by the time I got there, which meant that I would be heading into this man's territory in the dark. Ignoring the little warning bells at the back of my brain, I told him I'd be there as soon as I could.

Twenty-One

Fortunately, I thought to call ahead to the hardware store in Osprey Cove as I drove out of Kawshek. According to them, stockade fence wire was always sold by the roll and was definitely not available in shorter lengths. In desperation, I stopped by my house and simply used a pair of wire cutters to take loose a ten-foot section of Sal's play yard. I knew it would be a pain to replace later, but I didn't know what else to do.

I rolled up the wire and tried to get it into the back of my SUV without tearing the upholstery or the carpet. Hopefully, this would be worth all of this trouble. Once I delivered the wire, I could talk to Russell a bit about Eddie Ray and maybe get some more leads on my investigation.

I knew there was more to learn from Dewey and Murdock back at the store, too, but that would have to wait for another day. For now, I followed the winding highway to Russell's farm, the bale of wire tucked securely in the back, using the hand-scribbled map as a guide. The peninsula he lived on was certainly rural, though not as wooded as mine. Instead, it seemed to hold mostly fields and farms and not a lot of trees.

As I had expected, it was quite dark by the time I reached the farm, so I wasn't able to get much of an impression of the place. The mailbox was clearly marked "Lynch," and two wagon wheels decoratively graced each side of the entrance of the driveway. I turned in and drove about a hundred yards before coming to a large, white, old-looking farmhouse. In the sweep of my headlights, I could see a number of smaller outbuildings, including what looked like a chicken coop and, farther back, a barn. Even before I turned off the car, Russell emerged from the barn and started walking toward me.

I opened my door and got out, wondering if anyone else was home or if it was just the two of us here.

"Hey, thanks again for coming," Russell said, one hand extended. I shook his hand and smiled, thinking he seemed like a nice-enough fellow. "How were the directions?"

"Perfect," I replied. "I had no problem at all."

I unlocked the hatchback and let it pop open, the image of Eddie Ray suddenly filling my mind. If I paled for a moment in the moonlight, Russell didn't seem to notice. He simply removed the roll of wire from the back of the vehicle.

"So what's the wire for?" I asked, regaining my composure.

"Busted fence section," he said. "I drove the tractor too close to the wire, and the next thing I knew I had ripped out a good ten foot of fence."

"Good thing you weren't hurt."

"Nah, it was just a stupid mistake. I seem to make a lot of those around here."

"Have you had the farm for long?"

"I grew up here," he said, "but it was my daddy's farm until he passed on, 'bout a year and a half ago. That's when I moved back to make a go of it myself. Didn't know what I was getting myself into. It's a real job of work, I'll tell you that."

"What a nice place to be, though," I said. "Big spread of land out here on the peninsula..."

"I'm a waterman by nature," he said. "I'd rather be out there fishing it than standing here lookin' at it."

"I know exactly what you mean."

"Anyway," he added, "I'd like to thank you again for going to all this trouble. 'Specially since we've never even met. That was right nice of you."

"Oh, it was no trouble at all," I said. "Always good to help a neighbor in need."

"Yep."

My mind scrambled for something else to say, for some way to stall time. Finally, I decided that perhaps a bit of honesty was in order.

"To tell you the truth," I said, "I was hoping to get a chance to talk to you anyway."

"Oh?"

"I'm a private investigator," I said. "I'm working on behalf of Shayna Greer."

He blinked, stared at me, and then nodded.

"That's too bad about what happened," he said finally. "Shayna's a nice girl. I hate to see her in trouble."

"So do I," I replied. "I'd like to ask you some questions, if I could."

"Sure," he said. "But I've got the generator going out back with lights up for working on the fence. Can I work as we talk?"

"Of course."

He led the way, and I followed as we crossed the lawn and went around to the back of the barn. Sure enough, two big bright lights were mounted on sawhorses, aimed at a gaping hole in a wire fence. Russell picked up some tools with his free hand, dropped the wire next to a fence post, and went to work.

"So what did you need to know?" he asked, unrolling the wire.

"First of all, tell me about Eddie Ray. How long were you acquainted with him?"

"Well, we started first grade together, in Kawshek. We were buddies, off and on, our whole lives."

"I understand he moved away at seventeen."

"He couldn't wait to get out of here. Hated it. Dropped out of high school and said he was off to make his fortune dealing blackjack in Las Vegas."

"From what I understand, he tried to make his fortune running drugs out of Mexico."

Russell was quiet for a moment.

"Shayna told you that?"

"Yeah."

He nodded.

"Eddie Ray was an odd fellow," he said. "Grew up dirt poor, without a daddy or a lot of friends. Money was everything to him. It don't surprise me to hear he was running drugs. Although everything I ever saw him get involved in was legitimate."

"He tried to start a business with you, didn't he?"

"After his mama died. She left him the house and a little money, so he came back and tried to turn it into something bigger."

"And Shayna came with him."

"Yep. I believe that's when she first moved here."

"What was your business involvement with him?"

"We wanted to start a water taxi. Blue crabs were getting too scarce for me to make a living as a waterman, especially since I didn't have my own rig, but I wasn't ready to give up going out on the bay. So I let Eddie Ray talk me into buying a tourist boat. He said we could run tours out of Osprey Cove or even St. Michael's, maybe head up the Choptank to Denton. He made the down payment on the boat, but then we couldn't seem to get the business off the ground. There was already too much competition. Plus, Eddie Ray had lots of other things going at once, and I didn't have the wherewithal to finance a new business all by myself. The whole thing folded within a month."

"But you still have the boat?"

"Yeah, I took a job down at the menhaden plant, refinanced the boat, and took over the payments myself. At least I could still get out on the water, though it's not the same as working the crabs. I really miss that."

"And now you're a farmer."

He stretched the wire across a wooden fence post and clipped it into place with loud blasts from a staple gun. When he was finished, he looked up at me.

"Yep. 'Bout the only time I get out on the water any more is when I head over to Kawshek for a gallon of milk or an evening of pool.

Most of the fishing I do these days is at night, and only after a full day's work on the farm."

"That must be difficult for you."

He shrugged before slamming in a few more staples.

"We get by," he said. "Can't complain."

I reached out to help with the final stapling, since the wire kept curling away from the post. Together, we got it hooked on properly, and then he stapled it tight.

"Thanks," he said.

"So what was the argument about that you had with Eddie Ray last week?"

He looked at me sideways as he rolled the wire out to the next post.

"How'd you know about that?"

"I'm an investigator," I smiled. "I investigate."

"Probably big mouth Murdock. He doesn't miss a trick around here."

I didn't comment.

"Our fight last week. What can I say? Eddie Ray was back, looking for money. Said I owed him the three thousand dollars from the down payment he originally made on the boat."

"Did you give it to him?"

"No way! He owed me that much, at least."

"How do you figure?"

"When we went into that business together, he had big plans, big words. 'Gonna make a nice color brochure for us,' he said. 'Gonna get tourist contracts with the hotel. Gonna make a name for ourselves.' My job was driving the boat. His job was to fill that boat with people."

"You sound angry."

"'Course I'm angry! When things went sour, old Eddie Ray hadn't done a single thing he promised. Meanwhile, I had quit my job on a crabbing rig, co-signed the boat loan that put my credit in jeopardy, got all ready for this big new business—and then I didn't have a thing to show for it! The way I see it, *he* owed *me*."

"You must've been mad."

"I already said I was mad!"

"Mad enough to kill him?"

Russell stood up straight and glared at me.

"I'm not accusing you," I said evenly. "But you know that's what the police are going to ask you, if they haven't already."

He grunted, and then he knelt and took his anger out on the next fence post, pounding in more than enough staples to hold the wire in place. I reached over and helped again, wondering how much more information I could get out of this man before he physically removed me from the premises.

"Tell me about your affair with Shayna," I said finally.

"Good grief, lady!" he exclaimed, throwing the staple gun to the ground. "Is there anything you don't know? You'll be telling me next what I had for breakfast or what brand of cigarettes my wife smokes."

"Virginia Slims Menthol Lights," I replied.

For a moment there was a dead silence between us. Then Russell surprised me by throwing his head back and heartily laughing.

"If you don't beat all," he said finally, wiping his eyes. "I give up. Anything you wanna know. You've obviously done your homework."

"Tell me about your affair with Shayna."

"What can I say? It was short but sweet. We had a few good times. Then one night we got caught, so we gave it up. End of story."

"Was Eddie Ray still living here at the time?"

"Yeah, he was. But Shayna was mad at him for all the stupid business decisions and for taking a mortgage out on the house. I guess she was getting even."

"How about you?"

He rolled out the wire to the final fence post. It just reached, with only a few inches to spare. I held it while he stapled, neatly securing it from top to bottom.

"I was kind of messed up then," he said finally. "My dad had passed away, and I was trying to get over that, plus we'd had the move here, and I was feeling my way as a farmer. I was lonely. I was mad at my wife because she hated it out here and spent all her time back in Kawshek with her mama and them. It was a tough time. Shayna was a warm body, willing and able. That's all."

Russell stood and dusted his hands on his pants. He took a board the width and height of the fence post and lined it flush with the sides.

Then he began nailing it to the post as extra security for the stapled wire. When he was finished, he turned to me, the expression on his face earnest.

"That's the only affair I ever had," he said. "My wife loves me. She forgave me and let it go. It's all water under the bridge now. I'd appreciate it if you didn't go stirring all that up again."

I nodded.

"I respect your honesty and your privacy," I said. "I can't see any reason why this would have to go further unless it relates to Eddie Ray's murder. Of course, don't be surprised if the police come around asking you the same questions."

He went to the next post and nailed on another board.

"Eddie Ray was a real character," he said after he had finished. "But he was my friend. It tears me up that he's dead, especially considering how he went. It's a tragedy, is what it is."

I looked at Russell and wondered if he was a killer. There was some hostility in him, of course, but also a streak of decency. Either way, I thought my questions here tonight had been answered more than adequately.

"Did you see Eddie Ray the night he died?"

"No, I went to bed fairly early that night," he said. "I saw him that afternoon, though, when I took the boat over to Kawshek for some bait. He was there in the store, chewing the fat. We said hello, but I didn't hang around to chat. I wanted to get out on the water and do some fishing."

"Do you think Shayna killed Eddie Ray?" I asked. He hammered the last board to the last post and then slowly and deliberately put away his tools, turned off the lights, and took them down. He was quiet for a while. Then he turned to me in the moonlit darkness and spoke.

"For her sake, I hope not," he said. "But I can't imagine why anyone else would want him dead. I mean, he could be a big pain sometimes, sure, but he was mostly hot air. Never any real threat to anyone, far as I know."

Twenty-Two

According to the clock in the kitchen, I made it home with eight minutes to spare. Tom was usually quite punctual, so I expected the phone to ring any moment. In the meantime, I changed into sweatpants and a warm sweater. I made myself a cup of tea, and then I took the portable phone into the living room, started up the fire, and settled down on the sofa. Like clockwork, the phone began to ring the moment I swung my legs up under me and got comfortable.

"Tom?" I answered.

"Callie," he said, and suddenly I was transported to a place somewhere else, a place that was safe and warm and close to the man at the other end of the phone. "I'm so glad I finally reached you."

"Me, too," I said, wondering if he had missed hearing my voice as much as I had missed his. "I'm sorry I've been out so often. I've been volunteering."

"That's okay," he replied. "This is a good time. My mom's asleep and my sister's kids are down eating in the cafeteria."

"Where are you?"

"I found an empty waiting room on the first floor where I could talk without being intrusive. Otherwise, I'm keeping my phone off.

Except for the beeps and hums of all those machines, the ICU is actually a pretty quiet place."

"What happened, Tom?"

He proceeded to give me the whole story, how his mother had stepped out on her front porch yesterday morning to pick up the paper and crumpled to the ground, unable to speak or to move her right side. Fortunately, she lived on a busy street; and a pedestrian saw it happen and called 911.

"The neighbors contacted my sister first because she lives here in the city, and then she called me. At that point, I was already packed and ready to go to the airport anyway, so I took a look at the schedules and decided I could make the very next flight to New Orleans if I hurried. Of course, that meant I wouldn't be able to meet up with you after all, but I knew you would understand. I'm just glad that Janine was able to pull a few strings to rearrange my Singapore trip, not to mention deliver my message to you in the club."

I hesitated, wanting to know more about the blonde with the big engagement ring, but I was afraid it would be tacky to come right out and ask. Instead, I focused on the matter at hand, asking Tom how his mother was doing now. He launched into a detailed description of her condition, talking of things that were foreign to me like ischemia and heparin and embolisms. According to her doctors, she had a better than 50 percent chance of recovery, mainly because they were able to respond so quickly to the stroke by starting her IV medications well within the three-hour limit.

"How does she seem to you now?"

"Well, it's hard to say. They only let me in every few hours for just five minutes at a time. She's way out of it, kind of dazed and confused."

"Can she speak?"

"Not yet. Mostly, she just looks around. It feels like she's struggling for words, but nothing comes out."

I let him tell me everything, every detail, knowing that sometimes the best thing we can do for someone in a crisis is simply to let them recount it—again and again, if necessary—until they are able to get a handle on it. Certainly, I had needed to share my story after Bryan first died with anyone and everyone who was willing to listen.

Tom talked about the hospital and how impressed he had been with everyone on staff there. He described some of the nurses and the doctors, going on about all of the things they had done for her. I let him talk until finally he seemed to have talked it through.

"By the way, I'm sorry to leave you so high and dry without any work to do," he said. "I guess for future reference, we need to keep a few 'back burner' projects available for situations just like this."

I agreed, thinking that whatever process Tom used in his selection of grant recipients, it had always been a wholly personal choice, one case at a time, dictated by him and then acted upon by me. That was our procedure, and I thought it had worked well thus far. It was his money we were giving away, after all. However he wanted to do it was fine with me.

"The time off hasn't been so bad," I said. "I'm doing a little pro bono work for a young woman at Advancing Attire."

"Oh, good," he replied. "Then I won't worry about it. I plan to stick around here at least through the weekend. They'll do another CAT scan in two days, to make sure the clot is dissolving. After that, they can move her to a regular room."

"Great."

"Between now and then, I'll try to finish these files so I can get them to you by Monday. Unfortunately, I won't be able to deliver them in person after all, since I need to get on to Singapore as soon as possible. I'll be flying straight out from here."

"I understand," I said, disappointment settling around my heart. But at least now I knew I had the rest of the week off—which hopefully would give me enough time to find Eddie Ray's killer.

Tom and I talked for a while longer as he reminisced about his mother and what a character she had been when he was growing up in New Orleans. She sounded like a strong and admirable woman, which didn't surprise me at all, considering the caliber of son she had raised. This was the first time he had ever said much about his family to me, and I swallowed up the impressions and details like a starving man with a good meal. Tom was an incredibly private person, and glimpses of facts about his life were rare indeed.

Once we said our goodbyes, I called Harriet, as promised, just to tell her that Tom and I had finally spoken, and that the big emergency was that his mother had had a stroke. I got Harriet's machine, which was just as well. I left her a message, thinking I really didn't want to talk to anyone else right now anyway.

I hung up the phone and then sat for a while longer in front of the fire, sipping my tea and thinking about Tom and the origin of our relationship. He had become such an integral part of me that I sometimes found it hard to believe we had known each other only slightly more than two years. Oddly, as wonderful as things were for me now, Tom had first come into my life at what could only be described as the lowest point of my existence.

Three years ago, my husband, Bryan, had been killed by a man named James Sparks, an alcoholic who was too drunk to have been behind the wheel of a speedboat one August afternoon. But he was, and the resulting incident left my husband dead and me utterly alone. The months following the accident had been a horrific series of depositions and grand juries and sentencing hearings. In the end, Sparks pleaded guilty, so we never went to trial. Because of his long history of DUIs, he got 16 years in prison for manslaughter.

When the sentencing was complete and Sparks was in prison, I realized that since Bryan's death I had been driven by only one thing: procuring justice for my husband. Now that that had been achieved, all that was left was my own unspeakable loss. My heart sank to a depth of anguish I hadn't previously thought possible. Living in our home in Virginia, surrounded by all of our memories, was simply too hard.

So, exactly ten months after Bryan died, I left Virginia and came here to the Chesapeake, a place where I felt I could remember Bryan without constantly facing memories of him—an odd distinction but one that was important for me. I bought this house, moved in, and stubbornly severed nearly all ties with friends and family back home.

At first I simply lived off of my savings, holing up here like a hermit. There were entire days when the greatest distance I covered was from the bed to the bathroom and back. In retrospect, of course, I know I was still deep in the throes of mourning and suffering from a nearly crippling depression. At the time all I could think about was Bryan—how much I had loved him, how close we had been to starting a family. I had cried a lot of tears over the babies we would never have, over the milestones we would never celebrate. Even God seemed far away from me at that time, a selfish, vengeful entity who had taken away the person in the world I most loved.

But God was working in my life, even if I didn't know it. Eli Gold, the private investigator who had been my mentor, employer, and dear friend for many years, was really the only person who refused to be rebuffed by me. Now retired and living in Florida, Eli called me almost every day during that time, reading me Scripture, praying for me, and eventually forcing me to confront my misery.

Once he could sense that my depression was lifting somewhat, Eli began to insist that I could forge a new life—one without my beloved husband, but one that could still be rewarding and fulfilling. He insisted I go out and find a good local church, which I did, and then he talked me into taking up canoeing again. The canoeing ended up being a godsend for me, a way back to physical and emotional health. Out on the water, I found the freedom to reconnect with my past, contemplate my future, and reflect on all of God's beautiful creation.

Finally, about four months after I had moved to Maryland, Eli called and told me about Tom, a young techno-whiz friend of his who had made his fortune in the computer industry and was looking to share his wealth by creating a philanthropic organization.

I thought I wasn't interested in pursuing either of my former careers of law or private investigating, but I could see how this position with Tom's brand-new J.O.S.H.U.A. Foundation would be an unusual combination of both professions. I prayed about it and finally decided to give it a try. Once I started, it didn't take long at all for me to realize that my new position and I were a perfect fit.

Truly, it was this job that had saved me from my grief. At first, simply being forced to get back out into the world and interact with other people had seemed a monumental task. But slowly I had begun to cope with, and then eventually even enjoy, the contact my position necessitated. It also helped that the people I interacted with—both in the company I worked for and in the companies we donated to—

were for the most part exemplary human beings, folks who had dedicated their lives to helping others. Sure, there were plenty of bogus nonprofit groups out there, and many who were merely trying to cash in on their tax-free status. Since it was my job to ferret out those groups, it was always a distinct pleasure for me when their applications were denied. But I had found that the majority of the nonprofit groups I encountered were full of selfless, dedicated people who worked hard to make the world a better place. To me, it was an honor to be able to help Tom further their efforts, and the familiar little speech I gave every time I donated the money was always said with the utmost sincerity.

Tom, also, had been a great pleasure to get to know. In the beginning, our telephone conversations were brief and to the point. He hired me without ever meeting me in person, taking on faith the recommendation of our mutual friend, Eli. Together, Tom and I established the routine we would follow: He would screen the grant applicants, pass along to me the ones he was interested in helping out, and I would investigate them. I think together thus far we had given out nearly ten million dollars. Apparently, there was plenty more money where that came from, for the end was nowhere in sight.

The only question that remained for me, then, was who exactly was Tom, and why was everything about him such a secret?

In the beginning I didn't think that question was terribly important. He was a friend of a friend, a business genius, a multimillionaire many times over due to the invention of some integral part of the inner workings of the Internet. I even thought it was quite admirable that he chose to remain anonymous. In a world where everyone wants recognition, here was a man who refused it! But after I began to get to know him, other questions began to surface in my mind. Where did he live? Was he married? Did he have kids?

I tried asking the foundation's office manager, Harriet, and she told me she didn't know much about him either as she, too, had been hired over the telephone and had never met Tom in person. Though he traveled to the East Coast sometimes for business, she said he had made it clear to her that he wanted to remain separate from the mechanics of the foundation's operation, and thus he had never come into the foundation offices in DC. She knew his computer company was primarily based in California. Beyond that, she hadn't a clue about his personal family ties, married or otherwise.

Growing ever more curious, I realized it wouldn't be that difficult to turn my investigating skills toward my boss. At the very least, I could go online and search driver's license records, social security, things like that.

Or so I thought. I don't know what sort of security systems he had in place, but I hadn't done much digging at all one day when the telephone rang. It was Tom, and he was angry.

"You can work for me, or you can investigate me," he had said. "But you may not do both. Take your pick."

I was stunned. Never, ever, in my entire investigating career had I been caught red-handed poking my nose in where it didn't belong. Mortified and embarrassed, I responded defensively.

"It's very difficult to work for a man who is such a mystery," I said. "I was just trying to get a better feel for who you are."

"Does who I am have anything to do with how you do your job?" he challenged. After a moment of silence I had to admit that, no, it did not.

"Then leave it be, Callie. I really, really don't want to let you go, but you can't have it both ways."

I agreed that I wouldn't investigate him, but only because of our mutual connection with Eli. Eli had said that Tom was a good, but very private, man, and I would have to leave it at that.

Since then, surprisingly, I *had* been content to leave it alone, to get to know Tom on his own terms—slowly and carefully. The only mystery that still really bugged me was the acronym for our company. I had no idea what the "J.O.S.H.U.A." stood for, and according to Tom, I never would know.

"It's personal," was all he said the only time I ever asked him, though I frequently tried making up answers to that mystery on my own.

For a while, too, I had wondered if there were something wrong with Tom's appearance that kept him from meeting me face-to-face. I asked Eli straight out, but he just laughed and said no, Tom was a good-looking fellow with no facial scars or humpback or anything. Not that it would've mattered, really, but that was one more theory put to rest.

Now our relationship was two years deeper, two years stronger. In the intervening conversations, we may not have discussed many of the details of life, like how we spent our weekends, but oddly that left more time for talking about other, more intangible things. Slowly, I felt that I had come to know him as well as or even better than many people I did see frequently face-to-face.

Of course, the more I knew about Tom, the more I wanted to know. Over time, I had put together enough small clues from our conversations to figure out that he was in his mid-30s, that he wasn't married, and that the only children in his life were his sister's twin daughters. The ultimate mystery that remained was why we never could seem to get together. More importantly: Why did it even matter?

Two months before, we had nearly met in Philadelphia when we both attended the same funeral. Tom had known I was there, but at the moment he was ready to approach me, he saw that I was crying. According to what he told me later, he had wanted to come to me, to comfort me, but he was afraid that would have made me too uncomfortable.

"I realized it wasn't the right time and place for us to finally meet in person," he had told me later, over the phone. Such an important event, we both knew, needed to be just right. "Trust me," he had said then. "It *will* happen, eventually."

I clung to that promise more strongly than he could imagine.

For now, I thought to myself as I stood up from the couch and stretched, the potential for what we could, eventually, be to each other hovered out there on the horizon, sort of like the promise of springtime in the dead of winter. I was aware that there were many things I could work on in the meantime—like my reluctance to make friends, my tendency to isolate myself. Harriet was correct. I didn't have many friends anymore. I had cut most of them off when I moved here. But each day I prayed that the Lord would continue to heal my heart. If Tom had issues of his own, I felt sure he was dealing with them in the same way.

I closed the glass screen on the fireplace, picked up my empty mug, and turned off the lamp. I rinsed my cup in the kitchen and placed it in the dishwasher, wiped the counter next to the stove with the sponge, turned out the lights, and walked down the hall to my office. I decided I would work on the research for Verlene for a while and then go to sleep, content to know that Tom was okay and that we had finally been able to touch base.

Twenty-Three

My voice echoed in the morning stillness: "The Lord is my light and my salvation—whom shall I fear? The Lord is the stronghold of my life—of whom shall I..."

I faltered, closing my eyes, concentrating.

"...of whom shall I be afraid?" I finished, and then I leaned down to check the page in front of me to verify I had gotten it right. I repeated the sentences again, loving the way it rolled together so beautifully on my tongue.

Sal and I were on our morning canoe run, and since it was a Wednesday, it was my day for memorizing Scripture. This fall I was working on the psalms. I thought Psalm 27 was a good one for today, and I was determined to commit it fully to memory before the month was out, despite the limitations of my poor, aging brain.

I picked up my paddle and started again, moving with the current, heading toward home. We had done the full five miles today, as we had yesterday, and I loved the warm strength I could feel in my shoulders and waist as I worked the paddle. Between my two weeks of vacation and now the days I was having off this week, I had gotten more than my share of excellent rowing time lately, and I was truly grateful.

I tried the psalm one last time as I paddled, making it all the way through the fourth verse before my memory petered out. Ah, well, I had the whole chapter printed out on a page I could carry with me throughout the day. Maybe later I would make it through a few more verses.

For now I tucked the paper away in my pocket and enjoyed the lovely view of the last few strokes toward home. It was a little later than usual, nearly 10 A.M., but after staying awake again half the night, I had finally managed to get some sleep. This morning I felt surprisingly good, considering, and now I was feeling in an especially bright mood.

My e-mail inquiries about CNA on behalf of Verlene were already yielding some results. I had heard from three of the contacts I had e-mailed yesterday, and of those, two were familiar with the agency and its work. So far, so good, since both e-mails indicated that as far as they could tell, CNA was on the up and up. That was exactly what I had hoped to hear.

My third and fourth criteria, "plans and spends wisely" and "pays salaries and benefits on a par with nonprofit industry standards," were going to be a bit harder to research. I had heard back from my investigator friend in Akron, who said that he had received my e-mail and that he would be in touch.

Of course, the salaries of the CNA upper echelon would be on file with the IRS, but I was well aware that that didn't always tell the full story. Sometimes, nonprofit executives were able to hide their income by receiving disproportionately valuable benefits. I was reminded of the woman I once investigated who ran a soup kitchen at a mission in California. She earned a yearly salary that was at the low end for her region by nonprofit industry standards. On closer examination, however, I learned that her "company car" was a limousine, and that the "Director of Community Outreach" was actually her full-time chauffeur. On top of that, she received free housing in a home that had been donated to the mission by a wealthy widow—but what didn't show up on paper was that the house was a small mansion, worth millions of dollars, complete with a lap pool and separate servants' quarters. After that experience, I was always on the lookout for the types of financial abuse that didn't always show up on paper.

The literature from Verlene had shown the structure of the CNA organization, and there were about five people at the highest level of the company headquarters that I was concerned with. How much money were they making? More importantly, what was their *total* value of compensation from the company? I was always glad when a nonprofit could afford to offer reasonable salaries and benefits to their employees. It was hard to attract capable people from the corporate sector, and decent wages were always a plus. Still, no one should be getting rich from working at a nonprofit, either. As a good middle ground, I used industry standards to establish fair and logical pay rates. Now, I supposed I would have to wait to hear back from my PI friend in Akron before I would have the full picture on how CNA stacked up in that regard.

In the meantime, I was eager to get back to work on Shayna's case. Something told me that today was the day that investigation was going to turn the corner.

Sal startled me by barking, and I looked up, quite surprised to see a man standing at the end of my dock. As we got closer, I realized it was Kirby Collins, the handsome neighbor with the wooden nickels. He waved at me as we floated toward the shore, and when we got closer, he spoke.

"Greetings, Pocahontas!" he called. Sal started barking again, so I just waved and smiled and then tossed my rope up to him when we were close enough for him to catch it.

"Hey, Kirby," I said as he tied me off to the cleat. "What are you doing here?"

"I saw you row past my window in this direction, so I knew you were headed home."

Sal jumped onto the dock, stopped barking, and began furiously sniffing the cuffs of Kirby's pants. He let her, finally leaning down with an outstretched hand, allowing her to sniff it before he gently patted her on the back. She seemed not to mind.

"Hey, girl," he cooed softly, rubbing behind her ears. It was a done deal already, I could see. She snuggled up against him like they were old friends. I was surprised, for Sal almost never took to anyone quite that quickly.

"She's adorable," Kirby said to me. I climbed from the canoe to the dock and finished tying the boat off myself.

"Thanks. She's my pal, that's for sure."

"A Yorkie?"

"Maltese."

"Hey, cutie."

"Sal."

"Hey, Sal."

He stood finally and grinned at me, and I couldn't help but again admire the man's teeth. I had a thing about nice teeth, and his were about the most perfect I had ever seen.

"Guess what?" he said happily.

"What?"

"I solved the mystery of the wooden nickel."

"What do you mean?"

"My dad. I called my dad in New York. He knew exactly what you were talking about."

I *knew* this was going to be a good day! I met Kirby's grin with one of my own and invited him inside for tea. Chatting idly as we went into the kitchen, I busied myself with hot water and tea bags. Kirby waited until we were both seated at the table, steaming mugs in front of us, before he explained.

"Okay," he began, "here's what happened. A couple of months before my mom got sick, she went with my dad to a meeting of this club he belongs to. The club was trying to drum up activity for their website, and they had a bunch of these wooden nickels in a bowl by the door. Members were supposed to grab a handful and then circulate them elsewhere, like at work or other places. My dad already had a whole box at the office, so he didn't grab any, but my mom took one. According to my dad, it was for me. She said something like, 'Oh, look at this, Walter. Wooden nickels. Just like Kirby used to collect when he was little.' "

His face reddened for a moment, and I realized he was choked up about his mother. I took a sip of tea and allowed him to compose himself before he continued.

"She brought it home to give it to me," he said finally, his voice a little hoarse, "but she must've forgotten about it. So it stayed in the jacket pocket and eventually ended up making its way to Advancing Attire."

I reached for a paper napkin and dabbed at my mouth.

"What kind of club is it?" I asked. "What's the buried treasure?"

"How much do you know about GPS?"

"GPS? You mean global positioning systems?"

"Yeah."

"About as much as I need to know, I guess. GPS tells you where you are and how to get where you need to be, using satellites to do triangulation. Right?"

"Well, technically the correct term is trilateration, not triangulation, but yes. GPS calculates position by taking the time travel of radio signals from several different satellites and analyzing the resulting intersection of spheres."

"Gee, Kirby, you sound like an engineer or something," I teased, causing him to blush. "But what does this have to do with the wooden nickel?"

"My father's group, the one advertised on the nickel, is a GPS club. They do geocaching."

"Geocaching," I repeated, vaguely familiar with the term. "What's that, exactly?"

"It starts with a container or a capsule, usually small, about the size of a shoe box or maybe a toaster oven. That's the cache, which gets hidden in a publically accessible location, like under a rock near a hiking trail, or in a tree alongside a highway. After it's hidden, the coordinates are posted on a website, showing the points of latitude and longitude. To find that hidden cache, you look up those coordinates online and then use GPS technology to track it down. In a nutshell, that's geocaching."

"What's the point?"

Kirby shrugged. "Fun?"

I raised one eyebrow skeptically and then we both chuckled.

"My dad says that it's all about the thrill of the hunt, the challenge of the pursuit," he explained. "He originally joined the club for business reasons, being the owner of an electronics firm and all. But once he got involved he really liked it. Not me. I mean, I'm fascinated by GPS technology, and I've dealt with digital mapping and KML though my work. But I never really took to the sport of geocaching itself."

I nodded, trying to picture it. I could see doing it as a learning exercise, or maybe for some fun family time with kids. But in Kirby's father's case, it sounded more like just a bunch of rich old men running around in the woods with fancy gadgets, playing hide-and-seek.

"And the treasure?" I persisted. "What's in that hidden cache to make it all worthwhile?"

"Nothing of value. In fact, once you find a capsule, you don't take anything from it at all. Instead, you put something in, to prove that you found it. The goal is to do that with as many capsules as you can before time's up."

"Time's up?"

"Once a year. They get together monthly, but once a year they round up the containers, bring them to the meeting, and then go through them to see what's inside. You get points for every container you put something in. When they're done, the guys with the most points win trophies and stuff."

"I see."

"Then the whole process starts all over again. They hide the capsules somewhere new, you download the coordinates, and you try to find them. That's what the club does. They go geocaching."

"Okay. Wow. Thanks for explaining it to me."

I sat back in my chair, the mug in front of me empty. Even though I had never seen Eddie Ray alive, I could picture him following the trail of this wooden nickel, stumbling across a capsule full of trinkets, thinking he had discovered buried treasure worth a million dollars. Had he really been that dumb?

"Kirby, what kinds of things are these men putting inside the capsules when they find them? Is it valuable stuff?"

In other words, is it stuff worth killing for?

"No, it's kind of corny. At first, they used business cards, but some of the men were uncomfortable with that. They wanted it to be a little more secretive. So they came up with a 'thing' that they have, like a little object, to represent them."

"Like what?"

"Well, one guy is a car salesman, so he always puts in a key chain. Another guy collects eagles, so he bought a bunch of little plastic eagles, and he puts one of them in."

"What does your dad put in?"

"He's the electronics expert, so he said he always puts in a little tangle of electric wiring. About the size of a small bird's nest. He said that's his 'symbol.'"

I rose from the table and carried our mugs to the sink. Keychains? Plastic eagles? Tangled wire? This wasn't buried treasure, and even Eddie Ray had to have known that. So what was worth so much money?

"Did you go to the website yourself?" I asked. "Have you looked it up?"

"No, I came right over soon as I talked to my dad. But I wrote it down. Do you want to take a look?"

I nodded, gesturing for him to follow me down the hall to my office. Once there, I turned on the computer and sat at my desk. Kirby pulled up a stool behind me and watched over my shoulder. He read off the web address that his father had given him, and I typed it in, holding my breath as I pressed "Enter." The site appeared on the screen, large letters spelling out "SEARCH FOR BURIED TREASURE!" across the top. Below that was a smaller headline, "Official Website of the Chesapeake GPS Society."

The site was much as Kirby's father had described. Besides a history of the club and a list of contact numbers, it also provided all sorts of links to related websites, information about how GPS works, even instructions on how to set up your own GPS club. We had to sign in to access the "members only" area of the website, and there we found the coordinates list for the last four years. There seemed to be more coordinates each year than the year before, and Kirby mused that as the club increased in size and as the members became more GPS-savvy, they probably needed to increase the number of degree confluence points.

On a hunch I printed a list of this year's coordinates. I remembered next to nothing from geography class about latitude and longitude, but the website was very thorough, and after studying it for a while I felt as though I had a rudimentary grasp of the basics. Frustrated with the limitations of online mapping, I finally clicked away from the site, grabbed the list of coordinates from the printer tray, and walked back to the kitchen, Kirby following closely behind.

"We need a real map," I said, "something we can spread out on the table and study in its entirety."

I didn't know where any of this was leading, but I could guess as to how we should proceed. Obviously, Eddie Ray had also found the website and had probably pursued some of the coordinates, expecting the "treasure" to be valuable. I wasn't sure what he had found, but I knew I had to keep my mind open. Perhaps one of these rich men had played hide-and-seek with something a little more important than a trinket.

I led Kirby out of the door and across the lawn to the shed at the edge of the trees. I kept my lawnmower and a few tools in there, but now I was headed for the stack of navigational charts that were curled up in waterproof tubes in the corner. When I first moved here, I let an overzealous canoe salesman convince me I needed a full set of Chesapeake navigational charts for my canoeing, lest I get lost or confused. I had used them only a few times before realizing that getting lost was half the fun—and that finding my way along the waterways around here was a much safer and more intuitive process than he predicted.

Kirby and I carried the charts cradled in our arms back to the kitchen as I explained what they were and how I had gotten them. We dumped them onto the counter, and then I opened a tube, took out the map, and spread it open on the kitchen table.

"Yeah, see, here you go," I said. "It's got the latitude and longitude indicated along the edges."

I studied the list of coordinates we had taken from the website. The longitudes ranged from 70° to 164°, the latitudes from 20° to 42°.

"Hey, Kirby, this doesn't make sense. The coordinates on the list aren't anywhere around here."

"You got a globe?"

I pointed toward the living room, where I kept Bryan's beautiful old globe on a stand near the couch. It was a classic, ordered for him by his parents from *National Geographic* when he was 12. Bryan had always been more into geology than geography, and he told me once that he loved this globe more than the ones they had at school because it was a "relief" globe, with raised mountains and dented valleys and creased rivers. He said that as a teenager he used to run his fingers over the globe and wonder if that's what the earth felt like to God when He held it in His hands.

"Sweet," Kirby said now, bringing the globe into the kitchen. He had it up on one finger, spinning, like a basketball. "I haven't seen a globe like this since probably fifth grade."

I took the spinning globe from his finger and held it against my chest.

"Yeah, well, it's pretty fragile. You'd better not do that."

"Sorry."

I held the globe carefully, and we tracked the lines of latitude and longitude for the first coordinates on the list. It soon became apparent these were points in different parts of the United States, from Hawaii to Maine and lots of places in between.

"I guess I misunderstood," I said to Kirby. "I thought this was a local club."

"It is. The men are local, anyway. But the capsules are all over the country."

"How does that work?"

He was quiet for a moment, and then he smiled almost sheepishly.

"They're all rich, Callie. Rich, bored men who want an adventure. It's an excuse to travel."

I thought about these men who spent their time and money on such an expensive hobby. Truly, couldn't they have found better things to do with their cash? I had about a hundred worthy charities I could easily recommend!

"I know what you're thinking," Kirby said, "but don't judge my dad until you meet him. He's really a nice guy."

"Why the change of heart?" I asked. "Yesterday it sounded like you were feeling kind of bitter and angry."

Kirby shrugged.

"I am, sometimes. I still get mad at him when I think about the way he treated Mom when she was dying. But then I look out at Bertha—"

"The mermaid."

"The mermaid, and I remember that he really did love her. He just couldn't bear the sight of losing her."

"I'm sorry for your loss, too," I said. "Like I said yesterday, I know what it is to lose someone you love."

He looked at me, his deep green eyes holding mine for a long moment.

"I guess you do," he said finally.

Taking a deep breath, I broke our gaze and looked back down at the globe.

Bryan's globe.

"Let's look for points in the seventies and thirties," I said, feeling flustered. "Something closer to where we are."

We scanned the list together and discovered the one location at the same time: longitude 76°, latitude 38°.

According to my navigational chart, that put it somewhere in our general vicinity.

Twenty-Four

Soon we were in Kirby's Jaguar, flying much too quickly up the road in the general direction of the nearest hidden capsule.

"So what are we using to find our way? Is this thing portable?" I asked, gesturing toward the GPS unit that was mounted on the dashboard.

"Yeah, but it won't accept coordinates, just addresses."

"How about your phone? Do you have an app for geocaching?"

"Probably," he replied, "but I'd rather stop by my house and grab one of my dad's handheld GPS units, if you don't mind. That'll be far more accurate than anything I could get on here."

"Sure."

"On the way, maybe you can tell me more about why we're doing this."

"Of course," I replied, surprised that he hadn't asked sooner. After asking that he keep things confidential, I started by describing Shayna, saying how she was a young, recovering drug addict who had been working hard to make changes in her life since getting out of rehab. But then she made the mistake of letting an old boyfriend named Eddie Ray back into her home and her life. For some reason, when that wooden nickel popped up and Eddie Ray looked into it, he decided that it was going to make him rich.

"Then a few days ago," I continued, "Eddie Ray was killed by a bash to the head with a tire iron and dumped into the trunk of Shayna's car. Because her fingerprints were all over the tire iron, she's been charged with the murder. I'm investigating the case and working with her attorney by attempting to prove she didn't do it. It's probably a stretch, but right now I'm just trying to see if this wooden nickel is somehow connected. It seems improbable, unless you go back to what Eddie Ray said, that the nickel was somehow worth 'millions.' "

When I finished my explanation, Kirby let out a long breath, shaking his head.

"I hope it isn't connected," he said earnestly. "I'd hate to see my dad's club somehow linked to a *murder*."

I told him that we would find out soon if the two things were related or not.

"I read about that guy's death in the paper," he continued. "Sure sounded to me like the girlfriend did it."

"Shayna has made some stupid mistakes," I said, shaking my head. "But trust me, this kid is *not* a killer."

We got to Kirby's mansion and parked out front in the curve of the U-shaped driveway. I waited in the car, using my cell phone, while he went inside to find one of his father's old GPS units. It took him some time, which was fine, because it also took me a while to work my way through the proper channels of the legal system to get through to Shayna on the phone.

She was allowed to speak to me for just a few minutes, so I kept it brief. I assured her that I was hot on the case, and that I hoped we'd be able to clear her name soon. She sounded as though she was about to start crying, so I didn't inquire about how she was doing but instead went right to my questions. I needed more specific information about the chain of events following the discovery of the wooden nickel, I told her. I had brought my laptop, and I had it open now to my database for the case. According to my notes from the conversation I'd already had with Shayna at the jail, Eddie Ray first saw the nickel on Tuesday, two weeks ago. Two days after that, he declared to her that from that nickel they would make "millions." What I needed to know now was everything she could tell me about what transpired between the time he found the nickel to the time he made that statement.

Shayna thought hard, trying to piece together two seemingly ordinary days from her recent past—something that's usually not very easy to do. But the more she talked, the more she remembered, and by the end of the conversation, I had gleaned several more important facts. As we spoke, I quickly entered what I was learning into the database.

Apparently, Eddie Ray's first stop after discovering the nickel was a trip to the library in Osprey Cove, to go on the Internet and look up the website that was printed on the nickel. Shayna knew this because she went with him to check out want ads in area newspapers. They had stayed at the library for about an hour, during which time she found several leads on jobs while he sat huddled in the corner in front of a computer. She hadn't thought much about it at the time, assuming he had gotten bored with his original quest and was just playing around with games or something.

When they left the library, they drove to Easton, where they had dinner at a McDonald's and then drove out to see an old friend of Eddie Ray's, a retired fisherman originally from Kawshek who now worked at a marina in St. Michael's. Shayna hadn't been interested in visiting with this man she hardly knew, so while he and Eddie Ray chewed the fat at the docks, she strolled the quaint streets of the picturesque town, window-shopping. When she got back to the marina, Eddie Ray was ready to go, and he had in his possession a small electronic device. She said it looked like a cell phone, but with more buttons. When she asked Eddie Ray about it, he brushed her off and said it was just something his buddy was loaning him for a while.

From there, they went home. Shayna was tired and wanted to watch TV; Eddie Ray, however, was antsy and couldn't sit still. Finally, she told him to go on over to the bar and join his friends, because he obviously wasn't happy being there with her. Instead, he said, he wondered if by any chance he could please use the car. He said he had an errand he needed to run.

"At nine o'clock at night?" I asked.

"Actually, by then it was more like eleven o'clock," she said. "I let him go. He asked me so nicely and all."

Shayna continued her story, telling me how Eddie Ray didn't come home until five the next morning. She had been angry, but Eddie Ray had placated her, promising that what he had been out doing was as much for her benefit as it was for his.

"Did he bring anything home with him?" I asked. "Any trinkets? Any odd little items?"

"Just that electronic unit, a pair of binoculars, and a flashlight," she said. "But I remember thinking how weird it was that he didn't smell like smoke and alcohol this time—he smelled more like sweat and dirt. I guess that's why I didn't stay mad at him. He obviously hadn't been off fooling around in a bar or something."

"So what happened next?"

It took a few moments for her to recall much from the next day. She had gone on a job interview that morning, she remembered, and Eddie Ray slept until she got back. Then he borrowed the car for the afternoon and, exhausted from waiting up for him the night before, Shayna had taken a long nap. Eddie Ray had made it home that evening in time for dinner.

"He was like the best of his old self," Shayna said. "Happy and funny and charming. That night he didn't even go out. He just stayed home with me and watched TV. After Letterman, he went to sleep on the couch, and I went to bed. The next morning at breakfast is when he said the thing about that nickel being worth millions."

"And between that morning and the night he was killed, did he ever go out of town? Did he take any trips that you know of?"

"Gosh, no, Callie. Mostly, he seemed like he was just passing time, waiting for something. We drove back to St. Michael's one day, to return that electronic thingy. But other than that, he mostly just hung around the house or the bar."

"Were there any other nights where he went out late and came back smelling like sweat and dirt?"

"No, not at all. Though on Saturday..." Her voice trailed off.

"What?"

"Nothing. I was just thinking. He was out really late last Saturday night. That's not unusual, except that I know he wasn't at the bar, because I went over there looking for him. They said he hadn't been in all evening, and he wasn't sleeping at Stinky's."

"Where was he?"

"I don't know. I figured he was off getting drunk with one of his buddies. My car was still at home, so wherever he went, it was with somebody else."

"Did you ask him about it?"

"Yelled at him about it is more like it. He finally came home Sunday afternoon and we fought all evening. He said he had been doing business, trying to get us all this money. We were both pretty mad. In the end I went on to bed, and he stormed off to the bar. That's the fight we had that everyone overheard. I think that's one reason everybody thinks I killed him—because we had such a huge argument the night he died."

"So he was gone all night Saturday night, came home Sunday, went back out Sunday night, and ended up killed?"

"Basically, yeah."

"Time's up," a voice said sharply in the background, and then Shayna spoke again.

"I have to go now," she said.

"You hang in there," I told her, and then the line went dead.

I turned off my phone and sat there for a while, thinking about all that Shayna had said. I was able to draw a few conclusions, which I entered into the database now.

Obviously the handheld electronic device that Eddie Ray picked up in St. Michael's was a GPS unit. It made sense that a fisherman or a marina might have one for navigational purposes out on the water.

The next morning Eddie Ray came home smelling of dirt and sweat because he had gone out and found the club's local capsule. I didn't know what was inside or why it was worth so much money. And I couldn't imagine what he had been waiting for since then, or where he had gone all night Saturday night, the night before he died. But judging by Eddie Ray's suspicious and secretive behavior, I thought there was indeed something fishy about the whole wooden nickel angle. I felt strongly that Kirby and I weren't wasting our time looking for the capsule, though anything valuable that Eddie Ray had found inside of it had almost certainly been removed by him and wouldn't still be there.

As I was closing out the computer file, Kirby appeared again, bounding down the front steps of the house. He got to the car and climbed in, out of breath.

"I'm sorry I took so long," he said. "I couldn't find the one I was looking for, so I had to call my dad. Turns out, he has it with him. I grabbed this older one instead."

He handed me the GPS unit, which looked like a cross between a cell phone and a walkie-talkie with a rugged outer shell. On the screen was a topographical map of the area, our current position indicated by a pulsing red circle.

"It's fairly user-friendly," he added as he started up the car. "Feel free to play around on it if you want."

As he headed up the driveway, I did just that, pressing various buttons on the unit and bringing up a series of different images, including a compass, a bunch of numbers, and an assortment of maps.

"This is cool," I said finally, flashing Kirby a smile as I set the unit down in an empty cup holder between us and turned my attention to our surroundings. It was a gorgeous fall day, the air crisp, the sky a vivid blue. Despite my earlier reservations, there was something intoxicating about sailing down the winding highways at full speed in such a luxurious vehicle. I decided to relax and enjoy myself and the company of Kirby Collins. *We've got to get you more friends,* Harriet had said to me just a few days before.

Okay, Harriet, I thought. *I'm working on it.*

We chatted as we drove, and I found Kirby to be both witty and intelligent. I asked about his life and how he filled his days. He explained he was an electrical engineer and that he used to be in the research and development branch of his father's company.

"I took a leave of absence last year to help out my mom when she got ill," he said. "I still haven't gone back."

"Wow, she was lucky to have you around."

"Mostly I just took over all of her duties," he said. "Running the household, entertaining dad's clients. Keeping an eye on my grandmother."

"It must be exhausting."

"Exhausting. Frustrating. Boring. I don't think we ever realized how many different things my mother handled until she couldn't do them anymore. Beyond all the things I'm doing now in her place, she also served on two boards, worked with a couple of charities, did things at the church..."

His voice trailed off, remembering.

"When will you go back to your job?" I asked.

"I don't know," Kirby replied, a vague expression on his face. "It's hard to say."

"Surely you could hire someone to run the household for you. If you're not happy there, you should go back to work."

"Yeah, I guess," he said. "Though it's been a little hard to get motivated."

I nodded, remembering the weeks after Bryan died when I struggled even to get out of bed. I knew the kind of lethargy the mourning process could induce.

"In any event, I bet your dad appreciates having you around the house."

"Mostly for my grandmother's sake," Kirby said, nodding. "He likes knowing I'm around, just in case something happens."

"Like the incident with the broken pictures?"

"Yeah. Or if she walks off or something. Even though she wears a PTD, he's always worried about that."

"A PTD?"

"A personal tracking device. So we can always know where she is."

"Like the kind they put on prisoners?"

"Sort of. It uses the same GPS technology, but it's smaller and a lot more comfortable. She's not even aware it's there."

"It keeps track of her location?"

"Yeah, just in case. If she disappears, I simply log into the corresponding website and it shows exactly where she is."

"Impressive. That would be handy in my line of work. For keeping track of suspects."

Kirby laughed. "Handy, yes. Legal? Probably not. Though I do know some people use 'em to monitor the whereabouts of their teenagers."

"Oooh, sneaky," I said, thinking that GPS was one of those technologies that could be used in millions of ways, both good and not-so-good.

"Would you ever do that?" I asked. "Use a tracking device to keep an eye on your kids?" As soon as the question was out of my mouth, I felt embarrassed for having asked it. Maybe he was one of those people who didn't even want children someday.

Fortunately, he didn't seem startled or offended by my question but instead was obviously giving it some thought.

"Only if I had reason to believe they were in some kind of danger," he said finally. "Serious danger, I mean. And only as a last-ditch effort, assuming all else failed. How about you?"

I shrugged, turning to look out the window, thinking of the children Bryan and I hadn't had, would never have. Outside, the landscape rushed past at breakneck speed, the glorious fall colors a blur of reds and golds.

"I have no idea," I replied, wishing the conversation hadn't gone in this direction. As if sensing my sudden sadness, Kirby changed the subject, reaching out to grab the GPS unit from where it sat in the cup holder.

"Hey, Callie," he said softly, handing it to me, "we're getting closer. Why don't you plug in the coordinates? Let's see if this thing really can help us find our way."

Twenty-Five

"It says we're here," Kirby told me, studying the GPS unit as we stood in the middle of a big field. "It's supposed to be accurate within twenty feet or so, depending on certain variables."

"Twenty feet? That's a pretty wide margin of error." Fists clenching in frustration, I forced myself to relax and look around at the beautiful scenery. The drive had taken us about an hour, the coordinates leading us south of our peninsula, into the next county, and out to Carson Point, a piece of land that directly lined the Intracoastal Waterway. The bay was truly a mighty thing from this vantage point, wide and beautiful and strong. We had parked alongside the road and then hiked through low brush to the spot indicated on the GPS unit. Now we were here, but where were we?

Around us was simply an empty field, lined on three sides by trees and one side by coastline. There was nothing remarkable about the place, no big red "X" to mark the spot or anything—just sea grass and cattails and the remains of what looked like an ancient duck blind. Peering out toward the water, there was an abandoned osprey nest on a platform and, beyond that, what looked like a string of small, wooded islands. All very beautiful, yes, but fairly average terrain for the area.

"What next?" I asked.

"My dad said he usually looks for natural hiding places, like fallen logs, hollow trees, things like that. We'll use this point as our center marker and work our way out from here."

I could tell that Kirby was having a ball, though I didn't really see the thrill of it. I just wanted to find this thing and get out of here, but he acted like an ancient explorer: Ponce de Leon looking for the fountain of youth, when in fact we were just Callie and Kirby, looking for a capsule of junk.

We walked around the field for half an hour, growing itchy from the tall grass, our hands cold, our feet frozen. As much as I usually loved being out in nature, I couldn't imagine doing this as a hobby. The longer we searched, the more ridiculous I felt.

"I thought GPS units were more exact than this," I complained as we walked. "Twenty feet in every direction is a bit much."

"Well, remember, this is an older unit. A newer one could get us within about ten feet, maybe less, but where's the challenge in that?"

"Yeah," I said, rubbing my hands together. "Why do I get the feeling that, once this is all over, you might decide to join your father's club?"

Kirby laughed.

"Hey, you never know," he said. "It is a lot of fun."

"I just hope your girlfriend's a good sport about stomping around in the wilderness."

"Yeah, right. What girlfriend?"

"Your girlfriend."

He stopped walking and turned to me.

"I don't have a girlfriend."

His expression was genuinely puzzled.

"Sure you do," I said. "You told me about her yesterday. You said the two of you watched me paddling on the river. She made you study my canoeing technique."

"Oh, gosh, that was ages ago. We broke up last spring. I haven't gone out with anybody since then."

"Not at all?"

"Well, sure, I go out. But not any one person, not steady-like."

"I see."

He gave me an enigmatic smile, and I wondered if I *did* see. Certainly, there was an intensity to his expression that made me feel somehow disquieted.

"Hey, we haven't tried back by the duck blind," I said quickly. "Let's take a look over there."

I led the way this time, and Kirby trudged along in my wake. It was slow going, our feet methodically taking one step after another through the tall grass. I'd have to check myself for ticks tonight, I realized as I scratched at the back of my leg. We checked behind the duck blind but found nothing but a battered old rowboat, tipped over on its side. Finally, we just stood there, arms crossed, looking out over the land. It had to be here somewhere, unless Eddie Ray had removed it.

"Hey, maybe Eddie Ray stole the whole thing," I said suddenly. "Maybe he couldn't get it open, so he brought the entire capsule home."

"If that's the case," Kirby said, "then at the very least we should be able to figure out where it was located before he took it."

We looked around us again, wondering if there was any spot we had overlooked.

"How about by those rocks?" I said.

"Too close to the water. The capsule would've washed out with the tide."

"No, up there," I said. "On that rise. The back side of those rocks would be protected."

"Worth a look."

We marched up a slight incline to a point at the edge of the waterline where surf met rock. There was a cluster of black boulders at the point, and behind them, nestled into a crook of the biggest one, was a small gray container.

"Bull's-eye!" Kirby cried.

He wrestled the container from its hiding place, and we sat on the rocks and opened it, eager to pore through the contents inside.

"I can't believe we found it," he said excitedly.

"I can't believe it's just a Rubbermaid plastic box," I said. "I was expecting something a little more high tech than that."

The box was a rectangular shape with a snap-on lid. We knew it was the capsule because across the top, in bold black letters, someone had written the website address, along with the words "Property of the Chesapeake GPS Society."

Kirby popped the lid open, and we peered inside to find what had to be at least 30 little objects. I imagined this was probably their most popular capsule, considering that it was the closest to where these men actually lived.

We pulled out the items one by one—the tangle of wire, the plastic eagle, the keychain. Everything else was, as expected, just junk, like a small hairbrush, a bar of soap, a "C" battery. I wondered again how we could ever know what Eddie Ray had found here and why it was worth so much money.

"Hey, what's to keep these guys from cheating?" I asked. "If they're so dead set on winning the trophy, what's to stop them from removing some of the other guys' trinkets?"

"This log book," Kirby said, pulling a small spiral notebook from the pile. On the cover, the same hand that had printed the words on the lid had written here "Capsule invalid if logbook not present."

I took the notebook from him and flipped it open. The first page was dated the previous New Year's Day, and it was headed "Congratulations! Please log in." What followed was page after page of short notes, each written in a different hand, each signed by some sort of code name.

"Hey, look for my dad. His club name is 'Jolt.' "

"Jolt?"

"Yeah, like electricity. Collins Electronics. Get it?"

I flipped through the pages until I found an entry marked 'Jolt.' It was short and to the point: "Excellent cache! Took about 20 minutes to find, great coordinates. Capsule is in good condition and dry. Left wires."

Most of the entries were similar, I decided as I scanned through them. It was as Kirby had said: a bunch of men playing hide-and-seek in the wilderness.

"You know what this means, don't you?" I asked, waving the notebook at Kirby.

"Yeah. It means we have to do a quick inventory."

That we did, going through the entire notebook, comparing it with the items in the box. When we were finished, we had to admit that not one thing was missing.

Silent and disappointed, we put the lid back on, and then Kirby returned the capsule to its hiding place. I still wasn't sure if this had anything to do with Eddie Ray's murder or not. But if it did, I knew the answer wasn't going to jump out at me. I would have to work at it a bit more.

We walked back toward the car in a nearly straight line, finding it on the side of the road right where we left it. As I climbed inside, I realized it was nearly dark. We had wasted the entire afternoon clomping around in the bushes after buried treasure.

"Now remember," Kirby said as he shut the door, "not a word of any of this to my dad. He didn't mind telling me all about the club, but I don't think he'd appreciate finding out that we actually came and looked at one of their capsules."

"I understand."

Kirby nodded and then started the car. My hands were frozen solid, and I held them up to the heater vents as soon as he turned them on.

"Here, let me help you," he said. He reached over and took one of my hands between both of his. He rubbed his hands together, creating heat that radiated through my hand and even up my arm. It felt wonderful, and after a moment I switched hands and let him do the other one. When he was finished, I realized he was looking at my face, almost expectantly, still holding onto my hand.

We were close together, and suddenly it dawned on me that he was going to try to kiss me. I turned away and pulled my hand back, glad he couldn't see in the darkness that my face suddenly burned bright red.

"You're such an enigma," he said softly. He reached out a tentative hand and tucked a loose strand of hair behind my ear. Then he gently placed his fingers on the back of my neck, as if to pull me to him. My skin pulsed where he touched it.

"I'm a widow, Kirby," I said softly, not moving, not looking at him. "Lots of baggage. I think we'd do best to keep this on a purely friendly level."

My statement hung out there for a moment, and then he finally took his hand away and put the car in gear.

"Sure, whatever," he replied.

He turned the car around on the deserted road and silently sped off toward town.

Twenty-Six

The uncomfortable silence between us lasted almost all the way to Osprey Cove. But as we neared the bypass, Kirby turned to me and finally spoke.

"I'm a jerk," he said. "Can I take you to dinner by way of apology?"

"What's to apologize for?" I asked. "You didn't do anything wrong."

"No, but for the last hour I've been acting like a petulant child. All you did was turn me down. It's not like you deserve the silent treatment."

"That's all right, Kirby. I'm not exactly swift at these male-female things anyway."

"So, dinner? My treat, but friend to friend, of course."

I chewed my lip.

"Sure. Why not?" I said finally. "I...I'm starving, actually."

He took the road for Osprey Cove and steered through the congested streets toward the Harbor View Manor, a gorgeous, expensive restaurant situated on pilings out over the water. I had never eaten there, but I'd heard the food was the best in town.

"Shouldn't we go somewhere a little more casual?" I asked. "We're dressed for trooping around in the woods, not dining at the Harbor View Manor."

Kirby laughed and continued up the ramp toward valet parking.

"I'll give you a hint about how the very rich operate around here," he said. "In Osprey Cove, the only people who get dressed up are the tourists."

He came to a stop at the door of the restaurant and a red-jacketed young man appeared at my side almost instantly. We got out, and I noticed Kirby slipped the kid a twenty in exchange for his claim ticket.

"Evening, Tommy," Kirby said.

"How are you tonight, Mr. Collins?"

"Fine, just fine."

Kirby took my elbow and steered me into the restaurant. Despite a queue of people waiting in the lobby, we were whisked past all of them almost instantly and taken to a beautiful table for two right next to the window. As I sat and oriented myself with the restaurant and the gorgeous view of the harbor, Kirby chatted amiably with the maître d'. It was apparent to me that he must come here all of the time, a thought I found disturbing when I saw the prices on the menu. The least expensive entrée, a scallops-pasta dish, was $75! Prices went up from there, with several items costing in the three-figure range. Unbelievable.

"I hate to sound arrogant," Kirby said after the waiter had taken our order and removed the menus, "but women do not often turn me down. That's why I reacted like I did. I think mostly I was just surprised."

I took a sip of water and looked out at the white twinkly lights sparkling in the trees along the water.

"That's not arrogance, just realism. You're handsome, rich, and charming," I said. "I'm sure you can take your pick of women."

"But not you."

I met his eyes.

"It has nothing to do with you, Kirby," I said. "It's me. I don't date. Ever."

"Isn't that lonely for you?"

I thought about that. His question wasn't rude, just honest. I smiled, wondering how to explain.

"I have my faith to sustain me," I said.

"That's a crock."

"You think my faith is a crock?" I asked incredulously.

"No, your faith is admirable. But the notion that God alone can fulfill the need for companionship? Sounds like an easy excuse to me."

"I like my life as it is. I'm sorry if you can't understand that."

I knew I sounded defensive. But it seemed as though *everyone* was questioning my solitude these days.

Maybe, just a little, I was questioning it as well.

Our salads arrived, breaking the tension. Kirby waited until the server finished twisting pepper onto our plates before he graciously changed the subject.

"So tell me about this J.O.S.H.U.A. Foundation you work for. What do you do there, exactly?"

This was safe conversational terrain, and I gladly launched into an explanation of what I did and how it worked. Kirby seemed genuinely fascinated by the whole process, and he asked me a number of insightful and probing questions. I had fun sharing some of the more interesting tales of my investigations. Careful not to name specific people or organizations, of course, I told him about some of the good and the bad, the selflessness and the scams.

"And you mean to tell me that this guy Tom simply gives his money away? He just *gives* it away?"

"That's what philanthropy is, Kirby."

"Yeah, but to that extent? Incredible!"

We easily talked our way through dinner. The food was, indeed, the best I'd had since moving here. Kirby had ordered lobster, and I feasted on a broiled shrimp dish that was out of this world. By the time they rolled around the dessert cart, we were both too stuffed to take another bite.

"We'll just have some coffee, please," Kirby said to the waiter, looking to me for confirmation. I nodded.

"Decaf for me," I said.

The waiter left and we were quiet for a moment. I felt tired but strangely happy. The peaceful ambience of this lovely place was working its magic on me.

"I had a great day," Kirby said, smiling.

"Thanks for your help," I replied. "I'm sorry we didn't make any real progress on the investigation, but at least we can rule out the GPS connection."

"That's how investigating works, isn't it?" he asked. "By process of elimination?"

"Exactly. One by one, we take away what isn't relevant until we're left with what is."

Twenty-Seven

I arrived home at 8:30 to find a number of messages on my machine. The first was Denise Hightower, the hairdresser, calling to check on me after all that had happened with Shayna.

"I can't believe what you had to go through, seeing a dead body and all that," she said. "Barbara told me you used to be a private investigator, but that still had to be hard to take." She left her phone number, inviting me to give her a call if I needed someone to talk to or maybe go jogging with sometime.

The next message was from Denise's sister, Barbara Hightower, the cop. Her tone was much less warm and friendly.

"Callie, this is Barbara Hightower," the message said brusquely. "Looks like you worked things out with Shayna's attorney, because I know you're handling this case. I just wanted to give you a little word of advice. Call me."

I leaned against the counter, curious, and dialed the number she had left after the message. She answered on the second ring, sounding tired and a bit subdued.

"Hey, Callie," she said. "How's it going?"

"Coming along," I replied. "I'm wondering what your message was about. You have some advice for me?"

"Yeah," she said, "no offense, but you need to tread carefully where the authorities are concerned. Make sure you don't get in their way."

I reached back to let down my chignon, the bobby pins clicking softly in my hand.

"What do you mean?"

"Just watch yourself," she said. "If you interfere with this investigation, people might start getting mad."

"Did I do something wrong?"

"Not really," she said. "But I went out to Russell Lynch's farm today with Litman. He was a little concerned when Russell told him you had already been there asking the same exact questions we were asking."

I thought of Litman and his unfriendly manner when we first met. He definitely seemed like the type you don't want to cross.

"Hey, I'm just trying to help out a friend," I said.

"That friend is a cold-blooded killer," she replied.

My heart sank. If Barbara was now convinced Shayna was guilty, what hope did the poor girl have? Once the cops had their man—or woman, as the case may be—they often developed a sort of tunnel vision that blocked many other significant details from their view.

Still, I knew it would be a waste of time to try and convince Barbara of Shayna's innocence at this point. I thanked her for her "advice," hung up, and then listened to the rest of the messages.

They were from some of the charity directors I had tried to contact yesterday regarding references for CNA. Though it was too late to call most of them back tonight, I realized that the ones on the West Coast might still be at work. There was a three-hour time difference, after all. I called them back one by one and received testimonials praising CNA to the skies.

"I have nothing but great things to say about CNA," a woman from Seattle told me when I got her on the phone, echoing sentiments I had already heard from three other agencies. "When they came in and helped me expand, it was like a dream come true."

"They helped you expand?" I asked, thinking of Verlene and the soon-to-be-empty store next door to Advancing Attire.

"Oh, yes," she effused. "By joining with them, I went from three hundred square feet to nearly two thousand. Now, granted, we're not exactly in the high-rent district, but still. I couldn't be happier."

"Have you ever been to their headquarters in Cleveland?" I asked.

"No, I haven't," she said. "Haven't needed to, really. We had a few meetings and training sessions at first, but they always came out here to us, not the other way around."

I grabbed a pencil and paper and wrote myself a note: *Meetings and trainings on site.*

"Are you handled by the Small Agencies Division?" I asked, remembering the woman who said she'd had a personality conflict with the representative from that division. "Do you get along with the director?"

"Yes," she said. "Our rep is just the greatest lady, a real take-charge kind of gal."

"How about fund-raising?" I asked, thinking of the man in Houston who did his own fund-raising with monthly barbecues. My fifth criteria for judging a nonprofit was that they follow "standards of responsible and ethical fund-raising." That was often where the credentials of some otherwise-respectable agencies began to fall apart.

"That's the best part," she said. "Since we joined up with CNA last year, we haven't had to do a single fund-raising event. I haven't had to bother with any of those tedious grant applications, either."

I smiled to myself, thinking that our J.O.S.H.U.A. Foundation grant applications were so long and involved, they were probably among the most tedious of all.

"Where does your funding coming from?" I asked.

"Oh, donors, of course. CNA found a couple of local businesses that send them a big check every month on our behalf. It's amazing."

I doodled on the pad next to my note, absently penciling little question marks around a dollar sign.

"How many businesses support you, if I may ask?"

"Three."

"Three? Those must be pretty big checks! What's the size of your budget?"

She hesitated, obviously wondering if she should be sharing this kind of information with a total stranger.

"Well, I suppose I can tell you," she said finally. "It's not like you can't go look us up on Guidestar."

"True."

"Our annual budget is about a hundred and fifty thousand, give or take a bit."

"A hundred and fifty thousand," I said, thinking that was relatively modest by nonprofit standards. On the other hand, that was an awful lot of money to be coming from only three local business sources.

"So what are the names of these generous businesses?" I asked.

My question earned a moment of silence.

"I can't say," she finally replied. Though I dearly wanted that information, I thought it was prudent of her to keep it to herself. After all, though she was required to supply the names of her donors to the IRS in her agency's annual tax filing, she was also allowed, by law, to withhold that information from anyone else who wanted to know.

"I don't mean to pry," I added quickly. "I just wondered what types of businesses would be willing to help out a nonprofit with that much money."

"Well, if you want to know the truth," she replied, "our donors are anonymous. Even we don't know who it is that's supporting us."

"Any idea what kinds of businesses they are?"

"Yes," she replied, the tone of her voice indicating that that line of questioning was over. "Very generous ones. That's all we need to know."

I steered the conversation back to more neutral territory, moving on to criteria number six, "has an independent board that accepts responsibility for activities." She said her agency was small and had no real need for a board of directors other than to meet the state requirements. I bit my tongue to keep from telling her that every non-profit, no matter how small, needs an active board and instead asked about the national board for CNA. She'd never dealt with them directly, but she knew that one of the members was an author of children's books, and another was a popular psychologist with a call-in radio show.

That earned another note to myself: *Celebrity board members—merely figureheads?*

I could tell this woman was ready to conclude our conversation, so I thanked her for her help, saying I had one final question.

"Go ahead."

"When you were trying to decide whether to join up with CNA or not, how did you make that decision? Did you conduct an investigation of your own?"

"Didn't have to," she replied. "Gosh, when I saw what they had to offer, I knew it was the only logical choice. It was almost too good to be true."

Once I hung up, I reset the machine and then went back to the bedroom, replaying the conversation in my mind.

Too good to be true? That definitely set some alarm bells off for me, though I knew I might be overreacting. My instincts were fairly honed in these matters, but sometimes the gut feeling I carried around about a particular nonprofit turned out to be wrong in the end. For Verlene's sake, I hoped that was the case this time. Though the organization thus far was checking out okay, once I heard "too good to be true," I knew I needed to scrutinize things twice as thoroughly.

I changed into sweatpants and crossed the hall to the office to go online, thinking it might be a good time to check out criteria number seven, "is well rated by outside reporting sources." There were two categories there, both of which were important: independent ranking sources like the Better Business Bureau and voluntary watchdog groups like the Evangelical Council for Financial Accountability. Because of my job, I subscribed to all of the Internet information services, so I was able to pull up the rankings for CNA on each of them. I was glad to see that they were rated fairly well with the American Institute of Philanthropy's Charity Rating Guide, and there were no complaints against them with the Better Business Bureau's Wise Giving Guide. I checked the rest of my sources, noting that CNA seemed to rank well across the board.

So far so good, I thought, moving along to criteria number eight, "has a good reputation among its peers." This was often my least favorite part of any investigation. Frankly, most charity directors weren't comfortable talking about other charities, particularly if it involved criticism. Often, I had to listen to what *wasn't* being said as well as what was.

One of my contacts worked for another peripheral support-type charity, American Charity Assistance, and I thought she might be a good one to ask about CNA because they were basically competing for the same market and were thus truly peers. I looked up Carlotta in my Rolodex and dialed her at home in Richmond, Virginia. Carlotta was a frequent resource for me, since she was always easy to talk to and very laid back about the whole nonprofit arena.

Once I got her on the phone and we did a little catching up, I told her why I was calling, saying that I just wanted to get her impression of another peripheral services agency for an investigation that I was working.

"Sure, hon," she said, and I could picture her settling back in her chair, removing the bifocals from the end of her nose. "Who is it?"

"It's called CNA," I said. "Comprehensive Nonprofit Alliance. Are you familiar with them?"

"Oh, sure," she said. "We did a joint project a while back with them for some emergency relief. Flood victims in Central America or something, if I recall correctly."

"What did you think of their organization?"

She seemed to give the question some thought before answering, and her hesitation made me sit up and take note.

"Overall," she said finally, "I think they're fine. Good people at the top. Well organized."

"Do I sense a little hesitation?" I asked.

She took a deep breath and let it out slowly.

"Let's just say I think the bigger clients are probably much more satisfied with CNA than the smaller ones."

"What do you mean?"

"Well, CNA provides services for a number of major charities, as I'm sure you know. The man who handles the Assocation for Cardiac

Research, for example, is a great guy. A super rep. But since that's such a large client, serving them is practically his full-time job."

"I see."

"The little agencies," she continued, "obviously can't support that kind of service. They sort of all get lumped together into one division, which is where they stay unless they grow to the point where they're no longer considered small."

I thought of the woman I spoke to yesterday who said she'd had a personality conflict with the rep for the Small Agencies Division.

"Who's in charge of the Small Agencies Division?" I asked.

"A woman named Doreen, Maureen, something like that. She's a very brash lady and not at all the type of person I would've put in charge of the little guys. She's not very client-oriented. Kind of hard to work with."

I recalled my conversation with the woman in Seattle, who had nothing but praise for CNA. That was always my biggest problem in an investigation like this. Everything was so subjective. One person's "take-charge kind of gal" was another person's "very brash lady."

"If you had a small nonprofit," I said, "would you sign up with CNA?"

"Of course not, darlin'," she said. "I'd sign up with American Charity Assistance."

I smiled.

"If you couldn't go with your own agency," I said. "Would you sign with CNA?"

She seemed to hesitate again, and I let the silence remain between us. Sometimes you get more information out of a person by letting them become uncomfortable with the void.

"Well," she answered finally, "in general, no, I would not. Maybe for payroll services and little things like that, but I wouldn't sign on for the full package they're offering. It's not cost-effective unless you're one of those rare agencies that gets one of their sweetheart local-donor deals. Those are almost too good to be true."

There it was, that statement again. The problem with things that were too good to be true was that they usually weren't true at all.

"Can you elaborate?" I asked.

"I probably shouldn't say," she told me, "but in the past I've approached small agencies about using our services, and they all told me the same thing. They'd like to work with me, but only if I could meet or beat the deal they were getting from CNA."

"And could you?"

"In some cases, yes. In other cases, I couldn't even come close."

"Why do you think that is?"

"I don't know," she replied. "Connections, I guess? Local business contacts that CNA has that I don't? One friend of mine at an agency in Miami showed me her contract with CNA, and their quarter-of-a-million-dollar budget was entirely supported by a handful of local businesses that CNA had rounded up for them. It was most impressive."

"But not every place that CNA serves has that kind of deal?"

"No. I've seen it in Miami, like I said, and there's one in Norfolk. I think the rest are out on the West Coast. Oh, maybe Boston. Seems like they had a real sweet thing going, too. Always with direct corporate support. We don't get much of that for our small agencies, I'm afraid. Well, maybe some, but only in the hundreds. They're getting donations by the thousands. In some cases, by the tens of thousands, from what I've heard."

I thought about that, wondering if Verlene would be one of the lucky few with heavy local corporate support, or if she would find CNA to be not so cost-effective, as Carlotta had said. I thanked her for her help and then hung up the phone, thinking that I definitely had more work to do, though for now I would put the investigation aside until tomorrow.

Before turning my attention to my database, I decided to take a minute and check e-mail, mainly to see if Tom had written. As I typed in my password, I wondered how his mother was doing and if he planned to call me tonight. We hadn't prearranged a time, and I felt suddenly excluded and bereft. Maybe he didn't understand that I wanted to know how she was doing, how he was doing. Maybe he didn't understand how much I cared.

Looking at my in-box, I saw that Tom had, indeed, sent me a short e-mail. He was fine. His mother was still in intensive care, but she was stable. He would call me tomorrow. I sent him a quick reply, feeling much better.

There was also an e-mail from my mother, a chatty note about how she had run into an old high school pal of mine at the grocery store.

"She looks as though she's gained a few pounds," the letter said, "but she had two adorable kids with her, both very well behaved."

This was the nature of my current relationship with both of my parents. Though we traded newsy bits of info online, we rarely spoke in person and never, ever touched on anything but the most trivial of events. It had been this way since I had moved to Maryland, and it was a shame.

In those awful, early days following Bryan's death, my parents had been as solid as a rock for me. They had cried with me and supported me and tried to keep me from going out of my mind with grief. But once I moved out here, our relationship had changed. It was my fault, I knew. Essentially, I had cut them off—almost as if I thought I could distance myself from the pain if I distanced myself from them.

One day soon I would have to take steps to repair that relationship. One day soon, but not now.

Agitated, I closed up my e-mail and exited the Internet. I had questions about Shayna's investigation, and that was where my mind should be. I opened up my database and loaded in the information about my treasure hunt with Kirby this afternoon. Once that was done, I scanned the whole file, looking for clues, looking for ideas. Finally, I reached for the phone and dialed Eli, my mentor and old friend, who was now retired and living in Florida.

"Callie, you picked a perfect time to call!" he exclaimed as soon as he realized it was me. "Stella's off playing Bunco with the girls, and I'm sitting here flipping between two TV shows, both of which are boring as anything."

"Good," I said. "I'm glad you're free. I need some help."

"Fire away, sweetheart. The TV's off. What's on your mind?"

I told him about Shayna's case, starting at the very beginning and working my way through, trying not to leave out a single detail. This wasn't the quick version I had spelled out for Kirby. This was one investigator to another, looking for clarification and illumination on details that may or may not be significant. When I had finished with my tale, Eli exhaled loudly, and I could hear him pause to light up one of his signature cigars.

"Okay," he said finally. "I'm thinking whatever this guy was cooking up, it had to be of an illegal nature. Otherwise, why all the secrecy? Didn't you say the last time he was in town, when he went through his inheritance like wildfire, that the girlfriend was privy to every detail of his various businesses?"

"Yeah," I replied. "She said he loved to come home and talk about all of his big plans, item by item. At first she had thought it was exciting, but by the end, when the money was nearly all gone and he had nothing to show for it, she really couldn't stand to listen to him. So, you're right. He did used to talk about all of it. This time, he kept it a complete mystery."

"Not to mention that this time there was no start-up cash. The guy was flat broke going in."

"Correct."

"Okay. So we have this guy, obviously up to no good, all worked up over something he found when he went on a treasure hunt for one of these capsules. But nothing was missing from the capsule. You're positive you went to the right one?"

"The next closest capsule is somewhere in South Carolina," I said. "He wouldn't have had time to get there and back in one night, not to mention that I doubt the car would've made it that far anyway."

"Okay, so we know we've got the right capsule. I'm thinking maybe blackmail? Didn't you say the guys in this club were rich?"

"Yeah, but what's to blackmail? There was nothing significant in the capsule, and I doubt there would have been unless someone had been using it as some sort of drop-off or pick-up point for something else."

"Which you've already said is unlikely considering the large size of the club and the chances of it being found by the wrong person."

"Exactly."

"All right," Eli said, puffing loudly on his cigar. "Consider the murder scene. You think the killer came there by boat, right? So at least we can narrow things down to someone with access to a boat."

"Sorry, Eli, but around here *everyone* has access to a boat."

"Okay, then let's come at it another way. Look at this man's history. He's got drug smuggling in his past. Maybe tracking down this stupid capsule made him think of some new way to smuggle drugs."

"You mean the GPS idea? I'm sure drug smugglers have caught onto these things way before now," I said. "Nothing new there."

"Maybe when he was looking for the capsule, he stumbled across something else nearby."

"Now there's an idea. The area was very deserted, plus it was right along the Intracoastal Waterway. Maybe something valuable had washed onto the shore there or something. Ships lose cargo all the time. Maybe he found something valuable and planned to sell it."

We tossed that idea around, trying to decide how I should proceed. Eli gave me some good suggestions. Still, no matter how many ideas we considered, we still couldn't come up with something that would have led to Eddie Ray's death.

"And this whole bleach thing is bothering me," he said. "That's weird. Very weird."

"I know. Once the police confirmed that it wasn't a chemical spill, I wasn't sure what to think. They searched the area but never came up with any discarded bleach bottles or anything."

"Then, of course, you smelling it later at your house changes everything," Eli said. "My mind jumps to all sorts of possibilities. Someone cleaning something? Someone trying to mask a different odor? You know, bleach can destroy DNA. I wouldn't be surprised at all if someone was trying to mess up that murder scene with a hefty splashing of Clorox."

"But nothing was disturbed when I got there," I said. "In fact, the murder scene was perfectly intact. Besides, why would I smell it again later that night? My house wasn't anywhere near the scene of the crime."

"Maybe you were being watched," Eli said. "Maybe the person watching you had spilled bleach on his clothes and that's the smell you picked up at both places."

"Yes, I had thought of that, too."

"Of course," Eli added, "there is the drug angle."

"The drug angle?"

"Some addicts think you can use bleach to sterilize needles. Maybe somebody was shooting drugs nearby and you smelled them cleaning their needles."

"In both locations?"

"Maybe not."

We were both silent for a moment, thinking.

"You sure it wasn't just somebody cleaning out their swimming pool? Chlorine has that same smell."

"No, this was stronger than that. Completely concentrated, and then it disappeared."

"Maybe somebody was using bleach instead of black pepper or gasoline."

"You've lost me."

"To disguise their trail. From police dogs. Most people would use pepper or gasoline to throw off the scent. But maybe this guy didn't have any of that, so he tried bleach instead."

At the murder scene, that would've made a fair amount of sense. But later, at my house, it just didn't hold water. I told Eli to keep thinking, that one of us was bound to figure it out sooner or later.

"So before we hang up," he said, "tell me what else has been going on. The last time I talked to Tom, he told me the two of you still hadn't had a chance to meet in person. I wish you would. I think you'd really like him."

"I already like him, Eli. We've become very close, even if it is only over the phone."

"Such safety," he chided. "Sounds like every other relationship in your life. I tell you what you need to do. You need to go out and buy yourself a barbecue grill."

"A barbecue grill?"

"Yeah. Once you got a grill, you gotta have a party. You start having parties, you start making friends, you stop being such a hermit—"

"Hey," I said, "I'll have you know I spent the day with a very handsome man, and tonight he almost kissed me."

"Almost?"

"I...I turned away."

"Aha! And if this fellow was so handsome, why did you do that?"

I told Eli to mind his own business. He laughed and said that had never been his strong suit.

But once we hung up, I had to ask myself, why did I do that? I had told Kirby I simply wasn't interested in dating anyone, which wasn't entirely true. I didn't object to the *idea* of dating.

But the reality of it scared me to death.

Twenty-Eight

After yet another night spent tossing and turning, I finally sat up at 3:00 A.M. The room was silent and dark. Sal was asleep, curled against my side as usual, but I was wide awake, my head spinning, my stomach churning. I knew it was a combination of things, not the least of which was eating such a big, rich dinner. I took some Tylenol and some Tums, brushed my teeth, fluffed up my pillows, and laid back down.

Things weren't progressing quickly enough on Shayna's investigation, I decided, with too much of my time devoted to wild-goose chases. Still, something about that place out on the waterway pulled at me. I needed to return there, alone this time so I could concentrate and see if I could figure out what it was.

By 3:30 I had to admit I wasn't going to fall back to sleep. I got out of bed, showered, and dressed in black jeans and a black shirt. As long as I was awake, I might as well make myself useful.

Driving at a more legal speed than Kirby had used, it took me about an hour and 15 minutes to get to my destination. I glanced at my watch as I got out of the car. It was nearly 5:30, at least an hour before the sun would come up. I locked up the car, but instead of clicking on the flashlight, I tucked it into my backpack and flipped on my black light. You never knew what it might illuminate in the dark.

Now that the terrain was familiar, it wasn't hard to make my way across the field to the rocks where the capsule was hidden. Once there, I spent a lot of time with my light, shining it on different surfaces, looking for evidence of blood or sweat. I didn't know what I was looking for, but it seemed as good a place as any to start. Perhaps Eddie Ray had buried something out here. Perhaps this light would show me where or what it was.

It was no use. Everything was coming up shiny—a problem I attributed to the wildness of the area and to the abundance of animal urine and the like. Finally, I clicked off the light and sat down on the highest rock, peering out over the landscape.

I don't know how long I sat there before I realized that this area wasn't quite as deserted as I had originally thought. There were lights in the distance, obviously from a house out on one of the islands. That surprised me, because I was vaguely familiar with those islands, and I had been under the distinct impression that they were deserted.

After the sun began to creep close enough to the horizon that a ring of purple framed the edge of the sky, I took out my binoculars and trained them on the third island out, the one with lights on. As I watched, the lights were extinguished, and the place once again gave the appearance of being empty. I looked closer, trying to figure out if I could see what was there.

At first, all I could pick up were trees. But the more the sun came out, the more I thought I could make out a few things hidden there among the trees. A metal folding chair. Bits of trash on the ground. A discarded sneaker. Finally, I saw a man with straight black hair come out of the woods, set something down on the ground next to the chair, sit, light up a cigarette, and smoke.

Was there a park out there? Some sort of campground, maybe? I kept my eyes trained on the man, thinking that if it were a resort he definitely had to be an employee and not a guest. He was dressed poorly in a tattered jacket and darkly stained jeans. Perhaps he was an illegal squatter using the island as a temporary home.

The man finished his cigarette, stood, walked to the edge of the water, and flicked it in. Then he came back to the chair, folded it up against the tree, and bent over to retrieve what he had set down in the first place.

It was a gun, but not a hunter's rifle. It was a *machine* gun, which he proceeded to sling over his shoulder. Then he disappeared once again into the trees.

A machine gun!

Lowering the binoculars to my lap, I thought back to what Shayna had said, that Eddie Ray had come home that night with nothing but the GPS unit, a flashlight, and a pair of binoculars. *Binoculars.* Maybe, like me, Eddie Ray had seen something suspicious out on that island—something he wasn't meant to see. Sitting here on these rocks certainly provided the perfect vantage point.

I realized this could be another wild-goose chase. It was hunting season, after all, and not everyone used weapons that were perfectly legal. But something felt so creepy about what I had just observed that I thought it deserved at least a second look. Ignoring the goose bumps covering my arms, I gathered my supplies and walked as quickly as I could back to my car.

Twenty-Nine

I pulled up to the public boat launch at a few minutes before 11:00 A.M., nervous but ready to do a little exploratory paddling. I had gone home and changed from my all-black outfit into the "yuppie outdoorsman" coat my mother had given me for Christmas last year. I wore jeans with hiking boots, the red-plaid flannel coat, and a bright red wool cap. I looked like something straight out of an L.L. Bean catalog, which was exactly the idea I was going for. Knowing that an AK-47 might be trained on me from within the trees on that island, I also had a fishing rod, a picnic basket, and a tourist's guide to the Chesapeake Bay area. *When all else fails,* I thought, *just try to look like an idiot.*

Weighing in at 49 pounds, my V-bottomed ABS travel canoe was a good deal lighter than my regular canoe. It didn't handle quite as well in rough water, which made it a bad choice for today, but it was the only one I had that was light enough for me to get on and off the cartop rack all by myself. Now, I portaged it down to the edge of the water, loaded it up, climbed in, and pushed off.

According to the chart I had studied at home, it was about a mile, over water, to the island in question. I would be coming at the island from a different direction than I had seen it from this morning, but I felt sure I would know it when I got there. In the meantime, I had to concentrate on every stroke. The canoe felt wobbly to me, probably because I hadn't used it in a while. That, combined with the wind and the tide, made for some slightly scary conditions. A hundred feet out, I paused to strap on my life jacket. Better safe than sorry.

I continued paddling, making the right turn and then the left that would take me close to the island. When I rounded the final curve, I saw a pair of tundra swans floating ahead—graceful, beautiful, and startled by my appearance. They took off into the air and I watched them fly, hoping they wouldn't go far. This was the first pair I'd seen this fall, a sure sign that winter was well on its way.

I slowed my paddling to what looked like a leisurely pace, just in case anyone on the island was watching. Then I let myself coast to a stop as I put away my paddle and got out my fishing rod.

The water was a little smoother here, I was glad to see, primarily because the islands formed a protective string of land between the main waterway and this inlet. In the distance I could see the rocks where Kirby's dad's capsule was hidden. I felt more and more certain that I was on the right track, that Eddie Ray had blundered his way into something here that had gotten him killed. I knew I had to be careful, or I could very well meet the same fate.

I fished for over an hour, catching one little trout for my trouble, which I gladly unhooked and threw back. The point wasn't the fish; it was to establish a presence out here on the water, the aura of an innocent fisherman.

Finally, just before I was about to make some sort of move that would bring me closer to the island, I picked up the faint whiff of cigarette smoke. A casual glance told me my machine-gun-toting friend was back. He was simply sitting in the chair, smoking and watching me.

Gathering my courage, I sat up straight, turned, and waved. He waved back. Clenching my teeth, I reeled in my line, set the pole down into the canoe, and picked up my paddle.

"How ya doin'?" I called as I paddled closer. "Beautiful day, isn't it?"

The man smiled and nodded, and at that point I realized that he was Asian.

"Not much bitin' out here," I said. "I'm about ready to call it a day."

He smiled and nodded again, and I wondered if he spoke English. I knew a little Japanese, and I tried that instead.

"Anata wa nihon-jin desu ka?" I asked. *(Are you Japanese?)*

Excitedly, he began nodding and replied, in Japanese, that he was. I told him, also in Japanese, that I knew just a little bit of the language. I said I had a friend who was Japanese, and she had taught me.

I didn't add that I had studied two years of the language in college in preparation for what I thought was going to be a career in international law. It was a tough language to learn, and I would've given up entirely if I hadn't made friends with a foreign student who lived down the hall in my dorm. She tutored me through both years of study, and though I had never gotten very good with reading and writing, I wasn't half bad at conversation.

Now, this man was smiling and telling me, in Japanese, that he was fairly new to the country and that he hadn't yet learned to speak English. Then another man appeared from the trees. With a chill, I suddenly remembered Dewey and Murdock talking about Kenji and Shin Tanigawa, the Japanese brothers Eddie Ray had tangled with the week before he died.

"Can I help you?" the second man asked brusquely in perfect English.

"Just doin' some fishin'," I said. "Thought I'd say hi."

"He doesn't speak English."

"I know. He's very friendly, though."

Both men looked at me, the one in the chair still smoking and smiling, the other with two hands on his hips, obviously anxious for me to be on my way.

"I didn't realize anybody lived out here on these islands," I said. "I thought they were deserted."

He was quiet for a long moment, and then he spoke.

"We have a little processing plant out here. Oysters. Clams. Crabs. Nothing elaborate."

"Do you ferry the workers in? I didn't know there was a ferry that came—"

"We have a dormitory. This is private property. I suggest you be on your way."

"Oh, sure," I said, my heart pounding. "Before I go, though, do you suppose I could use your bathroom? I really need to go."

The man looked angry and irritated, but he didn't say no. Instead, he gestured with one hand toward a small green port-a-potty I hadn't noticed before, not far up the path from where he stood.

I paddled up to the muddy bank, climbed out of the canoe, and pulled it a little way onto the grass.

"Daijyoubu," the smiling man said, helping me. *(I've got it.)*

I left the boat with him and walked past the other fellow to the bathroom. It was a standard-issue fiberglass portable toilet with a hole on a bench inside. I pulled the door shut, and waited, disappointed that the bathroom was so close by and wouldn't afford me the chance to look around on the island. But then I glanced up and realized that there was a small vent near the ceiling. Gingerly, I climbed up onto the bench and peered out of the three parallel slats.

I couldn't see much. There was a little inlet of water on the other side of the bathroom, and there was a boat there, hidden among the pickerelweed. I couldn't make out the boat's name, but I could see the registration numbers that were painted on the side. I memorized them, climbed back down, and headed out.

Something told me not to fool around here anymore, and so I thanked both men, climbed back into my boat, and paddled slowly away. Once I was around the curve and out of sight, I dug in and began paddling furiously, my mind racing as I went. It felt as if I had just taken a very stupid risk, though what that risk was and what it had to do with Eddie Ray's death, I just wasn't sure.

Yet.

Thirty

By the time I got home, the adrenaline rush had passed and I was exhausted. After the lack of sleep last night and the activity of the morning, I decided to check my machine, make any necessary calls, and then take a nap. I needed to be rested for tonight, because I had full intentions of returning to the area around the island, this time for a more discreet surveillance.

There were two messages from Kirby, apparently just to chat. There was also a call from the receptionist at my dentist's office, reminding me it was time to schedule my six-month checkup.

"Oh," her message continued, "and a little birdie told me that you've been seen about town with Kirby Collins. I've got to say, Callie, he's quite a catch!"

Rolling my eyes, I deleted her message. Sometimes small-town life could be a real pain in the neck.

Three more nonprofits had responded to my request for a reference for CNA, so I called them back. Two of them were in the Midwest, both affiliated with CNA's Small Agencies Division, and both of them painted a picture that was a bit different than the mostly favorable responses

I'd been hearing thus far. One agency was about to cancel their association with CNA entirely, and the other had already done so last week.

"I don't know why I was on your list as a reference," the woman told me. "I haven't been pleased with those people since day one."

I didn't tell her that I wasn't really working from a list of supplied references but merely from the roster of affiliated agencies.

"What don't you like about them?" I asked.

"Well, for one thing, Maureen Burnham is a nightmare to work with. She's rude and opinionated and almost impossible to reach on the phone."

"Really?"

"Yeah, especially when you have some kind of problem. It's like, if we were such a burden to her, why did she sign us up in the first place?"

Why, indeed, I thought.

I listened as this woman described an absentee agency more interested in recruitment than in the actual execution of the services they had contracted for. I took ample notes, thinking this certainly threw a monkey wrench into the mix. Yes, she said, CNA had signed on to take over the fund-raising, agreeing to handle all of those duties in exchange for a reasonable percentage of the moneys raised. Thus far, however, CNA hadn't raised nearly enough. Now this woman's organization was in a budget crunch, forced to cut services just to cover the deficit.

"What about local donors?" I asked. "From what I understand, sometimes CNA lines up local companies with charities and gets support that way."

"Maybe elsewhere, but not here," she replied. "The most they've done for us was to send out a mailing which netted almost zero response. I've never been more frustrated."

The third call, to an agency in New York City, had a far more disturbing report.

"Yeah, they lined up local donor support," the man told me. "It was a sweet deal, for sure."

"Then what was the problem?"

"I got a look at the hard numbers," he said. "I mean, most people, if the donations are rollin' in, will simply take those checks and smile all the way to the bank. I'm not like that. Ours is a faith-based operation, and I want it to be fiscally impeccable. When I insisted that Maureen show me her entire fund-raising data for our agency, I hit the roof. It was unacceptable."

I sat forward, listening.

"They spent twenty-three thousand dollars," he said, "in order to raise twenty-six thousand. Another month, it was thirty-five thousand to raise thirty-eight!"

"Could she explain why the costs were so high?"

"Yeah, she did, and it didn't sit well with me at all. She used a 'donor broker,' she said, a place that matched donating companies with local charities. Most of the money went to them, as commission."

The little warning bells in my brain turned into out-and-out sirens.

"Did you get the name of the broker?" I asked.

"No, I didn't. And they wouldn't give me the names of the 'anonymous donors' either. I terminated our association with CNA that very day."

"I don't blame you."

We talked a bit longer and then concluded the call, leaving me to consider all that he had said. I had heard of donor brokers, of course, but never ones with that kind of commission rate. Though percentages like that were legal, they certainly weren't ethical. Since CNA had good rankings with the watchdog groups, I could only assume this wasn't a company-wide way of doing business but was limited to the Small Agencies Division. Perhaps once the figures were blended together on the CNA tax returns, everything appeared to be aboveboard across the board.

I picked up the phone and dialed Verlene.

"Hey," I said when she picked up the phone, "is Maureen Burnham the name of the woman you've been dealing with at CNA?"

"Yes," she replied. "It is. Why?"

"Tell me again what she promised you. She said if you signed up with CNA, they would cover the cost of the expansion? They would use local donors?"

"Exactly. She said they already had places lined up to donate and that it was just a matter of us signing on with CNA. That's why I'm hoping your investigation is going well. I so want this to work out."

"All right, Verlene, here's what I want you to do. Give Maureen a call and tell her you're still considering her proposal, but you need to know two things."

"Okay."

"One, who are the local donors she'll be connecting you with, and two, who is the donor broker?"

"The donor broker?"

"Yes, just ask her that. Then get back to me and let me know what she says."

Verlene agreed but then inquired as to how the investigation was going thus far. I put her off, saying only that I was "making progress." Eventually, I would give her a full report, but not yet. We chatted for a few minutes before concluding our call.

A wave of exhaustion swept over me as I put down the phone, so I pushed the button on my machine and listened to the final message, which was from Max Nealson, Shayna's attorney.

Max's message said that because Shayna's fingerprints were on the tire iron, it would be good if I could dig up evidence of that flat tire she'd said she had a few weeks ago.

"I don't have much information on it," he said, "but if you could find me a corroborating witness, that would be great."

I saved his message and decided to call him back in the morning. The flat tire issue was one I had already considered, but my hope was that soon this complicated case would be unraveled, and then Shayna wouldn't have to prove anything.

There was one more thing I needed to do before I laid down for my nap. First, I retrieved the navigational chart Kirby and I had used to find the general vicinity of the GPS club capsule. I unrolled it across the counter now, leaned over it, and studied the terrain, tracing my finger down the road to Carson Point, the spot where Kirby and I had driven. The string of islands dotted out from the mainland there like a series of tiny ovals. The island I was interested in was the third one out. According to this map, it was called "Manno Island," and it was small, maybe ten or 20 acres total.

Stifling a yawn, I looked up the number of the local coast guard office. My call was answered by a friendly young enlisted man. I told him my name and said I was calling about a navigational matter.

"Well, I'll sure help you if I can," he replied brightly.

I described the island and its location, trying to be as nonchalant as possible. Then I asked if he knew whether the island was inhabited and, specifically, if there was a seafood processing plant there. He didn't seem surprised or suspicious of my question, though he did put the phone down for a minute while he discussed the matter with the other people in the office.

Yes, he told me finally, they knew which island I was talking about, and they were fairly certain there was some kind of business out there, though they didn't know any of the particulars.

"But if it were seafood processing," I persisted, "wouldn't there be a lot of fishing boats coming in and out of there? Wouldn't the coast guard have to be aware of something like that?"

"Oh, not necessarily," he said. "If it's something as simple as a crab-picking house, they might only process a couple bushels of crabs a day. That's how it is around the Chesapeake. Crab pickers'll set up shop wherever they need to, long as the state health inspectors give it the go-ahead."

I thanked him for his help and hung up the phone. The thought came to me that I could probably get more information from my old fishermen buddies Dewey and Murdock down at the Kawshek General Store.

Still, it wouldn't hurt to investigate the legal paper trail as well. I dialed Harriet at the office, knowing she was just the gal for the job.

It wasn't hard to talk her into it. She was nearly caught up on her work, and she said she would welcome the diversion.

"I'm off to Chincoteague tonight for the competition," she said. "But I'll do what I can in the meantime. I've still got a few hours before I have to head home and pack."

"Thank you, Harriet. You're the best."

"Yeah. So what kinda things do you want me to check out?" she asked.

"Start with the state health department," I replied. "Then from there just do the usual. Tax records, workers' comp, unemployment. You know the drill. We need the lowdown on this business."

"Sure enough."

I described everything I had seen, and then I gave her the location of the island—the county, the township, even the coordinates. She said it wasn't going to be easy since she didn't have the business' name as a starting point, but that she would try.

"Begin with the boat registration," I said. "You should be able to trace it to an owner."

"Will do."

I thanked her, but before we hung up I told her there was one other matter, another personal favor for a friend.

"I downloaded some financial records from the web and sent them to you," I said. "For a nonprofit called CNA. Do you think you could give it your usual perusal?"

"I guess so," she said, "but this crab thing sounds like a lot more fun."

"Do the crab business first," I told her. "Then, if you have time, look into CNA as well."

"You got it."

"Pay particular attention to the fund-raising area," I said. "I've got some red flags out, and I want your opinion."

"Will do."

We said goodbye. I hung up the phone and whispered a quick, silent prayer of thanks for Harriet. If there was a job to be done that involved finances or fact-checking or paperwork, she was the one to do it.

I put away the phone book and the map and tiredly walked back to the bedroom, hoping that, with Harriet's help, I could verify criteria nine and ten from my list, "believes in full financial disclosure" and "has books audited annually by an independent auditor and receives a clean audit opinion." If both of those were the case, then maybe we could get to the bottom of the fund-raising questions I had about CNA.

I was also waiting to get the report back from my investigator friend in Ohio.

Yawning, I pulled down the shades and slid under the covers. Sal, lazy creature that she was, was thrilled to be going to bed in the middle of the day, and once she calmed down she found her customary spot next to me and plopped into position. It didn't take long for both of us to drift off.

I slept deeply, though at some point I was vaguely aware of the phone ringing and then, a bit later, someone knocking on the door. I felt sure it was probably Verlene calling and Kirby knocking. I rolled over and went back to sleep, planning on calling them both when I got up.

I awoke just as it was getting dark. Disoriented at first, I sat up and then remembered it was sunset, not sunrise. I had a long night ahead of me, so I got up and stretched, and then I went to the kitchen to make some strong coffee to help me wake up.

I was halfway down the hall when I hesitated. Something wasn't right. I saw that the door to the carport was open a crack. Then I realized there was a figure standing at the kitchen counter—large and hunched over, doing something in my purse.

"Hey!" I yelled. At the same moment, Sal started growling.

Without looking at me, the man turned and ran out of the door. I ran after him, heart pumping furiously. I was half scared and half angry. Sal was hot on his heels.

I ran out into the carport, chilled by the cold cement on my bare feet. I could see the man making his way across my wooded lawn to the main road. He was big but fast—way too fast for me to catch up with him. I noted his clothing, though there wasn't anything remarkable about it: black coat, brown pants, dark shoes. Shivering, I watched Sal nipping after him and realized he could hurt her much worse than she could hurt him. I yelled for her to return, which she obediently did, still growling, as the man disappeared into the brush.

Back inside the kitchen, I saw that my hands were shaking. I locked the door, hugged the dog to me, and then tried to see what had been stolen from my purse. Fingers trembling, I gingerly checked my wallet, which was lying open on the counter. I counted my cash, which was all there, as were my credit cards. From what I could tell, I had surprised him before he'd had a chance to take anything.

I had one hand on the phone, trying to decide whether or not to call the police, when Sal started barking again. I jumped at a sudden sharp rap at my door.

"Callie? Are you home? It's Kirby."

Exhaling loudly, I threw open the door and flung myself into his arms.

"Hey!" he said. "Hey, what's up?"

He hugged me back tightly, though I'm sure he thought I was nuts. To make matters worse, for some stupid reason, before I could explain what was going on, I started to cry.

"Callie, what's wrong?"

I cried against him, shocked at how good it felt to have someone broad and strong to hold on to. Had it really been that long since I laid my head against a man's shoulder?

"I'm sorry," I whispered. "I was just scared."

His arm firmly around my shoulders, he led me into the living room and over to the couch. We sat together and I struggled to turn my sobs into sniffles. He handed me a tissue, which I used to dry my wet cheeks. *Breathe in, breathe out,* I told myself. Soon, I had things under control.

"Now, what on earth is going on?" Kirby asked gently.

"I'm sorry," I said, blowing my nose. "I was taking a nap, and when I got up there was an intruder. I surprised him in the kitchen. He was digging through my purse."

"What? When?"

"Just now. I chased him off. I was about to call the police when you got here."

"I didn't see anybody."

"He ran away!"

"Are you sure he was alone?"

"I think so."

Kirby gave my hand a squeeze and stood.

"Let me make sure," he said. He looked around the room for a moment and finally grabbed the poker from the fireplace. Holding it over his shoulder like a bat, he went through the house, checking each room and all of the closets. When he was finished, he went outside and around the house.

I had to admit I was glad he was there. Though I was trained in self-defense and swung a pretty mean fire poker myself, it felt good to have someone else ready to defend me for a change—especially now that something like this had happened twice in one week. While he secured the perimeter, I checked the back door to see if I could figure out how the man had gotten inside. I also sniffed around for the smell of bleach, but there wasn't any.

From what I could tell, there hadn't been any force used on the door. Tiny scratches near the keyhole might indicate a lock pick, but I could've made those scratches in the past, myself, with the key. The man had been wearing gloves, so I didn't even bother dusting for prints. In fact, it was that realization that made me decide not to call the police. Now that he was gone, leaving no evidence behind, what could they do for me I couldn't do for myself?

"Whoever he was," Kirby said, stepping back into the house, the poker dangling at his side, "he's long gone now. Are you sure he didn't take anything?"

I shook my head no, my mind racing.

"Not from my purse, at least," I said. I walked around the kitchen and then the living room, but nothing was gone, nothing appeared to have been disturbed. There was only my wallet, open on the counter, my own face peering up at me from the little window that held my driver's license.

Perhaps, I realized, that was the point. Maybe the man had been digging through my purse not to rob me but to *identify* me. Maybe he was trying to find my license, or some other ID, so he could figure out who I was and why I was poking around in things that were none of my business. If that were the case, then that meant I had struck a nerve somewhere—probably at the island.

"Do you have a gun?" Kirby asked me.

I looked at him blankly.

"A gun," he repeated. "You're an investigator. Don't you carry a gun?"

I shook my head.

"I don't like guns," I said. "Long story."

I didn't add that years ago my brother, Michael, a cop, had been shot on the job and nearly died. The experience had been traumatic for the whole family, and after that I found I was not comfortable around guns or ammunition.

"So how do you protect yourself?"

"I have my ways," I said defensively. The truth was, I rarely found myself in much danger anymore. These days the majority of cases I worked had nothing to do with murder or death.

Suddenly, I was feeling very stupid for having cried in front of Kirby. I knew it had been mostly physical—a combination of having been so tired and then having been so startled. But now here he was thinking I was a helpless female, when in fact I could probably have him on the floor begging for mercy by the count of three.

"If you really want to know," I said, "I can do street fighting."

"Street fighting?"

"My dad taught me when I was a teenager."

"What is that, exactly?"

"Strategic defense. I'm not as big and strong as you are, but I can go for your weak points. Grind my heel into your instep. Knee you in the groin. Poke my car keys into your eyes."

"What if I grab you before you have a chance to do any of that?" he asked, looking skeptical.

"Then I use your weight and momentum as my defense."

"Hey, I know you're in good shape and all, but I doubt you could hold your own against me if push came to shove."

"Wanna try me?"

For some reason, I felt the need to prove my toughness. I knew it was immature, but there you go. I stared at Kirby with challenge, promising myself I wouldn't cry in front of a man again for a long, long time.

"You serious?" he said.

"Let's take it outside."

Grinning, Kirby followed me out the door and across the lawn to the softest part of the grass. I turned to face him and bent my knees slightly, arms loose at my sides.

"Attack me," I said.

"I'm not sure if I can."

"Scared?"

"No," he said, "but you're a girl."

"Don't think of me as a girl. Think of me as a victim. And you're the bad guy."

"If you say so."

He came at me halfheartedly, without much movement. The best I could do was grab his wrist and twist it around behind him, my knee to the small of his back.

"Ouch!"

"Do it again," I said, pushing him away. "This time try to act like you mean it. Don't be such a wimp."

He shook out his shoulders, obviously aggravated.

"Go ahead," I goaded. "Give it your best shot. You big baby."

Sure enough, this time he lunged. I turned and bent, using my body as a fulcrum, pulling him forward over my back until he flipped and was suddenly on the ground, upside down, staring up at me.

"That's street fighting," I said with a grin.

Groaning, Kirby got up and dusted off his pants, his pride obviously wounded more than his body. He rubbed the small of his back and grimaced.

"Okay, so maybe you don't need a gun," he said.

Together we went back inside. I felt much better, as if the score had been evened out somehow.

"Would you mind making me a cup of coffee?" he asked, sitting gingerly at the table. "I usually like a warm beverage after I've been ground into the dust by a girl."

I laughed and stepped toward the counter, more than happy to comply.

Thirty-One

A half hour later, the coffeepot was empty, Kirby seemed to almost have recovered from our bout in the ring, and I had filled him in completely on my morning's adventure at the island. He wanted me to call the police and tell them everything, but I forcefully declined. If I was already getting on their bad side, it would only be to my detriment to call them in now. I was afraid if that Litman guy heard about this he might try to put the brakes on my entire investigation, and that would leave poor Shayna without any outside help save for her overworked public defender.

Once Kirby got over his shock at my audacity for going to the island disguised as a tourist, he agreed with my thought that today's intruder in my home might've been on a fact-finding mission—and that I had probably stirred up a hornet's nest at the island with my appearance there this morning. He didn't necessarily agree that this was the road that would lead to Eddie Ray's killer, but he said that since it was a possibility it was probably worth pursuing. I told him that sometimes you have to follow your instincts, even if they seem a bit far-fetched.

Finally, we began to brainstorm about the island and what might possibly be going on there that would require the presence of an armed guard. Our suggestions ranged from "religious cult" to "crack laboratory"—and those were the least ridiculous of the bunch.

"Doesn't have to be crack," Kirby said. "Could be man-made heroin, ecstasy, or amphetamines. Maybe they're producing drugs there and smuggling them out with the seafood."

"Okay, so let's say it is a drug lab of some kind masked as a seafood processing plant, and Eddie Ray found out about it. What would have been his next move? Do you think he would've just gone out there and signed himself up as part of the team?"

"No telling," Kirby said. "More likely, he tried to steal some of the drugs and got caught. Or, maybe he was blackmailing someone with what he knew. Any of those actions could have led to his being murdered."

I stood and began pacing, thinking of what Eli had said about junkies using bleach to clean their needles.

"I've got to get back on that island and get a good look around," I said.

"No way," Kirby replied. "You said it yourself. They have machine guns."

"Yeah, I know. You're right."

I continued to pace, thinking I would have to go with my original plan of surveillance from a distance. Now that I'd had an intruder, however, before I could start watching them, I would first have to make sure that they weren't watching me.

"Hey, whatcha doing tonight?" I asked.

"Well, I came over here to see if you wanted to go to dinner."

"Forget dinner," I said. "Let's synchronize our watches. We've got more important things going on."

Before I could explain further, the phone rang. It was Verlene, and she was angry.

"Thanks a lot, Callie!" she cried. "Maureen Burnham is threatening to withdraw her entire offer."

"What?"

"I did what you said. I called and asked her about the donors and the donor broker. She started yelling at me, saying that their donors always remained anonymous, and that if I thought she was going to give me the name of her donor broker, I must be crazy. It was a very upsetting phone call, to say the least."

I waited a beat. We had obviously struck a nerve.

"Okay, Verlene," I said calmly. "Don't be angry. This is actually an important development in this case."

"It is? How?"

"I don't have time to go into it now, but I've got to tell you that I have a few concerns about CNA. There's something fishy there. This woman's response to your questions only confirms that for me."

"Oh, no," she moaned. "I *knew* this was too good to be true. Now what are we going to do? We need that money if we're going to expand!"

I told her not to get ahead of herself here. There was still a chance that things would check out okay in the end, but I had more investigating to do first.

"I just can't tell you how badly I want this to work out," she said. "Besides the bigger space, I was hoping to use their services for the accounting and the taxes and the purchasing and the—"

"Verlene," I said, interrupting her. "I know you're overloaded there with work and could use the help. But you said it yourself, we've got to be prudent. Let's not make a bad decision in haste just because of our immediate need. Okay?"

"Okay," she said, sighing loudly.

Once I had placated her somewhat, I got her off of the phone, and then I asked Kirby if he would mind waiting just a bit longer while I called my investigator friend in Akron, Gordo Koski.

"Sure," Kirby said. "Do whatever you need to do. I'm just enjoying watching you work."

I felt a blush creep across my face as I averted my gaze and dialed.

"Hey, gorgeous!" Gordo said loudly when he answered the phone. He wasn't hard of hearing, but he always spoke at top volume over the phone.

"Hi, Gordo," I said. "You gather any information for me yet about CNA?"

"Yeah, I'm done, but I haven't learned much, I'm afraid. They got a big building, one hundred and twenty-three employees, five divisions, nine board members. Good reputation, far as I can tell."

"Tell me about the board. I understand there are some big names on there. Are they primarily figureheads?"

"Well," he said, "you'd probably have to sit in on a board meeting to answer that question. But judging by their credentials alone, it looks like a pretty impressive group."

"How about the top executives of the company?"

"They check out. I did like you said, made a drive-by of all of their houses. By and large, the places were fairly modest. Nobody seems to be living high on the hog."

"By any chance," I said, "did you check out a woman named Maureen Burnham?"

"Maureen Burnham?"

I could hear the shuffling of papers.

"No, you said do the upper echelon. According to the employee roster I got, she's a little way down on the totem pole. She's not even a vice president. Just a division head."

"Do you mind looking into her?" I asked. "Her name keeps popping up, and I'm a little concerned."

"Sure, kid. What am I looking for?"

I leaned forward on one elbow and closed my eyes.

"I don't know. I'd love to have an idea of her work history, maybe her qualifications for the job she's in now."

"Go on."

Gordo was quiet at the other end of the line, and I smiled, picturing him with his flame of red hair and a stubby little pencil tucked behind his ear. An old PI buddy of my mentor Eli, Gordo had known me for ages, probably for as long as I had been a detective. Though he knew I didn't do regular detective work anymore, last year he had called and asked if I could help him out with a child support case since the man in question had moved to Baltimore. I hadn't minded. If fact, it was kind of fun to get back into the old investigating mode again.

The subject of the investigation was a fellow who hadn't paid child support in more than two years, claiming that he didn't have the funds. He had no inkling that I was following him, and on the second day of my surveillance I had been able to get some lovely photos of him out on the water in his new Cobalt 360 luxury sport cruiser. At a price tag of well over $200,000, I knew his kids wouldn't be neglected any longer.

Needless to say, now it was Gordo's chance to return the favor.

Of course, if I were doing an investigation on behalf of the J.O.S.H.U.A. Foundation, I would be flying to Cleveland to handle all of this legwork myself. But considering the situation, and my limited time and resources, I thought that using Gordo was a good solution.

"Here's the deal," I said. "This woman is the head of her division, and one of her responsibilities is to arrange fund-raising for smaller charities. To tell you the truth, I'm a bit leery of her methods. In one instance, she paid out about twenty-five thousand dollars in order to raise a net of *three* thousand dollars. That's just not right."

I went on to explain the woman used "donor brokers," but she was very tight-lipped about the identity of both the donors and the brokers.

"Ah ha," Gordo said when I finished. "So what you'd really like are some names."

I grinned.

"Do what you can," I said. "But, yeah, if you could get me some inside scoop there, I would really appreciate it."

"I'll give it my best shot."

We talked a few more minutes, and I gave him all of the information I could think of that might help him out. When I hung up the phone, of course Kirby was dying to learn what I was talking about as well. I gave him the quick version.

"But enough of that," I said finally, ready to change gears back to Shayna and her problems. I flashed Kirby my most persuasive smile. "How'd you like to do a little detecting of your own?"

Thirty-Two

By 7:30 I was pulling into the parking lot of the Kawshek General Store. My hope was that Dewey and Murdock were hard at work inside, maybe mending another net, and that they would be in the mood to talk. I wanted to ask about Manno Island, and I wanted to find out more about the Japanese brothers, Kenji and Shin Tanigawa.

"I'm here," I said softly into my cell phone, "just pulling into the parking lot now."

"Okay," Kirby replied, talking from the cell phone in his car. "You should see him any minute. Probably coming around the curve right about now."

I twisted my rearview mirror so that I could look up the way I had just come without appearing to be watching. Sure enough, after a moment a gold Pontiac minivan rounded the curve and then slowly drove on past the parking lot. Two beats later, I could see Kirby's car also coming around the curve.

"Howdy," I said into the phone.

"Hello," he replied, though when he drove past me, we didn't acknowledge each other with a look or a wave. "Okay," he said. "He's pulled to a stop on a side street. Should I park, too? I can stick with him on foot."

"No," I replied. "I just wanted to know if I was being followed. Now I know. You got the plate number, right?"

"Right, but don't you think you're in danger?"

"Not here," I said. "Too public."

"Okay," Kirby said. "Well, I've driven past him now, but I'll double back so I can watch the watcher. I don't think he's spotted me."

"I'm going inside," I said. "I'll call you back when I'm done."

I hung up the phone, slid it into the pocket of my red-plaid coat, got out of the car, and headed to the door. The bell jangled as I stepped inside, and I realized immediately that no one was there except Stinky. He was on a low stool in front of a shelf of canned goods, marking the cans with an old-fashioned ink-stamping pricer.

"Excuse me," I said, watching him work, wondering if he even knew that scanners and bar codes had been invented. "I'm looking for Dewey and Murdock."

"Not here," he said.

"Have you seen them this evening?"

"Yep, a while ago."

"Do you know where they are now?"

Stinky paused in his stamping to look at me over his shoulder. He seemed to size me up before finally returning to his stamping. He said they were over at the community church, as far as he knew, printing up the bulletins for Sunday's service.

"Where's that?" I asked.

"Go out the back door and walk up the pier 'bout two blocks. Big white community chapel. Can't miss it."

"Super. Thanks."

I did as he instructed, walking out of the store's back door and onto the dock area. There were quite a few people sitting around or milling about the boats in the marina. Music blared from the bar next door, and people came and went from there noisily.

Pulling out my cell phone, I called Kirby and told him what I was doing.

"I'm about a block and a half over," he said softly. "I can see him, and he's just sitting there, watching your car. I think you're okay."

I turned and walked away from the din. Though the sun had already set, a number of streetlights illuminated the whole place, so at least it seemed safe and exposed, not dark and hidden. I was glad. I was feeling a little spooked despite Kirby's protective presence.

"I'm going to hang up now," I said, "but call me if he gets out of his car."

"Will do."

Slipping the phone back into the pocket of my coat, I ignored the chill and headed up the pier away from the store and the bar in the direction Stinky had indicated. I could see the white building with a cross in front at the end of the next block, and it looked as though my walk would be lighted all the way.

As I went I thought about the church and its place in this fishing community. I wondered how many members it had and if they always made a practice of caring for newcomers as thoroughly as they had embraced Shayna. *God's love in action,* my old pastor used to call it. Some churches were so intent on saving souls they ignored anything that came *after* the moment of decision. Conversely, this church had really followed up with Shayna, helping her get her life together, showing her a way out of her destructive cycle. I thought that any group with that kind of compassion and dedication had to be on the right track.

The place wasn't locked, and I could hear talking from inside the building as soon as I opened the door. Following the voices, I found Dewey and Murdock at the far end of what looked like a fellowship hall, sitting in a small alcove next to a copy machine. The machine was printing bulletins, and the two men were sitting side by side at a table, folding the bulletins in half and putting them into a small pile between them.

"Evening, gentlemen," I said. "Remember me?"

"Well, if it isn't our friendly neighbor!" Dewey cried, looking up. "Candy, right?"

"Collie," corrected Murdock. "Like the dog."

"It's Callie," I replied. "Callie Webber. Do you guys have a minute? I need to talk to you."

"Well, sure," Murdock said, starting to rise.

"Don't get up," I told him. I grabbed a folding chair from the fellowship hall and set it next to the copy machine. As I sat, the machine finished its run, so I took the stack of bulletins from the tray and joined the two men in their folding.

"Do you get a lot of people here on Sundays?" I asked, surprised at the size of the pile.

"This time of year, 'bout two hundred," Murdock said.

"Two hundred? From Kawshek?"

"From all over. This is a watermen's church, which is why it's near the marina. We serve a couple of other fishing villages that don't have a church of their own. They come over here for our services."

"That's great."

"Yeah, well, we don't kid ourselves," Murdock said, shaking his head sadly. "A lot of 'em are just coming to socialize. I'd say half the folks who are in here on Sunday morning will be back in the bar by Saturday night."

"So what can we do for you?" Dewey asked. "You looking for a church for yourself? We'd be right glad to have you here, you know."

"Thank you, no. I already have a church," I said. "I'm here on a different matter."

I folded a bulletin in half and then ran my thumb down the crease, smoothing it out.

"I wasn't completely honest with you fellows the other day," I said. "I am a neighbor, and I am a friend of Shayna's. But I'm also a private investigator—"

"You're a what?" Dewey asked.

"She's a private investigator," Murdock explained. "A PI!"

"Anyway," I interjected, "I'm working for Shayna Greer. Right now, I'm trying to find out who really killed Eddie Ray Higgins."

Murdock let out a low whistle.

"Shayna didn't do it?" he asked.

"She says she didn't. And I believe her."

"Well, how do you like that? It did seem awful shocking, but then again I learned a long time ago not to be surprised by the things people do."

"I truly believe she's innocent," I said. "I think Eddie Ray was mixed up in something that got him killed, and it was just set up to look like Shayna did it."

"Could be," said Murdock. "Could very well be."

"In any event," I continued, glancing at my watch, "I need some information, and I was hoping you fellows might be able to help."

"If we can. Shoot."

I placed a folded bulletin on the pile and leaned forward, elbows on my knees.

"Either of you guys ever heard of Manno Island?"

"Manno Island? Yeah, I think so. South of here? Not very big. Runs out from Carson Point."

"That's the one."

"What about it?"

"What do you know about what's on it?"

The men looked at each other and then at me.

"Golly day," Murdock said. "You think one of the Tanigawa brothers killed Eddie Ray?"

My pulse surged.

"Is that where they live?"

"Yeah. That's the place."

"What's out there? I thought the island was deserted."

"I ain't never been there," Dewey said, shaking his head. "I don't trust those fellows. Don't do business with them."

"I been a few times," Murdock said. "Last spring, when my daughter was in a cast. She does all my crab picking, see, at the co-op here in town. But she slipped at the dock and broke her wrist and ended up with a cast all the way out to the end of her fingertips. She was bound up like that for 'bout six weeks. So, in the meantime, I sold some crabs to the Tanigawas. They got a picking house down there."

"A picking house?"

"Yeah. You know, crab processing."

"Other people work there, too?"

"Oh, sure, lots."

"How many?"

"Let's see. When I was there, I'd say I saw 'bout thirty or so, all Japanese, all of them picking crabs."

I was about to question him further when he burst out laughing.

"If you could call it picking," he said. "I tell you what, those folks didn't have a clue what they was doing. It's a miracle they didn't cut their fingers off."

"Or smash 'em with the mallet," Dewey added.

"But they paid good for the crabs," Murdock continued. "I figure if they can't pick right, it's no skin off my nose. I got my money up front."

"Where do the workers live?" I asked. "There on the island?"

"Yeah. There's a little cinder-block dormitory behind the picking house."

"Do they ever come into town? Do they come here to your church?"

Murdock picked up the stack of folded bulletins and rapped them against the table, squaring the pile.

"Well, the Tanigawa brothers are here in town kind of frequently," Murdock said. "Probably a couple times a week. But now that you mention it, I never do see any of those workers here. I suppose they keep to themselves. Dewey, you ever see any other Japanese people around town?"

"Never. I know a couple nice Japanese families that live in Easton. But they don't have anything to do with the Tanigawas."

"Yeah, I don't think anybody 'round here wants to have anything to do with those brothers."

I sat back, thinking. I knew that everything Murdock had told me fit with my theory of a drug lab—particularly the fact that the people who worked in the picking house hadn't a clue how to actually pick. The Tanigawas must buy a small but steady quantity of crabs to provide a cover for what was really going on there.

"How much can you tell me about the layout of the island?" I asked. "How much of it did you actually see?"

"Oh, just a little bit," Murdock said. "They've got a dock on the northern tip, with a kind of a rough ramp that goes up to the picking house. When I went there, I usually just tied off at the dock, helped unload some bushels into the picking house, and then I left."

"Would you say that they get a fair amount of boat traffic in and out of there?"

"Gosh, no," Murdock said. "I only know one other fella who sells to them regular, and even then it's only fifteen, twenty bushels a week. That's probably all the traffic they get. I think Shin runs the picked crab out to the distributor himself. He's got a nice little eighteen-foot runabout."

"Which one is Shin? The one who speaks English?"

"Yeah. From what I understand he's lived in the States most of his life. Kenji just moved over from Japan a few years ago."

"Do the brothers live in the dormitory with the crab pickers?"

"No, there's a little house there on the island, too. They stay there, I believe."

"How long have they been there?" I asked.

"Gee," Murdock said, scratching his chin. "Couldn't tell you. Two years? Two and a half? I don't remember exactly."

I nodded, pleased with the amount of information these men had been able to give me. I thanked them for their trouble and told them I would be on my way.

"You going back to the marina?" Dewey asked. "We'll walk with ya. We're done here."

Grateful for the escort, I stood where I was and waited until they walked into the sanctuary with the pile of bulletins before making a quick, quiet call to Kirby. I told him the men were going to walk me back to the store, and he could go ahead and leave.

"You've got lots to do," I whispered. "You'd better get moving."

"You're sure you'll be safe coming home?"

"He didn't try anything on the way out. I doubt he'll try anything on the way back."

"Okay," Kirby said. "Call me if you run into trouble."

We disconnected just as the men returned.

"Alrighty," Murdock said. "If you'll get the lights, we'll be on our way."

I turned off the light, they locked the door, and we headed out. It had grown colder while we were inside, and I pulled my coat tightly around me as we went.

We hadn't gone far when I noticed a movement to one side. It wasn't much, really, just a shadow that flickered across the next building as we walked past. I hesitated, my heart pumping. A moment later, I distinctly heard the soft crunch of gravel behind us.

We were being followed.

We walked on. Murdock was chattering away, though I wasn't really listening. Without question, I could sense that someone was behind us, by my guess only about ten or 15 feet back. I was tempted to spin around, and I kept thinking, *Does this person mean me harm, or is he simply keeping tabs on me?* Worse than that, if I was in danger and he was about to make a move, had I now endangered these two sweet old men as well?

I kept walking forward, ears alert, adrenaline flowing, my body ready to spring into action if necessary. I thought if we could only make it to the marina safely, then I could confront the person without as much risk to my two companions. I increased our pace and my two buddies followed suit, though Murdock began to sound a little breathless as he talked. Deep in my coat pocket I fingered my car keys, holding them so that the longest, sharpest key pointed forward like a dagger. I thought about using the other hand to call Kirby, but I knew he would already be several miles away by now and unable to be of any real help.

Finally, I realized, there was a boat docked just up ahead, a trawler, that had several big, strong men on board. They were working on something mechanical, and one held a bright light while the other two clanged away with wrenches and pliers. I knew it was my time to make a move, though before I could turn around, one of the men on the boat waved and called out.

"Evening, Murdock. Dewey. Ma'am."

"How's it going, Claude?" Murdock replied loudly with a wave.

"Just fine. Is that you back there, Hank?"

I spun around to see the man behind us. He was walking with both hands in his pockets, head down from the cold. It was Hank Hawkins, the great big fellow with the scar who had been dating Shayna before Eddie Ray came back to town.

Hank Hawkins had been following us.

"Yep," he acknowledged, waving at the men on the boat. "It's me. How ya doin'?"

We kept walking, though in our hesitation Hank caught up with us. Dewey and Murdock greeted him as well, and the four of us continued on toward the store together.

My mind was spinning. Was he merely walking into town after us, and I had mistaken him for a tail? I didn't know whether to feel like an idiot or to be doubly on my guard. It seemed just too much of a coincidence that a man on my list of suspects for Eddie Ray's murder had been the one behind us on this dark night, hiding in the shadows.

Then again, this was an awfully small town.

"Howdy, folks!" a woman's voice called.

I looked toward the marina to see Russell and Tia Lynch in the back of a large boat. It looked like a tourist vessel, with double-decker observation areas and a small snack bar. Usually, these kinds of boats could be seen cruising up and down the rivers, blaring narration or music over their loudspeakers, offering either nature tours or party trips, depending on the company running the show. But this boat was devoid of people or chairs, its decks wide and empty. I realized this must be the water taxi, the vessel that had led to the dispute between Russell and Eddie Ray.

Tia was sitting on the back of the boat, smoking and drinking from a bottle of beer. Russell was leaning down over a toolbox, fooling with the engine.

"Evenin' to ya," Murdock called. "How's the water tonight?"

"Getting ready to go fishing," Russell said, glancing up at us. "But it was smooth as glass coming over here."

Our group of four walked to the edge of the dock where we could converse. I needed to keep moving, but I thought I had a few minutes to spare.

"Hey, Callie," Russell said, tipping his hat to me. "I didn't see you there. Thanks again for bringing that wire out to me."

"What's that?" Tia asked, leaning slightly forward.

"This is the lady I told you about, the one who brought me the wire for the fence."

She looked me up and down. Suddenly I felt exposed and defensive.

"That was a long way to go for a little wire," she said evenly. She wasn't an unattractive woman, but there was something harsh about her features.

"I didn't mind," I replied, trying to sound as warm and friendly as possible. "I know what it's like to run out of something you need."

"I bet you do," she said, still eyeing me. I realized suddenly that she was half drunk, and a chill ran up and down my bones. James Sparks had been drunk when he drove the boat that killed my husband.

"Are you going to drive this boat?" I couldn't help but ask her.

"Me? Are you kidding? I don't even like to ride on it. I just caught a lift with my husband so I could visit my mama."

Dewey hooted.

"Is your mama in the bar, Tia?" he cackled. "'Cause I'd be willing to bet that's where you're headed next!"

To my surprise, Tia just laughed.

"I'll get down to Mama's eventually," she said, winking at Dewey.

"Hey, Murdock, can you give me a hand with this winch?" Russell asked, oblivious to all of the interaction around him. Murdock stepped closer to the boat, and I took that moment to say my goodbyes and make my exit. I had lots to do, and time was ticking away.

I left them all clustered there at the dock and went up the narrow walkway along the side of the store.

As soon as I got in the car, I turned it on and cranked up the heater, holding my hands in front of the vents for warmth. I glanced at the spot up the street where Shayna's apartment sat looking dingy and forlorn in the darkness. There was no police tape there anymore, and I could only assume that the pool of Eddie Ray's blood had been washed from the driveway by somebody's garden hose.

I put the car in gear and looked back over at the people who were still there at the dock: Russell and Murdock, busy with the engine. Tia, leaning back to take a long swallow of beer. Dewey, his shock of white hair whipping loosely in the wind.

And Hank, standing on the edge of the group, watching me intently. Looking back at him, I gasped as I realized what he was wearing: a black coat, brown pants, and dark shoes.

Thirty-Three

According to my watch, I made it back home on schedule. The place was dark except for the lamp I kept on a timer.

I pulled into the driveway and parked in the carport, as usual. I made a lot of noise getting out of the car, rattling my keys, banging my purse against the door. Fortunately, my noise caused no barking, because Sal was safely ensconced elsewhere. Whistling a tune, I unlocked the house, stepped inside, and shut the door firmly behind me.

I had to admit, it was creepy coming into my home—the home that had earlier been invaded—knowing there was already someone inside. I put my purse on the counter and walked back to my bedroom. The door was slightly ajar. I pushed it further open and clicked on the light.

Mr. Buchman—Kirby's butler—was sitting on the edge of my bed, as planned. He was looking grim but willing, which was about what I had expected.

"I sure do appreciate you doing this," I said, peeling off my coat and handing it to him. He was already wearing black pants and a black shirt, the same as me.

"I don't know how I let that young man talk me into these things," he said, sighing.

I pointed toward the chair at my dressing table and waited as he stood, stepped over to it, and sat.

"Kirby says you're a very, very good sport."

"Would I be here if I weren't?"

He handed me the brown wig he had brought with him, a remnant of Grace Collins' struggle with cancer. According to Kirby, she'd had several wigs, one of which was just about the color and length of my hair.

I worked with Mr. Buchman, smoothing his own hair down with bobby pins, pulling on the wig, and then styling it in the familiar chignon I always wore. It was a lot harder to do to someone else than it was to myself, and it took several tries before I got it right.

As I worked, I told him a little about Shayna and her plight so he would understand what was at stake here—and that the favor he was doing wasn't just for Kirby, but for a poor girl who had been unjustly accused of murder.

He seemed appropriately impressed, so much so that by the time I was done, he actually smiled.

"In broad daylight," he said, looking at himself in the mirror, "about the only person who might mistake me for you is my poor mother, who has cataracts so bad she can barely make out the side of a house."

"That's why we're lucky this isn't broad daylight," I replied, grinning.

Truly, the man was a sight. He had my hair, but underneath was the unmistakable face of an older man, complete with silver sideburns and full jowls. My only hope was that the bright red coat would be the clincher—and that whoever was following me didn't have binoculars.

"I think we're ready," I said.

He stood and put on the coat.

"The window is still unlocked," he said. "Oh, and the little dog seems perfectly happy back at the house."

I nodded, handed the man my keys, and wished him luck.

"You understand that you must stay on the main roads at all times," I told him. "Though I don't think this fellow is going to do anything, I don't want you in any danger whatsoever."

"Kirby wrote out my directions," he said. "I'm going over the Bay Bridge and then down to Alexandria, buy a box of donuts at Krispy Kreme, and then drive all the way back here."

"Do you have a cell phone with you?"

"Check."

"Keep your speed down," I said. "You want to stretch this out as long as possible. 'Operation Decoy,' you know."

"I understand. Good luck to the two of you as well."

We shook hands and then he turned off the bedroom light, leaving me in darkness. I watched from the doorway as he stepped down the hall, grabbed my purse from the counter, and walked out the door, whistling the same tune I had whistled when I came in. Heart pounding, I listened as he locked the door. A few moments later, he started the car and drove away.

All was silent. I checked my watch and decided to wait ten minutes before I, too, headed out.

In the meantime, I crept to the window and peeked out, not surprised to see the familiar Pontiac pass by, driving off down the road in the same direction Mr. Buchman had just driven. So far, so good.

Back in the dark bedroom, I stripped down and then pulled on my "dry suit"—a scuba getup that would be a bit warmer than my wet suit. It was snug but not uncomfortable. I added rubber socks, and then I pulled the outfit I had been wearing back on. Two more layers of warm clothes completed my outfit, which I topped off with a black cap and my black vinyl jacket.

I sat on the bed and dialed Harriet's cell phone, feeling guilty for disturbing her on the way to her dancing competition. But I needed some answers, and I hadn't had a chance to check in with her before now.

"Hello!" she yelled into the phone. There were loud voices and music and lots of background noise. "Hold on!"

I heard her telling everyone to be quiet. The music was turned down, and she came back on the line.

"I'm sorry," she said in a more normal tone. "This is Harriet. Can I help you?"

"It's Callie."

"Callie! Can you believe the noise these women can make in a car? My goodness, a person can't hear themselves think!"

"I'm sorry to bother you," I said. "You must be on your way to Chincoteague."

"Yep. Just crossed into your county now. My land, I don't know how you drive over that Bay Bridge all the time. It's so high! I swear, it would scare the stuffing out of a roasted turkey. I had to close my eyes."

"I hope you weren't the one driving!"

She laughed.

"No," she said. "I wouldn't do anything *quite* that stupid."

I glanced at my watch, aware I had to keep things moving.

"I was wondering if you were able to find anything for me," I said.

"Yeah," she replied. "A whole lot."

"Can you talk right now?"

"I can do better than that," she said. "The girls want to stop in Cambridge for dinner. Why don't you come and meet us there?"

We figured out the timing, and I thought it might work. She named the place they were going, and I said I would see her there. We hung up, and then I stood and took a deep breath.

It was time to go. I slipped two pairs of hand warmers into my pockets, tucked some power bars and a bottle of water into my backpack, and checked to make sure that I had my binoculars, night-vision goggles, hood, scuba mask, and my portable air tank.

Finally, I went to the window, slid it open silently, and climbed from the bedroom out onto the deck. I listened to the stillness, thinking again how awful it was to have had my peaceful home invaded by an intruder this afternoon. Always my sanctuary, the house felt a little less perfect now, a little less mine.

I slid the window shut, turned, and climbed over the rail to the ground below. I hit the grass with a gentle thud and took off across the lawn, keeping to the trees, listening for any other activity. I didn't hear or see anything suspicious, and finally I reached the dock. As expected, the little motorboat was waiting there for me—the same boat that Mr. Buchman had used to get here.

I climbed in and pushed off, grateful that the sky was clear so the moon could shine through. I didn't like rowing at night, and it was particularly tough in such an unwieldy craft. But I was afraid of the noise the motor would make, so I hooked the two oars in the oarlocks, turned around, and rowed the whole way, hoping there were no hidden obstacles floating in my path.

It took only about 15 minutes to get to Kirby's, and he was there waiting for me at his dock. He, too, was dressed all in black, though I had a feeling his jacket was not off the rack, as mine was. I enjoyed wearing designer clothes, too, a luxury I had grown to appreciate in connection with my job. When I went out on business for the foundation, Tom expected me to dress as an upper-level executive; he even provided me with a generous clothing allowance so I could do so. But on my own time, for an all-night surveillance that might get kind of dirty, I was more comfortable in something that wasn't nearly as expensive.

"You made it!" Kirby cried, eyes bright with excitement. I smiled at him, but as I climbed from the boat and handed him the rope, I knew we needed to have a little talk. Investigating could be fun, especially on a night like tonight, but level heads were what we needed now, not uncontainable enthusiasm.

I watched as Kirby stepped onto the grass and pulled the boat along the shoreline toward a little shed that was nearly hidden in the trees. As he secured it there, I took off my hat and let down my chignon. The bobby pins were pinching my scalp. But before I could pin it back again, higher this time, Kirby whispered to me across the lawn.

"Wait!" he said.

He jogged over to me and, much to my surprise, came to a stop right in front of me.

"Don't do a thing," he said. He looked at me with a startling intensity, and it took a minute for me to understand what was going on.

"Pocahontas," he whispered. "I knew it. With your hair down, you could be Pocahontas."

"Kirby, don't—"

"You're so beautiful," he said. "Why do you try to hide it?"

His eyes locked onto mine, and for some reason I met his gaze with my own. It had been an odd couple of days, but something about this man attracted me at a very basic level.

Slowly, he reached up and ran his hands through my hair. It felt good. It felt better than good. Bravely, I went with the moment and closed my eyes.

"Callie," he whispered, leaning into me.

To my surprise he didn't try to kiss me. Instead, he brushed his lips against my cheek, my ear, my hair. Then he pulled me into an embrace, holding me tightly against him.

"I know you don't feel the same, but I'm so crazy about you," he whispered.

I held onto him, realizing I didn't really know how I felt about him. Yes, he was handsome and charming and imminently likeable.

But he was no Bryan.

"We have to go," I said brusquely, regretting it even as I said it. He released me and stepped away, and suddenly I felt mean and selfish and stupid. Kirby was in the here and now. Bryan was not—and never, ever would be again.

"Kirby."

There must've been something in my voice, some note that gave him hope, because he looked at me, expression open, for what I would say next.

"I'm sorry I keep pushing you away," I said. "I like you, too."

At first, surprise widened his eyes. Then slowly, ever so slowly, he placed his hands on each side of my face, leaned forward, and touched his lips to mine.

It wasn't an urgent kiss. It wasn't an earth-shattering kiss. But then he came back a second time, his lips pressing into mine and then lingering sweetly, and I felt something in me awaken, some memory of being held and being loved and being treasured this way. I closed my eyes and kissed him back and tried not to let thoughts of Bryan fill my head.

Finally, the kiss ended and he stayed very close, his forehead touching mine, his fingers gently teasing at my hair. He exhaled slowly, his breath sweet and warm against my skin.

"I've wanted to do that since the first time I saw you out on your canoe," he said.

"Baggage," I whispered. "Please remember that I come with a lot of baggage."

"I have no expectations," he said.

"And I make no promises," I replied.

That established, we finally stepped apart. He comfortably took my hand, and together we went to his car. There was still much to do on this night. I could only hope that what had just happened wouldn't be a distraction—especially one that might put us in danger.

Thirty-Four

I heard the women before I saw them. They were in the side room of a roadside café, and as Kirby and I came through the door, the chortle of Harriet's laughter filled my ears.

"We're meeting someone," I said to the waitress at the hostess booth. Then we headed for the side room and wove our way among tables toward the group of five ladies who sat in the back corner.

"Callie!" Harriet cried, waving at me. She stood up, and I realized she was dressed in a costume. A white cowboy hat with silver trim was perched high atop her head of orange curls, and the outfit she wore was a white, turquoise, and silver vision of a cowgirl, complete with fringe. "You girls remember Callie, don't you?"

The other four women, all similarly dressed, smiled and nodded and extended their hellos. I had met them at a line dancing contest in the spring, when their group had made it into the finals and Harriet had insisted I come along for good luck.

"Don't you look fancy," I said, gesturing toward their elaborate outfits. "Are you performing tonight?"

"Naw, these are just our traveling clothes," Harriet replied, grinning.

I introduced Kirby all around, and then Harriet took my arm and suggested we take a table in the main part of the restaurant.

"I won't be long, girls," she sang out as we walked away.

This time, we let the waitress seat us. We ended up in a booth two down from the door. Kirby and I sat on one side and Harriet slid in across from us. Except for the three of us, this part of the restaurant was nearly empty. Kirby and I ordered coffee for there and burgers to go. Harriet just got coffee, saying she had already ordered food at the other table.

"I didn't realize you'd have someone with you, Callie," Harriet said, grinning at Kirby. "How'd she manage to rope you into this?"

"Kirby's been helping me with my investigation," I answered for him. "He's a neighbor."

"Well, goodness," Harriet replied. "If I'd a known they grew 'em like that out on your river, Callie, I'd a moved there myself years ago."

Kirby gave Harriet one of his prize-winning smiles.

"It's a good thing you didn't," he replied. "Otherwise, all the other girls in town would never have had a chance."

The two of them giggled.

"I'm sorry to interrupt this flirt fest," I said, "but we've got important business to take care of here."

"Well, this shouldn't take long," Harriet said, patting at her elaborate hairdo. "I just thought it might be easier in person than over the phone."

"So what'd you find out?"

She put her hands on the table and focused in on me, suddenly all business.

"The company out on that island is called 'Manno Seafoods,' " she said. "The boat is registered to the business."

"And is the business legit?"

"They've certainly done all their paperwork. I found quarterly state and federal tax filings, quarterly state unemployment, annual federal unemployment..." Her voice trailed off as she counted on her fingers. "Workers' comp. I-9 forms. The works."

"Sounds like the real deal," I said.

"To anyone else," Harriet replied, but then she lowered her voice. "Maybe not to yours truly."

"What do you mean?"

"It works on paper," she said. "But I've got my suspicions."

"How so?" Kirby asked.

"For one thing, they've never filed a single workers' comp case despite the fact that crab picking is a relatively dangerous occupation."

"Crab picking?" I asked. "What's dangerous about that?"

"According to my source at the Board of Health," Harriet said, "crab pickers are prone to cuts and infections. Statistically, there should've been several claims by now."

I thought about Murdock's description of the way the people there had been such inept crab pickers. *It's a miracle they didn't cut their fingers off*, he had said. *Or smash 'em with the mallet*, Dewey had added.

"What else?" I asked.

"Not a single unemployment claim, either," she said. "Statistically, it doesn't hold up."

"You said they had I-9 forms filed?"

"For ten employees."

"Just ten?" I asked. According to Murdock, he had seen about 30 people working when he was there.

"Yeah. I wrote down the names, if you want them."

Harriet dug in her pocket for a moment and then produced a slip of paper.

Kirby and I held it and read the list of names, none of which I recognized, and none of which sounded Asian, even though I distinctly remembered Murdock telling me that the workers he saw there were all Japanese.

I sat back and thought, wondering how all of it added up.

"So what's your take on this?" I finally asked Harriet.

"They're flying under the radar," Kirby interjected, and Harriet nodded.

"Exactly," she said. "With good, clean records like these, no one would have any reason to question any part of their organization."

"It's all spit and polish?" I asked.

"It's smart thinking," Harriet replied. "If there is any funny business going on out there, it certainly won't be discovered from a paper trail."

"I see."

Our coffee arrived then, and I leaned forward to take a sip, thinking. In the silence, Kirby began asking Harriet about her methods of investigation. He seemed quite impressed with all she had been able to do.

"That's why Callie and I make the perfect investigative team," Harriet explained to him. "Callie's the brave one who does all the scary footwork, trooping around in the dark and peeking in windows. I'm the chicken who sits back at the office and investigates with the phone and the computer."

I smiled, thinking that we all had our ways in which we were "chicken." Harriet may have been afraid of heights and bad neighborhoods and fast cars—but you wouldn't have caught me dead on a dance floor doing the Double Split Pony in front of 300 people.

"Hey, what about the other matter?" I asked. "The financial records for CNA."

"Oh, yeah, that," Harriet replied. "You didn't give me much to work with there, but what I saw looked good."

"Any red flags? Any questions?"

"Nah, things seemed fine. Of course, none of the figures were broken down. If I were going to do a full audit, I'd ask for separate records for each division."

"What do you mean?"

"The data from all of their divisions was combined. To fully analyze the Small Agencies Division, I would need separate data just for them."

"Yeah, that's what I was afraid of. But the report I sent you was all that was available."

"Well, the totals were fine, but I wouldn't sign off on it without a closer look."

"Okay," I said. "Thanks for checking."

It was time for us to leave, but we chatted a few more minutes while we waited for our hamburgers to be wrapped up in take-out boxes.

Harriet prattled on about the line dancing competition, saying how much better it was going to be now that she'd found out a certain someone else wasn't also going to be there.

"There's a cowboy who's got his spurs set in my direction, if you know what I mean," she said. "But I don't cotton to him at all."

"He's not coming?" I asked.

"No, thank goodness. He tore some ligaments doing the Achy Breaky, so now he's down for the count. I mean, I'm sorry he got hurt and all, but I'm glad he won't be there messing up my good time."

"If you don't like him," I asked, "why did you encourage him in the first place?"

"Aw, 'cause nobody can two-step like he can," she replied. "As they say down at the Longhorn, 'I just wanted to dance him, not romance him.'"

I laughed, thinking, *I know what you mean.* In a way, and despite tonight's kiss, that was how I felt about Kirby. He was fun to be with, but I certainly wasn't looking for a boyfriend!

Finally, our burgers were ready. We got up from the table and said our goodbyes. I hugged Harriet and thanked her for her hard work, especially since it had only been done as a favor to me and not as a function of the foundation.

"No sweat, sweetie," she replied. "Anything for a pal."

She and Kirby shook hands, and then he went to the counter to pay. Once he was out of earshot, Harriet gripped me by the wrist and pulled me to the side.

"You have *got* to be kidding me," she whispered sharply. "You're going out with that hunky-hunk thoroughbred over there, and you didn't even bother to tell me about it?"

"We're not 'going out,'" I whispered back. "We're just friends. We're neighbors."

"Neighbors?" she hooted. "Well, then, honey, he can borrow my cup of sugar anytime!"

Thirty-Five

"I've got it, I've got it," I whispered, holding my end of the two-person boat up over my head. Instead of the Jaguar, we had driven another of Kirby's vehicles, a plush Mercedes SUV. I had been nervous about eating the messy hamburgers in such a nice car, but fortunately we had managed to consume them without dripping ketchup all over the interior. Now we were parked at Carson Point, trying to wrestle Kirby's boat off of the carrier and down to the water.

I knew we should've brought one of my canoes, I told myself as we struggled with the unwieldy craft. This was a gorgeous, extremely expensive Kevlar racing boat. Leave it to a rich person to have top-of-the-line equipment that was totally impractical for our purposes.

Our portage was slow going, particularly because there was no entry point to the water here, just weeds and muck. But we couldn't go in at the boat launch, as I had done the day before, because that would bring us out to the island at a different point and in full view, no less. This time, we were slipping in the back way. Our intention was to paddle past island number one to island number two, which hopefully would afford us the right access to island number three, Manno Island.

We finally managed to get the boat in the water. While Kirby griped about the mud on his fancy Martin Dingman boat shoes, I climbed into the vessel and took my position at the rear. My boots were muddy, too, but at least inside my feet were dry and warm in their rubber socks, and that was the important thing.

Kirby pushed us off and climbed in, and then together we struggled with the paddles until we found our rhythm. Fortunately for us, the water was as smooth as glass, and I had to admit that the long, narrow hull gave us impressive speed. We paddled straight to the first island and skimmed along closely to its shore, moving then across open water to the second.

We went ashore on the second island at the tip, dragging the boat safely into the weeds before running ahead for the cover of trees. This was the smallest island, and you could practically see one end from the other. I led the way through the brush as we crossed right down the middle. Nearing the other end, we crouched low and found a dry, grassy spot behind a bush to kneel and set up our surveillance of island number three.

So far, the forces of nature seemed to be working in our favor. Besides the smooth water, the air was dry and still, so the cold wasn't unbearable. The moon was bright and the sky was clear. I felt optimistic that from where we sat we would be able to learn more about Manno Island and what was going on there. In the meantime, it was fun to be so close to the main waterway. Giant ships slid gracefully through the water in the distance, their bows lit, their wakes barely visible in the dark.

Kirby seemed to lose some of his initial excitement once the reality of our mission set in. I don't think he realized that surveillance was mostly uncomfortable and boring and mindless. Finally, I let him have the night-vision goggles, thinking that would entertain him while I got situated. Sure enough, soon he was whispering excitedly as he peered through them, telling me of the things on Manno he was able to make out in the darkness.

The first hour passed fairly quickly, though the second and then the third began to drag. We took turns looking through the goggles, waiting for activity. All we had been able to glean thus far was that there was, indeed, an armed guard, and that he seemed to wander out to different checkpoints along the water periodically, look up and down the river, and then step back into the trees. It felt as if he were waiting for someone, and I hoped that meant we would see something of significance happen here tonight. I hadn't yet told Kirby that we might have to come out here for quite a few nights in a row before we actually saw anything important.

He also didn't know I was prepared to get a little closer to Manno Island on my own, if need be.

Kirby was still using the goggles when he clamped a hand over his mouth, stifling a scream. Skin tingling, I got up to my knees and took the goggles from him.

"What is it? What?"

"In the water!" he whispered sharply. "Ahead and to the left. Giant rats!"

I looked where he had indicated, and saw a pair of nutria swimming toward us. Indeed, they did look like big, 20-pound rats, particularly when they reached the shore and climbed out, their long rodent tails poking out behind them.

"That's nutria," I said softly. "Not rats."

"You told me there wouldn't be anything wild out here!"

"I meant like snakes. I never said anything about mammals."

"Do they bite?"

I studied the animals without the goggles, trying not to smile.

"Look," I whispered. "They're leaving. You're safe."

"Ewww, yuck," he said. "Those are the nastiest creatures I've ever seen."

"They're usually marsh animals," I said. "I'm surprised they're out this close to open water."

"Is there anything else I need to know about here? Like giant spiders or man-eating lizards?"

"Just turtles," I said. "And maybe ducks. Everything else keeps farther inland, like muskrats and raccoons and things."

"This is great," Kirby griped. "Stuck in the dark on an island with a pair of giant rodents."

"Hey, I'm here, too."

"Yeah, well if those rats come back, I'm not. I'll be outta here."

I chuckled.

"They're more scared of you than you are of them," I said, and I was about to launch into a brief zoology lesson when a big boat in the distance caught my eye.

I'm not sure why it was different than the other ships we had seen. Perhaps because it seemed to be making a direct course for Manno Island. I put on the goggles and watched, trying to decide what kind of vessel it was.

My heart leaped into my throat when it came close enough for me to see that it was Russell's boat—the same one I had seen at the dock in Kawshek not five hours before. Now, however, it was headed north from *below* us, which meant that soon after I saw him at the dock he must have gone out into the bay and sailed to some point south of here. Obviously, he had picked up something and was bringing it back, because now there was a sort of large, rectangular box sitting squarely on the deck of the boat. Together, Kirby and I watched as the boat made a wide sweep toward the far end of Manno Island, where the dock and the picking house were supposedly located.

Making a decision, I handed the goggles to Kirby and then began to take off my clothes. He watched me in awe, his eyes widening as each layer came off.

"What are you doing?" he finally whispered.

"I want to get closer," I said.

"Here? Now?"

I paused to make a face.

"To the other island, Kirby. I'm sorry I didn't tell you about all of this, but I thought you might object."

He seemed to figure out what was going on once I got down to the dry suit and the rubber socks. From my bag I pulled my little air tank, mask, water shoes, and Kobalt hood.

"This two-liter tank will give me enough air to swim around to the northern side of the island and get a closer look at that boat."

"What's to look at?" he asked. "It's probably someone delivering a load of crabs."

"Not this time," I said, snapping on my hood. "Not this fellow."

I explained that the boat belonged to Russell Lynch, a man who was connected to Eddie Ray in more ways than one.

"I have to get closer," I said. "I need to see what he's doing here."

"This is so James Bondish," Kirby said admiringly, helping me on with my tank. I was glad he wasn't arguing with me about going. He must have realized I knew what I was doing.

"What do I do in the meantime?" he asked.

I slid my cell phone down into my suit where it would stay dry and then carefully put my other clothes into my bag and zipped it shut.

"You keep observing," I said. "Just watch closely, take note of everything, and stay here till I get back."

"What if something goes wrong for you?"

"I'll call you. Turn your phone on, set it to vibrate, and put it in your pocket where you'll feel it if it goes off."

"Okay."

"If I haven't called or come back in two hours," I said, "call the coast guard and tell them what's happened."

"Do you have that much air?"

"I won't be underwater the whole time," I said, double-checking my waterproof watch. "I'm just using the air tank to get there and back."

"But what about the armed guard?" he asked. "What if he sees you?"

I shrugged.

"I'll try not to let that happen."

I put the mask over my eyes, tested the respirator, and then gave Kirby a thumbs-up.

"Is there anything I can do to stop you?" he asked desperately.

I pulled out the respirator and grinned.

"Not unless you want me to flip you again," I replied.

Thirty-Six

Man, the water was cold! Despite the layer of rubber, I could feel the chill of the mighty Chesapeake. I knew that with the suit I wasn't in immediate danger of hypothermia, but that still didn't mean it was comfortable.

I slid into the water from the muddy bank and then dove down about five feet. I didn't want to go too deep, just deep enough so that I wouldn't be seen from the shore.

Heart pounding, I set off. I soon discovered I would have to surface frequently because I could see next to nothing in the black water. I had a small diving light built into my hood, but I didn't dare use it for fear of being seen.

Flippers, also, were a luxury I hadn't taken advantage of—mostly because I didn't want to fool with them at the other end. But that made it much slower going. I was an excellent swimmer, but these weren't exactly ideal conditions.

Still, I eventually got into a rhythm. I would go 15 strokes, surface, and then down for 15 more. In that way I managed to come alongside the island and then moved slowly toward the tip at the far end. As I went, I tried to block all fear from my mind, though it wasn't easy.

Besides the machine guns on the shore, I knew there was also a danger of sharks or stingrays or even snapping turtles in the water. *Not to mention the deadly nutria,* I thought with a smile.

Finally, I paused and floated, gauging my position, trying to get a feel for what was going on. There was a lot to see. Besides Russell's boat, which was now tied up at the dock, lights illuminated the ramp and the picking house, and I could see a number of Japanese people milling about. They weren't saying much, but there was an intensity to their actions that seemed deliberate and disturbing. Vaguely, I tried to recall what I had read about the Japanese mafia, and I wondered if this might be somehow connected with that.

I needed to get on that island. I decided my best approach would be to swim along the shoreline until I found the inlet where they stored their own little speedboat. I gave the well-lit dock area a wide berth so as not to be seen, then I fought the current as I swam around the northern tip of the island. Just as I had expected, once I rounded the curve I found that there was a small break in the land that led to the inlet. I floated all the way up the inlet to where the speedboat sat in the water, dark and quiet, securely tied to a wooden stake.

The water was more shallow here, and I found the bottom with my feet. As quietly as possible, I climbed out and stood on the muddy bank, getting my bearings. The port-a-potty was behind me, which meant the picking house and all of the activity must be in front of me. I could detect lights through the trees, so I crept toward them now, keeping my head low, my heart beating wildly in my throat.

I stole toward the back of a gray cinder-block building, wondering if this was the dormitory Murdock had told me about. I wanted to peek in a window, but there were too many people milling around. Instead, I hid behind a nearby tree and examined my options.

A row of garbage cans lined one wall, and finally I sprinted to them and crouched down, using them as my cover. From what I could make out, this whole area was a scene of organized confusion. Men with guns were barking orders in Japanese—short, clipped commands like "Come here!" "Stand there!" and "Wait!" Other people were basically following those orders in a daze, as if they were being herded like cattle. Directly across from me, a group of women stood in a row against a metal fence as a man sprayed them with a hose. When the hose was shut off, I could see that most of the women were rail thin and sickly, their ribcages poking out through their wet shirts.

Slowly, I began to understand what might be going on.

"Over there! Over there!" a guard yelled suddenly.

Gasping, I ducked down into the shadows behind the trash can, arms wrapped around my head, listening as footsteps crunched in the gravel toward me. The metal lid from one of the cans was lifted, and then trash rattled into the can. One piece missed the can and landed in the darkness at my side. Squinting, I could just make out what it was: a crumpled box of head lice remover.

The lid slammed down, and then I heard the same footsteps marching away. I took a chance and peeked out between the cans, watching the man hike back toward the dock. Just as he was passing the group of women against the fence, one of them crumpled to the ground. The man stopped to help, kneeling down and using a hand to lift her head off the ground.

"*Daijyoubu?*" he asked. *(Are you okay?)*

She answered him, but not in Japanese. Her words tumbled out in some other tongue, and by her gestures it seemed as if she were asking for food or water. The man produced what looked like a strip of beef jerky from his pocket, which he then gave to her. Between bites, she continued talking, though I doubted he could understand her any better than I could. Straining to listen, at first I thought she might be using some odd sort of Japanese dialect, but finally I decided that she was speaking Chinese.

I looked around, realizing suddenly that although the guards were Japanese, all of the people who were being herded around, who were being hosed down, were Chinese.

That confirmed my suspicions, telling me what I needed to know.

Silently, I crawled backward to the relative safety of the trees, taking one last look at the people before I turned and quietly sprinted away. I kept going until I reached the inlet. Gasping from the cold, I slid down into the black liquid and started swimming. I knew I needed to hurry. I had to get on board Russell's boat before it sailed away.

I swam back around the tip of the island and made my way to the boat. Once there, I stopped and floated in the shadows behind it, listening, trying to decide if there was anyone else still on board. I could hear voices on land, in the distance, but it didn't sound as if anyone were nearby. Finally, taking a chance, I swam around to the back, gritted my teeth, and pulled myself up by the built-in ladder.

Water dripped loudly from my dry suit and I held my breath, waiting for someone to come running. When no one did, I climbed the rest of the way up and then flattened myself against the back deck of the boat.

For now, at least, I had been lucky: The boat was empty, and no one on shore seemed to have heard me come aboard.

Gathering my nerve, I crawled over a little dinghy and stepped onto the main deck, heading for the big black box that filled the wide surface. It was a hard fiberglass-looking structure, about ten feet wide, thirty feet long, and maybe six feet high. I stood and ran my hands along it, feeling slit-like holes that had been drilled through the side. At the front, I found a jagged sort of door that had been cut into the fiberglass. I pulled, trying to peel it back noiselessly so that I could peek inside.

I had it open perhaps an inch when I was hit by the smell—a smell so nasty and overpowering that bile surged in my throat and filled my mouth. The odor was like a sewer, a mix of feces and urine and vomit. I let go of the box and stepped to the rail, leaning over as I tried to quell my own heaves. I still was there a moment later, gulping deep breaths, when I heard men's voices, very nearby.

I needed to hide. Frantically, I looked around the boat, but except for the big container, the deck was clear. I knew I'd never make it up front to the bathroom or the closet without being seen, but I also knew there was no way I could force myself to climb inside the container and hide there.

"...packing 'em in too tight," I heard Russell say angrily. "If I end up with any casualties, it's on your head."

"We got one more shipment tomorrow. What's the difference how tightly they're packed?"

"I just don't need any dead bodies to deal with."

"What're you gonna do, Lynch? Call the police?"

"Shut up, Shin. And get my bumpers."

A man laughed, and then the boat lurched slightly in the water as it was boarded.

Heart pounding, I inched my way along the container until I was at the very back. I could hear Russell fiddling near the wheelhouse, up front, and once the ropes were tossed on board and Shin barked out the "all clear" from the shore, I waited a minute and then took a chance and darted through the shadows to the end of the boat. I climbed down onto the diving platform and lowered myself into the little dinghy that was strapped there.

The engine roared to life near my head. I shut my eyes, gripped some straps inside the dinghy, and prayed—that I wouldn't be caught, that I wouldn't be killed. I wasn't sure if Russell would have any reason to come back here or not, but I knew that if he did, I was nothing more than a sitting duck.

Having second thoughts—but helpless to change my situation at this point—I laid there in the dinghy on the diving platform as I felt the boat pull away from the dock and slowly edge its way into the bay. After a few minutes, I dared to take a peek over the edge of the dinghy at what we had left behind. I could see Manno Island clearly, all but deserted now, with only a single light shining at the end of the dock. As I watched, the light went out, and then all was dark.

Thirty-Seven

Wham!

The boat hit a giant wave and nearly flung me into the air. *It must be another ship's wake,* I realized, as I gripped onto my little dinghy for dear life. I counted the stomach-churning leaps—two, three, four...and then it was back to smooth sailing.

I laced my hands more tightly through rope handles on the dinghy and held on, praying we wouldn't hit any more wakes before we reached our destination. I needed to call Kirby to give him an update, but I didn't have a hand to spare. According to my watch, we had been apart for more than an hour; I knew I had until the two-hour mark before he would be calling the coast guard.

"Not yet, Kirby," I whispered into the darkness. "Not yet."

We drove up the Chesapeake, continuing on for half an hour or so. In that time we hit four more ship wakes, the last of which very nearly did me in. Besides the jostling, I was also freezing to death, my dry suit scant protection for a nighttime boat ride in these temperatures. At least I was out of most of the wind since I was at the back of the boat and not the front.

Just when I thought I couldn't last much longer, the noise of the motor changed, and I realized we were slowing down and turning in toward shore.

I knew I needed to be ready to act fast. Wherever we were heading, there could be lights and people and activity—and a woman in a dry suit clinging for dear life to a dinghy might be a bit suspect, to say the least. Based on the direction and duration of the trip, I had the sinking feeling we were going to end up back at the Kawshek marina, which meant that my death-defying trip hadn't been worth it after all. When I climbed on board, I had hoped that Russell would sail south to return the empty container from where he had gotten it, thereby leading me to the missing link in this chain of crime. Instead, I feared, he had merely turned toward home.

Bracing for the cold, I slid out of the dinghy and crouched low on the ladder, listening to the motor, waiting for the sound to tell me it had been switched into neutral. Finally, I took the chance and lowered myself into the water, letting go of the ladder and pushing back away from the boat as firmly as possible.

I made it away without injury. Kicking softly to stay afloat, I fit the respirator into my mouth, slid the mask down over my eyes, then submerged just to eye level, where I could see without being seen.

From what I could tell, we weren't at the marina after all. We were at a private dock. There was a sort of camping lantern hung from a pole, and one man was standing near it at the dock, waiting for the boat. It was Hank, the man who followed me at the Kawshek pier and who had broken into my home.

He caught the rope Russell threw to him and then held it while Russell cut the motor and tossed out the bumpers. Together, the two men tied the boat up to the cleats.

I needed to get a little closer. My tank felt as though it was almost out of air, so I made my way underwater as quickly as I could, surfacing over to the side among some marsh grasses where I could see better.

"What's the matter?" Hank asked.

"Stupid snakeheads," Russell snapped. "They had eighteen in there this time."

Hank let out a low whistle.

"That's too many."

"What about the girl?" Russell asked. "She still snooping around?"

I blinked, feeling sure they were talking about me.

"I've got someone on it," Hank said. "I have to check in with him, but at last report she had driven over the bridge and was headed toward DC."

"Good," Russell said. I closed my eyes, thankful that our ruse with Mr. Buchman in my car had worked.

Russell reached up and took the lantern from the pole, and then the two men walked off across the grass toward what I now realized was the Lynches' farm. Seizing the opportunity, I climbed up onto the bank among the reeds, pulled out the cell phone, and dialed Kirby, who sounded nearly frantic when he answered the phone.

"You've been gone exactly one hour and fifty-five minutes!" he cried. "My finger was ready to dial for help. *Where have you been?*"

"I'll explain later," I whispered sharply, cutting him off. "Here's what I need you to do. Get our stuff, get in the boat, and get back to the car." I explained that I had taken a little trip as a stowaway, and I gave him directions to come and get me, telling him to meet me on the side street just before the farm.

I hung up the phone, tucked it back down into my suit, and looked around, trying to decide how to get out of there. Before I could make a move, however, I saw a light coming across the lawn. It was Russell and Hank, swinging the lantern, heading back to the dock.

"...shouldn't take long," Russell was saying as he walked up the dock and hung the lantern from the pole. "I wanna get this done before Tia gets home."

"Why didn't you make *them* do it?" Hank asked.

"I did," Russell said. "They got all the garbage out, but we still have to spray it down."

"I'll get the hose," Hank said wearily.

I moved further into the cover of the reeds, my body shivering from the cold. I watched as the two men slowy began cleaning out the container. Russell held open the makeshift door while Hank sprayed the hose. After a while, Hank stopped spraying and Russell went inside with two big white jugs.

Bleach, I realized, the acrid smell striking me like a slap across the face. *They're using bleach to disinfect the big container!* The smell grew stronger after Russell came back out, the jugs obviously empty. My eyes watered as the smell lingered and, once again, Hank sprayed the whole interior down with the hose. It must've taken a good 15 minutes, but finally the men seemed satisfied. Hank put away the hose, Russell locked up the boat, and they retrieved the lantern and walked back across the yard to the house.

At that point I realized I was chilled to the bone, my teeth literally clicking together. I knew I needed to get out of there and get into something warm very soon.

Slowly, I crept through the tall grass until I reached some trees. Staying in the shadows, I worked my way around the perimeter of the entire farm, finally passing the area where Russell had used my wire to repair the hole in his fence. I found the road and walked up it a half mile before I finally saw the side turn where I had told Kirby to meet me. Luckily, no cars passed me in either direction as I walked.

About 20 feet up I found a rock on the side of the road and sat down. I was exhausted and cold, my feet hurt, and I felt fairly sure I was getting sick. Still, I knew that I had solved the mystery of Manno Island. My initial suspicions were incorrect: They weren't smuggling drugs there.

They were smuggling people.

Thirty-Eight

Kirby was worried about me.

"If you haven't stopped shaking by the time we reach the house," he said, "I'm calling a doctor."

"I don't n-need a doctor," I replied, shivering under his coat and mine. "I think a w-warm bath will be sufficient."

Kirby drove quickly toward home, scolding me part of the way and questioning me the rest. He seemed more concerned with my well-being than with what my investigation had turned up. Though he was surprised to learn our theory about drugs was wrong, he took the news of people-smuggling in stride.

"It makes sense," he said. "The logistics, the easy access to international shipping channels, the anonymity. They've probably been working illegal immigrants in and out of that island for months."

"But if they're coming from China," I said, "why are they ending up on the East Coast rather than the West?"

"I think illegal Chinese immigrants are brought into this country from every direction. Remember the ones who washed up on the shore in New Jersey?"

I nodded, thinking.

"I have a feeling I know now what Eddie Ray saw," I told him, "the night he went hunting for buried treasure."

"You think he saw a man with a machine gun, like you did?"

"No," I replied. "I think he saw Russell's boat—what he still thought of as *his* boat—pulling up to that island and unloading people out of a shipping container. I'd bet you anything he went straight to Russell's farm, waited there until he got back, and then confronted him about it. I think ol' Eddie Ray saw a good thing and somehow tried to get himself in on the action."

"I've read that the smuggling of people is incredibly lucrative."

"Lucrative, perhaps, but also reprehensible. And Eddie Ray ended up getting himself killed."

We talked about that for a bit, wondering if the killer was Russell or Hank or one of the Tanigawa brothers—or someone else connected with the smuggling. I wasn't sure how to find out, though I knew the next step in clearing Shayna's name was to go to the police, or perhaps to the Immigration Bureau.

"Whoever it was," I said, "they must've brought in a boatload the night I found the murder scene. That bleach smell must've come from the boat, which for some reason they had parked at the deserted boat repair shop. I bet at least one of those guys was watching the road—watching me find the spot where they had killed Eddie Ray—from that roof, with some night-vision goggles."

"What about the bleach smell later, at your house?" Kirby asked.

"The boat could've been nearby, maybe even tied up to my own dock."

"Too shallow, " Kirby reminded me.

"Then maybe that stink was on their clothes," I said. "The way they were splashing around cleaning that container tonight, I wouldn't be surprised if Russell had gotten bleach all over himself. I bet one of them came to my house to check me out, and I smelled traces of the bleach on their clothes. Sal *was* barking at an intruder, just one that chose not to let himself be seen."

"You're still shaking," Kirby said.

"I'll be okay," I replied, suddenly feeling a bit claustrophobic at the intensity of his concern. It was one thing to have someone care about you, and quite another to have them fawn over you. Kirby didn't seem to pick up on my mood, however, because he kept going, telling me how the time we had been apart was the longest of his life and that he'd thought for sure I was dead.

"I was blaming myself," he lamented, reaching over for my hand. "I couldn't bear the thought of losing you."

I was flattered, but it all seemed a bit melodramatic to me.

"This is what I do, Kirby. I investigate."

He shook his head.

"I know," he told me. "I thought I'd like it, too, but tonight has given me a new appreciation for sitting at a desk with the paperwork. Believe me."

"I'm sorry for dragging you into all this."

"Don't be," he replied. "It's been a real trip. Is your job always this exciting?"

"Not nearly," I said. "Not usually, anyway. Maybe once in a while, an investigation might get a little dicey…" My voice trailed off with thoughts of past investigations, some quite exciting, some incredibly mundane. I didn't elaborate further, and he didn't ask.

Kirby held my hand all the way to his house. Once there, he helped me up the front steps and inside. He had called ahead, and a female member of the staff met us at the front door, fully dressed in a uniform despite the fact that it was four o'clock in the morning.

"Come with me," she said warmly, as if this were the most natural thing in the world. I followed her as she led me upstairs to a huge, sumptuous bathroom.

A hot bath had already been drawn for me, and there were towels and a robe hanging on a warming rack nearby.

"Please make yourself at home," she said. "There's soap and shampoo on the shelf right there."

She pulled the door shut, and I proceeded to peel off the dry suit and climb into the tub.

It felt heavenly. The longer I soaked the more I felt myself returning to normal. Finally, I shampooed and rinsed, then I just lingered there a bit longer, relaxing in the warm water until I almost fell asleep.

Not only was the towel rack heated, I realized as I climbed out, but the floor was, too. I dried off and pulled on the robe and slippers, then I used a comb that was in a basket on the vanity to comb out my hair.

There was a knock on the door when I was nearly finished. It was the maid and she had with her some clean, dry clothes for me to try. I chose a pair of jeans that were about my size, a worn but comfortable T-shirt, and a thick fleece sweater.

Finally, I picked up my things and went back downstairs in search of Kirby. I also wanted to find my dog, and I wanted to make sure Mr. Buchman had made it back from his adventure in Operation Decoy.

Kirby was waiting for me in his study, sitting on the sofa in front of a blazing fire with Sal on his lap. It was such a cozy, homey scene, and for a moment as I stood in the doorway, my breath caught in my throat.

If only I could feel for this guy what he apparently felt for me! Seeing him there, staring into the fire and gently stroking my beloved Sal, it struck me again how handsome he was, how genuinely sweet.

"Hey," he said, spotting me in the doorway. "Look at you."

I came into the room and joined him on the couch, greeting my little dog and her wagging tail. She switched over to my lap, and I clutched her to me, exhaustion suddenly overwhelming every other emotion.

"They haven't heard from Bucky yet," Kirby said. "I'm getting a little worried."

"I told him to drive slowly and take his time," I said, looking at the clock. "Maybe he's just really stretching it out."

"I hope so."

"Are you sure he knew to come here and not to my house?" I asked.

"Yeah, but while you were taking your bath I drove over there anyway. He's not back yet at either location."

"I'm sure we'll hear soon. Let's say thirty more minutes, and then we'll do something about it."

"Okay."

We sat side by side on the couch in relaxed silence. Sal jumped down from my lap to curl up in front of the fire. After a while, Kirby began tracing a pattern on the back of my hand with his fingers.

Eventually, he moved his fingers lightly up my arm, across my shoulder, and to my chin. Shifting ever so slightly, he leaned forward and tilted my face up until I was looking at him. Then he bent down and pressed his lips to mine.

He kissed me harder this time, with an urgency and a passion that he'd held in check earlier. I felt myself responding, my own urgency increasing, a soft moan escaping from my throat. Finally, I broke the kiss and simply held onto him, my arms tight around his neck, my body feeling shielded and protected in his embrace. *Oh, Lord,* I prayed, *You created us to need each other. Why, then, is it so difficult to get it right?*

"I don't want to hurt you..." I said, leaning back again to look at him.

"Shhh," he replied, putting a finger against my lips. "We'll just take this as it comes. I told you, I don't have any expectations. And we've got all the time in the world."

"Do you realize," I whispered, "that you're the first man I've even held hands with since my husband passed away?"

He nodded.

"You made it very clear that you don't date, Callie. But I'm honored that you're giving me a chance. I want us to have a chance."

Before I could reply, there was a knock at the front door.

Kirby excused himself and went to answer it while I attempted to pull myself together. Did the pounding of my heart show on my face?

I was just smoothing out my hair when Kirby came back, a strange expression in his eyes.

"What is it?" I asked.

He stepped farther into the room, and behind him came Mr. Buchman, the wig off but the coat still on.

Behind him came Hank Hawkins, the gun in his hand pointed firmly at the small of Mr. Buchman's back.

Thirty-Nine

"Over to the couch," Hank said, motioning with the gun as Sal barked furiously. "All of you."

I scooted down to one end and commanded Sal to be quiet. She obeyed but remained alert, a soft growl rumbling from her throat. Kirby sat next to me and a pale-looking and exhausted Mr. Buchman sat next to him. I felt so bad for poor Mr. Buchman. He didn't need this kind of trouble!

Once they were seated, I realized that another man was with Hank. Instead of a gun, though, he held out a wallet which sported a badge.

"Special Agent Jeffrey Litman, INS," he said. I studied his face, remembering that he was the suited man who had hovered around the fringes of the police investigation the night we found Eddie Ray's body. With his slender face and hook nose, he was the one the lieutenant had deferred to, the one I had assumed was with the DA's office.

"INS?" I asked.

Hank lowered his gun and tucked it in at his waistband.

"Immigration and Naturalization Service. And I'm Special Agent Hank Quinn."

"I thought your name was Hank Hawkins."

"That's my cover," he said, "which you very nearly have blown."

I exhaled slowly, closing my eyes. They were with the Immigration Bureau! Suddenly, it felt as if a great weight was sliding from my shoulders. We weren't alone in this. The government was already on the job.

I leaned forward to pull Sal onto my lap, and I stroked her reassuringly as I spoke.

"Wait a minute," I said to Hank. "I thought you were from Kawshek. I thought you were a local."

"I've spent over a year here," he said angrily, "building my cover, learning the ropes, fitting in. Then you show up with your big mouth and your rinky-dink investigation and threaten to ruin everything."

I thought back to the night I had first seen him, the night people were gathered in the parking lot of the Kawshek General Store and Wendy Lentil told me that Hank was "kinda new here," but that he seemed like "a good fella." He looked so much like a waterman that it hadn't sunk in he wasn't a Kawshek native born and bred.

"I'm so confused," I said. "Who was driving the Pontiac van tonight, the one that followed me to Kawshek?"

"I was," Litman said. "Once you got out of your car, I radioed Hank and he followed you on foot."

"So who tailed Mr. Buchman in my car to Alexandria?"

"Again, I did," Litman said. "And a big waste of time it was, too. Thanks a lot."

I felt a blush creep across my face. I guess the whole decoy thing had been a bit much.

"Meanwhile, our surveillance team tells us you took yourself a little boat ride tonight," Hank said to me. He looked angry, and I didn't blame him. Obviously, I had wormed my way right into the middle of something major. No wonder Barbara Hightower had called me and tried to warn me off. She must have known the INS was involved.

"Please, have a seat," Kirby said suddenly to the two men. "Would anyone like some coffee?"

"That would be good," Agent Litman said. "Black, please."

Kirby went to his desk, lifted the phone, and spoke softly to a maid.

"It goes without saying," Hank began as soon as Kirby returned to the couch, "that your little investigation has crossed over into our big investigation. Guess who's going to back off now? You are."

"Hey," I replied, "I'm sorry if we messed anything up for you people. But we couldn't possibly have known what was really going on. I'm thrilled you're already involved, trust me, but we don't deserve this attitude from you. We were well within the bounds of our own investigation. It's just unfortunate the way things played out."

Hank seemed to listen to my little speech, and when I was finished he stood and crossed to the fireplace.

"All right, fine," he snapped. "Right now I'm just trying to sort out what's been done and what hasn't. You'll excuse me if I'm a little miffed that Agent Litman here just wasted five hours following a cross-dressing butler to Alexandria for a box of donuts."

I stifled a smile and turned to Mr. Buchman.

"Are you okay?" I asked.

He nodded.

"I'm sorry, Callie," Mr. Buchman said. "I guess the wig slipped while I was waiting for my order. Agent Litman stopped me when I came back to the car with the donuts. He made me follow him back to his office in Barrington. I had to tell him everything I knew."

"That's okay," I said. "Considering what we discovered tonight, this is actually a wonderful development."

He looked relieved.

"So what's going on out on Manno Island?" I asked Hank. "Obviously, they're smuggling immigrants."

"Oh, no," he said. "You first. Tell me about your investigation."

"Well, considering you were in my home without a warrant," I said, "why don't you tell me what you were able to figure out about my investigation on your own?"

"*What?*" Agent Litman asked, sitting forward.

Hank ran a hand through his hair, and I found my eye drawn to the scar on his chin. It was funny, but now that I knew he was one of the good guys, I could see what everyone was talking about when they said he was a "gentle" person. His very size made him appear threatening, of course, but in the parlor by the light of the fireplace he looked like nothing so much as a giant teddy bear, just as Shayna had said.

"May I speak with you in the hall?" Hank said to me.

I nodded and walked out, curious as to what would happen next.

"Look," he told me softly once we were alone, "you're an investigator, you know how it works. I was in a hurry. I was desperate. Here we are about to take down a major operation after a lengthy investigation—and then suddenly you pop into the mix, threatening to blow it all up in our faces. I needed to know who you were, why you were there. I did what I had to do. Just like sometimes you do things you have to do."

"Was Litman in my house, too?"

"No, he's strictly a by-the-book kind of guy. And this could get me in a lot of trouble."

"What are you offering to keep me quiet?" I asked.

"What do you want?"

"Shayna released from all charges."

"I'm afraid I can't do that."

"You can pay a visit to the DA," I said. "At the very least, show him there's more to this situation than meets the eye."

"The DA is marginally aware of our presence here," he said. "Beyond that, I'm powerless."

"Can you talk with Shayna's lawyer, at least tell him?"

"Again, no. I'm sorry, but there's nothing I can do to help her. The scope of our investigation is just too great to take such a risk."

"Come on, Hank," I said. "You dated Shayna yourself! You know she's innocent."

"Yeah, I feel sure that she is. And I would do something about it if I could, but right now I can't. That's just how things are."

I stared at him, wondering if he was being completely truthful. Shayna had broken up with him, after all. Maybe there were some sour grapes here. Maybe he was paying her back by letting her fry.

"If you can't help Shayna, then why should I keep quiet about you breaking into my house?" I asked.

Hank shrugged, looking desperate.

"I don't know, Callie. Maybe just to be nice? Maybe so I could owe you one?"

We glared at each other for a moment.

"Look," he pleaded. "Believe it or not, I have strong feelings for Shayna. We didn't date all that long, and I know it wasn't exactly mutual, but I really liked her. I still do. Don't you think this mess she's in now is killing me?"

"Then do something about it."

"I can't! My hands are tied."

I exhaled slowly.

"You saw those immigrants out on Manno Island," Hank added softly. "Do you really want to do something that might jeopardize the apprehension of the criminals responsible for that?"

He had me there. I thought of those women standing against the fence, their ribs poking through their soaked shirts. I didn't know much about human smuggling, but I did know those people were suffering.

Finally, I let out a frustrated sigh before turning and walking back into the study with Hank following behind. As we entered, Agent Litman was eyeing us suspiciously.

"Was Agent Quinn in your home without a warrant?" he asked.

"Well, sir," I replied, "I truly never got a good look at the man, so I can't be sure. But I think I was mistaken. I think the man who broke into my home was much bigger than him." I smiled at my own joke, as I doubted it was physically possible for a person to be much bigger than him.

"Now may we hear the details of your investigation?" Hank asked, more nicely this time.

As succinctly as I could, I recounted the steps I had taken to try to uncover the true murderer of Eddie Ray Higgins. I explained about the wooden nickel, the GPS club, the man I saw with the machine gun. I didn't have to provide much detail about our activities tonight, since we had been observed by their surveillance the whole time we were observing the island.

"And have you solved your case?" Hank asked.

"Not yet," I replied. "But from all that's going on, I feel certain that Eddie Ray was killed by these smugglers. I just don't have the proof yet."

Hank looked at Litman and then shook his head.

"You could've frozen to death in that water, you know," he said. "Not to mention getting blown up by their machine guns or hacked to death by the boat motor."

"That's what I've been telling her," Kirby said, placing his hand on mine.

His public display of affection bothered me, and after a beat I casually extricated my hand from his grasp.

"Now tell us what you can about your investigation," I said. "I think we deserve to know a little, at least."

Hank looked at Litman, and he nodded.

"As you guessed, Manno Island is being used as a processing station for illegal immigrants coming to the U.S. from China," Hank said.

"Are they always transported in containers?"

"They're brought here in lots of ways, but yes, that's one way. They put the people in a container and then load the container on a ship, surrounded by similar containers that are full of legally imported goods. Those people you saw on the island tonight came all the way from Suriname to Norfolk in that ten by twenty box. Eighteen of them, in that one little box."

"No wonder it smelled so bad," I said.

"Suriname?" Kirby asked. "In South America?"

"Yeah, it's one of their standard routes to the U.S.," Litman said. "Illegal immigrants come into America from nearly every direction, but this is the route we've been assigned to. We're very close to making some arrests."

"What's Russell Lynch's involvement?" I asked.

"He picks up the containers in Norfolk and brings them to Manno," Hank said. "He's convinced himself that what he's doing isn't all that bad, but the truth is, he's just another cog in a big, nasty machine of snakeheads. He'll go down with the rest of them."

"Snakeheads?"

"That's what we call Chinese human smugglers. Manno Island is part of a series of stops where the people being smuggled are taken and hidden as they wait for the next step on their journey."

"What's their ultimate destination?" Kirby asked.

"From here? The immigrants will be under the control of other snakeheads in DC, Philly, and finally New York City. The snakeheads have to get these people to Chinatown where they can blend in. Then the immigrants will go to work to pay for their lovely trip to America."

"Don't they pay before they leave China?" I asked.

"Just a small deposit. Once they get here, the real work begins. The price is usually fifty, sixty, seventy thousand dollars. With a thousand-dollar deposit up front, you do the math. They'll be slaves in sweatshops or restaurants or brothels for years just to make up the difference—if they ever do."

"Wow."

"Sometimes the money they can't raise is extracted from relatives and previous immigrants. Essentially, the ones being smuggled in are held hostage. They're beaten, raped, starved—whatever it takes to get their loved ones to pay the money."

"That's horrible."

"Make no mistake, Ms. Webber, this is a terrible, evil business. The profits for some smuggling rings can run into the billions *per year*. They're not going to let you or me or the Department of Immigration and Naturalization stop them if they can help it."

"Unbelievable," Kirby said.

"Now do you understand the problem here? We have a situation where we're closing in on this particular ring, we've almost got a handle on the leadership involved, we've got Hank planted well undercover—and then along you come to mess everything up! Even the leaks we've had from inside our own agency were nothing compared to what you have almost done to our investigation."

At that moment, the maid entered with a large coffee tray, which she set on the table in front of us. Kirby thanked her and she left, and then we all busied ourselves with fixing coffee. I had mine black, with a small slice of coffee cake on the side. I was smarting from their harsh words, and I was grateful for the distraction as I considered a new approach.

"So who killed Eddie Ray Higgins?" I asked finally.

"We're not sure," Hank replied. "But we do know he found out about the smuggling, and he was trying to blackmail Russell."

"Did Russell kill him?"

"Perhaps, but we can't prove it. That's not what we're after here, anyway."

"What do you mean?"

"We're on an INS investigation," Litman said. "Illegal immigration. As far as we can tell, the murder had nothing to do with the smuggling."

"Nothing to do with it?" I cried. "Eddie Ray was blackmailing snakeheads—and then he ended up dead? Of course it had something to do with it!"

"Perhaps. But, again, unless some sort of direct evidence shows up linking the two, his death is not our concern."

"Not your concern!" I repeated.

"Trust me, Callie," Hank said, "we would love to find a link there. But so far there's simply no evidence tying the murder to anyone except Shayna."

I stood and began pacing, the coffee cake forming a solid lump in my stomach. I kept picturing Shayna, behind bars, the image of her fading as the clock ticked her chance at freedom away.

"What if I don't back down from my investigation?" I challenged, hands on hips, my eyes locked on Agent Litman.

"Then we'll bring you up on charges of obstruction of justice," he replied calmly. "And, trust me, you really don't want to go there."

Forty

"I can't believe they're just going to hang Shayna out to dry!" I ranted, pacing the floor. The two agents were gone, and I was alone in the study with Kirby. Poor, tired Mr. Buchman had gone to bed the moment the agents left, but I was far too agitated to think of sleep.

"I can see their position, Callie," Kirby said gently from his place on the couch. "What they're doing here is a lot more important than just one dumb kid cooling her heels in jail. They're trying to bust an entire smuggling ring."

"I still don't see why they think we're at cross-purposes here," I said. "It seems to me that each side of this investigation can only help the other."

I plopped down on the couch next to Kirby and looked into the fire.

"They weren't being completely honest with us anyway," I said. "Acting vague, insinuating that one day soon this thing will come to a head."

"So?"

"I heard it with my own ears, Kirby. Out at the island, when I was hiding on the boat behind the empty container. Shin told Russell, 'We got one shipment left.' That shipment's going to be tonight. I think everything is coming to a head tonight."

Kirby ran a hand through his hair, and then he stood and went to the fire, putting the screen to the side. He used the poker to stir up the embers, and then he carefully placed the poker back in the rack.

"Oh, no," he said, once he turned and looked at me. "Don't even think about it."

"What?"

"I know where your mind is going, and you're crazy."

"What?" I asked again, trying to look and sound innocent.

"Callie, I don't care how dedicated you are to learning the truth, you heard what Litman said. If you interfere, they will charge you with obstruction of justice."

"But someone's got to be there tonight for Shayna's sake," I said. "I wouldn't get in the way. I just want to be there as an observer. To look out for her interests in all of this."

"No," Kirby said adamantly. "First of all, they've got that place too well covered. You'd be caught before you even got close. Second, it's too dangerous. It's bad enough what you did there already, sneaking around and stuff, but if there really is going to be a bust, then you're talking about gunfire, tear gas—who knows what else? That's no place for a civilian."

I exhaled slowly, knowing he was right.

"Third," Kirby said softly, walking to the couch and kneeling in front of me, "if you even try to sneak out there, I will personally—physically, if need be—stop you myself. I care about you, Callie. I will not let you put yourself in harm's way."

He reached up one hand and brushed it along my cheek.

"Then what do you suggest I do?" I asked.

"You're a resourceful woman," he said. "Think of something."

He looked into my eyes, concern for me evident on his face.

"There are proper channels for this sort of thing," he said softly. "Don't you know anyone in the government? Don't you have any contacts who might be able to work this from another angle?"

I looked back at him and took a deep breath, trying to think.

"Tom!" I said finally, my face breaking into a smile. "Of course."

"Tom?" Kirby asked, rocking back on his heels. "Your boss?"

"Yes."

"He works for the government? I thought you said he was in computers."

"He is. He doesn't work for the government, but he's got lots and lots of connections. I'm fairly certain his business dealings with the government go to pretty high levels. If anybody can make this happen, he can."

Suddenly, I wanted nothing so much as to go home, call Tom, and set things in motion. I looked at my watch and realized that the sun would be up soon. I could leave a message on Tom's voice mail now, and he could get back to me later in the morning, as soon as he had a chance. In the meantime, I would try to get a little sleep. Suddenly, I felt overwhelmed with exhaustion.

"I'm sorry, Kirby, but I've got to go," I said, my mind already two steps ahead. Without waiting for his reply, I jumped up and gathered my clothes.

"Let's go, Sal," I said, feeling vaguely insulted when it looked as if she would rather stay there in front of the fireplace with Kirby than come on home with me.

"Come back for breakfast," Kirby said as I shooed Sal out the front door to the driveway, where Litman had left my car.

"I'll be sleeping."

"A late lunch, then," he replied. "Say, one-thirty?"

"Sure," I agreed, holding the car door open for Sal and then climbing in myself. Right now, I just wanted to make my call and get to bed. I would've agreed to anything, I think, just to get out of there and go home.

Forty-One

I awoke at noon with a pounding headache and stiff, achy shoulders. I was a little surprised Tom hadn't yet returned my call. I snuggled under the covers and just played with Sal for a few minutes, wondering if the world would spin to a halt if I spent the entire day in bed. *Soon,* I told myself, *soon.* For now, there were still miles to go before I could sleep.

Finally, I got up, threw some water on my face, and then checked my messages. There was nothing from Tom, though I did have a disturbing call from Gordo Koski, the PI in Akron who was investigating CNA.

"I don't know what you've gotten me into," his message said, "but there's been a tail on me all afternoon. We're hitting some nerves here, girlie."

I picked up the phone and dialed his cell phone number, glad when he picked up on the first ring.

"You still have a tail?" I asked.

"I shook him a few minutes ago," he replied. "But I'm sure it'll pick up again once I go back to the office."

"What do you think it is?"

"I asked somebody the wrong question, I guess."

I felt bad, especially since Gordo was just doing me a favor. The case I had worked for him last year had never put me in any personal danger.

"Tell me what you've learned," I said.

"Plenty," he replied. "Miss Burnham might be working for a nonprofit, but she's got some profit coming in from somewhere."

"Go on," I said, echoing Gordo's favorite phrase.

"The lady has a taste for gold," he said. "Not to mention diamonds and pearls and anything else that sparkles as it appreciates in value."

"How do you know?"

"I got lucky. I was doing a drive-by of her house—very modest, by the way—when she got in her car, also modest, and headed off toward town. On a hunch, I followed her. She went to a jewelry store and made a layaway payment on a pearl necklace. I was right there in the store. I saw her hand over several thou *in cash*."

"Maybe she's been saving for a long time," I said.

"Nah. Once she left I flashed the sales guy my fake police badge, and he told me she was one of their best customers. Always buys the big-ticket items, always pays in cash over time. Rubies, emeralds, you name it. Been coming there for a couple years."

"Sounds like she's doing some laundry to me."

"Some folks swear by gold and jewels," he replied. "And if you have to wash your dough, it sure beats real estate, because jewelers are willing to take cash."

My stomach grumbled. I reached absently into the fridge and pulled out a stick of celery, which I rinsed under the faucet.

"What else have you got?" I asked.

"I sent you the data you were looking for. The breakdown of both income and expenses at CNA, divided out by division."

"You've got to be kidding me. How did you get that information?"

"You don't really want to know. Suffice it to say, it should be waiting for you in your e-mail inbox."

"Fantastic," I said. "That'll help so much."

"Well, there's more," he said. "Names. I got a list of names for ya."

I bit into the celery, trying not to crunch over the phone.

"Names?"

"Of companies. I haven't found any donor brokers connected with CNA, but I did manage to get a list of the companies that donated money last year. The 'sponsoring businesses,' I think you called them."

"How'd you do that? Nonprofits are allowed to keep the names of their donors private. They don't have to supply that information anywhere."

"Anywhere except to the IRS."

I took another bite of celery and shook my head.

"Ah, Gordo, your endless resourcefulness never ceases to amaze me."

"Well, when I take this lovely IRS agent out for the steak dinner I promised her, I'll send you the bill."

"Oh, great. I don't mind buying you a steak dinner, but don't ask me to be a party to your questionable methods of investigation."

"Yeah, yeah, yeah, here you go, the good conscience of the PI world."

"Come on, Gordo," I said. "If you're crossing the line on my behalf, I don't want to know about it."

"Fine," he grumbled. "Do you want these names or not?"

I waited while he dug out the list of businesses that his IRS contact had supplied. Then he read them off to me and I jotted them down, one by one. Smith Consulting. Freemont Ironworks. Townsend Financial. Nothing struck any chords until he got near the end.

That's when he listed Manno Seafood.

"Did you say Manno?" I asked, heart pounding. "M-a-n-n-o? Here in Maryland?"

"Yeah. Why? That ring a bell?"

I sat down heavily, my head spinning.

"Say that again," I told him. "Manno Seafood donates money to CNA for the support of nonprofits?"

"Yeah. Doesn't say how much or how often, but they're on the list of donors. I take it that's significant to you in some way?"

My stomach lurched at the thought of the danger I had put Gordo in by involving him in this investigation.

"Gordo," I said firmly, "I don't want you to do any more work on this. I'm sorry, but I got you in way over your head."

"Why? What is it?"

I hesitated, wondering what to tell him. I didn't want to violate the confidences that had been shared by agents Litman and Quinn; on the other hand, Gordo needed to know the kind of danger he was now in.

"Human smuggling," I said finally. "Manno Seafoods is a front for a group of people who smuggle illegal immigrants in from China."

Gordo let out a small whistle.

"Thanks a lot, Callie," he said. "You coulda warned me."

"I had no idea," I told him. "I'm working a completely different investigation that has to do with them. But somehow there's a connection. It doesn't make any sense."

And it didn't. Once Gordo promised me he would watch his back and we hung up the phone, I sat in the kitchen for a long time, trying to fit the pieces of the puzzle together.

How could Manno Seafoods be connected to CNA? It made no sense! These were two investigations I was running, two totally separate inquiries on behalf of two totally separate people in two totally separate situations. And yet, they intersected. What—or who—was the common denominator, either wittingly or unwittingly? Shayna? Earl Ray? Verlene?

I pressed my hands against my eyes and tried to think it through.

Manno Seafoods was on record with the IRS as being a donor to CNA, a group that arranged funding for charities. But since Manno wasn't really a legitimate business, then obviously their donations to CNA weren't legit either.

CNA itself had to be a decent company, or they wouldn't have such good ratings across the board with all of the watchdog groups. I needed to get a look at the breakdown of their finances, so I went down the hall to the office, got online, and downloaded the file Gordo had said would be waiting for me.

Sure enough, once I took a look at the file, I realized that the breakdown of figures provided a very clear picture of the financial workings of CNA. Figures that had essentially been "hidden" when looking at CNA as a whole were now strikingly obvious when examined division by division.

For the Small Agencies Division, the percentage of fundraising costs versus the total amount raised was appallingly high. If this division stood alone as an agency, there is no way I could ever recommend anyone to become affiliated with them. Why this had never become an issue to the company as a whole, I didn't know. I had a feeling CNA concentrated its scrutiny on the larger, more prominent divisions and left Maureen pretty much to her own devices. Sadly, I had seen this before with other nonprofits; usually, once we turned down their request for a grant, they would finally catch on to what was happening within their own agency and clean up their act.

In this case, I now felt certain that this connection with the smugglers was a singular effort by Maureen Burnham conducted within the boundaries of her position as the head of the Small Agencies Division.

But why? What was she trying to do?

I thought about it and decided that all of these machinations must be providing a way for working some money through the system. Maybe when Manno "donated" a chunk of cash to CNA through Maureen Burnham, she would apply just a small percentage of that "donation" to a corresponding charity—to make it look legitimate—then pay the rest back out as a "commission" to a "donor broker." Perhaps, then, the broker kicked back some to her, ergo the need for her to invest that cash somewhere logical, like jewelry. The remainder of the money then would be given by the broker to whomever it was down the smuggling chain who was waiting for it. Or maybe the broker was the mastermind for the whole thing, the one to whom the money was due, and he kept it for himself.

I thought back over all of Maureen Burnham's references, good and bad, and I realized that I hadn't been seeing the picture that was being painted in front of me. Apparently, Maureen spent her time recruiting small nonprofits, promising a full range of services once they signed up with CNA. That was her job, after all. But once they signed up, she either ignored them and sent almost no money their way at all, or she gave them plenty of attention along with full funding. I guessed that the places in the latter group were the only ones she really cared about, since they were the ones who were unwittingly instrumental in providing a secondary paycheck in her direction. I looked at the list of nonprofits that had received the greatest funding, and I realized that those charities were located in areas known for heavy smuggling: Miami. Seattle. California.

And now here on Maryland's Eastern Shore, with Advancing Attire.

I reached for the phone and dialed Agent Litman. He didn't answer, so I left him a voice mail, stressing it was urgent he contact me as soon as possible. I was just about to send him a text as well when the phone rang in my hand. It was Litman, calling me back.

"That was quick," I said, answering the phone. "Thanks so much."

"You said it was urgent. What do you want?" he snapped.

Forcing myself to remain calm and professional, I asked if he had ever heard of CNA, or the Comprehensive Nonprofit Alliance.

He was silent for a long moment.

"Why do you ask?" he said finally.

"Because I think I've made a connection between them and Manno Seafoods. I think Manno is somehow working money to the smugglers through CNA. More than that, I have a whole list of CNA donors that are probably bogus, that are likely doing the same exact thing."

Litman cursed, demanding to know where I had gotten this list. I told him that I had my sources.

"We've got a leak in this department!" he exclaimed. "If you got that information from one of my agents, I need to know about it now."

"No," I said, thinking of the poor woman whom Gordo had charmed at the IRS. She didn't know what she was getting herself into. "This information came from somewhere else entirely. Trust me, it wasn't from the Department of Immigration and Naturalization."

"Where is this list now?" he asked. "Do you have it there?"

"Yes."

"Then listen carefully to what I'm telling you. I need you to fax that list of agency names to my office, and then I need for you to destroy it. That list could put you in a lot of danger, Callie. You aren't safe as long as you have those names in your possession."

He wasn't telling me anything I didn't already know!

"I've got your fax number on your card," I said. "I'll send over the list now."

"Go ahead. I'll wait."

He didn't disconnect the call, so I set down the phone, carried the list to the office, and faxed it over. Once it was feeding through, I returned to the kitchen and picked up the phone.

"Are you getting it?" I asked.

"It's coming in now," he said. When it was finished, he told me he would hold on and wait while I burned it.

I retrieved the paper from the fax tray, but when I carried it back into the kitchen, I had no intention of burning anything. Knowing Litman was listening, I picked up a piece of scrap paper from the counter, carried it over to the sink, then loudly struck a match and burned the paper to a crisp, washing the ashes down the drain when it was finished.

"Done," I said into the phone.

"Good," he replied. "Now, do you remember what we discussed about obstruction of justice? I need to know where you got that list, Callie, and I'm not going to take no for an answer."

I shook my head firmly, though of course he couldn't see me through the phone.

"Bring me up on charges if you want," I told him, "but I'm not going to reveal my sources. Suffice it to say that I came at this information in a very roundabout way. It has nothing to do with you or the INS."

"Understand that I can have you held for an uncomfortably long period of time," he threatened. "Sometimes the wheels of justice turn very, very slowly."

"Hey, Litman, at least I called you and told you about it," I said. "Look, I'm investigating CNA for a local charity, that's all. Obviously, you've heard of them. There's a woman there named Maureen—"

"Maureen Burnham, yes, we know. She's been under investigation for quite a while."

"Well, I was kind of digging around about her, and I turned this stuff up. That's all."

I took his silence as acquiescence, for the moment at least.

"Webber," he said, "you are about to push one too many of my buttons. Don't the words 'cease and desist' mean *anything* to you?"

"What can I say?" I replied. "Up until a few minutes ago, I had no idea that CNA was connected in any way with smuggling."

"Well, now I hope you'll choose to forget it, and let us do our jobs."

I agreed to stay out of his hair and hung up the phone.

Then I called Tom and left a message on his voice mail, asking him if there was any way—any way at all—that he thought he might be able to use his connections to get me in on that INS raid tonight.

Forty-Two

While I was waiting for Tom to call back, I went outside with Sal, wondering when I would have time to fix the gaping hole in her fence. I went to the shed, bringing the list that Litman thought I had burned. Now that I had faxed it to him, I doubted I would need it myself, but I still was reluctant to part with such weighty information. Instead, I dug out an old aluminum canoe paddle from a pile, pulled off the end cap, rolled up the list, and dropped it down inside. Then I tucked the paddle back where I had found it and closed the shed up tight.

Once we were back inside, I headed for the shower, leaving the bathroom door open so I could hear the phone. It finally rang as I was getting dressed; it was Tom, sounding in excellent spirits. He told me they had taken his mother out of intensive care and moved her to a private room.

We talked about that for a few minutes as I pulled on tweed slacks and a cream-colored sweater. Apparently, his mother's CAT scan had turned out well, and there was good movement in both hands and feet.

"Anyway," he said finally, "enough about us. I know you called for a reason. It sounded important. What's up?"

"I need a favor," I said, thinking this was the first time in our relationship I had ever uttered those words. I didn't really like favors and obligations, but Tom was a master at pulling strings, and it seemed like such a small request in the grand scheme of things.

As simply and benignly as I could, I explained that I had been doing some investigating for Advancing Attire and that I had run up against a brick wall, because it turned out that the INS was already involved with the situation, from a different angle. Did he know anyone, I asked, who might have the authority to allow me to ride along on an immigration bust? I wouldn't get in the way, I said, I just wanted to be there, to help close out my own investigations.

Fortunately, Tom didn't seem unduly alarmed by my request. I knew I had sugarcoated things a bit, but the fact remained that I needed him to help me become part of an official government operation. He said he knew someone important with the Department of Justice, which had jurisdiction over the INS, and they might be able to help.

I provided the details, reminding him that this was all quite confidential. He assured me he would look into it discreetly and get back to me, one way or the other, in the next couple of hours.

That done, I hung up the phone and stood in the kitchen, trying to decide what to do next. Though I was sick and sore, my main draw was to the water, to my trusty canoe. I decided to go for an abbreviated ride up the river. I didn't have the strength or the time to paddle the full five miles, especially since I had agreed to have lunch with Kirby at 1:30. But as long as I kept it short, I should be able to get a little time on the water.

First, however, I needed to spend a few minutes updating the database on my computer. Once that was finished, I went online and did some quick reading about Chinese human smuggling. Primarily, I was interested in the money chain and how it worked. What I read reaffirmed what Litman and Hank had told us, that it could cost anywhere from $30,000 to $80,000 to be smuggled from China to the U.S., and that it usually involved payments at both ends: a deposit to get started on the trip, and then the balance at the other end, either in the form of years of backbreaking labor by the immigrant or heavy payments by relatives already established in the U.S.

If money had to change hands along the line, I thought as I signed off and then shut down the computer, then perhaps the nonprofit angle was a clever way for them to do it. The money that needed to be moved from both ends to the middle could be given as "donations" to CNA. And as long as Maureen Burnham funneled most of that money out to a broker, who then facilitated its distribution to the snakeheads, their plan worked. Since Manno Seafoods seemed to be some sort of immigrant processing station, then I could only assume that the donations they were giving to CNA were actually what was left of the "front-end" money, the deposits, after expenses had been deducted along the way.

My head hurts too much for this. I grabbed my coat, called Sal, and headed out to the canoe. We hit the water at a slower-than-usual pace, and I tried to let the beauty of my surroundings temporarily erase all thoughts of snakeheads or immigrants or money laundering. But in the end I finally just took it all to the Lord in prayer, asking for wisdom and closure with Shayna's and Verlene's cases—and tact and grace with Kirby.

Kirby. Such a dear man, and yet I knew in my heart of hearts that our relationship was going nowhere. I found him attractive, and he was a lot of fun to be with, but there was a major element missing. What, I wasn't sure.

"Is it just fear that's holding me back, God?" I prayed out loud. "Or is he really not meant for me?"

I asked the Lord to show me the true nature of my heart and what His will was for me in this matter. I had been hiding many sides of myself since Bryan died, and I confessed now the sin of not giving over every single part of my life to God.

Slowly paddling along, I passed the point where the lovers' pine leaned out over the water. Studying the trunk, I tried to understand—as I had many times before—what would make two trees somehow grow into one. It had to have been something else that wasn't present anymore, some outside force that had caused them to intertwine. But what? A vine that had pulled them together? Maybe a storm that had tangled their branches until they could no longer be untangled?

Whatever it was, the two had nearly become one, and now they formed what looked like almost a single unit, one mighty, majestic pine. To chop down one of the trunks would mean certain death for both.

That's what Bryan's death was like for me. His removal from my life was like what the removal of one of those tree trunks would be: painful, brutal, even fatal.

And yet…

And yet it hadn't been fatal. I was still here, still living in this world, still trying to understand where the other half of me had gone. Time does heal. I could openly admit that now, for every day after Bryan's death had seemed ever-so-slightly less of a heartache than the day before. With enough days piled together, I had slowly learned that I could function, that I could exist, that I could find moments of happiness and sometimes even joy.

But what was the lesson waiting for me now, with Kirby pressing so urgently into my life? Was it to open myself to the chance of love again? I paddled away from the tree, wondering if this wasn't about love or romance at all—but about fellowship in general.

Connect, I could almost hear the Lord saying now. *Reach out to others. This is what I want for you.*

I blinked away tears, wondering why it was so much easier in the midst of my pain to draw into myself and pretend I didn't need anyone. Yet, all I ever heard from the few people who I did let into my life—Harriet, Verlene, Eli—was that I was hiding, that I still needed to open up more, that I wouldn't really begin true healing until I could start making some connections.

Once I grasped that, I could see, suddenly, why God had given me someone like Kirby, a man who was pushy enough to work his way past all of the walls I had so carefully constructed around me. The common bond of our mutual grief had disarmed me from the beginning, and his enthusiastic nature—combined with his good looks, charming ways, and the feelings he professed to have for me—had all served to make me vulnerable at a time when vulnerability was exactly what God desired most for me.

Yet Kirby probably wasn't who God wanted for me as a love interest. If he were, I think my heart would've known. I would always be grateful for what he had shown me, that I could dare to open myself to others, that I could risk making new connections, and, most importantly, that I could take a chance at romance without betraying the memory of my husband. But I just felt, deep inside, that God had someone else in mind for me to love. Someone else down the road a bit, when I had healed even more.

In my heart, I had a feeling that person was Tom.

Suddenly, an image of Bryan's smile, his laugh, filled my mind, and with the clarity of a photograph I could suddenly picture him there in a canoe next to me. *Come on, Callie,* he called to me in my imagination. *Race you home!*

Despite the tears that streamed down my face, I lifted the paddle high and plunged it into the water, my heart suddenly soaring. I could almost hear him singing out one of his favorite hymns, his voice ringing across the water like a bell:

Blest be the tie that binds
Our hearts in Christian love;
The fellowship of kindred minds
Is like to that above.

I paddled to the rhythm of the song, singing each verse myself, finally reaching my dock as I got to the verse I loved best. I tied up my canoe and then stood at the end of the dock and sang out my favorite lines:

When we asunder part,
It gives us inward pain;
But we shall still be joined in heart,
And hope to meet again.

Forty-Three

I got to Kirby's a few minutes late, after taking the time to fix my hair and repair my makeup. I felt kind of sad but also at peace. I needed to be honest with him. I needed to let him know there was no future for us as a couple.

I parked in front and rang the bell, and eventually he came to the door, grinning. Over nice slacks and a dress shirt he was wearing an apron, and in his hand he held a big spoon.

"Callie!" he cried. "Come in. Guess what? We're slumming it."

"Slumming it?"

He leaned over to kiss me hello. I turned my face so that his lips brushed my cheek.

"Yeah, come on back," he said, without seeming to notice. "Not thinking, I gave the cook the day off. So we're having chili, the one and only thing I know how to make myself. I hope that's okay with you."

"Of course. Can I help?"

"No, no, you're my guest," he said. "Come on in and sit down. It's almost ready."

I followed him into the dining room, where I was surprised to see his grandmother, Eleanor, and her nurse, Carol. They were sitting at the large table, which had been set for four down at one end. Cheese and crackers were arranged on a center platter, and tall glasses of ice water had been put next to each place.

"Hello again," I said to them as Kirby took my coat and then held the seat for me directly across from the two women. "This is a pleasure."

"Eleanor's having a good day," Carol said, placing a napkin in the lap of her charge, "so we thought we'd join you."

"Stop treating me like a baby. I'm perfectly capable of managing a napkin," the older woman said to the nurse, taking it from her. Slowly and deliberately, she spread it on her own lap.

"I'm Eleanor Collins," she told me when she was done. "I understand we've met before?"

She looked at me, eyes lucid and clear. *How disconcerting,* I thought. The last time we met she was in a complete fog, sitting right here and having an imaginary tea party.

"Yes, ma'am," I said. "It's good to see you again."

"Now, Grandma," Kirby said loudly, "we're all having chili, but I made you some oatmeal. Okay?"

She looked from Carol to me and then up at him.

"No, it's not 'okay,' " she said. "But I suppose it will have to do."

He left the room, and then she winked at me.

"He's a good boy," she said.

"Yes, ma'am. He certainly is."

Kirby returned juggling the bowls of chili and oatmeal, explaining that everyone except Carol had been given the day off.

"It's not often I wake the staff at four A.M. to draw hot baths and serve coffee," he said. "I thought it was the least I could do."

"How is Mr. Buchman?" I asked.

"Sleeping like a baby the last time I checked," Kirby replied, smiling.

He sat to my right at the head of the table and led us in a short grace, and then we all started eating. The chili was perfectly fine, albeit a bit spicier than I usually liked. I ate mine with a lot of crackers and plenty of water.

The meal was very pleasant. I could tell Kirby had a nice relationship with his grandmother's nurse, and Eleanor herself was sharp and funny. At one point, after she made a little joke, I noticed Kirby looking at her wistfully. How difficult it must be, I thought, to live with someone who was there all the time—yet only rarely really *there.*

After lunch, Kirby and I did the dishes together while I filled him in on my conversation with Tom. Afterward, he gave me back my coat and suggested a walk, which I welcomed. The air had turned rather warm, much more so than in recent days, and I barely needed my coat as we stepped out into the sun. Stepping outside, Kirby took my hand and I let him, wondering how long it would be before I held hands with anyone else again. I thought of Shayna, grabbing onto Eddie Ray out of loneliness. *Part of me just wanted a man around again,* she had said. *Somebody to hold my hand. Somebody to say nice things to me.*

I, too, had found it nice to have a man around again. But the difference between me and Shayna was that it was important to me that it be the *right* man and not just any man. Kirby deserved to know the truth.

We walked slowly, without talking. Finally, we reached an ornate iron bench near the dock. We sat, looking out at the water, silent for a while longer. I was thinking hard, trying to come up with the right words, when Kirby finally spoke.

"You're awfully quiet today," he said finally. "You okay?"

"I have a lot on my mind."

"Shayna's case?"

"Well, yeah," I said. "But us, too. I've been thinking a lot about us."

He hesitated and then looked at me. Finally, he bent over and picked up a few shells from the ground, stood, and began tossing them one by one into the water.

"Oh man, here it comes," he said. "The great kiss-off speech."

"I'm not kissing you off."

"Yes you are," he said. "I know that look. I've felt it on my own face. I've given the speech myself about a hundred times. Save yourself the trouble, Callie. You'll always think of me fondly, we'll still be friends, blah, blah, blah."

"Kirby—"

"I know I've been coming on too strong," he said, tossing the last shell into the water. He dusted off his hands, and then he turned and knelt on the grass in front of me, taking both of my hands in his and looking at me earnestly. "But you've got to understand that you're one of the most interesting, unique people I've ever met. Not to mention you're beautiful and smart and kind and just about everything else I ever wanted in a woman. If I've come on strong, it's because for the first time in my life I've found someone I can look at and actually envision a future with. Do you know how weird that is for me? The rich playboy meeting someone who makes him want to grow up and settle down? You make me want to be a better person, Callie. You make me want to be worthy of you."

"You are such a special man," I whispered, tears filling my eyes. I reached out to touch his cheek. "But I'm sorry, Kirby. My heart just isn't in this."

"I know," he answered softly, stroking my hair. "Your late husband. In time—"

"No," I said. "This isn't about my husband."

Kirby met my eyes and held them for a long time. I could tell he was trying to put it all together, how this independent woman who lived alone and hadn't even kissed a man in three years could now afford to turn him, the great Kirby Collins, down.

"Your boss," he said finally, incredulously, pulling away from me. He stood and ran a hand through his hair. "You've got a thing for your boss!"

My face reddened.

"What? We've never even met in person, for goodness' sake."

"It doesn't matter," he said. "I've seen the way your face lights up when you talk about him. You're in love with him!"

Taken aback, I shook my head.

In love with Tom? Of course not. How could I love someone I didn't even really know?

I shook my head and forced the conversation back on track.

"Listen, Kirby," I said. "I'm sorry it's not going to work out between us. But there isn't anyone else, and this isn't a typical kiss-off speech. You showed me something about myself this week, and for that I will be eternally grateful."

"Oh yeah?" he asked, a hint of sarcasm in his voice. "What'd I show you? How quickly I can make a fool of myself?"

I tried not to be offended by his tone, knowing he was speaking from his own wounded pride. I spoke softly and evenly, wanting this to be an honest conversation and not just angry words between hurting people.

"Being with you this week has made me realize that it's time for me to start living again. I'm ready. And I have you to thank for that, Kirby. You'll never, ever know what a change you've made in my life."

He stared off toward the water for a long time.

"I can't even hate you for this," he said finally. "Because I understand what you're saying. In just a few days' time, I've watched you change. It's like I've seen you come alive."

He met my eyes. Then, slowly, he sat down on the bench next to me, wrapped his arms around my shoulders, and pulled me in for a hug. I hugged him back, hoping we could still be friends. I really didn't want to lose him completely.

"It's time for you to come back to life, too," I said.

He relaxed the hug and kept one arm casually draped around my shoulders. I leaned into him, resting my head there, feeling the warmth of his body next to mine.

"I don't know what you mean," he said.

"I mean, you obviously loved your mother very much. You miss her."

He was quiet for a while, looking out at the water. On the other bank, I could see a tree, vibrant orange, its leaves falling one by one and then floating away. I thought about the cycles of nature, about life and death and rebirth, and I wondered if Kirby knew the Lord well enough to understand that physical death wasn't just an ending—it was also a beginning. For me, that knowledge was all that could comfort me after Bryan's death.

"My mother was a wonderful lady," he said. "It wasn't fair how she had to go."

"No," I agreed. "It wasn't. But she is gone now, and you're not. It's time to get your own life back. Time to focus. As you said, time to grow up."

"It might help if I knew what I really wanted out of life," he admitted. "Do I stay here and care for my grandmother until she dies, too? Is that my lot in life, to keep marking time while the women I love slowly waste away and die?"

"Oh, Kirby, of course not."

"There were parts of my old job I really liked. The research. The fiddling around with new things. The inventing. But I don't want to go back to the workaday world. I like knowing I'm helping out around here."

"Then do both. Work from home. Combine research and development with taking care of your family. Seems to me, if it's your father's company, you can structure things almost any way you want."

"I suppose that's true," he said.

"At least give it some thought."

"I will. I mean, I hate to sound like a whiny rich kid, but it's hard when you grow up getting everything you ever asked for. If it's all available to you, how do you ever learn what really matters?"

"At the risk of sounding simplistic," I said, "you go to the Bible. It tells you, straight out, what is and what isn't important here on earth. Base your life on God's Word and on His will, Kirby, and you cannot go wrong. I promise you that."

"Is that what you do?"

"As much as I can."

He nodded.

"By what I've seen," he said, "it really works for you. I mean, you seem to go through life the way you paddle a canoe, Callie. Like you know where you're going and exactly how you're going to get there."

"Ah, but there's where you're wrong," I replied, smiling. "In life, my hands aren't even on the paddle. I'm just holding on to the side of the boat, trusting the Lord—I guess you could call Him the Master Paddler—to take me wherever it is He wants me to go."

Forty-Four

The phone was ringing when I walked in the door, and I caught it just before it went to the machine. It was Tom, calling to tell me he had been able to work things out for me with the INS, and that I would, indeed, be allowed to go along with them tonight, as long as I adhered to their lengthy list of rules.

"An Agent Litman will be in touch with you in a little while to work out the details," he said. "I had to pull in some major favors for this one, so you need to be as unobtrusive as possible."

"Don't worry," I replied. "They won't even know I'm there."

Sal was eagerly trying to say hello, so I cradled the phone against my shoulder as I bent down and scooped her up in my arms.

"Apparently, civilians are *never* allowed on something like this," Tom continued. "But they're willing to make an exception this time, especially given that you are already so involved with the case. Just keep a low profile, okay?"

"Okay," I promised.

"Now, officially, you're going to be under the watch of Agent Litman."

"I've already had the pleasure," I said, trying not to sound sarcastic.

"Well, listen, if you're out there tonight and there's any kind of problem and this Litman fellow isn't available, I want you to ask for the other guy, Hank Quinn."

"All right."

"According to my contact, Hank's a real stand-up guy. You can rely on him completely."

"Okay. I will."

I could hear something in his voice, some hesitation.

"What is it?" I asked. "Is there something else?"

"I was just wondering about your new boyfriend," he said, an odd note to his voice. "Is he wanting to go along, too?"

I let that sit between us, trying to figure out how Tom had learned about Kirby so quickly. From one of the agents who had been there last night, I supposed. So Kirby holding my hand had not gone unnoticed!

"No, he's not interested," I said breezily. Let Tom decide how to respond to that.

He was quiet for a moment.

"Is it serious?" he asked, his tone more subdued. "This relationship with this guy?"

"Are you asking me that question as my boss? Because you know by law you have no right to intrude in my personal affairs."

"It's been a while since I was merely your boss, Callie."

"I'm just saying you can't ask me that."

The line was silent for a moment.

"You're right," he said finally. "I'm sorry. I hope it works out for you. I'm off to Singapore tonight anyway, so I guess it's all for the best."

He was quiet, though I could almost hear the tension crackling between us. I set Sal back on the floor and went to the cabinet to get her a treat. Kirby had accused me of being in love with Tom, which was crazy. *I can't love a man I don't even know.*

Can I?

"What about Janine?" I asked finally.

"Janine?"

"At the airport? The beautiful blonde with the big engagement ring?"

"What about her?"

I held out Sal's treat in front of me, and she jumped up and snatched it in her mouth.

"Who is she to you, Tom? Was that your ring on her finger?"

Much to my surprise, he laughed.

"Is that what you thought?" he said. "Me and *Janine?*"

"She implied—"

"Callie," Tom said, "Janine was just helping me out. In an official capacity."

"Oh?"

"She and her fiancé are old friends of mine. Janine is a high-ranking official with the FAA."

"The FAA?"

"She was just doing me a favor, getting me on a flight at the last minute. Then she agreed to meet you to pass on my message in person."

I wasn't sure what to say. I was quite surprised and a little embarrassed. Primarily, however, I was overwhelmed with a great sense of relief.

"I...I broke things off with Kirby today," I admitted. "We're not going out anymore—not that we ever really were."

Sal finished her treat and then ran to the door and scratched at it. I let her into her play yard, watching to make sure she didn't run off through the gap in the fence.

"Would I be presumptuous," Tom said softly, "if I told you I was really, really glad?"

I blinked, a surge of some emotion I couldn't name clouding my vision.

"I wish I could understand," I said, "the true nature of what you and I are to each other."

"It is confusing," he replied, "but we both know there's something there. There always has been, since the very beginning of our relationship."

"I know," I said, "but considering the fact that I don't know what you look like, that I don't know any of the details of your life, that you seem to have spies in every tree watching me while I'm not allowed to delve into even the most minute, insignificant detail about you—I don't know if I could call this a 'relationship' or not. A relationship requires participation by both parties, Tom. Alive and usually in person."

"I don't have spies in every tree. That's not fair."

"Then how did you know about Kirby?"

"The agents who were there last night said you weren't working alone. They said that you and this Kirby guy seemed to be a couple."

"A couple of what?"

"You know what I mean. A couple. Involved."

I thought about all that Tom and I had shared, albeit over the telephone, and I wondered if part of the attraction for me with Tom was the very inaccessibility of it all. For a woman dealing with issues of seclusion and withdrawal, this fellow, who seemed to exist mostly in my imagination, provided a dangerous and convenient situation indeed.

The important thing, then, was not what had taken place with us so far, but what we were willing to do now. Could we take this relationship out of fantasy and into reality? And if we did, would the reality of who Tom was come anywhere close to the man I had created in my imagination?

"Where do we go from here?" I asked.

"I don't know."

We were both quiet, confused by what was taking place. I let Sal back into the house and looked out at my wooded yard, at the sun setting behind the trees, and prayed for guidance.

"I just want to get this right," he said finally, and I knew exactly what he meant.

More than anything, I wanted to get this right, too.

Forty-Five

We rolled at midnight. Wearing enough layers to stay warm even at the North Pole, I parked my car at the designated spot (the parking lot of a grocery store in Osprey Cove) and waited for Agent Litman to pick me up.

Since talking to Tom, I had eaten dinner, updated my database, and then tried taking a nap in preparation for another all-nighter. I'm not sure how much sleep I actually got, but it had still been restful to spend a few hours just lying down, drifting in and out. Now it was midnight. My mind felt sharp and clear, and my body was in much better shape than it had been earlier in the day. My sleep patterns had been so messed up the last few days, I wondered if I might need a week off to recover from my week off!

Agent Litman showed up exactly on time, and I left my car in the parking lot and got into his. As I sat down and shut the door, I braced myself, knowing I was about to become the target of his wrath.

"I don't know who you know," he said with controlled fury, "or how you managed to get yourself included here tonight. But I just want to make certain you understand that this is highly irregular. The INS does not allow civilians to come along on a bust. Ever."

He prattled on about security clearances and the Department of Justice Privacy Act, steering out of the parking lot as he ranted. I remembered Hank saying that Litman was strictly a by-the-book kind of guy. I would imagine someone pulling a few strings to get me here had really rattled his cage.

"So who is it?" he pressed, heading down the dark road at a pretty fair clip. "Who do you know who was able to get you on this mission?"

I shook my head, hoping we would get to wherever we were going soon.

"Someone important in the Department of Justice," I said. "I don't think you need to know anything beyond that."

The fact that *I* didn't know anything beyond that almost made me smile. *This is just how things work with Tom,* I thought but did not say. *Somehow he has the power to open doors.*

Litman grunted but left it alone, turning instead to a long list of warnings about tonight's mission. Apparently, this bust was to be the culmination of a nearly two-year investigation. No wonder he didn't want me nosing around and messing it up!

Litman drove us to the marina in Cambridge, where we boarded a small vessel about the size of a tugboat. According to him, from there we would sail out to the Intracoastal Waterway and blend in with the other ships as we approached Manno Island. I understood their operation was multifaceted, and we would not be with the team who took the island. Instead, we would be with the observation and coordination forces at a nearby vantage point.

On board, the mood seemed somber but efficient. Litman positioned me inside the lower cabin at a window and told me that under no circumstances was I allowed to leave that spot. I gave him my word that I would stay put.

"We may seem like a peripheral part of tonight's operation," he warned me, "but our presence is as integral to this bust as any other part of the team. We're monitoring the activity electronically. In fact, I'm linked to Hank's wire," he said, pointing to a small earphone clipped over one of his ears. "I can hear everything as it happens."

Once he felt that I was suitably impressed by the gravity of the situation, he went out the door and up some stairs to what I assumed was the main control room. I watched from my vantage point at the window as a number of people made their way around the small ship, some heading up the stairs after Litman, some preparing the ship to set sail. Everything was quiet except for the low hum of the motor, punctuated occasionally by the groans and creaks of the vessel itself.

Even being stuck out of the way of the main action, I was excited to be there. Once we pulled out of the harbor and got going, my heart was actually pounding. The night was dark away from the lights of Cambridge, and I pressed my face to the glass and looked out at the passing shoreline, glad I had brought my night-vision binoculars for later.

We sailed for about 30 minutes before slowing to a stop in the middle of the river and just sitting there, engine idling. I was afraid something was wrong with the ship. When a uniformed officer crossed through the small room I was in, I stopped him, and he told me we would be waiting here until we got word that it was time to close in on Manno Island.

We waited nearly an hour and a half. In that time, I occupied myself by devising different escape routes in my mind, should something go wrong. The longer we waited, the more I began to have second thoughts about being here at all. It was just a nagging feeling of doubt, but it had begun creeping up on me as we idled, and now it was growing stronger. This sense of foreboding wasn't strong enough to make me pull out, but it was keeping me on my toes.

As I waited for something to happen, I realized the mood was different for me than when I was doing surveillance. This time, the knowledge that something big was going to happen—as opposed to the thought that it *might* happen or *could* happen—nearly drove me crazy with anticipation.

Tonight, it was just a matter of time.

Finally, a little after 3 A.M., I could sense a difference in the atmosphere. Suddenly, people were milling about overhead, and there was a change in the pitch of the engine sounds. Soon we were on our way again. I wiped the window clear in front of me and held my goggles to my eyes, studying the dark, empty shoreline ahead.

About ten minutes later, we rounded the curve that brought us from the Choptank River out into the Intracoastal Waterway. The water was rougher here, though the boat absorbed most of the waves fairly well.

We moved as slowly as possible, hugging the far side of the channel. A larger ship eventually overtook us and passed us by. We rocked in its wake, and I thought of my terror the night before, clinging for dear life in the dinghy on the back of Russell Lynch's boat. Tonight, Russell would be one of the ones arrested, his nefarious nighttime activities ceased permanently.

I was thinking of him, wondering what had driven him to take part in such a horrendous crime as human smuggling, when I saw the unmistakable silhouette of his boat up ahead. He was heading toward us, but as we drew nearer he veered off to our left, cutting in to the dock at Manno Island. Obviously, he wasn't yet aware he was being observed or that he was going to be greeted at the island not just by the smugglers but by a cadre of INS agents as well.

I watched through my binoculars as his boat pulled into the dock at Manno. Even with my goggles, it was hard to see what was going on from such a distance, but it looked as though a big man, probably Hank, had come out on the dock to meet the boat and was tying it off. I could see Russell step onto the dock and have some sort of discussion with Hank. Suddenly, there was a flash of gunfire from the trees, and then the dock area was crawling with men dressed in black, sporting big guns and taking the operation under control. Hank and Russell stood with their hands up, and they were soon joined by several other smugglers, hands also in the air.

Our boat went up to full speed then, straight for Manno Island. I had so many questions. I was relieved when I could hear pounding footsteps coming down the stairs, and soon Agent Litman appeared in the doorway of my little room. He was pressing the earpiece against his ear, listening intently and grimacing. Finally, he looked at me, shaking his head.

"Good news and bad news," he said curtly. "The good news is, we've taken the island without any fatalities."

"What's the bad news?" I asked.

"The Tanigawa brothers aren't anywhere to be found."

Forty-Six

There had to be 20 people squeezed into a container that really wasn't big enough for a fourth that many. I had been allowed on the island, though I was relegated to the sidelines, and I watched as the people filed off of Russell's ship all in a row, hands clasped at the back of their necks, their bodies decimated, their eyes terrified. One or two looked as if they might drop dead of exhaustion or illness on the spot.

The agents were corralling them together in a group on the grass, and they huddled there looking scared and confused. I wished I spoke Chinese so that I could reassure them: You won't be hurt here, you're in America. You're safe now.

But for how long, really, were they safe? In the car, Litman had told me that despite the arduous journey these people had taken to get here, they would not be allowed to stay in the United States unless they could prove that they would come under direct physical harm if returned to their country. Since most of them were simply peasants who had come here to seek a better, more prosperous life, it was doubtful that any of them would be able to meet that criteria.

I sat on a log, exhaustion suddenly overtaking me as well. It had been such a busy, exciting night, but now the reality of the INS raid was setting in. Again, that strange sense of foreboding clouded my mind, but I brushed it aside and tried to concentrate on all that was happening around me.

Someone brought out some food for the immigrants—what looked like a case of bologna and some juice boxes—and they devoured it all as if they hadn't eaten in days. I watched as agents with guns led Russell and then Hank, both handcuffed, on board a coast guard cutter, one of the several ships that now crowded the island. A few minutes later, three other prisoners were taken aboard, Japanese men who had been armed guards for the island.

I could only assume that Hank being carted away in handcuffs meant that he was still undercover, and that his identity would not be revealed in front of the other smugglers for his own safety. I wondered where they would all be taken, if I would be allowed to listen to any of the interrogations, and how I could possibly find out which one of them was responsible for Eddie Ray's death.

Once the Chinese people had been fed and then led into the picking house en masse, I felt a little more free to move about. I had promised Tom I would follow all of the INS rules to the letter, and thus far I had done just that.

Still, that didn't mean I couldn't explore a bit. Out of curiosity I strolled the small compound, peeking in the windows of the various buildings. First was the picking house at the end of the walkway, just as Murdock had described it. Inside, I could see the immigrants being lined up in rows between long, narrow tables. Apparently, the ones who had arrived last night were also still here and were being herded into the picking house from the dormitory next door.

I moved beyond those two buildings to the third structure, which was set back into the woods a bit. It looked like a small home, a quaint place with a broad, dark wood porch and attractive double doors. The Tanigawas must have lived there, though where they were now was apparently anybody's guess.

The house was wide open, well lit, and swarming with agents. The mood inside was one of angry frustration. Agents were going through drawers, cabinets, closets—and carting off boxes of papers, confiscating bullets and machine gun casings, cursing at each other and the situation.

"Heads will roll for this," one agent yelled, brushing past me as he stormed out the door.

I followed him, wondering how the Tanigawas had known not to be here tonight. Obviously, there was a leak somewhere in this carefully orchestrated operation. I thought of how Agent Litman kept referring to "leaks from inside our own agency." I wondered who the mole was and how long they had been working both sides of the operation.

I had just returned to the dock area when I heard someone calling my name.

"Callie! Callie Webber!"

I looked up to see a woman walking toward me, dressed in the dark clothes and heavy boots of the other agents. When she reached me, she took me by the elbow and began to lead me up the ramp of the same ship where they had taken Hank and Russell and the other prisoners.

"You'll have to come this way, ma'am," the woman said, even as she practically dragged me up the ramp. I hurried along with her, nearly tripping over the lip of the doorway at the top.

"What's this about?" I asked.

She didn't reply but instead led me down a narrow hall and into a small room lined with metal benches. She indicated that I should sit, so I did and waited to hear what she had to say.

"Am I to understand," she said, "that you are a private citizen and not an employee of the Department of Immigration and Naturalization or of the Department of Justice?"

"Yes, that's correct."

"Can you tell me please by whose authority you were brought here on this mission tonight?"

I took a deep breath, heart pounding. I didn't know by whose authority I was here. "Someone who knew someone" was all I could think of—but how could I tell her that?

"Agent Litman is my liason," I said, sitting up straight, trying to look dignified. "Why don't you ask him?"

"Just a minute."

The woman turned on her heel, crossed the hall, and banged once on a metal door. It swung open to reveal another agent.

"I need to see Litman," she said.

"He's translating for the prisoners," the other fellow replied. "What do you want?"

"I need more information about this woman who was allowed to come along on the raid tonight."

She gestured toward me, and the other fellow leaned forward to peek in at me.

"What about her?"

"We had a leak," the woman said. "I need to understand why a civilian was allowed—"

She was interrupted by the man, who spoke in hushed tones, saying something about "the AG's office." In turn, they each looked at me and whispered some more. Then she stepped back into my room.

"I'll be back in a minute," she said gruffly. "Don't move a muscle."

"Yes, ma'am."

She stomped away and I sat there, feeling suddenly sick in the pit of my stomach. Obviously, my being here was causing a big ruckus that would eventually have some sort of an impact on Tom. He had gotten me on this trip by calling in a favor, so if my presence here made for complications, it could only look bad on both Tom and whoever it was who pulled the strings that had gotten me here. I realized now I should've just stayed home.

I reached into my pocket for my phone, thinking I needed to contact Tom and warn him things hadn't exactly gone off without a hitch. Calculating the time difference, I decided that he was well on his way to Singapore now, probably somewhere out over the Pacific. Though I couldn't call him on the airplane, I could at least leave a warning message on his voice mail. Before I could even dial, however, I saw the screen was showing five missed calls.

They had told me to turn my phone off while on the tugboat, and since then I had forgotten about it. I pressed the button to bring up the numbers of the missed calls, wondering who had been trying to reach me so late at night.

I looked at the number—the same number for each of the missed calls—and realized it was the code for Cleveland, Ohio.

"Gordo," I whispered, quickly pressing the buttons that would allow me to return his calls. Despite the uncomfortable churning in my stomach, my hope was that he was calling to tell me of some new development in the investigation. Perhaps, I thought, even though I had told him to stop poking around, he had persisted and somehow managed to learn some of the missing elements to this equation, such as the connection between these two investigations, or perhaps even the name of the donor broker himself. I put the phone to my ear and heard a busy signal, so I hung up and decided to try again in a few minutes.

I sat on the metal bench, shifting to find a more comfortable position before finally giving up. There was no comfortable way to sit there. I turned my attention instead to the room across the hall. The agent had left the door slightly ajar, and I could hear sounds of the interrogation taking place. Someone was questioning the armed guards, and Litman was acting as the translator.

"How long have you known Kenji and Shin Tanigawa?" a man asked.

"*Tanigawa Kenji to Tanigawa Shin wo itsukara shitte irunda?*" Litman repeated in Japanese.

"*Roku nen desu,*" one of the prisoners replied. I translated in my own head, six years.

"Six years," Litman repeated.

"How long have you been working out of this island?" the man asked.

"*Donokurai kono shima de hataraite irunda?*" Litman said.

"*Daitai jyuuhaci kagetsu desu.*" *Approximately eighteen months,* I thought, trying again.

"About eighteen months," Litman translated.

For being so rusty, I thought I was doing pretty well.

Turning my attention to the phone, I pressed the redial button, and this time I was able to get through. Much to my surprise, instead of Gordo, a woman answered.

"Hello?" she said, sounding soft and tentative.

"Hello?" I replied, a bit confused. "Were you calling me?"

"Is this Callie Webber?" she asked.

As I was saying yes, the female INS agent returned to the room, her face contrite. I asked the woman on the phone to hold for a moment.

"Uh, ma'am," the lady in front of me said, much more subdued than before. "I apologize for the misunderstanding. You are certainly free to return to the main area until we're ready to leave the island."

I wondered what to make of her extreme shift in attitude.

"I don't understand," I said, covering the mouthpiece of the telephone. She lowered her voice and leaned toward me.

"You should've told me you were here by special request of the Attorney General of the United States," she said. "None of this would've happened."

The U.S. Attorney General himself? Unbelievable. And Tom had said he knew "someone important" in the Department of Justice! I grinned in spite of myself at the sheer audacity of it. This was so like him.

"If you'll wait just another minute," she said, "I'll show you back out."

"Okay."

She stepped away to confer with someone while I returned my attention back to the phone.

"I'm sorry," I said softly. "Yes, this is Callie. Who is this?"

"I'm Gordo Koski's secretary," she said. "I got your number from his address book."

"Yes?"

"I just wanted to tell you that...to let you know what's happened. He kept saying your name all the way to the hospital. He wanted me to call you."

"The hospital?"

"Gordo got...Gordo's been hurt. Real bad. The police think somebody roughed him up."

I felt a surge of bile rise into my throat.

"*What?*"

"They found him in an alley in downtown Cleveland. Gosh, it was really awful. He's all banged up and his jaw is broken. He's in the operating room right now. They said it might be a while before they're done."

My own legs began wobbling beneath me, and I sat on the metal bench, steadying myself with one hand against the wall.

"What did Gordo say? What did he want you to tell me?"

"I think he was talking crazy. With his face all messed up, I could hardly understand his words."

"What was it?" I pressed.

"He said to tell you he got the name of the broken donut?"

"You mean the donor broker?" I asked, heart pounding.

"Yeah, I think that was it. He was pretty sure. He said 'Callie's got to know, Callie's got to know.'"

"Who is it?" I asked.

"He kept saying the name over and over. It sounded like…gosh, I can't remember. Hold on a second. I wrote it down."

I sat there and waited, my mind a blur, unable to think or feel anything other than numb. This was my fault. Gordo was in the hospital all because of me.

The secretary was taking forever. As I waited, I could still hear the translating that was going on across the hall.

"Do you know the whereabouts of the Tanigawa brothers at this time?" a male voice asked.

"*Tanigawa kyoudai ga ima donoatari ni iru ka shitte iruka?*" Litman asked.

"*Hai.*"

"Yes."

"Where are they?"

"*Yatsura wa doko ni irunda?*" Litman repeated.

"*Kareraha wa moutaabouto de boruchimoa ni mukatte kita e hashitte imasu,*" was the reply. By my rough translation, I thought absurdly, that meant the Tanigawa brothers were on a speedboat, headed north to Baltimore.

"They're riding in the back of a commercial truck, heading south toward Florida," Litman said.

I sat up straight, my lungs suddenly devoid of air. I may not have been fluent in the language, but I knew what they had said, and "south" toward "Florida" in a "truck" was not it!

"Okay, here we go," the girl said into the phone. "It's Litman. That's the name. The donor broker is Jeffrey Litman."

I inhaled sharply, the hot sting of tears piercing my eyes.

It was Litman! Litman was the donor broker, the person who was working with Maureen Burnham to run tens of thousands of dollars through CNA.

Now, right here across the hall, Litman—the fellow everyone deferred to, the one everyone said was so by-the-book—was deliberately mistranslating the prisoners' statements, giving the Tanigawas a chance to get away. My heart pounded. Though he had been feigning outrage at the leaks from inside the INS, it was Litman himself who had been the one responsible!

And even though he hadn't been there to actually do it himself, it was also Litman who must've called the shots on what had been done to Gordo Koski—and probably Eddie Ray as well.

I needed help. I was on Litman's territory now; I couldn't go up to just anyone and report what I had learned. They were already suspicious of me, and they all respected and trusted him. What was I going to do? I didn't know who to turn to or where to go. Then I thought of Hank. Hank was the one person Tom had assured me I could trust.

Numbly, I thanked the secretary and told her that I would get back to her soon. I hung up the phone, but before I could do anything else, the INS agent who had brought me onto the boat now concluded her conversation and reappeared at my side.

"Sorry about that," she said. "I can show you out now."

I followed her until we were outside, out of earshot, and then I grabbed her elbow and spoke urgently.

"I need to speak with Hank Quinn immediately."

"I'm afraid that's impossible," the woman replied. "Hank is still...he's still *under*."

"For how much longer?"

"As soon as we separate the prisoners," she said. "Any time now."

"I'll wait. But please tell him it's extremely urgent."

"Can I help you with something?"

"No," I said, "I need to see Hank."

The woman escorted me the rest of the way off of the boat, and I stood near the ramp, waiting for Hank to come ashore, wondering if I should take a chance and tell someone else what I knew. Not only was Litman bad, but the Tanigawa brothers were getting away—and I might have the information that would stop them!

I decided to wait exactly five more minutes and then tell someone else. At three and a half minutes, however, Hank came down the ramp with several other men as the boat started up and prepared to set sail.

"Hey, Callie, what's up?" Hank said, looking tired and distracted.

I told Hank in no uncertain terms exactly what I had learned, and what I had overheard.

"Are you absolutely positive?" he asked, his brow deeply furrowed. Behind him, the boat eased away from the dock, letting out three short blasts of the horn as it went.

"Yes."

"Why didn't you tell someone?"

"I didn't know whom to trust," I said. "I was waiting for you."

He nodded.

"Come with me, then."

Together, we half walked, half ran down the dock to another boat, a smaller, faster police boat. Barbara Hightower was at the wheel, and she nodded at Hank in recognition.

"Officer Hightower, we need to commandeer this boat," Hank said. "Will you drive us?"

"Yes, sir," she replied, starting it up. "Which way?"

"North, as fast as you can."

"Do we need to radio ahead?"

"Please," he said. "We need units to stand by. Coast guard, too. Tell them we'll radio back with coordinates as soon as we have them."

Hank and I climbed into the boat as Barbara spoke into her microphone. I found a seat near the back, and Hank pulled out his cell phone, dialed, and spoke into it sharply.

"It's Quinn," he said. "Give me—"

"Oh, I don't think you need to make that call."

We looked up to see Agent Litman climbing into the boat, a gun pointed straight at Hank.

"Now hang up the phone, nice and easy," Litman said. "That's it. Toss it over."

Hank held up both hands and promptly threw his phone overboard into the water. I stared at Litman, still amazed that this man who had pretended to be so good was, in the end, so truly evil. Looking away, I searched the dock area, hoping to see help coming, but there was no one there. The boat carrying the prisoners had sailed, and the rest of the agents were obviously busy inside the buildings.

Litman sat on the bench between the bow and the main part of the boat, bracing himself firmly, the gun still pointed at Hank.

"Now let me see all weapons overboard," Litman said. "You too, Officer Hightower."

Hank and Barbara both dropped their guns into the water.

"Telephones, too, Miss Webber."

I pulled mine from my pocket and dropped it into the bay.

"Word of advice," Litman said as he gestured for Hank to take a seat near me, in the back. "If you're going to talk about someone, make sure they're not still on the receiving end of your wire."

He pulled the black earpiece from his ear and tossed it onto the floor of the boat. We all looked down at it, as if it were alive.

Litman told Barbara to get us moving, rattling off directions. Frozen, she just looked at him.

"Let's go!" he hissed.

Flinching, she quickly untied the ropes, pulled in the bumpers, and started the engine.

The boat roared to life. I braced myself as we backed away from the dock and then turned and sped northward into the cold. As we went, my eyes cast about in the boat for something I could use as a weapon. I could sense Hank doing the same thing, but we both came up empty. I thought of jumping overboard, but I knew that even if I managed to swim away without being shot, I would be hypothermic in a matter of minutes without a dry suit.

We drove for a while, and at that speed, the air was freezing. I held my arms tightly around me, my mind racing. As we drove on, I tried desperately to think of something I could do to change the situation. I came up with nothing.

Finally, Litman told Barbara to slow down and turn to the right. In the distance, I could see what looked like a small town, and as we came closer I realized it was Kawshek. I thought perhaps we were going just north of there to the dock at Russell's farm—the same place I had ridden to the other night in the dinghy. But then Litman had Barbara make a sharp right turn, and we headed along the river that flowed inland south of Kawshek. I knew the sun would be coming up soon, and already there was a faint purple glow along the horizon.

"Do you know where we're going?" I yelled to Hank over the roar of the engine. He shook his head.

Barbara drove for about five minutes, and then Litman told her to slow down.

"Turn on the spotlight," he barked, pointing the gun at her now. "Flash it three times."

She did as he instructed. A moment later, up ahead in the distance, I could see a light flashing back at us three times as well.

"Looks like somebody's waiting for us," Hank whispered to me.

Heart pounding, my eyes searched the shore for some sort of landmark. Finally, just ahead, I could see the shape of the tin building hanging out over the water—the boat repair shop near where Eddie Ray had been killed! My mind raced, realizing the Tanigawas must be using this place as the meeting point for their getaway with Litman.

"Pull up nice and slow," Litman said to Barbara. "No fancy moves."

Barbara lowered the throttle, and we eased under the roofline and up to the concrete abutment. There was already another boat there in the water, a six-seat ski runner, tied over to one side, on the cleat I had spotted as suspect several days before.

"Okay," Litman called, and then suddenly people emerged from the shadows.

There, guns drawn, stood the two Japanese brothers, Kenji and Shin Tanigawa. Behind them was a woman, attractive with black frizzy hair.

Tia Lynch, Russell's wife.

Forty-Seven

"All right," Litman said, his voice calm, "cut the engine."

"What's going on here?" Shin demanded angrily.

"Slight change in plans," Litman said. "The woman overheard me throwing the feds off the trail. Just my luck, she speaks Japanese."

Shin looked at me, venom in his eyes, and raised his gun.

"C'mon, Litman," Hank said, stepping forward. "You can't just have her killed like this. Don't forget, she's connected directly with the attorney general. You'd better watch your step."

"And you'd better watch yours," Litman said. Then he raised his gun and shot Hank cleanly in the chest.

I screamed, watching in disbelief as Hank's huge body was flung back by the force of the bullet. He hit the side of the boat and went over, his bulk crashing loudly into the water.

"Now out of the boat!" Litman demanded. Stunned, Barbara and I did as he said.

Following his gestures, we climbed onto the cement and leaned against the cold, corrugated tin wall. Roughly, Shin patted us down for weapons. He came up empty, though he pulled a pair of handcuffs from Barbara's belt and proceeded to jerk her hands behind her back and lock the cuffs around her wrists.

"All right, Ms. Webber," Litman said, his voice close to my ear. "Let's hear what you have to say about the attorney general. You're not like the guy's daughter or something, are you?"

I refused to reply but simply stood there, staring at the wall.

"Are you?" he demanded, yelling directly into my ear. I remained silent, still looking at the wall.

"What difference does it make?" Shin demanded finally, putting a gun to my head.

"'Cause what we don't need," Litman barked angrily at him, "is the entire DOJ on a mission of vengeance."

Shin lowered his weapon. Litman stepped away and pulled out his phone, dialing a number.

"I'll make a call," Litman said, more calmly this time. "We'll find out."

The Tanigawas separated me from Barbara, Kenji pushing me toward the back wall without smiling now, and Shin forcing Barbara to go to the end of the walkway. Pulse surging, I realized he was pushing me toward the table strewn with old, discarded tools. Barbara must've realized it, too, because she shot me a significant look and then suddenly began creating a distraction.

"You won't get away with this!" she yelled at Shin, struggling to break free.

Discreetly, I reached around behind me for a wrench or knife or screwdriver that I could use as a weapon. My fingers closed around something that felt like a small fish scaling knife, and I tucked it up into my sleeve just as Kenji turned and jerked me away, closer to him.

"The police boat's got a GPS radio signal!" Barbara continued. "They'll find us before you can escape."

"Then I guess we'd better hurry," Shin said calmly. He pushed her to the edge of the dock and pulled out the switchblade-type knife Murdock had described: long and curved and deadly-looking. No wonder Eddie Ray had run away from it in the bar.

Barbara struggled valiantly, so much so that Shin yelled for his brother to help him. Tia took over guarding me, and, without a qualm she put a semi-automatic pistol to my head.

Quickly and smoothly, as Kenji held Barbara still, Shin plunged the long knife blade into her abdomen. Then he pulled it out and pushed her forward into the water.

Barbara's body landed with a splash and then bobbed back up to the surface. Thrashing. Gasping. Choking for air. I started to go to her, but Tia pressed the gun more firmly to my scalp and told me to freeze. Helpless, tears streaming down my face, I had to watch as the current pulled Barbara away from us and into the dark, black river. When she was gone, I tried to meet Tia's eyes with my own, but she was staring firmly at a point beyond my right shoulder.

"Why are you a part of this?" I cried. "Did you see what they just did?"

"Comes with the territory," she replied coldly.

"What about Russell?" I said.

She feigned innocence, putting one hand to her mouth in mock surprise.

"Oops. He got caught. He'll go to jail. Meanwhile, I get away with the money."

"You helped set him up," I said incredulously.

"He's an idiot and a cheat. He deserved it."

My mind reeled. The sheer heartlessness of it all was astonishing. Suddenly I gasped as realization struck me.

"*You* killed Eddie Ray," I said. "You killed him and then set it up to look like Shayna did it."

"The backstabbing little sneak was playing around with my husband."

"Russell told me that affair was over and done with."

"Maybe done but not forgotten," she said. "This way, I got two birds with one stone."

"Eddie Ray had to die just so you could frame Shayna for murder?"

"Don't be stupid," she snapped. "Eddie Ray had to die because he was nosing around in our business, threatening to ruin a good thing. Do you know how much money we've made in the last year? Just for

Russell and me alone, we're talking over a million dollars. And then Eddie Ray shows up, thinking he can worm his way in, get in on the action. We killed him on Litman's orders. Framing Shayna for the murder was my own doing, just a nice little touch on the side."

"A nice little touch?"

"Why not? All Eddie Ray brought to the table was that place, that Advancing Attire. Otherwise, he was just trying to get rich off of *our* backs."

"Advancing Attire?" I asked. "What did Eddie Ray have to do with Advancing Attire?"

Tia rolled her eyes. "Litman had us looking for a local charity, something small, preferably run by someone who wouldn't pay much attention to how the fund-raising was being done. When Eddie Ray showed up talking about the wooden nickel and this charity that gave his girlfriend free clothes, we decided to give the place a look. Considering the idiot who runs the joint, it seemed like a perfect choice."

The idiot she was referring to was Verlene, I supposed. A part deep inside of me laughed, for they had underestimated Verlene by far. Maybe she came across as a bit flighty, but she was smart enough to leave the decision about signing with CNA to her board of directors, smart enough to ask me to investigate. Of course, considering the situation I found myself in now, maybe *I* was the real idiot. Soon I would be dead, the same as Hank and Barbara. My only hope was to keep Tia talking and maybe seize a chance to escape when her attention was diverted.

"So how did you get Eddie Ray to pull over to the side of the road way out here in the middle of nowhere?" I asked.

"We told Eddie Ray to meet us out here. He thought he was getting his piece of the pie. Instead, I distracted him while Shin gave it to him with the tire iron. It wasn't much trouble to load him in the trunk and drive the car back. Shin met me at the dock in town with the boat. Then we sailed away into the night, nobody the wiser."

Tia's face was hard and ugly in the dim light. She dug in her pocket for a pack of cigarettes and managed to get one out and light it with one hand, the other still holding the gun that was trained firmly on me. I thought about the little knife in my sleeve, and I wondered if I would be any match for these people when it was my turn to die.

"What about the next night?" I asked. "When we found Eddie Ray's body and I came out here to the scene of the crime?"

"We were supposed to have a shipment that night," Tia said. "Return one container and pick up another. But then we saw all the cop cars and flashing lights in Kawshek and decided against it. We came here instead, watching from the roof to see if or when they might discover the place in the road where we killed Eddie Ray. Thanks to you, soon this whole place was crawling with cops."

"And the bleach I smelled?"

"Bleach?" Tia asked. "Oh, that was probably the container. Russell cleaned it out before we left the farm."

"How about later, at my house? I smelled the bleach again."

"I made Russell go check things out, see if he could figure out who you were and what you had to do with all of this." She laughed out loud. "You pretty near scared him to death! He heard the dog barking, but he didn't expect you to come charging out the back door in the middle of the night. He almost didn't get out of sight in time. Don't you know you can get killed doing something stupid like that?"

I looked into her mocking eyes, thinking that *she* was the killer in that marriage, not Russell.

"So how did your husband feel when he found out you helped murder his friend Eddie Ray?" I asked.

Something flashed in Tia's eyes, a mix of anger and guilt that told me Russell probably didn't know that his wife had been involved.

"Why don't you shut up and quit asking questions," Tia hissed, jerking my arm and dragging me toward the worktable in the corner. Once there, she tied me to the old, rusted motor that hung from the winch over the table. I could tell she'd grown up near the bay, because the knots she used were boating knots, sturdy and tight. My only hope at this point was the little knife that remained securely up my sleeve.

"They have to call me back," Litman said, hanging up his phone.

"Fine," Tia snapped.

Once I was securely tied, she reached for a switch on the wall and flipped it upward. Suddenly the winch overhead sprung to life.

Creaking and groaning, it raised up the motor—and me with it—and then swung it out across the floor. I kicked and twisted and struggled, but it was useless. I was swept out over the water. Finally, Tia turned off the winch and I hung there, suspended, my arms straining, my heart pounding in my head. Below me and off to one side, I could hear the Tanigawas laughing at my predicament.

Litman barked at them to get the other boat ready to roll, shouting in Japanese that they needed to get out of there fast, that the sun would be up any minute. Watching them work, I thought of Harriet, chasing the paper trail of Manno Seafood, and suddenly I understood how the company had known to cross all of their "t's" and dot all of their "i's" with taxes and I-9 forms and all of that. As a bureaucrat, Litman knew exactly what needed to be done to legitimize a business. He was the one who kept Manno Seafood flying under the radar.

"How can you do this?" I yelled to Litman. "You're supposed to be one of the good guys."

He walked to the edge of the cement and spoke in a voice that was eerily calm.

"I *was* one of the good guys," he said softly. "For thirty-two years, I was one of the good guys. I may have been surrounded on all sides by ineptitude, sloppy work, and bad attitudes, but I did my job. And I did it better than anybody else in that bureau. It wasn't much of a leap to see that I could work the system just as well for my own benefit."

"But I don't understand," I said. "How could you become a part of the very thing you were fighting against?"

He surprised me by turning and kicking the nearest bench with a vengeance. It clattered across the cement, a couple of screwdrivers flying across the pavement and into the water. Even Tia looked startled at his loss of calm.

"It's *my* system!" he yelled, a vein throbbing at his neck. "*I* put the policies into place. *I* traced the smuggling routes. In thirty-two years of doing my job, I brought down the Herraras and discovered the Valparaiso connection and turned up the Chengdu family. I've had a whole career of righting these kinds of wrongs!"

"So what happened, Litman?" I asked. "How could you cross over?"

"I finally realized," he hissed, pulling out his gun and pointing it at me, "that I could use my skills just as well on the outside, for myself. I knew those idiots would never catch me. I was smarter than anyone in that agency."

Regaining his calm, he lowered his gun and slipped it into his waistband. Then he walked over to the switch on the wall and turned it, kicking the winch to life again. Slowly, it began lowering me toward the water.

"Frankly," he added, "I don't know what took me so long. The benefits are much better on this side of the game."

Our eyes locked and held. I could see a coldness in his heart, a total lack of conscience. I wondered if he were a sociopath or merely a man who had lost his soul, swept away by the temptations of his own knowledge. Breaking our gaze, he turned to Tia.

"Don't worry about her connections to the AG," he said, walking to the door. "Just kill her."

I heard the bullet from Tia's gun before I even had time to flinch, and then, instantly, pain seared across my side. The force of it set the motor to spinning as it continued to lower me toward the water.

"Did you get her?" I heard Shin ask.

I felt a warmth spread over my right hip, though the sharp pain of the bullet had quickly faded to a dull throb. *Did* she get me? Judging by how I felt, my guess was that I had only been grazed.

"Of course I got her," Tia barked. "Look at all the blood."

Despite my terror, despite my pain, as the motor spun on its cable I knew my only chance at this point was to let them think I was injured worse than I was, to let them think that I was dead. I forced myself to go limp, the full weight of my body hanging from the ropes that bound my wrists.

There were no more shots fired. I remained still, wondering how much I was bleeding, how long I could wait before it would be too late. Surely, they would leave now. Surely, they would give me up for dead and go away.

Eyes closed, I strained to listen. I could hear Tia and the Tanigawas untying the boat. I stopped spinning when my feet reached the water, though it took all the strength I had not to flinch from the icy cold.

How I dreaded that cold! Even the other night when I had worn my dry suit, the freezing water had been nearly unbearable. Now I was to plunge into it without any special protection at all! I shuddered at the thought and then realized that after a few minutes the cold wouldn't matter anyway. I would have drowned by then—if I hadn't already bled to death.

As the water reached my knees, only a supernatural, God-given strength kept me from moving, kept me from screaming. I could hear the boat starting as the water climbed to my hips. By the time the water reached my waist, I heard the boat leave, gunning its motor and speeding away into the dawn.

I was alone.

I opened my eyes, pulling myself higher on the motor, trying to get my hands free from the ropes. It was no use. Instead, I carefully worked to dig the fishing knife out of my sleeve. By the time I got it out, the water was up to my shoulders and I was trembling so hard it felt as though I were in spasms. I needed to move fast, but not so fast that I would drop the knife. Despite my violent trembling from the cold, I went to work cutting at the rope, inadvertently slicing my palms and wrists with the knife as I worked.

Soon, the water had reached my chin. I took a deep breath and let myself go down. As the water closed over my nose, my eyes, the top of my head, I could feel the ropes giving way, one by one. Counting in my mind, I kept cutting, kept slicing. I had been holding my breath for 40 seconds when, suddenly, my hands were free! I pushed off toward the surface, only to realize that part of my hair had come loose from my chignon and was caught in the engine.

No! I nearly choked from the shock. Screaming into the water through my open mouth, I gripped the knife and began hacking away at my hair. It was no use. It was too tangled and caught. I was starting to lose control. I needed to breathe! I wanted to breathe! Then the knife slipped from my frozen hands and it sank down in the murky, dark water.

I had no more options. Despite the pain, I spun around as best I could and placed my hands and my feet on the giant motor. I simply pushed as hard as I could, ripping my hair out by the roots, forcing myself loose. My consciousness waved in and out, like a bad movie, like a flickering film. My lungs burned but I didn't breathe. I just pulled. Finally, thankfully, something gave way. With a great searing pain, I pushed one final time and then I was suddenly loose. I popped to the surface like a cork. I sucked in great gasps of air, trying to pull myself out of the water by the chain that hung over me.

That's when I realized I wasn't alone. The sun had broken over the horizon, and in the misty rays of morning light I saw Kirby, coming through the door, looking at me in shock. Our eyes met, and then he was running to me, reaching out for the chain I held onto, pulling me toward him.

He managed to get me to solid ground, holding me tight and lowering me to the cement as my legs ceased to function. I had been under water for too long—probably two minutes, at least.

"You're half frozen," he said, tears filling his eyes. He pulled off my wet coat and flung it away, and then he covered me with his own and held me close.

"You're bleeding," he said. "There's a lot of blood."

"Hurry," I whispered. "We've got to c-catch them b-before they all get away."

"No," he said. "We have to get you to a hospital. You're freezing. Oh, Callie, did they shoot you?"

I shook my head, trying to make him understand.

"The police," I rasped. "Use the radio on the b-boat to call the police."

He pulled off his shirt and wrapped it around my waist, the pressure tight against my wound. Then he laid my head gently on the ground and then ran to the police boat, which was still tied there to the cleat. He climbed on board and grabbed the mike. He told them what was happening, reading off to them some coordinates from the GPS unit he held clutched in his hand.

"Tell them," I said, speaking as loudly as I could, "tell them the Tanigawas and Tia Lynch are on a b-boat headed to Baltimore. They are armed and d-dangerous."

I described the boat and even remembered most of the serial numbers, all of which he repeated into the radio.

"I think Litman left here by land, also armed," I rasped. "And there are two officers down."

I felt myself drift toward unconsciousness. The cold feeling was replaced by an odd weightlessness, a sort of floating sensation. *Maybe I'm flying,* I thought, but then I opened my eyes to see that Kirby was carrying me and we were outside. I wouldn't have thought he was that strong, but he held me gripped in his arms and pressed his way through the thick brush, straight toward the road, my head tight against his chest, his heart pounding beneath my ear. He was sweating, even though he wore only a thin T-shirt in the morning cold.

"Don't go to sleep, Callie," he pleaded, moving as quickly as he could in the heavy undergrowth. "Stay with me now."

"How did you find me?" I asked, drowsiness nearly overtaking me. I didn't feel cold anymore. I felt warm now. I felt very, very warm.

"I tracked you," he said, breathing heavily from the exertion. "Yesterday, when you came to my house for lunch. I put my grandmother's Personal Tracking Device in your coat so I'd know where you went."

"You did? I didn't see it."

"I told you, it's tiny. I clipped it onto the back of your jacket. You wouldn't even have known it was there."

"But why?"

"Because I knew you were going to include yourself on that INS raid, one way or another. I didn't want you in danger. As it was, I almost didn't make it in time."

We finally reached his car, the Mercedes SUV, which was parked on the side of the road. Kirby lowered my feet to the ground and then dug in his pocket for the keys. I felt a giggle well up inside of me as I tried to stand. I felt delirious, despite the pain that coursed through my side.

"Oh no," I said. "I'll get blood all over your seat."

"Why are you laughing?" he asked, unlocking the door and swinging it open.

"Because I thought it would be ketchup! Now it's blood, but I thought it was gonna be ketchup! From the hamburgers!"

I kept laughing as Kirby lifted me onto the seat and buckled me in. He slammed the door, and wild laughter filled the car as he ran around to the driver's side and climbed in.

"Callie!" he said, taking my face in his hands. "Pull it together for me, honey. Come on. You can do this. I don't want to lose you."

I realized that the wild laughter was coming from me. I held my breath and looked up at Kirby, his features blurring in front of me until he became someone else.

Eyes. I could see his eyes. Nothing but his eyes, looking back at me, knowing me. Loving me.

"Tom?" I whispered. "I knew you would come. I love you. I love you so much, Tom."

Tears filled my eyes, but when I wiped at them I realized it was Kirby again, pain written in his expression as he gently smoothed my hair away from my face.

"We have to get you to the hospital," he said softly, leaning me back against the seat and turning on the car. "Let's take your wet shoes off, Callie. Can you feel the heater?"

Like a mother with a child, he tended to my shoes, pulling them off, pulling off my socks, and pointing the vent toward my toes. Using his hands, he rubbed my arms up and down, trying for friction, trying for warmth.

"Isn't this how the whole thing started?" I asked drunkenly, seeing us in the car the night we first used the GPS unit. "You tried to kiss me."

In the distance, I could hear sirens coming closer.

"Do you still want to kiss me?" I asked, trying to remember if he ever had kissed me or not. I think he had. Someone had. Someone recently, and not Bryan.

"Just hang on, Callie," Kirby said, still rubbing my arms. "Maybe that's the ambulance."

I don't know what happened next. My eyes blurred. My ears roared with a sound like rushing water. But suddenly Kirby's door was flung open, and he was pulled from the car and dragged to the ground, a gun pointed at his head.

Litman.

"You must have nine lives," Litman said to me, incredulous. He weaved in and out of my focus, and all I could think of was how easily he must have issued the order to harm Gordo, how quickly he had pulled the trigger on Hank. Now he was about to do the same with Kirby. Sweet Kirby, who was only trying to be my knight in shining armor.

"Leave him alone," I said, my mind momentarily clear. "He has nothing to do with this."

"He's in the way," Litman said, shrugging. "And so are you. I'm just glad I recognized his fancy car when he passed me on the road."

Then I was hallucinating again. Dewey and Murdock were there with their fishing nets, floating in the morning mist behind Litman.

"I bet mending nets gets pretty tedious," I said to them, wondering if I was back in the Kawshek General Store. Stinky was there with his chowder pot, raising it up in the air to hit Eddie Ray across the head.

Only it wasn't Eddie Ray. It was Litman.

And it wasn't a hallucination.

Bong!

Stinky slammed the pot down onto Litman's head, knocking him to the ground. Dewey and Murdock followed, casting their net over his body. Kirby kicked at Litman's gun, knocking it out of reach.

"We got him!"

I blinked, trying to figure out what was real and what was not.

Kirby was real, and he wasn't dead; I knew that. The net around Litman, trapping his thrashing body, was real. The police cars screeching to a stop on all sides of our car were real. The lights that danced around inside my eyes were maybe not so real.

"That was for Gordo!" I yelled at Litman's ensnared body.

Then I fell back against the seat, and everything simply went dark.

Forty-Eight

I awoke in a hospital room. Sunlight from the setting sun was softly shining through vertical blinds. Swallowing, I simply laid there, looking at the window and wondering where the day had gone.

Funny, but things were mostly one big blur. I remembered waiting for Litman to pick me up in the grocery store parking lot. I remembered studying the shoreline from the tugboat with my night-vision goggles.

I closed my eyes, trying to bring it all back, working my way through the night step by step. Talking to Gordo's secretary. Hearing Litman mistranslate the Japanese. Getting kidnapped on a police boat.

"Barbara," I whispered, recalling her death.

"Shhh," I heard, and then I realized I wasn't alone in the room. Kirby was there, sitting on the other side of the bed, and now he leaned forward to touch my arm, gazing at me with concern.

"Don't worry," he said softly. "She's going to make it. She's still alive."

"Barbara is?" I asked, my throat feeling as if it were lined with sandpaper.

"Yeah," he answered. "She spent most of the morning in surgery, but for now she's stable. They've got her in ICU."

"But I saw her float away. I saw her drown."

"Hank pulled her out of the river and kept her hidden until the police got there."

"Hank?"

I tried to sit up but my arms were weak. Kirby reached for the bed control and raised the head of the bed. Dizziness clouded my vision for a moment, and then receded.

"Hank got shot," I said, and Kirby nodded.

"That's right, but he was wearing a bulletproof vest."

"Is he okay?"

"He's right down the hall," Kirby said. "They're treating him for hypothermia and three broken ribs—not to mention a big, nasty bruise on his chest. But he'll be all right. Without that vest on, he would've been dead. Barbara, too, probably, since he wouldn't have been there to pull her out of the water and keep her alive until help came."

"What about me?" I asked. "Am I okay?"

Kirby smiled, relief evident in his eyes.

"You, my dear, had a low body temperature of eighty-eight degrees. It's been a long day, but you're pretty much back to normal now."

I looked down at my hands, which were both wrapped in bandages.

"Stitches?" I asked, remembering the cuts I'd made as I tried to slice free of the ropes.

"A few," he replied. "They also gave you a tetanus shot, and you're on antibiotics to prevent infection."

"My head hurts," I said, reaching up to feel more bandages.

"You lost a chunk of your scalp," Kirby said. "But there's not much they can do for it. They expect it to heal eventually."

"What about my side? I was shot."

"Actually, you weren't. You were cut quite badly, apparently from a shard of flying metal. The police have sort of reconstructed everything, and they figure the bullet hit that big motor you were hanging from and knocked a sharp piece of it loose. It sliced into the side of your waist, but no organs were hit, thank goodness."

"More stitches?"

"Oh yeah, a few. But they didn't have to operate or anything. Mainly, they've been worried about your body temperature."

I closed my eyes and swallowed, thanking the Lord for keeping me safe. Then I remembered Dewey and Murdock and Stinky, how I had thought they were a hallucination. Were they?

"My memory's kind of blurry," I said. "Was Litman really taken down by a big pot?"

"A chowder pot and a fishing net," Kirby said, grinning. "I've never seen anything like it."

"How did they know to go there?"

"The three of them were out fishing, and they heard things. The gunshot. The motor on the winch. Litman yelling. They came ashore on the other side of the peninsula and had just reached the road when they realized what was going on. Their timing was just good luck."

"Their timing was the good Lord," I said. "He sent them to protect us."

"True," Kirby agreed. "though I never thought I'd have a guardian angel named 'Stinky.' "

I smiled, though it hurt to do so.

"Did the others get away?" I asked.

"Nope. The coast guard caught them outside of Baltimore. The newspapers are giving you lots of the credit, calling you a hero."

I looked at Kirby, remembering how he had swept in and pulled me from the icy water when I didn't have the strength left to save myself.

"*You're* a hero, Kirby," I said. "Did you really track me with your grandmother's PTD?"

He nodded.

"Followed your progress with my laptop most of the evening," he answered, looking embarrassed. "The tracking device shorted out once you went into the water, but by then I was almost there."

I placed my bandaged hand over his, feeling a surge of gratitude for this sweet man. I remembered how he carried me through the brush and tried to warm me in his car. I wondered if maybe our talk yesterday, where we sort of broke things off, had been a bit premature. He was a very special guy. Maybe if we dated a bit I could learn to feel about him the same way he felt about me.

"Hey, Kirby," I said, meeting his eyes. "Listen. Maybe yesterday, at your house, when I said those things...I don't know. Maybe I was wrong. Maybe we should try dating for a while and see what happens."

He looked away and then surprised me by standing and walking to the window. For a long moment he didn't speak, and when he did his voice was somber.

"You don't remember everything, do you?" he asked.

I looked up at the ceiling, thinking through the memories, trying to put it together.

"Did I do something?" I asked, feeling him slip away from me. I could tell a wall was slowly going up between us.

Before he could reply, a nurse bustled into the room.

"I see we're awake!" she said loudly, coming to the bed. "How are you feeling?"

"A little dizzy," I replied.

"That's to be expected," she said to me, and then she turned to Kirby. "Would you excuse us for a minute, hon?"

He nodded and left the room. I watched as the nurse checked my IV and then recorded the readings from some machines behind me. She pulled down the covers to examine the dressing on my wound and then she made some more notes in my chart.

"The doctor should be around shortly," she said finally, pulling the sheets back up and then tucking the chart into its holder at the end of the bed. "I expect he'll want to keep you overnight. But unless there are complications, you'll probably be discharged in the morning."

"Good."

"Try to drink some water," she said, pointing to a pitcher and a cup on my side table. "Oh, and you've got a line of people out there waiting to talk to you."

"Police?"

"Police, reporters, friends—practically a whole waiting room full of folks. Once your boyfriend's gone, we'll let them in one at a time."

"Kirby? Oh, he's not my boyfriend."

"He's not?" she asked, a bemused expression on her face. "That's good. Because from what I heard, you've spent half the day moaning for somebody named 'Tom.'"

She bustled out as quickly as she had come in. My face was still bright red when Kirby returned and began gathering his things. Finally, he straightened and put his jacket over his arm.

"Kirby?" I asked, looking up at him. "I'm so sorry."

"I just stayed until I knew you were okay," he said. "Now I'm going to go."

"But what about us?"

He leaned forward and kissed me lightly on the forehead.

"Ah, Callie, there is no 'us,'" he whispered, looking into my eyes. "Believe me, your heart is definitely elsewhere."

Forty-Nine

Six days later, my head wound and side were better, most of the bandages were off of my hands, and I was feeling stronger. I had intended to spend the week holing up quietly in my house and healing, but that wasn't exactly how it had gone. Instead, I had received a steady stream of visitors—from officials who needed to question me, to Shayna, who was like a new person now that she had been released from jail. And Verlene had put herself in charge of seeing that the church kept me well supplied with pies and casseroles for my entire convalescence.

I'd like to say that all of the commotion was bothersome to my solitary soul, but the truth was I was grateful for all of the people who had come into my life and were surrounding me now with such love and care. Dewey and Murdock had come by several times just to check on me, and the two of them had even spent a morning repairing Sal's fence and then assembling my new barbecue grill, compliments of Eli Gold. If the Lord wanted to teach me a thing or two about making connections and accepting help from others, He certainly threw me in feet first! I just loved it when God showed His sense of humor.

In fact, the only person who seemed conspicuously absent was Kirby. We had spoken on the phone a number of times, but we hadn't seen each other in person since he walked out of my hospital room.

I wasn't sure how I felt about that. One part of me missed him, missed his sense of humor and his enthusiasm for adventure. Another part of me, however, felt an odd sense of relief that he was out of my life in that way. I wondered if we would ever be able to forget about the hint of romance we had shared and simply become good friends. I hoped, eventually, that we could.

Now there was another knock at the door, and I opened it to see a man in a suit, huge and handsome in a rough sort of way, the familiar scar shining from his chin.

"Hank?" I asked.

"Hi, Callie."

"Wow! You clean up real nice!" I told him, laughing. Gone were the fisherman clothes and the scruffy two-day growth of beard. Even the scar on his chin, rather than making him look fierce, now simply lent an exotic touch to his rugged face.

"Yeah, well, now that I'm not undercover anymore, I thought it was time that Shayna saw the real me."

"She's in for a treat. Would you like to come in?"

"No, no," he said, and I realized that his car was sitting in the driveway with the engine still running. "I was on my way to Kawshek, so I thought I'd just stop off and say goodbye. I'm driving Shayna to her new apartment in Annapolis today, and then I'll be going on back to DC. I'm all done here."

"Aren't you coming to the ceremony this afternoon?"

"Oh, right, we might drop by," he said. "It's at five, right?"

"Yes."

"Maybe we'll see you there."

He looked almost nervous as he stood in front of me, hands tucked in his pockets, and I realized there was more on his agenda than just a friendly goodbye.

"You know," he continued shyly, "with Shayna living in Annapolis and me in DC, I really think this could work. It's not that far of a drive for us to get together sometimes. I mean, I know she broke things off with me before. But maybe now that the situation has changed, she might give me another chance. You're her friend. Do you think so?"

I tried to remember what Shayna had told me about Hank. The only real reason she had broken up with him in the first place was because she thought he was a waterman content to live his life out in Kawshek, the one place she wanted desperately to leave. I smiled at him now, thinking how cute it was that he had felt the need to stop by and ask my opinion before trying to find romance again with Shayna.

"I wouldn't be surprised if things work out for the two of you very well this time," I said, winking. "Just a hunch, you know."

"Thanks, Callie."

Hank and I hugged, the connection of our traumatic experience bonding us in a way that not many other things could. He stiffened as he stood back up straight, and I realized he was still in pain with the broken ribs—and probably would be for a while. At least he was still alive.

Once he was gone, I decided to make my lunch. I was just heating a bit of a casserole in the microwave when there was another knock at the door. It was Denise Hightower, proffering a yummy-looking coffee cake and a big smile. She had already called me a few times this week, but this was the first chance she'd had, she said, to stop by.

She sat at the table, declining my offer of lunch, and filled me in on her sister's condition. Apparently, Barbara was still in the hospital but was doing very well and would probably be released in a few days. Denise talked about the trauma of having a sister who was a cop, and I realized that was something we had in common. My brother, Michael, had put me through many a sleepless night in his years on the force, too. It was the price we paid.

After I finished eating, Denise got around to what she'd wanted all along. She gestured toward the scarf I had wrapped snugly around my head, suggesting politely that I take it off and let her see. Blushing, I removed the covering to reveal the disaster that until now I had managed to ignore. The place where my scalp was injured had formed a scab, fortunately, and since it was at the nape of my neck it barely showed under the back of my hair.

But the rest of my head was a nightmare, a chopped-up mess I had a feeling I would have to hide under hats and scarves for a long time to come.

"Oh, it's not that bad," Denise said, standing behind me and fingering the layers carefully. "The important thing is that your head wound is healing."

"True."

"Besides," she said, "you're a beautiful woman, Callie. You'd probably look good bald."

"Thank you."

She crossed to where she had hung her purse on the chair.

"No, thank *you,*" she said, and then she grinned.

"For what?"

She dug into her purse and pulled out a little black case. I watched as she opened it to reveal, nestled in satin lining, a shining pair of silver scissors.

"For the opportunity," she said, "to finally give you a decent haircut."

Fifty

The ribbon-cutting ceremony was brief but touching, with Verlene giving a quick speech and then Kirby unveiling the temporary sign that would hang on the door of the new, expanded Advancing Attire until the permanent brass plaque arrived. Kirby held up the sign and read it out loud: "This building is lovingly dedicated to the memory of Grace Collins."

I stood off to one side of the crowd, tears inexplicably filling my eyes. Only I knew how far Kirby had had to grow just to get to this point. Just a short while ago he had been marveling at Tom's philanthropy, wondering how a person could just give their money away. Now, today, he had joined forces with the J.O.S.H.U.A. Foundation, offering a combined grant that would cover the cost of the lease and the necessary alterations for the building next door to Advancing Attire. Through our joint efforts, Verlene was going to have her big expansion after all.

I thought it was a wonderful venture, and I was glad that Kirby had been willing to work with me to make it happen. I looked at him up there in front of the crowd, and I felt almost motherly, as though the Lord had allowed me to have some small part in helping him grow.

If so, it was only fair, I realized, since he had certainly helped me to grow as well.

Standing on the other side of Verlene was her daughter, Joanne, and I studied her for a moment, thinking what an attractive girl she was. At nearly six feet in high heels, she was tall but willowy, with long blond hair, a perfect nose and chin, and intelligent eyes. As I watched her, I noticed she was eyeing Kirby a bit, and when he glanced back at her and smiled, I was surprised but pleased. Joanne was a great person. I thought she and Kirby might have a lot in common.

I turned my attention elsewhere, to Verlene's cutting of the ribbon, to the applause of the small crowd that was gathered there on the sidewalk to watch. It was a gorgeously sunny fall day, and as the ceremony ended, I couldn't help thinking that my only regret was that Tom couldn't be here now, too. I fingered my new hairdo self-consciously, wondering what his reaction would be when he found out I was no longer the "lady with the bun." Denise had done an amazing job, blending the parts I had hacked up into a layered cut that came just to the midpoint of my neck. Though I hated to admit it, the style was perfect for me. Not only was it flattering and chic, but it also seemed to take several years off of my appearance. Chalk one up for my friend and hairdresser, who, when she was finished, had beamed and said, simply, *I told you so.*

Tom, meanwhile, was far away in Singapore, and our communications were spotty and ill-timed at best. It was just as well, since I hadn't wanted to burden him with all that had happened here. Compared to his mother's health issues and the work that had been waiting for his attention on the other side of the world, I didn't think that my cuts and bruises were all that significant.

But I missed him. How I missed him! We had spoken just a few times in the past week, and each conversation hadn't been much more than matters of business, working out the details of the grant to Advancing Attire and making arrangements for my next investigation. Each time we spoke, he sounded tired and distracted; and though he had asked about the INS raid and how things had gone, he obviously hadn't received any sort of update from his own sources, because he took me at my word that the situation was "fine" and that all of the loose ends had been "wrapped up."

I knew that if he ever found out all the details of that night—particularly my injuries and subsequent hospitalization—he'd be angry that I had kept so much from him. For once, he didn't know everything there was to know about me, and to my surprise I found that oddly unsettling.

"Oh, Callie, I can't ever thank you enough," Verlene cried now, interrupting my thoughts and hugging me tightly. "I'll never get over all you went through just to investigate that horrible company."

"Now remember, Verlene," I said, "it wasn't the whole company that was awful. Just the head of that one division. And you can rest assured that she won't be conducting business of any kind for a very long time."

I thought of the list of charities that Maureen had used to funnel money through CNA, the list that Litman thought I had burned. According to the authorities, in the end it had turned out that every single one of the donor businesses on that list was a fake, just like Manno Seafood, each one set up to help facilitate the smuggling process in one way or another. I thought, as I often did when I uncovered fraud hidden in a charity, just how frustrating the nonprofit world could be. In the case of CNA, they had violated one of the basic tenets of any company—for-profit or nonprofit alike—and that was to make sure that there are good internal controls so that one person can never subvert operations to their own purposes.

"How's your friend," Verlene asked me, "the detective who was in the hospital?"

"Gordo went home yesterday," I said. "He's still a mess, but they think he'll eventually have a full recovery."

"I sure hope so."

"In the meantime, my friend Eli and his wife are going to stay with Gordo for a week or two, to help him get settled and to make sure he's got the proper in-home care. Eli's wife is rich, you know, and apparently she's decided to make Gordo her new pet project."

"Lucky him."

"Well, not really," I said. "But he's a survivor. He'll be okay in the end."

"How about you?" Verlene asked. "How are you feeling?"

I smiled.

"I'm almost fine," I said. "I just seem to tire more easily, but the doctor said that's to be expected."

"Well, good," she said, flashing me a brilliant smile and stepping back to take in my new look. "I've got to say, you look absolutely stunning. I do believe this is the single best makeover I've ever seen!"

"Now wait a minute," I heard from behind me. "Isn't that the same thing you said to me when I had my hair done?"

We turned to see Shayna looking positively radiant in one of her new outfits from Advancing Attire. She was holding firmly to the arm of Hank, who beamed like a kid on his birthday.

Much to my surprise, I realized that standing next to them was Shayna's public defender, Max Nealson.

"Ms. Webber," he said, shaking my hand. "Nice to see you again."

I must've seemed shocked to see him there, because he laughed and then told me to wipe that look off of my face.

"What was it you said to me that day in my office?" he asked. "'Better late than never'?"

"I'm sorry," I told him. "I was just worried about my friend."

"Don't apologize. Thanks to you, I decided that some changes needed to be made down at the Public Defender's office. I've started advocating for a more realistic workload, and apparently my concerns were heard. They've just put through a request to hire two additional attorneys."

"That's wonderful," I told him, meaning it.

We shook hands again, and then I turned to see Dewey and Murdock and even Stinky, who didn't look half bad all cleaned up and changed into slacks and a sports jacket. We all chatted for a while and then I made my exit, happy to walk back toward my car and head home. I still wasn't fully recovered, and the business of the afternoon had completely worn me out.

"Callie!"

I was just climbing into my car when I turned to see Shayna running toward me. She stopped in front of me, breathless, looking like a beautiful bird that was almost ready to take flight.

"I just wanted to say goodbye!" she said, grinning. "Goodbye and thank you. I don't know how I'll ever be able to repay you for what you did for me."

I looked at her, at the kid who had made some dumb choices that had very nearly ruined her life. My deepest hope was that she had learned her lesson and that she wouldn't settle for less than she deserved ever again.

"You want to pay me back?" I said, noticing movement out of the corner of my eye. I glanced over toward Main Street, where I watched as Kirby Collins pulled out of his parking space and drove away, Verlene's lovely daughter comfortably buckled into the seat by his side. Seeing them together gave me a sense of happiness, and that made me realize, once and for all, that although I enjoyed being with Kirby, there wasn't, and never had been, anything between us except friendship. I focused my attention back on Shayna.

"You want to pay me back?" I asked again. "Then do this for me. Promise me you'll never allow a man into your life simply out of loneliness. There are plenty of good reasons to have a relationship, Shayna, but 'just so there's someone there to hold my hand' isn't one of them."

She seemed to consider what I had to say. Finally, she nodded.

"I promise," she said earnestly.

"You have a second chance here," I said. "You've already accepted Christ as your Savior. Now you need to give your life over to Him *fully*. He has a plan for you. I know it's a good one, but now you've got to put Him at the very center of your life."

She thanked me and then we hugged and said our goodbyes. I got in my car and was just pulling away when I heard my name shouted, once again. This time it was Verlene, waving at me from among the small crowd on Main Street.

I rolled down the window and leaned out.

"Yes?" I called.

Verlene stood there among the gathering of friends and well-wishers, looking for all the world like a woman who was in her element.

I was reminded again of the good works she did, of the way her efforts rippled out from small acts like waves from a stone thrown into a pond. With enough people devoting their lives to full-time nonprofit service, we really could change the world, I thought, one little person at a time.

"Don't forget about next Sunday!" she cried. "The Ladies Circle Dinner, at church. Are you going?"

I wanted to roll my eyes. I wanted to step on the accelerator and get out of there. But then I looked back at her expectant face, and I knew what the Lord wanted me to do.

"Count me in," I told her, trying not to groan. "I'll be there."

I drove straight home, hoping I would be able to grab a few moments on the water. Once there, I didn't even take the time to change out of my tweed slacks and into something more comfortable. Instead, I simply let Sal out of the house, and we walked down to the dock together. There was going to be a lovely sunset this evening, and despite my fatigue I wanted to enjoy it from the canoe.

I started slow and easy, because this was the first time I had gone out since being discharged from the hospital. After a while, though, I found myself soaring across the water, my exhaustion disappearing, my heart suddenly light and free. As I went, I thought about all that had happened in the last two weeks, and how it all had seemed to start with a silly little wooden nickel.

Don't take any wooden nickels was the saying, which I took to mean "Don't grab onto something that only looks valuable, because it may not be." Someone like Eddie Ray hadn't known the difference, and he had managed to get himself killed.

I realized that, as a Christian, one of my jobs was to keep in mind, always, the things that truly are of value: Faith. Hope. Love. All the fruit of the Spirit.

It was time to pray. As I continued to paddle, I talked to God out loud, thanking Him for the lessons He had sent my way these past two weeks. Then I went down my list, praying for the people who had recently touched my life. I prayed for Shayna and her new start. I prayed for Hank and Dewey and Murdock and Stinky. I prayed for Barbara Hightower and Denise. I prayed for poor Gordo. I prayed for repentance for Russell and Tia Lynch and Agent Litman and the Tanigawa brothers. I prayed for the immigrants, for their health and their plight.

I prayed for Kirby, asking God to draw him into a closer relationship with Him and to provide him with guidance and new opportunities in the days ahead.

I prayed for my parents, and I asked for help in restoring our relationship.

Finally, I prayed for Tom, thanking God that He had put such a wonderful man in my life. As the sun set on the water in front of me, I raised the paddle over my head with both hands and looked up at the brilliant blue-and-purple sky.

"Thank You, God," I said. "For this beautiful world, for Your awesome power."

I lowered the paddle and looked at Sal, who was perched on the deck plate of the canoe, facing forward, ready for whatever might be coming her way.

"Thank You, God," I added softly, "for helping to make me whole."

Filled with a warm sense of well-being, I paddled on toward home, watching the sunset in the distance, gazing in wonder at the myriad of colors that streaked the autumn sky.

My reverie was broken, however, by the muffled ringing of my cell phone. I didn't usually bring it with me out on the canoe, but I'd had it in my pocket at the ribbon-cutting ceremony and had forgotten about it. I hesitated before finally digging it out and answering, a little unwilling to lose the moment.

"Hello?" I said absently.

"Callie?"

It was Tom. My face broke into a smile, thinking that in the entire world, his was the only voice I felt like hearing on the other end of the line.

"Hey, Tom," I said, much more warmly, "I didn't expect it to be you."

"Is this a bad time?" he asked, the connection sounding clear and strong even though he was half a world away. "Are you busy?"

"I'm out on the canoe. It's okay. What's up?"

I cradled the phone against my ear with my shoulder and attempted an awkward maneuver with the paddle. I'd made a few strokes before I realized he wasn't answering me.

"Tom?"

I could hear him exhale slowly.

"Callie, did you really think I wouldn't find out?" he asked finally, a tinge of sadness in his voice.

"Find out what?"

"How hurt you were. Exactly what happened that night."

I closed my eyes. Even though I had hoped we wouldn't be having this conversation, I had known all along that it was inevitable. He knew too much; he learned too much. Eventually, he'd had to find out.

"Obviously, it took a while for the news to catch up to me," he continued. "It seems you weren't ever going to tell me about it yourself."

"It's just that you're so far away, Tom. Between your work and your mother, I didn't want to burden you with my problems, too."

He was silent for a moment.

"Didn't you think I deserved to know?" he asked, his dear, familiar voice cracking with emotion. "Didn't you think I cared?"

I'd never meant to hurt him. "I know you care," I whispered, my heart fluttering in my chest. "Believe me, I know you do."

I switched the phone to the other ear and tried again to paddle. The sun had dipped below the horizon now, and it would be dark soon.

"I'm sorry, Tom," I said earnestly, wanting to reassure him. "I'm doing so much better now that I didn't think it was necessary to give you the whole story."

"You're really doing better?" he asked, sounding somewhat placated.

"I am," I said. "I promise."

Floating with the current, I slowly rounded the final bend toward home. In the gathering darkness, I could see up ahead that someone was standing on my dock. Distracted, I asked Tom to hold on while I brought the boat in, telling him that I needed both hands free. I carefully set the phone in my lap and then paddled quickly, guiding the canoe toward the landing.

At first I thought it was Kirby standing there waiting for me, especially given the nice shoes, the creased gray pants, the tasteful black dress coat. But then as I drew closer, I realized that it wasn't Kirby after all. This man was just as handsome, but he was taller, with dark hair and broad shoulders.

"Hang on another minute, Tom," I said, picking up the phone and speaking into it. "I'm just home, and somebody's here at the dock."

I set the phone by my feet, coasted in, and then climbed from the boat, pulling it onto the shore. As I tied off the rope, Sal jumped out and ran to the man, sniffing at the cuffs of his tailored slacks.

"Can I help you?" I asked, grabbing the phone from the bottom of the canoe and holding it at my side.

The man didn't reply for a moment, but when he did, it was to say my name, his tone deep and instantly familiar.

"Callie," he said, looking down at my phone and then back at my face. "It's me."

It wasn't until that moment that I noticed the cell phone in his hand as well. He pressed the button to disconnect it, and then he took a step toward me on the dock. As he did, I saw that on the front of his suit jacket, peeking out from under his coat, was a big red mum.

I gasped, air rushing to fill my lungs. He stepped toward me again, but I backed away.

"You're in Singapore," I said, shaking my head, trying to align reality with what I was seeing and hearing. I held my phone to my ear, but the line had been disconnected. As I fumbled to turn it off, tears sprung unexpectedly into my eyes.

"No, I'm not. I needed to be here with you," he replied gently. "Business in Singapore can wait."

I swallowed hard, my heart pounding, my voice caught somewhere in my throat. I didn't trust myself to speak, didn't trust myself to do anything but stand there and gaze at him, trying to match the voice of the man I knew so well with this handsome stranger. Finally, I dropped my phone onto the grass and took a tentative step toward him.

That's all he needed. A smile teasing at his lips, he crossed the wooden slats of the dock, walking until he stood on the grass in front of me. He reached out and put one warm hand on my arm. I looked up at him, searching for the person I knew inside, thinking that even if I didn't recognize his face, the man behind those beautiful eyes was already my very best friend in the world. I smiled, and then I whispered his name.

"Tom."

Mindy Starns Clark is the bestselling author of 16 books, including:

The Million Dollar Mysteries Series
- *A Penny for Your Thoughts*
- *Don't Take Any Wooden Nickels*
- *A Dime a Dozen*
- *A Quarter for a Kiss*
- *The Buck Stops Here*

A Smart Chick Mystery Series
- *The Trouble with Tulip*
- *Blind Dates Can Be Murder*
- *Elementary, My Dear Watkins*

Standalone Mysteries
- *Whispers of the Bayou*
- *Shadows of Lancaster County*
- *Under the Cajun Moon*
- *Secrets of Harmony Grove*

Contemporary Fiction
- *The Amish Midwife* (cowritten with Leslie Gould)

Nonfiction
- *The House That Cleans Itself*
- *A Pocket Guide to Amish Life*

Gift Book
- *Simple Joys of the Amish Life* (cowritten with Georgia Varozza and illustrated by Laurie Snow Hein)

Mindy is also a popular inspirational speaker and playwright. Originally from Louisiana, she now lives with her husband and two daughters near Valley Forge, Pennsylvania.

Visit Mindy's website for more information about the Million Dollar Mysteries, including book club questions, fun freebies, and many other exciting extras.

www.mindystarnsclark.com